WAR BODIES

NEAL
ASHER
WAR BODIES

TOR

First published 2023 by Tor
an imprint of Pan Macmillan
The Smithson, 6 Briset Street, London EC1M 5NR
EU representative: Macmillan Publishers Ireland Ltd, 1st Floor,
The Liffey Trust Centre, 117–126 Sheriff Street Upper,
Dublin 1, D01 YC43
Associated companies throughout the world
www.panmacmillan.com

ISBN 978-1-5290-5008-0 HB
ISBN 978-1-5290-5009-7 TPB

1 3 5 7 9 8 6 4 2

A CIP catalogue record for this book is available from the British Library.

Typeset in Plantin by Palimpsest Book Production Ltd, Falkirk, Stirlingshire
Printed and bound by CPI Group (UK) Ltd, Croydon, CR0 4YY

Visit **www.panmacmillan.com** to read more about all our books
and to buy them. You will also find features, author interviews and
news of any author events, and you can sign up for e-newsletters
so that you're always first to hear about our new releases.

More years ago than I care to think about, I heard of this thing called 'podcasting' and pretty much ignored it. I then got invited onto a few and saw their utility but did not get involved beyond that. I am of the generation that spent its evenings getting soma from the TV. But like so many, learning from diverse opinions on the internet, steadily more appalled by the partisan nature of current affairs and agendas shoehorned into entertainment, I've turned away from the TV.

Social media has become the source of dopamine hits, but where could I go to learn and be entertained during those periods when my mind was tired from writing and my body from exercise? Over the last four or five years I've found these from the independent podcasters on health, science, current affairs, politics and more besides. The long form of many of these doesn't allow for much in the way of bullshit from interviewees, and allows for deep dives into detail. Their independence cuts out the producer shouting through the earphone, 'You can't say that!' I've learned more from these podcasts than I ever did from TV soma.

So, I dedicate this to the independent podcasters. Keep up the good work!

Acknowledgements

Thanks to the staff at Pan Macmillan, and elsewhere, who have helped bring this novel to your e-reader, smartphone, computer screen and to that old-fashioned mass of wood pulp called a book. These include Bella Pagan (editor), Georgia Summers (assistant editor), Samantha Fletcher (desk editor), Neil Lang (jacket designer) and the Pan Mac marketing team; also freelancers Claire Baldwin (editor), Jessica Cuthbert-Smith (copy-editor), Robert Clark (proofreader), Steve Stone (jacket illustrator) and Jamie-Lee Nardone (publicity); and others whose names I simply don't know.

Glossary

Augmented: To be 'augmented' is to have taken advantage of one or more of the many available cybernetic devices, mechanical additions and, distinctly, cerebral augmentations. In the last case we have, of course, the ubiquitous 'aug' and such back-formations as 'auged', 'auging-in', and the execrable 'all auged up'. But it does not stop there: the word 'aug' has now become confused with auger and augur – which is understandable considering the way an aug connects and the information that then becomes available. So now you can 'auger' information from the AI net, and a prediction made by an aug prognostic subprogram can be called an augury.

– From 'Quince Guide' compiled by humans

Cyberat: A faction of humanity who feel that AI is a danger to humanity, and that people must therefore incorporate that technology, and others, within themselves rather than separately. They are cyborgs, steadily replacing their human bodies with that which is machine-based and, to their minds, better.

First- and second-children: Male prador, chemically maintained in adolescence, enslaved by pheromones emitted by their fathers and acting as crew on their ships or as soldiers. Prador adults also use the children's surgically removed ganglions (brains) as navigational computers in their ships and to control war machines.

Golem: Androids produced by the Cybercorp company – consisting of a ceramal chassis usually enclosed in syntheflesh and syntheskin outer layers. These humanoid robots are very tough, fast and, since they possess AI, very smart.

Hardfield: A flat force field capable of stopping missiles and energy beams. The impact or heat energy is transformed and dissipated by the hardfield projector. Overload of that projector usually results in its catastrophic breakdown, at which point it is ejected from the vessel containing it.

Jain technology: A technology spanning all scientific disciplines, created by one of the dead races – the Jain. Its apparent sum purpose is to spread through civilizations and annihilate them.

Nanosuite: A suite of nanomachines most human beings have inside them. These self-propagating machines act as a secondary immune system, repairing and adjusting the body. Each suite can be altered to suit the individual and his or her circumstances.

Polity: A human/AI dominion extending across many star systems, occupying a spherical space spanning the thickness of the galaxy and centred on Earth. It is ruled over by the AIs who took control of human affairs in what has been called, because of its very low casualty rate, the Quiet War. The top AI is called Earth Central (EC) and resides in a building on the shore of Lake Geneva. Planetary AIs, lower down in the hierarchy, rule over other worlds. The Polity is a highly technical civilization but its weakness was its reliance on travel by 'runcible' – instantaneous matter transmission gates.

Prador: A highly xenophobic race of giant crablike aliens ruled by a king and his family. Hostility is implicit in their biology and, upon encountering the Polity, they immediately attacked it.

Runcible: Instantaneous matter transmission gates, allowing transportation through underspace.

Spatterjay virus: An alien virus on the world of Spatterjay. It infects life forms to make them a tough and reusable resource for their main hosts, the leeches of that world. Having incorporated elements of an alien technology, the virus is able to infect creatures from other worlds. Those infected are practically indestructible. Left unsuppressed, it can cause extreme physical changes to its host, especially if the host has received life-threatening damage, in which case the virus will use genomes collected from other creatures to make grotesque changes.

USER: Underspace interference emitters are devices that disrupt U-space, thereby stopping or hindering both travel and communication through that continuum. They can also force ships out of U-space into the real, or realspace. They can consist of ship-mounted weapons, mines and missiles whose duration of disruption is variable.

U-space: Underspace is the continuum spaceships enter (or U-jump into), rather like submarines submerging, to travel faster than light. It is also the continuum that can be crossed by using runcible gates, making travel between worlds linked by such gates all but instantaneous.

1

Piper visualized the thing inside him, wound through his skeleton and his guts, ready to uncoil and snarl at the world at the slightest provocation. Whenever it occupied him fully, his eyes seemed to become a sick yellow, and claws threatened to break from his fingers. It was as if he had donned it like a suit, or perhaps it had donned him. Anger was what it evoked in him mostly, but also excitement, excess, often clarity and certainly brilliance. He called it his reptile, because surely it was some expression of his reptile brain. Although in reality it was him – just a facet of his being – he always envisioned it as something separate, to try and exert control over this aspect of himself. For here, on Founder's World, the punishments for not controlling your organic self could be severe.

I have too much imagination, he thought.

He had no clear recollection of when it had first started manifesting, though its influence had increased when he went into puberty. This was longer ago than he cared to remember, and it was only briefly ameliorated by the customary drug implant to suppress his equally raging hormones. The anger had been very evident to his teachers at the time too, which led to the addition, at age fifteen, of a behavioural modifier – a device commonly used in Cyberat society to control their weak organic emotions. Unlike others, he hadn't been able to have it removed in the ensuing five years. After surgery in a Cyberat 'progression' hospital, and then subsequent adjustments in his father's factory, the reptile, as he thought of it, had started waking up more often. It ignited aberrant thoughts and impulsive behaviour which, of course, the modifier punished. And following a new surgical adjustment recently, it had become even worse. Perhaps that was because he still felt sore, wooden and slightly clumsy after this final upgrade to match the data channels running through his bones to his adult frame. Whatever the reason, the only option the state had left was to put him to work hard enough to exhaust him of this malevolent energy. And so he'd spent the last five years working on building sites.

'Why are you standing there gaping, boy?' Mallon snapped.

Mallon was one of the Old Guard who'd recently taken charge of the site, and she controlled the swarm of robots which were digging the foundations for the new houses. Silhouetted against lavender sky, she floated on a sphere over the tanks containing the foamstone mix – three cylinders five metres long and two wide running pipes to mixer drums then to the injector bots. She was a Cyberat rumoured to be over a hundred years old – her upper torso that of a wrinkled old woman with an oversized head. He resented her pointed comment, reminding him he wasn't regarded as an adult yet, even though he was twenty-five Founder's World years old. The necessity of the implant had stalled his progression.

'I'm waiting for more girders,' Piper replied.

Mallon waved a mechanical arm, the end of which terminated in a bayonet fitting. This could be inserted into a variety of hands and other tools.

'Very well,' she said, unable to find another reason to berate him.

Piper winced a smile at her as she swung away to look at

something else further across the site. With her gaze no longer on him, he took the chance to study her more closely. Various grey metallic protrusions and interfaces studded her upper body, while snakes of shiny ribbed metal ran up, stitched through her back, to draw together into the horseshoe of the cerebral linkage and support unit wrapped around her skull from behind. Her wrinkled torso, below flaccid breasts, transitioned into a blockwork tech of interfaces, which itself extended down in a cone. He couldn't see that portion of her since it was currently plugged into the floating control sphere. This object measured two metres across and was covered in squared-off spirals and emitter protrusions of other kinds. On its side sat the tube of just one weapon: an ionic stunner – meagre armament for one such as her.

Piper lowered his gaze as she swung back, feeling his inner reptile writhing for expression, then turned his attention to her walking body, which she'd left squatted over to one side of the building site. This was a quad form, with blocky legs folded in below the main body, which itself sported heavy assortments of weapons tubes on either side. On top a chain-glass dome folded back to reveal the socket she would later plug herself into when she occupied the thing. No doubt Mallon could control it remotely if she needed to. She was also able to summon Enforcers to her command, or even a huge war body to occupy. Fifty years had passed since the rebellion in which she'd taken part, yet, apparently, these visible displays of power remained necessary to maintain order, especially now.

Things had become more tense lately, with the arrival of interstellar visitors from a civilization grown out of old Earth – a world the Cyberat had abandoned long ago to its own, supposedly inevitable, destruction. Piper gave Mallon a second glance then quickly lowered his gaze again, still baffled as to why his reptile anger always seemed to increase in the presence of Old Guard. Perhaps it was just a hatred of authority figures. Whatever. He needed to get his mind onto other things while he waited, or the modifier would soon be giving him a jab. So he looked out across the site and thought about the visitors from the Polity instead.

Their technology was highly advanced – this much at least the citizens of Founder's World had learned through the netlinks they'd provided over the last year. Their augmentations were much smaller, and their nanofibre connections to the brain, as well as the neural meshes there, didn't need skull expansions, cooling, cell hardening or an increased venous system. And though Polity citizens did incorporate some tech inside themselves, they mostly retained their full human bodies intact. Most importantly, however, they were ruled by AIs. Such things were a matter of heated debate among the Cyberat, and political infighting had now reached hysterical levels. The arrival of the Polity, with its new technologies, had created a schism between the old established cyborgs and a large contingent of those still *progressing*. Because maybe, just maybe, their thesis that artificial intelligence should only be allowed to develop in conjunction with the human brain had actually retarded Cyberat development. The worry that AI, rising independently, would result in human extermination had certainly been proved wrong, and that belief had been a founding principle of the Cyberat.

As a general rule, Piper tried to avoid thinking about these things. Although he of course agreed with those on the opposite side of the schism from the Old Guard, his concerns were more personal, focused on his difficulties with self-control and the modifier. He reached up and touched the lump at the base of his skull where it resided, and grimaced. The device was, in essence, a temporary version of the permanent modifier usually installed in criminals – something that identified aberrant thought processes by neurochem profiles and then administered punishment by stimulating afferent nerve pain.

'Your girders are coming,' Mallon called, pointing with one bayonet fitting.

'Thank you,' he replied politely, teeth gritted.

He looked out to the construction road winding in from the city through undeveloped land. Either side of the road, indigenous lichens smeared the rocky ground with pastel shades of red, purple, blue and green, scattered here and there with spore spikes and fans reaching five metres tall in some places. The sled came into sight – just a floating slab heaped high with bubble-metal girders. It was time to get back to work.

Piper turned to the four construction robots he'd been controlling. They were similar to Mallon's walking body, with their blocky limbs, except they had six of the legs, terminating in heavy grabs. He lowered his VR band over his eyes, to give him a holographic overlay running projected movements for the robots, schematics of the site and scrolling subsidiary data in Cyberat code. Touching a code sequence invisible to others, he activated the robots. With a whining, rumbling sound they rose from their squats in readiness. This method of control was laughably antediluvian, for both Polity and Cyberat technology, but why waste resources on exterior body tech when it would be steadily displaced during *progression* into a full Cyberat? This process, which saw the human body ultimately discarded and internal data channels linked to more *efficient* machines, was something he should have begun seven years ago. Gazing down at his arms, and then his torso, he recognized that billions of years of evolution and selection had created his body. But, as was the Cyberat way, he also understood it to be grossly organic and full of redundancies, and he knew that he could be better.

Piper frowned in concentration and set the construction robots into motion as the sled arrived. He could only manage the four – those that Mallon had allowed him – but he'd been getting the job done. Over the next hour he directed them to unload the sled and move the girders into position, inserting cross-connections too and blobs of foamstone to secure them in the foundations before the final pour. His intense focus on this task banished any other thoughts, except a brief realization that perhaps the state had been right to put him here, calming as this work was for him. After positioning most of the girders from the sled, he ran laser measurements, ensuring they were precisely where they should be according to the schematic he'd called up in virtual reality. With that finally done, he then released the four robots back to Mallon, raised his VR band, wiped away the sweat and took a look around.

House construction was proceeding apace. Robots swarmed around stacks, tanks and drums of materials. In many cases they were difficult to distinguish from the older Cyberat, whose secondary bodies were essentially just robots with Cyberat insertion sockets. And those plugged into them were sufficiently *progressed* to have little in the way of a human body remaining. From the various castes of Cyberat, it was mostly Builders and Engineers who worked here, though he did see a scattering of Medics and one or two Bureaucrats. Among them all were iterations of the various stages that led to the likes of Mallon. There were people with cyber limbs, extra limbs, or metal torsos, but also with smaller additions ready to take something larger. All of this was part of the usual Cyberat *progression*, and their bodies would continue to be steadily stripped away until only a core of humanity – a plug form – remained, wrapped in interfaces.

There were also many who looked similar to the way he'd been seven years ago: apparently completely human but likely possessing internal additions in readiness for their progression. This struck him as odd since they'd be as inefficient as he was. He then turned his attention back to Mallon and saw her watching him. Like many Old Guard, Mallon was a puzzle. She seemed to have gone far down the accepted route, elevating herself to the perfect amalgam of human and machine, and then stopped. Why had she retained the upper half of her human body – that wrinkled, ineffective flesh? This had been a matter of debate among Piper's contemporaries, especially since the arrival of the Polity. In hushed tones it was proposed that perhaps many of the older Cyberat no longer truly believed the dictums of the Founder, but just enforced those tenets as a way of retaining power. Piper, always painfully aware of his modifier ready to stamp down on his every bad thought, didn't take part in these risky whisperings, though he did guardedly ask his parents about them. As usual, they'd been didactic and parsimonious with information, telling him to think through the matter himself. Another conundrum about Mallon was why someone who was so high up in the Old Guard hierarchy would concern herself with overseeing the construction of Cyberat homes.

Feeling uncomfortable under Mallon's attention and the resultant uncoiling of his anger, Piper turned away. He then suddenly found himself faced with a construction robot, heading straight for him, fast. Before he could do anything, the end of the girder it was transporting struck him at the waist, sprawling him across it, then carrying him along with it. It ran him straight into another upright girder, one set in ready for the pouring of the foundations, and crushed him against it. The horrifying impact had surely shattered his pelvis, though thankfully he felt nothing at first. He glimpsed a split in his side with his intestines poking out – all that soft organic ephemera – and then the pain hit. He hung there screaming as Mallon quickly descended. The construction robot abruptly drew back, leaving him stuck to the girder end for a second, before dropping heavily to the ground. There was blood everywhere, now jetting from severed arteries, and with a surge of adrenalin the reptile erupted within him, ready for fight or flight. But then the massive drop in blood pressure released him from the agony and into the dark.

Piper woke in a surgery, but definitely not a Cyberat one. A large chrome and white plastic autosurgeon was folding itself up on top of its pillar, cleaning its sparkling instruments as it did so. Meanwhile, a subsidiary pillar was also folding up its arms on the other side, as it retreated on a mobile pedestal back to an alcove in the wall. He at once recognized Polity technology and a thousand speculations arose in his mind. A surge of anxiety ensued as he feared how his modifier might react to these thoughts. He then realized that his clarity of mind was stunning. He'd taken a hit that nearly cut him in half, leaving the organic, replaceable machine of his original form severely damaged. How was it that he could feel so well, so sharp, when other recent surgery had left him sore, angry and out of it for weeks? Preparing himself for the worst, he raised his head and looked down at his body.

He couldn't see his feet because a thick metal cylinder, with numerous tubes and wires running into it, was wrapped around his torso and blocked the view. He wondered if, as was usual when people suffered such accidents on Founder's World, the organics below his waist had been removed. It wouldn't be before time. However, although he couldn't move them, he could still feel his feet and legs. Perhaps that was due to nerve memory. Many Cyberat struggled with 'limb ghosting'. His gaze strayed to a viewing window in the room, with a clean lock beside it; through the glass he could see his parents. He felt his usual rush of mixed emotions about them.

Doge, his father, was a plug-form Cyberat, slotted into the top of a cylinder carrier, so it looked as though he consisted of this cylinder topped by a human head. Multiple arms, similar in style to those of the now-inert surgeon, were folded up against the cylinder, while below the whole thing moved on two caterpillar treads. This was one of the bodies Doge used for visual factory inspections and repairs. Otherwise he plugged into the control centre of the factories, where he manufactured the hardware interfaces for plug-form bodies. He did not favour antigravity carriers, though he still had that option. He expressed a prefer-ence for connection to the ground, which was an opinion almost heretical to the establishment. He gazed at Piper with watery eyes, his long beard spilling over the edge of the cylinder and his mouth moving as if he was chewing something tough and unpleasant.

Piper felt a rush of irrational fear, but no reptile anger response, which he strangely never did feel in the presence of his father. Instead the thing was watchful, wrapped around his mind and seemingly covered by an overlay – one of the information and control holograms used for VR control of external machines. His father had always been a dark and dangerous presence for him, until he was moved to the building work crews. However, though Doge was a disciplinarian, Piper had actually received more of that from his mother Reema. She was the one who'd slapped him across the face when he showed a lack of control. And she was the one who'd enforced his mental exercises and supple-mentary education, even now still pushing him to do them. Yet it had been Doge, just watching him, and occasionally expressing disappointment, who had scared him the most.

At fifty years, Reema was much younger than Doge and not so far along in her progression. She still retained a human shape but one seemingly patched with metal and composite. Piper had learned that when she'd had her womb removed to the birthing facility at the age of sixteen, something about her had changed. She'd not been so eager to continue losing her weak organic components after that. Her attitude, just like Doge's, was frowned upon by the hierarchy. However, having lost her eyes and part of her face in a factory accident, her visage was now mostly pink enamelled metal, while her eyes were blue sapphires in dark pits. It had been considered a strange and unnerving choice by many. Maybe it was a kind of rebellion that nobody could fathom. She didn't explain the matter and managed to stay clear of any tribunal set up by the Old Guard to investigate such things.

Alongside them at the window were two more individuals. One appeared to be a perfectly human male. He was a dignified-looking man with cropped grey hair, grey eyes and a beak of a nose, with a boosted physique under an Earth Central Security uniform. But he wasn't human at all. This was Albermech or, rather, a Golem android avatar telefactored from the AI of the Polity ship which was in orbit above. The number of these Golems scattered about Founder's World were all the same and instantly recognizable. The other individual, whose spider carrier body tilted him close to the glass, was a Cyberat. He retained all of his human body up from his waist, including his arms, in a similar format to Mallon. He looked incredibly old and wrinkled, his severe black eyes glaring at Piper from below a jutting brow that was etched with cubic sensory tattoos. It took a moment for Piper to recognize him as Castron – perhaps the highest up of all in the Old Guard – and he felt an unusually intense flash of sick rage. He immediately visualized this rage as the reptile, gaining substance under overlay and leaping forward to occupy his body. In this way he managed to get a handle on it and worked to suppress it. Weak emotions such as simple dislike or anger usually escaped the notice of his modifier, but Piper was sure this would garner punishment.

That he disliked this Cyberat, just as he disliked all the Old Guard, might again have had something to do with a hatred of authority figures, for Castron was the ultimate of those. Yet, even as Piper thought this, he knew he was rationalizing. The sick rage felt too personal – and it scared him.

Finally, having managed to shove the reptile into abeyance, and surprised his modifier still hadn't reacted, Piper studied the four of them and wondered what the hell was going on here. Why had he been operated on by a Polity surgeon and not taken straight into a Cyberat progression hospital? And why was such a senior Cyberat here? Perhaps they could hear him.

'I don't understand why I'm here,' he said out loud. His voice was surprisingly clear and easy, considering the circumstances.

Castron swung round to face Albermech. At first Piper couldn't hear him but then a microphone kicked in. '. ... should be able to move him to progression soon?' he was asking. Piper felt a surge of emotion, but couldn't tell if it was gratitude or fear.

Albermech urbanely replied, 'As you are well aware, the accident would have killed him had not one of our observers been nearby. Our medical technology saved his life, but it's not so advanced that he can be moved just a few hours after being under the knife.'

Castron remained expressionless as he folded his wrinkled arms. Piper sensed his deep disapproval.

'How are you feeling?' asked his mother, quickly adding, 'Not so good after what happened to you, I imagine.'

Piper stared at her for a long moment. Because of her rigid face and generally bland way of addressing people, it was difficult to read anything beyond what she was actually saying. However, since the Cyberat hadn't yet managed to complete their full suppression of the nuclear family, he'd been able to spend a great deal of time with her before the state intervened. So now, along with the strange new clarity he seemed to possess, he was able to see the implied warning in her words. He put his head back, closed his eyes and coughed, wincing a little, then replied in a lower, weaker tone. 'I feel like I was crushed by a beam end. It's like I'm going to fall apart.'

He closed his eyes again, as if fighting back tears, but was actually preparing himself for a jolt from his behavioural modifier for the lie. Under this facade, his mind began to race, and a stark memory suddenly came to him: the image of Mallon watching him just prior to his accident. He speculated on just how many young Cyberat recently put to work on the sites had been taken in for progression in the last year. What he had previously uncomfortably assumed to be a conspiracy theory started to take on new weight.

'I want all your data on him,' said Castron, still facing Albermech. 'It should be sent to me now, and I want regular updates. Hourly.' Castron unfolded his arms and moved towards Albermech as though he was about to launch into one of his lectures about Polity interference, but then he jerked back, reaching up to clutch at his skull.

'There, you have it,' said Albermech. 'As you can see . . . Oh, sorry, was that a bit too fast? But you should be able to take apart the information packet in time – it's in your required format.'

Castron glared at him, eyes watering and obviously in some pain.

Albermech continued, 'I can give you the highlights. We repaired bone structure, sealed all the bleeds and, as instructed, haven't tried to reconnect his legs since you'll be removing them. We have saved his testicles, since you asked for that. However, the massive blood loss has caused tissue damage throughout. His body and brain are full of dead spots, so we injected a temporary nanosuite to break down any dead matter and allow regrowth. The process may take weeks. If we move him to a progression hospital now, he will probably die on the slab.'

Castron looked in at Piper, and Piper got the impression the man was weighing up the value of this. He then swung his gaze back to Doge and Reema and held it there for a long while.

'Keep me updated,' he finally said, before moving away abruptly and departing. Piper felt some tension seep out of him – the rage within had been mollified. The remaining three stood silently until Castron was gone, then Doge turned to Albermech.

'Why was he here?'

'More demands. Another inspection.' Albermech waved a dismissive hand.

Reema now interjected, 'My son . . . you said "bone repair"?'

'Of course not,' Albermech replied. 'It would take more than that to break his bones. I wasn't lying about the tissue damage, though, just how long it'll take to repair. It's nearly done now.'

Piper was shocked at the blatant lies given to such an important figure as Castron, then puzzled over their content. He'd felt sure his pelvis had ended up in splinters from the accident. Before he could think on this further, his mother continued, 'We are going to have to speed things up. It won't be long till they start taking more control.'

Albermech nodded and looked to Doge. 'How many factories now?'

'Fifteen,' Doge replied. 'But we're starting to get Old Guard interference. Demands and inspections there too.'

'It's time to push distribution – we need at least sixty per cent before we go online.'

'I hope that will be enough,' said Doge. 'I need to go back

there. Maybe distribution of the upgrade interface and cerebral components could now be done by micro-drone. The rumour is already going around that they're Polity tech.' Doge swung back to face into the surgery room. 'Piper,' he said, and Piper found himself frantically trying to think what he might have done wrong, 'we'd hoped for more space to prepare, and that you'd have the choices you deserve, but time is running out. Listen to your mother and Albermech.' Doge then swung away and disappeared the way Castron had gone. Again Piper experienced a release – something sighing out of him. With Castron and Doge gone, he felt less on his guard.

'What's this all about?' he asked.

'It's about keeping you from the butchers,' Reema replied, heading over to the outer door of the clean lock and opening it. 'Here, right now, it's about personal considerations, though I swore I wouldn't allow them to affect my decision-making.'

She came through into the surgery room, with Albermech following. As they entered, the cylinder covering Piper's torso parted along a castellated line and folded open, revealing the rest of him below. He expected to see further support hardware, but his lower torso, hips and upper legs were still perfectly intact, as if nothing had happened to him at all. A warm flush started at his chest and spread down, with full feeling gradually returning to his body. He twitched his feet and shifted his legs. He felt really good – even the ache in his bones was gone. But then he puzzled over his instinctive gladness to see the damage repaired. What he'd been about to have replaced, over in the progression hospital, with something machine-based and better, was still there. This wasn't something he should be happy about.

'Come on, get off there,' said his mother. 'We have things to discuss.'

He sat fully upright and swung his legs off the side of the slab.

Albermech came over with a bundle from the Polity fabricator set in the wall, dropping a stack of clothing beside him. Piper gazed down at the garments, fondling the soft underwear and studying the ECS uniform. He had a momentary flash of distaste, since an organism shouldn't be so pampered by comfort, or so he'd been taught. This disappeared as he started to dress and found he quite liked it, but then he expected another jolt from his modifier for entertaining such organic pleasure. As he put the pants on, he felt a warm surge in his groin and hurriedly pulled the trousers up on top of these – embarrassed about something he hadn't felt since before his drug implant in puberty. Still no jolt, however.

'How many have you managed to grab?' Reema asked Albermech.

'Just twenty-four, while over a thousand have gone in for progression. It's not as disastrous as it might seem. While human tissue remains, a body can be reconstructed. Even Castron . . .' Albermech waved in the general direction of where that individual had gone.

Piper finally slipped on comfortable boots that automatically closed about his feet. Standing up, he observed the perfect fit of the uniform. But of course, they would have known his measurements exactly. He wondered how he looked and recognized vanity as his mind strayed to how his contemporaries might see him. He ran his hands down the front of it, his fingertips touching his penis through the cloth. No jolt again, but Reema stepped closer and slapped his hand away.

'His hormone levels are rising,' she said to Albermech. 'I need him sharp. He's not stupid and we've ensured he knows what questions to ask.'

Albermech dipped his head.

Piper, standing there flushed with embarrassment, felt

15

something shift inside him. His intense awareness of his body began to diminish.

'I've turned off his implant because his hormones are integral to proper healing. Of course, they also interfere with Cyberat indoctrination which is why they are suppressed. If they weren't, the history of revolution here would be far more extensive than it is.'

'Perhaps take it down gradually,' his mother suggested.

'I've set it for that. It's presently down to the level of an elderly, base-format adult so won't interfere with his thinking as much. The snap back, since he's been under the implant for so long, would have been harsh.' Albermech gave Piper a slightly amused look. 'But otherwise, the hormonal effect on his brain will clarify his thinking, and is already doing so. I also shut down his behavioural modifier to allow breadth of thought.'

Shut down my modifier?

Piper reached up to the back of his skull and touched the nodule of the modifier under his skin – ready to be removed whenever his behaviour was judged sufficiently correct and adult. He felt a surge of what he identified as freedom to think any way he liked, quickly followed by a fear of that freedom. But he was soon able to quash the fear, deep anger from his shifting reptile pushing it aside as he suddenly felt very painfully alive.

'Mother,' he said, testing the modifier. Usage of that word would definitely have been punished, but the lack of reaction confirmed the thing was off. On having this proof, he suddenly felt an intense loathing of it. Whether that arose from the rational Piper or his reptile he couldn't tell, but he would certainly be doing everything he could to ensure it remained off. He continued, 'What the hell is happening?'

'I'll deal with this now,' she said to Albermech.

The Golem avatar nodded. 'Things to do,' he said, then dipped his head and froze to the spot. Doubtless Albermech, Polity AI, had now shifted his attention through to other avatars and systems as he studied their world with his complete omniscience and omnipresence.

Reema reached out and took hold of Piper's arm, guiding him towards the clean lock. They walked through into the viewing room, then through a sliding door into a corridor. Piper inspected his surroundings with curiosity, wondering where he was. The Polity had numerous small installations scattered around Founder's World – perfectly enclosed and no interaction allowed outside of them. There was also the Embassy in Ironville. As she brought him to a canteen, he gazed out of the panoramic window to one side and saw that they were in the Embassy.

She led the way over to a table beside the window. Only one other of the meagre scattering of tables in here was occupied. He studied the four sitting at it. Two women wearing Polity monitor uniforms. A man, casually sprawled back in his chair, in a silvery grey suit seemingly copied from some old age of Earth. The fourth, in blue overalls, was a Golem android, made obvious by the fact he was sans skin on one arm and the side of his head. He turned to look at Piper, revealing his silver skull, white teeth and a bright blue lidless eye that matched the one on the skin side.

Piper and his mother sat at their table and the Polity people continued their low conversation. He turned to the view of Ironville, with its trapezoidal buildings, low factory blocks, and air buzzing with Cyberat and big grav-transports. Reema concentrated on the table top to work a touch screen, then sat back.

'What is the population of our world?' she asked.

Piper dipped his head, remembering their times together before he'd joined the building crews. It was going to be one of *those* conversations.

'Eight hundred and forty million, at the last count,' he replied. The familiarity of being in one of her lessons pushed away the anger, but it worried him that his reptile now seemed permanently lodged under an overlay in his mind. As ever, he couldn't tell whether it was driving him or he driving it, but did that matter if the result was a clarification of thought?

'That is a very low population,' she told him. 'When we departed, Earth had a population of twelve billion, with a further six billion scattered through the Solar system. Why is the population here so low?'

Piper blinked. This was a question she had never asked before, perhaps because she knew that he previously couldn't think beyond what was allowed.

'Because we limit population to food production.'

'Wrong. Try again.'

'Solar radiation causes high DNA damage and selection—'

'Wrong again.'

'We are limiting our environmental footprint because—'

'Wrong.'

'Technological processing must match human increase because—'

'Wrong, and of course these are all the answers you've been given through Cyberat schooling: the permitted answers. But, within the constraints of your modifier, I taught you to think, to question and to assess.'

'Within constraints,' he said. Yes, his constraints were off. He felt in some integral ways as if he'd suddenly jumped forwards to his true age. Without the pain, and threat of pain, would he still be able to partition and control that part of him which seemed to be utterly irrational and yet, on other occasions, also seemed to drive extreme rationality?

She nodded sharply. 'I know you're not stupid – you are in

the highest percentile through birth genetics *and* genetic modification. I also used nootropic therapy and growth factors to increase this during your schooling.' She flicked a hand up beside her head in a gesture he'd learned to read as an apology. 'It's because of your alterations you ended up under the behavioural modifier in the first place. An intended and beneficial corollary that in part saved you from progression until now.'

Piper gaped, the shock of her words tightening his guts and sending a hot tingling through his limbs. He fought to maintain the overlay and keep the reptile down. It was simply against the law for parents to intervene in any way like this – that was the purview of the progression hospitals. It was also criminal to delay progression. Right now, his modifier should have been repeatedly jolting him to report such infractions, for them to be punished severely. A person could end up with a permanent modifier installed, perpetually punishing aberrant thought processes until, with their minds shaped to the purpose, they eventually became Enforcers. Now, having found his body completely restored, he understood that his parents had already gone way beyond the law. There was a bigger picture here of which he was only just getting the first pieces.

Anger swirled up. He dipped his head to try and think carefully, then raised it as a floating tray crab drone settled in the middle of their table and began distributing dishes.

Distraction . . .

He goggled at the colours, shapes and textures of the food, doing his best to derail the anger. Food, like sex, was frowned upon by the Cyberat. Both were organic activities which, if they couldn't be eliminated completely, were tightly controlled. His usual daily nutrition consisted of a slab of proteins, fats and vitamins and measured quantities of liquids containing similar nutrients. He took these in quickly and without pleasure, annoyed by the necessity of having to maintain his organic body in this way. And *apparently* looking forward to the time he'd only need to top up an internal reservoir to keep his remaining organics functioning.

'Eat,' said Reema.

So Piper ate, expecting annoyingly organic gratification. At first he found the experience uncomfortable and his stomach seemed to agree. The textures weren't right and the tastes were strange. Then he tried something else that gave a sudden rush of incredible pleasure. It was so intense, and so good, his eyes filled with tears.

'What is that?' he asked, pointing at a piece of what looked like brown foamstone with white layers, soft and glutinous.

'Gateau,' Reema replied. 'You're experiencing this reaction because it's the first time you've tasted unencapsulated sugars. In the ancient past they caused all sorts of health difficulties. No problem in the Polity now though, especially with the nanosuites.'

'Nanosuites? I have one inside me?'

'A limited suite, because of other factors,' she said dismissively, then continued, 'You still haven't answered my question correctly. I taught you not to be distracted by ephemera when you have some thinking to do.'

He stopped eating and drank from the beaker provided. The liquid tasted bitter, pretty much on a par with usual Cyberat food. He put it down and turned his thoughts inwards, the anger having receded: the distraction had been sufficient. He'd always known that both his parents, like many mid-generation Cyberat, greatly disagreed with the dictums of the Founder and the way they were applied by the Old Guard. Now he realized their disagreement went further than just comments and attitude. Retrospectively, he could see that his mother's choice not to hone herself down to plug form reflected that.

He also remembered his father's disparaging comments about his own machine body, and regrets about losing touch with the world, hence his dislike of using grav. This knowledge acted like a key to much he had learned on the sites. Now he again picked at the fragments of conspiracy theory and began to patch them together.

'The Old Guard want to keep the population low because a lower population is easier to control,' he said.

Reema nodded and her mouth twitched, which was the closest she could get to a smile. 'The failure rate in the birthing facilities is close to seventy per cent. Albermech has analysed this and informs me that even with the old technology they have, it should still be below twenty per cent.' She paused, perhaps feeling some emotion that simply couldn't show on her face. 'Now think about the mechanism of control. Think about how Old Guard have died in the past, and that even the likes of Castron were not one of the first.'

'The Old Guard were the New Guard fifty years ago, during the last rebellion,' said Piper as he tried to keep his thoughts in order.

'A cycle that has been repeated many times here, though that reality has been removed from the education system,' she replied. 'Continue.'

'As we adopt more and more of the cyber and lose more and more of our human bodies, we come to think like the . . . Old Guard.'

She nodded sharply. 'It's actually a system that has operated throughout human history, and without any cyber technology involved. The new rebelling against the old, but following that rebellion becoming the old. The establishment. It's almost comedic when you see it that way. However, with us it's done by dint of eliminating numerous options for human advancement,

21

and ways of living, confining them to the cyber and the acquisition of power.'

Piper didn't consider it comedic. He felt his reptile rising, seeking to lock on to something. The logical thread had led him here, yet it denied so much he'd previously accepted. He looked down at his body and still saw it as something inefficient – something that needed to be replaced by the machine.

'Surely the machine is best?' he said, looking up.

Reema shrugged. 'And that is what we have been convinced of ever since we first came here, and even before the Cyberat were building their colony ships to leave. The reality is actually perpetual loss of the whole to be replaced by inferior parts.'

'Inferior!' He felt a flash of anger, and yet rather than the inner anger of his reptile, it was something not so deeply rooted.

'Oh we can have stronger limbs and different limbs. We can control technologies as extensions of ourselves, and we can expand the processing of our minds. But then we get into the philosophy of it: to what purpose are we doing this? Do our lives have more joy in them? Do we gain greater satisfaction from our power? These desires, in the end, arise from our human aspect. Even Castron has recognized this and so keeps what remains of his body, while at the same time fighting to maintain the system. Because of his human need to cling onto power.'

This felt like too much of a stretch. Piper's intensive education had given him a deep understanding of the science. All Cyberat physical enhancements made them stronger, faster and more efficient than plain biological humans. They became perfect mentalities, with hugely enhanced control of their environment!

But to what purpose?

He reviewed what his mother had just said, now in the light of some simple experiences: how he'd felt seeing his organic body restored, the soft cloth against his skin, that brief surge of sexual feeling, and the taste of that gateau. Deeper memory played its part too. He looked back on brief joyful times in the past, of growing up between the constant lessons, before hormonal suppression and before they'd put him under the behavioural modifier. He remembered friendships, swiftly clamped down upon. And he remembered a repeated dream, arising out of memory, of a young girl by a river and how they'd spent many hours together there on bright sunny days. This had occurred just when he entered puberty, and he realized that once put on the drug implant, he'd never seen her again, or ever felt the same again. His mind catalogued these moments and then compared them to the arid, intellectual and mechanistic future of the Cyberat. It seemed his new mental clarity would allow no denials.

'Indoctrination,' he said, and felt another surge of that deep reptile anger.

Until that moment, he had simply perceived everything done to him as correcting his organic faults, in preparation for him becoming a full Cyberat and a productive member of society. He understood the displacement of the human as a way of being rid of his angry and irrational inner self. Now he saw it for what it was: suppression of the human to make individuals more malleable slaves of the ruling Old Guard. This mental transition felt radical – as if whole blocks of his consciousness had shifted round to different positions. Was this something of that 'snap back' Albermech had mentioned earlier? The reptile overlay broke and shifted, and it seemed almost as if elements of his identity were fading in and out of focus.

'Outstanding,' his mother replied. 'You have been taught from an early age to sneer at the organic human and place cyber enhancement on a pedestal. The Founder knew what he was doing when he first established our world. His vision of a cyborg future required complete suppression of the organic. We had to be prepared from a young age, so we would be willing to accept our integration with the technology calmly.' She reached up and touched her plastic face.

'So how is it you've *not* accepted it?' Piper asked, feeling daring in asking such a question.

'One moment.' She held up a finger. 'There is further information you need at this point. The original thesis of the Cyberat was to enhance the human through integration with technology, not to *replace* the human. Perhaps on other worlds this has happened, since the Founder was only one leader aboard one colony ship from Earth, and subordinate to a ruling council.'

'What?'

'Why do you think you were kept from progression for so long?'

'Because I needed to learn how to control my anger issues before going through that process, otherwise I could become a societal danger.'

'No, not really. If you became a danger, the modification would have continued and you would have ended up an Enforcer. We were able to delay your progression by arguing the original thesis, and we only managed that because of your father's position in the hierarchy.'

'I see.' His mind started fizzing with this new input.

She continued, 'Throughout our history here, the original thesis has been distorted to show contempt for the human and the organic, and a need for its removal. The five rebellions we've had have all been by those who didn't accept this distortion. Even Castron and the present Old Guard rode on that idea, until they obtained power. Then they quickly abandoned it. But others, and I, still agree with the original, which is about enhancement, not replacement.'

'Five—'

She interrupted, 'In fact, much as they are doing in the Polity.'

Piper sat there absorbing another blow to his past thinking. He felt he couldn't encompass all this properly – it was too contrary to his Cyberat education. However, the more he turned over these facts in his mind, the greater his acceptance. At first, he felt oddly relieved. When he realized he was being presented with the truth, not political expediency, that reaction wasn't so strange.

'How do you know this?'

'Albermech has given me access to much information not available in the netlinks the Polity has provided more widely to our population. And you might be interested to know that the limitations on that information do not come from the Polity, but have been imposed by the Old Guard's censorship.'

'Fuckers,' said Piper, teeth gritted and suspicions confirmed.

His mother's arm flicked out and she slapped him across the face. The education she'd provided had often been as harsh as general Cyberat education. She didn't frown on profanity, but on loss of control, and Piper had just displayed the angry thing constantly boiling inside him. He noted the four at the other table briefly look over. The guy in the suit looked amused as he turned back to their conversation.

'I apologize,' said Piper, feeling embarrassed.

'Do you now understand why I taught you not to show your emotions?'

Piper struggled with the anger, again using the mental technique of attributing it to the reptile and distancing himself from it. He finally dipped his head and the anger hardened into a cold exactitude; it was the clarity he felt from the reptile overlay on the rare occasions he countered an argument or expressed an opinion. Only now it was much stronger.

'Because you were preparing me for the truth about the

25

Cyberat, and needed me to conceal that truth inside me. You tried initially to help me avoid getting a behavioural implant, but that failed. And you were preparing me for . . . rebellion?'

'It was a long game. It could have led to you becoming a teacher just like me, and rebellion would still lie sometime in the future. But now, with the arrival of the Polity, things have changed.'

Piper understood this, but cycled back to his previous question again: 'How is it that the indoctrination didn't work on you?'

'The information about the original Cyberat thesis can never be completely erased. There are those who maintain it but keep their heads down, and it's available for anyone who's prepared to look. I was one of them, and I found your father, who had long known how things are. We connected to others and I've steadily learned the truths of our society. This is how it's happened every time, leading into the previous rebellions too.'

'And yet they've all failed.'

'Old structures reasserting, as I said before.'

'And now the Polity . . .' he prodded.

'The Polity is prepared to intervene, but only if certain circumstances prevail. A high percentage of the population needs to be aware of what has been happening here, and to that end your father is distributing secret software in the latest upgrades and tech replacements. When he has distributed a sufficient quantity of these items, the Cyberat in receipt of them will be presented with the data you now have, and more.'

'Why is that necessary for intervention?'

Even with her enamelled face Piper could see the question made Reema uncomfortable.

'When it reaches a certain number of recipients, the information will spread to all, and everyone will know the original Cyberat thesis, how they've been indoctrinated, what has been taken away from them, and what the true aims of the Old Guard are. For most of them, it will just be confirmation. But they'll also learn what they can gain from the Polity – how much can be restored. The paradigm will change and the Old Guard will fall.'

Piper noted that she hadn't actually answered his question. He tilted his head and gazed at her in query. She remained silent for a moment, then snorted.

'I taught you well,' she said. 'Rebellion and intervention. If eight hundred and forty million Cyberat think they are under attack from the Polity, many will respond. However, with the right information, most will not respond and a portion will join the rebellion. These matters are always decided by the minorities of major populations.'

'But the Old Guard is powerful, and they have their Enforcers . . .'

'They are already responding. Why do you think that accident happened to you?'

He again remembered Mallon looking at him, and understood.

'Deliberate,' he snapped, then leaned back to avoid a slap that didn't come.

'The accident rate has always been high here,' she said. 'At one time I simply accepted that, until Albermech pointed out that it shouldn't be so. It's been mostly deliberate, to hurry Cyberat into progression from their youth. Now, knowing just what a threat the Polity poses to them, the Old Guard has accelerated the programme. In the past, the accident rate was thirty per cent and it has gone up above sixty. And there have been many full deaths. Yours would have been one of them, without the Polity's intervention.'

'It seems illogical,' he said. 'By pushing people into progression, they're not necessarily creating supporters.'

'Except, of course, they've decided that newly progressed Cyberat will receive modifiers for the duration of the *emergency*.'

'What emergency?'

'They have classified the Polity as a potential threat, since it arises from the artificial intelligences of old Earth, from which the Cyberat fled.'

'That's ridiculous.'

Her shrug was eloquent.

'What can I do?' he asked.

His mother stood up abruptly. 'I would rather you did nothing, but unfortunately we've reached the point where inaction is no longer an option. Being protective of you would simply be a selfish act on my part.' She turned to the suited man, who'd also stood up and was approaching their table. 'Inster here will show you some things . . . I must go and prepare the others for what is to come.' She walked off with no further word.

Piper stared at her retreating back. A stray thought then arose: Mallon was a powerful Cyberat of the Old Guard, yet she had visited and taken control of a house construction site. The one where Piper had been working, and he was the son of rebels . . . how much did they suspect?

2

'Why are you showing me weapons?' Piper asked as he studied the inside of the Embassy armoury. 'I don't have the training for such things. They're the province of the Enforcers.'

Inster looked down at the pulse gun he was cradling lovingly and replied, 'Because your mother, even with her great hopes of a relatively bloodless transition of power, is a smart woman and she wants you to survive.'

'The Old Guard, the Enforcers . . .' Piper said, and his reptile rose eagerly. Even after all he and his mother had discussed, and the resultant shift in his thinking, he'd never really entertained the possibility of proper violence, of warfare – in short, what rebellion really meant. He suddenly felt stupid; he should have realized. His mother had explained to him how the Old Guard currently clung to power covertly. But as soon as the threat against them became clearer, they'd order the Enforcers out to implement an overt crackdown. The Old Guard's ostensible acceptance of the Polity would disappear and the Embassy would likely come under attack. He reached for the pulse gun and Inster handed it over to him.

Piper repeated verbatim what Inster had said to him after presenting the weapon: 'Ionized aluminium dust flung out by, and incorporating, electromagnetic pulses. Has the same impact value of slugs from an Enforcer rotogun. It can kill the human

29

components of a Cyberat, but a lot of shots are required because of their physical support systems. Best to aim for extraneous, unshielded hardware, like cerebral supports.' He worked the controls, noting numerous settings and vaguely recognizable code appearing on a small screen in the side of the thing. 'I don't want to kill my own people.'

'You may not have a choice,' Inster replied. 'But you are, apparently, highly intelligent. So tell me what else it does.'

'Power supply value?' Piper enquired.

'It's on the screen.'

Piper studied the thing further. The code wasn't what the Cyberat used, nor was the written language he next brought up, but there were similarities, and the numerals hadn't changed. He pieced things together and, with his Cyberat technological education, worked out the basic premise of the weapon.

'It can fire dispersed pulse shots that deliver an electric discharge,' he said.

Inster smiled. 'You worked that out on very little information. Perhaps your mother was right about you.'

'Probably not sufficient to knock out an Enforcer and his hardware,' Piper opined. 'Nor is it likely to have a big effect on one of the Old Guard. If they decide to go to war, they'll plug into their war bodies.' He now looked around the armoury Inster had brought him to. There were racked laser carbines Inster had pointed out earlier, and the rifle version of the weapon he held, as well as other things, such as the armoured suits, hand-held missile launchers and munitions.

'That's why this is only a backup weapon,' said Inster. He paused contemplatively then added, 'Interesting that they retain these "war bodies" when this world hasn't had a rebellion in fifty years, and has no extraneous enemies.'

'Perhaps having been rebels they're always prepared for rebellion,' Piper said. 'And this gun still is not enough.'

Inster nodded, reached over to another rack and took out a different weapon – one of about twenty. It looked vaguely like the carbines but was thicker and had some canisters screwed onto the underside. 'This will be your main weapon.'

Piper put the pulse gun back on the shelf next to its holster and took the new weapon. The pulse gun had been heavy but this was much heavier and, though he knew it wasn't quite logical, Piper equated this weight with danger.

'What's this?'

'It's specifically designed for taking down Cyberat,' said Inster.

'Nice to be prepared,' said Piper dryly.

'Do you think we didn't know what was likely to go down here?' Inster pointed to the gun. 'It's a combined weapons system. It has a laser carbine function but the main guts of the thing are an ionic warfare beam – a disruptor. It puts a high power discharge through the target, along with induction viral warfare. All programs are loaded and prepared. It should be enough to take down the systems of one of your Enforcers and severely hamper one of the Old Guard, no matter what they're plugged into.'

'This isn't going to be easy, is it?'

Inster sighed, then said, 'Let me enlighten you with some harsh realities your mother probably didn't elaborate on. We're short-handed here in this embassy and in our ship in orbit above. A proper intervention mission on a world of this population, with the level of tech of the Cyberat, should involve at least five capital ships, and no fewer than fifty thousand soldiers with plenty of equipment to deploy. We have four thousand marines presently coming out of hibernation up there. That's all.'

'Why?'

'Before I tell you about that, perhaps you'd like to start trying on one of those suits?'

Piper shrugged, walked over and began inspecting one of them. When he turned back, shaking the heavy thing out, he saw Inster had his fingers up against the object behind his ear – some kind of communications device. He was frowning. Piper looked down again to concentrate on the suit. The armour sections were soft and light and, on tracing some pipework, he saw they were filled from reservoirs around the torso section of the suit. The joints had bearing surface assist motors. Judging from the connections in the thick helmet ring, and the chain-glass visor lying hinged back from it, the visor ran a head-up display. Seeing no toilet arrangements inside the suit, he began to pull it on over his clothing. Inster lowered his fingers from his ear device and returned his attention to Piper.

'Okay,' he said. 'We were sent here to try and pull this world into the Polity. Not because of any wish to save you from your-selves, but because, strategically, it sits at the back door of our realm. Intervention was planned for this place some time ago, through instigating a vote and then a force to back up its result. But our mission, with limited resources, is to push most of the population out of the fight and to assist the rebellion. It will be bloody but will result in regime change.'

'Back door?' Piper repeated, abruptly aware he was being told things he probably wasn't supposed to know about, and wondering why.

'The main front is over the other side of the Polity,' said Inster bluntly.

'You're at war?'

The man nodded. 'It all seemed so wonderful when we encoun-tered our first alien civilization. Didn't turn out that way. The prador are like your tree crabs, only the size of an Enforcer. Totally hostile.'

'Why are you telling me this?'

'To get you acquainted with the harsh realities as quickly as possible, since the shit has just started to hit the fan.'

'What other harsh realities do you have for me?' Piper asked.

Inster looked at him with a flat expression. 'Your mother and father have just been arrested,' he said.

A distant rumble reached them and Piper felt the floor shift slightly. 'Seems the Old Guard are on the move,' Inster told him.

Piper noticed the man hadn't touched the device on the side of his head this time. Evidently there was now no need to convey to Piper that it was a method of communication, a data source, additional computing for the man's brain. Piper studied the device more intently and guessed that it had connections woven into his skull.

'It's called an aug – short for augmentation, though there are many varieties of the same. You'll understand the terms in time.' He was sharp. Inster had divined the direction of his attention straight away and seemingly read his mind. The man turned away, eyes briefly glazed. Piper took the opportunity to step back to a shelf, to surreptitiously sweep up an object and close it in his fist.

'My parents?' he said tightly.

'Castron has them at his villa which, you may know, is large, fortified and has prison cells underground.' Inster turned back, studying him intently. 'Come with me – I have some people I need to introduce you to.'

As the man headed out, Piper quickly scanned all the weapons before following, glad to have at least retained the suit and the object he'd stolen. Under reptile overlay, his mind was working fast now and all his youthful misconceptions seemed to be shrivelling in its intensity. His parents were captives. Almost certainly Castron had known they were working against him. Mallon's attack on Piper had likely been intended to push them to reveal themselves in some way, and this also explained Castron's presence outside the surgery room. They would be questioned and Castron would then learn of the other rebels. After this, they'd be discarded or so radically altered they'd no longer be the people he knew. Inster closed the door to the armoury, palming a lock. Piper studied the door for a moment, then went on after the man.

Yes, his parents would surely be killed, in one way or another, and attempting to free them was quite likely not on the Polity agenda, since it seemed to be only big picture with them. He would have to act himself, and soon.

'Reema and Doge are important to what will happen here and important to me,' said Inster. 'I'll not allow Castron to ream them out.'

Again, it was almost as if the man was reading his thoughts.

They hurried through the Embassy. Around them other people were also on the move: soldiers in suits like his, some carrying equipment, and what looked like civilian staff heading for shafts. Piper paused, seeing them step into what appeared to be a straight drop downwards, but then descending slowly out of sight. Some form of grav tech unfamiliar to him.

On a platform outside a long curved window, he saw two women in green and grey overalls. One was operating a tablet, while the other had climbed into a seat and was strapping herself in. She wore a strange helmet and, even as he passed the window, Piper saw a heavy, pedestal-mounted gun rising out of the terrace ahead of them. Shortly after this, through another window, across which armoured shutters were drawing, he saw amber hexagons

34

appearing in the sky. He understood it to be shielding, though again it was a technology he didn't recognize.

'They'll be in for some surprises when they try to hit this place,' said Inster. 'Our war tech is, of necessity, rather advanced.'

'When will they?' Piper asked.

'Over eighty per cent chance in the next hour – it's in the log-tac assessment.'

Piper nodded at that.

Finally, Inster brought them to a door. Piper stepped through it and noted a scattering of chairs, a table, with equipment and packs neatly but temporarily stacked here and there around them. Tool racks ran along the walls, and benches had been pushed up against one of them. Some kind of workshop? Inster stepped in after him, then caught his shoulder. 'Stay here. You'll be coming with us to go after your parents.' With that, the man left.

The door swung closed and Piper stared at it. Why would Inster bring him, a young untrained man, along on a rescue mission? It seemed unlikely and, even if it was so, he felt he would most probably be kept at the back, safe, and not be allowed to get fully involved. He started to step towards the door but then it opened again and a huge man loomed through it.

'Meersham,' he said, holding out a hand like a scrap grappler. 'And you're Piper.'

Aug on the side of his head, updated from Inster, layers of information transmitted. This man was big and Piper suspected he'd had some form of organic enhancement. His head was bald, his face scarred and he had a big grey moustache. Piper shook the hand, then moved back as others crowded in behind this giant. Meersham seemed utterly relaxed, and walked over to sprawl in a chair, then tilted it back against the wall. Piper studied the others following and knew his chances of getting out of here, to go his own way, had just dissolved.

All four soldiers wore suits similar to Piper's, but he noted they had a more battered look, with variable additions and personalization. They all carried disruptors like those Inster had shown him in the armoury, but also heavy pulse handguns, quantum-cascade hand lasers and, in two cases, swords. One thin, acerbic-looking man sat at the table and set to work with the objects there. A black-haired man sat in a chair, one along from Meersham, while a beautiful black-haired woman squatted to open a pack and inspect its contents. Piper wasn't sure what to do or say, until Meersham pointed at the man behind the table.

'That's Sloan – he's our explosives tech, mainly because he really loves blowing things up.'

Piper shrugged himself into motion. He had to make himself part of this. He stepped out hesitantly and pointed at the objects on the table. 'Those spheres are grenades, I think, but what are the others?'

The man was sorting through the grenades, various small cylinders as well as other objects that looked like small coins, and inserting selections of them into bandoliers.

Sloan indicated one of the coins. 'These are chain-glass decoders – they unravel its molecular structure and turn it to dust.' Next the cylinders. 'These are explosives, with a variety of blast profiles including planar and line-punch.' He added, 'The grenades are antipersonnel, predicated on a conventional Polity human without armour, within a three-metre blast radius.'

Piper nodded and stepped back, looking around. Meersham gestured with a thumb at the black-haired man, then to the woman. 'This here is Cheen and she is Geelie.'

Piper noted the close physical similarity between the two, with their dark hair and perfect chiselled features. They could be twins, he realized, but then he focused in on the weapons both of them carried.

'Why a sword?' he asked Geelie.

She looked up at him with vague interest in her deep blue eyes and he felt his legs growing just a little weak. Closing the pack, she stood upright and abruptly drew the sword out of the sheath on her back. It made a fine ringing sound as it came free. From where he sat on the other side of the room, Cheen reached up to a tool rack behind him, took down a torsion spanner and threw it at her. Her movements were a blur, the sword making a crackling sound as it cut arcs through the air. The spanner fell in four pieces, the cut faces gleaming.

'Show-off,' said Meersham.

'Quite enough to remove the robotic limbs of any Cyberat who gets antsy,' said Sloan. 'Of course, while a ceramal sword with a meta-material, cat-claw edge is atomically sharp and can cut through just about anything, it's pretty much useless in the hands of us weak humans.' He held up one full bandolier and Geelie stepped over, sheathing her sword, and took it from him.

'What?' said Piper, staring at him in puzzlement.

'Are we all getting nicely acquainted?' Inster asked as he stepped back into the room.

Piper let the last comment settle in his mind for later review, and turned his attention to Inster. He was now wearing a combat suit too, had a disruptor on his back and handguns at each hip. Or at least they had a gun shape but looked surprisingly flat and thin. He also carried a second disruptor and the pulse gun sidearm he'd shown Piper earlier.

'The boy is coming?' Sloan asked, standing up.

Piper bridled, reminded of what Mallon had called him. He then suppressed the reaction as immature. He might be twenty-five Founder's World years old, but perhaps he was still a boy to them.

'Yes,' Inster replied.

Piper half expected there to be objections, but Sloan simply nodded, picked up a bandolier and tossed it to him. He caught it and looked over the series of grenades and decoders. 'There's a four-second detonation setting on the grenades – you only have them and a couple of decoders. Make sure you're at least five metres from any blast, with your visor closed.'

They were all on the move now, picking up bandoliers from the table and various packs, power supplies and other equipment. Piper hung the bandolier over his shoulder as he had seen the others do, where it engaged against pads on his suit. Inster then handed him the two extra weapons he'd brought. Piper pressed the sidearm holster against another pad on the suit's belt, where it stuck, and hung the disruptor on his back by the strap. By the time he'd done this, the four were already heading out of the door. He moved to follow but Inster caught his shoulder and held him in place for a moment.

'Any questions?' he asked, once the others were through the door.

'Why are you letting me come?' Piper asked.

'Because you're safer with us than out there trying rescue missions on your own.'

'What?'

Inster gave a tired smile. 'I'm old, Piper, and I've had years of experience dealing with people in many ways, and judging them. How long after we left before you were in that armoury, getting weapons to rescue your parents?'

Piper felt briefly annoyed and, at the same time, oddly reassured. He hadn't thought himself so transparent, yet the fact that Inster could see through him indicated the man's professionalism.

'How would you have got through the door?' Inster asked.

Piper pondered this for a moment, then pulled the object he'd stolen from his pocket. It was a grenade – just like those on his bandolier.

Inster nodded. 'I never saw you take it. You're interesting. Come on.'

He led the way out after the others into a corridor through the Embassy. There weren't so many people about now, and those that were wore uniforms and/or armour, with weapons. He felt the floor shake again and could hear the distant rumbling of explosions.

'Put your helmet up,' said Inster, watching him out of the corner of his eye.

Piper had already ascertained how some of it worked. Most of the suit's controls, when not operating through the visor's HUD, could be worked through the console on his right arm. It had come on when he donned the suit, showing a keypad with icons that were only vaguely familiar. But he realized the thing should also have other quicker options. He reached up and tapped a flat pad just below the collar. With a gentle whirring, ribs lying around the back of the collar hinged up, creating a helmet over his skull to the top of his forehead. They also brought up the visor, now hinged out to one side. He swung it across and clicked it into position, seeing Inster nod approval as he did so.

As soon as the visor was in place, the whole thing tightened and sealed around his head, and more whirring produced metallic air to his nostrils. Piper frowned at the HUD as it appeared. The language was again only vaguely familiar.

'I can work out some things, but I am not completely familiar with Polity Anglic,' he said.

'It's very similar, but I get you,' said Inster. 'I and others here tried learning your language bare-brained, but found that wasn't enough.' The man's voice came through a speaker somewhere in the helmet. 'Albermech?' Inster continued.

'On it,' replied the familiar voice of the Polity AI.

The HUD display disrupted, shifted and reformatted, then converted into easily readable Cyberat machine code and text. Piper glanced at the console on his forearm and saw that had changed too. He began to experiment with the HUD and quickly found it operated by eye tracking and blink control. As they hurried along, he scrolled through the menus, soon finding connections to his weapons, the com icons of the others and some incredibly complex, but useful, data feeds. He linked up the weapons and got crosshairs, one up at the top of the visor and one below. No use to him yet, since right now the disruptor was pointed at the ceiling and the pulse gun at the floor.

'Activate your com icons,' said Inster.

Piper noted that one was active: a flat thin gun like the ones Inster wore, his name in text below that. He activated the others. These were small pictures of ancient warriors carrying spears, almost naked but for helmets and some armour. He focused on them, activating each with a blink. Next, because they were on the move, he did an unfocused blink then swept his eyes to one side, shifting and compacting the menu to the edge of the visor so it wouldn't interrupt his vision.

Having so easily adapted to this new technology, he felt sharp, smart and happy. The reptile still seemed to be sitting under or in overlay, or rather some expression of it did, while the thing itself remained coiled inside. Action, and the necessity of thought, suppressed its irrational aspects, just as work on that building site had done, but this wasn't a long-term solution. Perhaps now, without the threat of the modifier, he would be able to incorporate what he felt sure was just a part of himself. Maybe he could become complete, and not someone suffering from a split personality disorder. Yet, even as he thought this, the reptile stirred in response and he feared its effects on him.

They soon caught up with the other four at the top of a long staircase, opening a door there and moving out onto a landing platform on top of the Embassy. Piper looked around. Over to his left, hanging in the sky, were hexagons of the force field he'd glimpsed before. Far down to his left, in the conglomeration of buildings, sat the weapon he'd seen earlier too. It fired, the flash of a blue-purple particle beam stabbing through the air and hitting something in the distance. Black debris silhouetted against a blast.

'The fuckers,' said Inster.

'Not slinging quite so much our way now,' Meersham replied.

'No real regard for their people,' commented Geelie.

'No regard?' Piper wondered.

Inster turned to him. 'The hardfields are stopping the small stuff, but we're taking out the other things with particle beams. Things such as nuclear warheads – yields in kilotonnes.'

Piper got it instantly and looked out at the city all around the conglomeration of embassy buildings. A nuclear warhead here, in that yield range, would take out a lot more than just the Embassy. Many Cyberat would die, many would be injured, and more would lose their systems to the EMR pulse and quite possibly die too. He almost felt satisfied that his anger at the Old Guard had received further justification and, as a consequence, the reptile stirred again. Next, finding visual enhancement and magnification on his visor, he focused outwards. Numerous Cyberat were in the sky, moving away swiftly. Between the buildings he could see further hordes of his fellow citizens, who didn't have the option of flying, fleeing through the streets instead. They clearly all knew about the nukes.

They finally arrived at a vehicle parked on the landing platform. The long Polity grav-car had thrusters protruding from nacelles at the back of it, and looked as solid as a brick. As they approached,

41

wing doors opened down the sides, revealing the pairs of seats inside. By this he understood that someone had sent a signal via aug to open it, and also inferred that there was probably a further level of communication between the group to which he wasn't privy. They threw packs in the back two seats and piled in. Inster and Cheen were in the front two – one of them evidently for the pilot, which Cheen took, and one for another set of controls. Piper suspected they were for weapons and or defences. Geelie and Meersham went in the next two seats behind these, and so he found himself strapping in beside Sloan at the back.

'Be fast, Cheen,' said Inster.

'No, really?' said Cheen dryly.

The doors folded down closed and locked in place with numerous solid thunks. A second later the car was lifting off, upward acceleration pushing Piper down in his seat. He wished he had a view, then searched his HUD menu for something. The link to the car he found quickly and, sorting through options, opened a screen in the HUD. Now, wherever he looked, it was as if the car had become transparent around him. The Embassy fell away below, Ironville then opening out and dropping too, turning into a small collection of human habitations amidst the pastel palette of the lichen. Piper could see explosions down there and the brief bright stab of beam weapons. He focused in and it became clear that the exodus continued – Cyberat flying out over the lichen and those on the ground moving fast along transport roads between the slab-like greenhouses on the outskirts of the city.

'Cheen has much faster reactions, obviously,' said Inster. It took a second for Piper to realize that the outline appearing around Inster's com icon indicated this was a private communication between them. He focused on the compacted menu and brought it back across his visor over the view, then found that focusing on one of the background squares behind each icon opened up private com.

'Why, specifically, can Cheen and Geelie use swords?' he asked Inster.

'Because they're Golem.'

Piper was starting to get used to Inster presenting him with only meagre information. Was the man perpetually testing and assessing him because they were about to go into action? Piper had searched out his memories of the word 'Golem' after finding out this was what the Albermech avatars were. It had been just a small segment in history class. Back on old Earth, increasing mechanization had inevitably led to increasingly independent and capable machines. And, of course, since it was almost a fictional imperative, they had created humanoid robots – androids. The main company that had swept the market for androids, used in medical care, had been called Cybercorp. And their main product had been called Golem – a name that was related to some ancient history about manufactured humanoids.

'They're AI avatars, as Albermech uses?' he asked.

'They'd be insulted if they heard you say that.'

'But they're robots . . .'

'Don't call them that to their faces. They're sensitive about such things.'

How then did all this relate to artificial intelligence? It had been steadily on the rise before the departure of the Cyberat and, apparently, they had missed the AI takeover of Earth by a couple of decades. The Cyberat doctrine had presupposed this eventual ascendance of AI, and had been the reason they built their colony ships. Their idea to keep AI suppressed and incorporate it was to avoid the eventual AI extermination of humanity. Again Piper pondered on the fact that they had been right about the ascendance of AI, but wrong about the extermination.

'They are free individuals,' he said.

'Yes, you got it,' said Inster happily.

Piper grimaced at Inster's happiness. It was the same as past reactions of his mother and other teachers whenever he made a leap. The *boy* done good. Later, the reactions of those teachers had become more muted when he continued to make further leaps. Piper had then tried to hide his intelligence but struggled to do so with his reptile prodding him. This had become increasingly difficult when he was working the sites too. He blinked off private com, shunted his view to one side and went back to studying his menu – learning all the functions of his suit and weapons at a frenetic pace.

'What do we have on log-tac?' Inster enquired. 'And remember we're not all auged.'

'The villa is by the sea, and it also seems to be a tertiary operations centre,' said Geelie. 'Interesting, the politics of this. The Old Guard council ran the world, but what's happened now reminds me of the Roman senate.'

'Elaborate on that,' said Inster.

'In some circumstances, the senate would elect a dictator, and then sometimes make him dictator for life. It was this that led to the emperors of Rome. Castron has recently been elected "war leader" but, as with old Rome, the election involved some . . . pressure.'

'Pressure?' Meersham asked.

'Albermech informs me a number of "moderate" Old Guard have met with accidents over the last year. In the last few days, more of them have been either arrested or taken down by Enforcers. Projections are that there will be no return from this dictatorship.'

'So the villa,' Sloan prodded, glancing aside at Piper.

'Heavily fortified against air and land assault. A few hundred

Enforcers in place, along with Castron and some of his supporters.'

'Our way in?' asked Cheen.

'The sea.'

At the mention of that body of water, Piper felt a surge of atavistic fear, but just then the car jerked to one side. Piper's minimized screen view filled with fire and he expanded it. The car was flying out of a blast, then a particle beam licked out from it and hit something in the distance. The second blast was a ball of orange fire and Piper realized this must have come from a chemical explosive.

'The order went out about a minute ago,' said Inster. 'All Cyberat other than Enforcers and select war bodies are to remain on the ground.'

'We're not Cyberat,' Meersham drawled.

'That doesn't seem to matter to the Enforcers chasing after us.'

'Missiles were from them?' enquired Sloan.

'No – ground battery,' Geelie supplied. 'We'll soon be over the sea, so clear.'

Piper looked down. He could see no battery amidst the lichen, but they did pass over another Cyberat town, again lit with explosions and beam trails. On seeing this, something strange occurred. He'd always seen Cyberat construction as a desirable implementation of order, but now he saw that town as an aberration, like a pustule breaking through clear skin. Other reactions were expected: he felt tight inside and very much awake. Fear and excitement ran through him too, and with so much to occupy his mind and body, his reptile was keeping to itself. So he recognized his reaction to the town as another sign of the radical change going on deep inside him since he'd awoken in that Embassy surgery. Meanwhile, the soldiers around him had shown

45

very little reaction to the attempts to blow them out of the sky and were even continuing their commentary for his benefit, though perhaps they just liked to talk.

'So tell me about the sea,' said Inster.

'A blind spot,' said Geelie. 'Castron's villa extends into it but doesn't have a lot of defences there. They only use the sea to net up big shoals of adapted krill for protein, and for a scattering of abiotic oil platforms. Very few Cyberat have altered themselves to move effectively in that environment.' She glanced round her headrest at Piper. 'It's like it's irrelevant to their dogma. But that's not all of it.'

The fear Piper felt acquired a new dimension.

'Water,' he said, feeling that age-old paranoia of the Cyberat creeping up.

'Indeed,' Geelie replied.

'You said not a lot of defences, so that means there are some,' Meersham noted.

'Semi-sentient hunter torpedoes,' she replied. 'A recent addition. I suspect Castron has been reassessing his defences since our arrival here. But I don't think that's all that's driving him.'

'Wanted to be the boss for a long time,' commented Sloan.

Lichen-clad land slid along below them, then rose up into mountains, undergoing a colour change to darker shades of the alien growth, raising thousands of spore fans. The car turned, tracking along a mountain chain and then slowed. Piper couldn't see the purpose of this, puzzling over their current location in relation to Castron's villa on the coast. The car began a slow descent.

'We want them to think we are running to hide in the caves up here,' explained Inster.

Ah . . .

'Albermech,' Inster continued. 'Four Enforcers are on our tail.'

Piper directed his attention back the way they'd come but could see nothing. He magnified and scanned, and then drew the menu across to search the data on his links to the car's exterior cams. Here he found highlighted coordinates and long-range focus, then turned his head precisely and linked into it. Magnification increased, finally bringing four Enforcers into sight. Two wore large bacilliform bodies, with weapons protruding all around them and grappling tentacles bunched up underneath. One was a large man form riding on one of these – essentially a human-shaped robot twice the size of a conventional human, with his organic components stretched and tangled up in the hardware. The last was just a knot of pipes and cylinders around a misshapen armoured centre, all resembling some ancient engine. Image enhancement was nigh perfect and Piper focused in on this one. He could see the Enforcer's head behind a chain-glass screen – skull almost twice the size of normal, the back of it sunk into support tech, with a protruding forehead, and optic data cables plugged into the eyes. These must have been a recent addition, otherwise why would he have bothered with the chain-glass screen? The fact that he questioned this Piper recognized as another sign of change in his thinking.

'I have them,' Albermech replied.

A second later, three explosions disrupted the view. Piper drew back to see the blasts expanding and debris tumbling out, the man form still intact and dropping fast. Three vapour trails spearing down from above were now breaking up in the wind, and he realized the Enforcers must have been hit by railgun shots from the Polity ship in orbit. He felt a brief moment of sorrow at the loss of life, but hard practicality quickly kicked in. The Enforcers had been hunting them and would have tried to kill them. Another harsh reality was that little of what they'd been remained anyway. Under constant *modification*, they had ceased to be the people they once were, becoming merely the physical manifestation of the Old Guard's power. People never came back from being turned into an Enforcer.

'Keep any others away,' said Inster. 'How go preparations?'

'Hypersonic drop shuttles are ready and the marines are aboard. We'll knock out ground defences from up here prior to drop. I'm also running cover for you. Time to disappear.'

'Cheen, engage the chameleonware,' said Inster. 'Let's do this.'

The car abruptly rose and huge acceleration threw Piper back in his seat, his suit compensating and dampening some of it. He reviewed his memories and found 'chameleon' in a brief glance, from when he was two years old in a museum of old Earth biology. From this he understood this technology must now be hiding them, as they closed in on their destination.

It took minutes only. Piper wondered about this chameleonware, since his view outside showed him the thruster nacelles burning hot. How the hell could that be hidden? Brief analysis offered him the hypothesis of viral warfare from the ship above hitting detectors on the surface.

'Chameleonware . . .' Piper said.

'Yes . . .' said Inster privately, waiting.

Piper opened up the menu tracking down something he'd seen earlier but dismissed because he hadn't understood it, and it hadn't seemed relevant. The word was different, 'chameleoncloth', but apparently the outer layer of his suit was made of it and could be activated.

'We can be invisible too?' he said, activating the function and looking at his hand.

'Open your visor,' Inster instructed.

Piper did so and his hand disappeared. Peering down, all he

could see was an empty seat, but line edges and flickering that hinted at something there. It was an utterly weird experience. He closed the visor again and it reappeared. The logic was apparent: if they all activated this cloth and couldn't see each other, they might end up shooting their own side. The visor somehow negated the effect.

'Don't rely on it too much,' said Inster. 'It was developed for prador ambush in a unit Sloan served in. It weakly covers the prador spectrum of vision, which includes our own but little else. Cyberat sensors can detect more.'

'But still gives a good edge.'

'Indeed.'

The landscape slid away below, then he saw the first flash of waves crashing against the rocky coast as they shot out over open water. The car turned hard, moving fast up the coast, and then abruptly decelerated. Piper's mouth went dry.

'The sea,' he said, then felt annoyed his innate fear had driven him to comment.

'Did you have any problem with us killing those Enforcers?' Inster now asked, still privately, and Piper recognized this as a distraction.

'Very little of the human remained in them anyway,' he replied.

'Interesting that you should think in those terms. Others might consider that entirely the Cyberat's objective.'

Piper nodded, astonished to find how he now utterly rejected Cyberat dogma, at least as it stood under the Old Guard. He recognized that, despite his indoctrination, his mother had prepared him for such a shift in perception, yet it still seemed radical. He searched for the root of his rejection and found it in the example set by the Polity. A key tenet of Founder's World dogma was a fear of AI, yet the AIs hadn't exterminated humans but worked in partnership with them to propel greater advancement. In a flash of insight, he understood that the idea of AIs wanting to wipe out humanity had been based on humans being a threat, or even just a hindrance, to them. But this obviously wasn't the case. And why not keep humans around? Humans kept pets, and apparently still did in the Polity, and AIs were in essence just post-humans. He noted in passing that Cyberat didn't keep pets, which attested to a degree of fanaticism that dismissed such ephemera.

'The Cyberat objective is no longer mine,' he replied. And he really felt this in his core, boiling out into his overlay.

'Okay,' said Inster, 'but perhaps you need to take some time to decide what you are, or perhaps *find out* what you are.'

This seemed an odd thing to say, Piper felt.

The car dropped abruptly and he was weightless for a second, then it hit the water with a huge splash. His suit went semi-rigid around him, and internal layers instantly expanded, dampening the impact. The car then sank fast, into the emerald depths of the sea. Piper felt a surge of panic and began breathing fast. He thought about all the electronics and technology around him, all the EMR communication and data transfer, and how the salty and acidic seawater of his world could interfere with that. Then it was as if his inner reptile saw the ridiculousness of all these thoughts, and reached out to turn them over and sink them. His breathing remained rapid, however, and he still held himself rigid, as he searched for a logical response. He fell into an analysis of his reaction as the car settled just above the seabed, then moved forwards with the deep hum of turbines.

'Are you okay?' asked Inster.

'Psychological quirks,' he said abruptly. 'Avoidance of environments that can interfere with Cyberat technology, as it was. Accelerated adaptation. Cyberat avoid the sea because of this . . . history.'

50

'Outstanding,' said Inster, again echoing what his mother would often say to him when he did well.

'She certainly did a number on him,' said Geelie.

'That's a discussion for later,' Inster warned.

Piper didn't like being talked over this way and said, 'I presume you are referring to my mother. She used genetic alteration and nootropic therapy to increase my intelligence.'

'Did she indeed?' said Geelie flatly.

'She intended me to be a teacher, like her,' Piper felt the need to add.

'Of course,' said Geelie.

She was a machine, and a highly intelligent one – being artificial intelligence she couldn't be otherwise. What purpose would there be in making stupid AIs? She didn't believe what his mother had told him. More interestingly, she had clearly shown him her doubt by the tone she used.

'Limited Cyberat preparation,' said Inster, his voice dry. 'You have data hardware in your bones and, apparently, connections ready to interface with hardware as your body is *progressed.*'

'Yes,' Piper replied.

'From your father's factory,' said Geelie.

'Of course it was from his father's factory,' Inster interjected before Piper could confirm it.

Did Inster want him to know that something more had been done to him than he'd supposed? Analysing the brief conversation, Piper perceived that Inster's warning to Geelie had in essence also been to alert him to pay attention.

'Something in my bones,' he said, noting the car now settling to the bottom.

'You're fast,' said Geelie.

Piper nodded an acknowledgement.

A crump sounded, and then a rushing noise. Looking down,

he saw water flooding in around his feet. Again he felt a surge of panic, but this time angrily suppressed it. Having worked through the HUD menu, he understood perfectly that the suit provided air, while Cyberat technology, and certainly Polity technology, was way beyond being affected by seawater. The fear was an atavistic hangover and he could no longer countenance it. To one side, he noticed the nearest door steadily opening. In fact, all the doors were opening. Water began to boil in and the fight in his own mind was on. He put aside his queries, at least for now. Fear and excitement were organic and the same, while the words applied only to how the mind interpreted them. They were going into action and he felt a *thrill* about that, while his reptile anger was now almost non-existent. Fear was irrelevant and instead he saw the world with a harsh, fierce clarity. He unstrapped, picked up his weapon from the pocket beside him and wondered if it would fire under water. He had the answer via his HUD a second later: it would.

'Cloth on,' said Inster.

Though he hadn't turned off his chameleoncloth, Piper knew that was for his benefit – a reminder, an affirmation. He looked at the others and they were still visible. Good to remember they wouldn't be if he opened his visor.

'Cavitators,' said Sloan. 'Two of them in the compartment next to you, Meersham.'

'Got it,' Meersham replied.

The water reached Piper's visor, then went over above it. The visor adjusted instantly and it was as if the water had faded out of existence. When he stood up, he could only just feel it too, noting the suit had gone partially into assist mode to counter the water's resistance. Both of these things helped quell the dregs of that fear he supposedly wasn't feeling.

'Remora your boots,' said Inster privately.

Piper used the console on his forearm – just to ensure he knew how to operate it. The boots had gecko function, which was fine for walking on relatively clean surfaces, usually in vacuum, but not here. Looking out, he could see a rocky bottom with ribbons of green weed laid across it. Remora function of the boots turned out to be what the name implied, but with a cleaning cycle in the stick pads so the soles wouldn't get clogged up.

'We're about negative,' said Cheen.

Piper understood this meant they were about negatively buoyant. And, since Inster had told him to use the remora function, leaning a little towards floating away from the bottom. The others were soon out of the car, grabbing packs from the back seats. Meersham had two weapons like long slim rifles with impossibly narrow barrels, one of which he handed to Inster. Piper climbed out after them, then Geelie led the way, trudging off along the bottom.

'Funny how, when people are scared of a thing, they still like the thrill of looking out at it,' she said.

'Method of entry?' Sloan enquired.

'The part of the villa under the sea which has chain-glass bubble viewing windows.'

'Defences actually on the villa?'

'None that I know of.' Geelie looked over to her left. 'They're out here and a couple are coming right now.'

They moved through the water at a steady, slow-motion lope, kicking up debris from the sea floor and heading towards a large rocky outcrop. Focusing in on this, Piper noted scimitar mussels and penny oysters – a GM product of Earth that the Cyberat had sown in the oceans, along with a lot of other modified life. What the intention had been he had no idea, because such life didn't fit in with their dogma, beyond the netting of the krill for protein. From this he speculated on the change from then till

53

now. Society had been more open then, with a wider focus, but this had soon been crushed by those who came after the Founder.

As they rounded the outcrop, the lower parts of Castron's villa came into sight. It was a composite slab of a building running down a rocky slope and leading up into the shallows, a lip of which extended along the bottom with chain-glass bubble windows along it. Lights were shining from inside. At the very same time, two torpedoes appeared, coming straight for them: metal, hammer-headed devices, spurring steering fins and turning, white-tailed, as they accelerated. Meersham fired his cavitator. The beam initiated around what Piper had thought to be a barrel, and stabbed out through the water like a shiny braided cable. It struck one torpedo on the nose and it detonated, sending the other one tumbling away. The sea around Piper turned instantly glassy and he could see the meniscus of the shock wave approaching. It hit, as if he had run into a wall, and he found himself up off the bottom and flailing. A hand snared his foot and hauled him back down again just as Inster fired, hitting the other torpedo as it righted itself.

Once again engaged with the bottom, Piper felt embarrassed to have failed at the first action. Inster would be disappointed with him. But his clarity of mind swiftly dispelled this, for it wasn't necessary. He also noted how quickly the torpedoes had come after them – a reminder that he was only partially invisible since those weapons would have been using sonar. He followed Cheen, who'd pulled him back down, and found flat clear rock as the second blast wave passed, then stayed rooted to the spot until it was safe to continue on. Soon they were much closer to the lower lip of the villa. Four chain-glass windows bulged out into the depths, with shoals of krill dancing before them. Through them he could see bare rooms, and occasional portal doors for Cyberat plug forms, but no sign of occupancy.

'Piper, take the one on the right,' said Inster. 'Cheen, go with him.'

The others needed no verbal direction, doubtless being instructed via aug. Each went to a selected window and took out the chain-glass decoders from their bandoliers. Inster was over to the left with Geelie, while Sloan and Meersham took the middle two. Piper pulled a decoder from his bandolier as they drew closer. All it had on it was a simple button, and he guessed the delay was similar to that of the grenades. Cheen moved ahead and to the left, then halted abruptly, turning.

'Defences!' he shouted, just as a barrel protruded from the wall beside the window and fired. What came out whirred through the water towards Piper, but Cheen stepped into its path. Weapons fire flashed underwater to Piper's left, just as a blast picked up Cheen and rolled him to one side. Piper's own weapon was suddenly in his hands without a second thought, crosshairs up and laser selected, and he fired at once. The laser cut through the water, leaving a boiling trail, and struck another shot that was just coming out from the barrel of the weapon. He then moved in, leaning into the shock wave, wanting to get as close as possible, not knowing how much energy the laser lost firing through water. As detritus of shattered krill, and perhaps some parts of Cheen, cleared he saw a second shot wasn't required. The barrel had tilted down, a chunk missing out of the wall above it and some of its workings were exposed. He scanned the rest of the wall, looking for further weapons, then turned in case more torpedoes might be incoming. What he saw gave him pause.

'Don't stand there staring,' said Cheen. 'Stick that decoder on!'

The man, or rather the Golem, had lost a good part of his body between the chest and waist. Artificial skin and flesh were gone, to expose shiny metal spine and ribs, though a knot of artificial intestine still floated in place, trailing one loose end. Fractured optics, tubes and s-con wires also hung free, but Cheen must have routed round these because he moved as smoothly as before. Piper absorbed the sight and turned back to the window. He'd lost the first decoder so took another from his bandolier. As he put it in place and pressed the button he found himself wondering: why the gleaming, polished bones? Surely some form of composite would have been better, perhaps with binding surfaces for the overlying artificial flesh? Such things he thought.

The decoder bound to the glass and he stepped back. Noticing water flooding into the room beyond from his left, he looked over and saw that the others had already blown their windows. A second later, the one before him turned white, then disintegrated, spreading milky debris in the water as it collapsed inwards. The water rushing in sucked Piper forwards and he let it take him, going feet first into the far wall of the room, beside a door.

'Location,' said Inster briefly, with no other explanation.

Piper estimated he had learned eighty per cent of functions and data available to him via the present iteration of the HUD and linked systems, and this was an easy question. A 3D block appeared in his visor as the room filled up, and he got his feet back down to the floor. It was a map of the building around and above him. This showed the four rooms they had just broken into, along with corridors and rooms leading upwards, towards the surface.

'We converge here,' said Inster.

A flashing dot appeared high up in the block. Piper fixed it with a blink, then chose one of the icons scattered around the block. The map and icons disappeared to show a directional arrow, which centred on the door when he moved out from the wall and turned.

'You first,' said Cheen, moving up beside him.

Piper nodded and ducked through.

'And remember that the tech, while very useful, is a target for disruption in warfare.'

Moving along the corridor on the other side, Piper dipped his head in agreement. He recalled the map, stared at it and fixed it in his mind. He hadn't tried to remember it before. Now he knew he would never forget it.

3

Before Piper and Cheen had reached the convergence point, Sloan joined them. They all finally came together again in an oblate chamber, still under water, with a shaft running up at the angle of the rocky slope the villa clung to. Piper counted floating figures higher up, then glanced towards Inster, who was hanging onto the lower rung of a ladder leading up this shaft, then at Meersham and Geelie. There was another body here.

'Casualties are an unfortunate reality of war,' said Meersham.

Piper studied the man's grim and angry face behind his visor. It was a reminder that those around him had already been fighting a war and had faced loss. He wondered if the comment had been deliberately aimed at him, as it seemed so much was. He pushed off and swam over to the corpse, which was up against the curved roof of the chamber. It was held within some kind of veined suit caught on a protrusion there. Judging by the body shape, this was a woman. She seemed heavily damaged, so Piper surmised she must have been caught in an explosion or shot by one of the others. Only as he drew closer did he see the oddities about that damage. The top of her skull was missing, while one arm had been ripped away at the elbow, as well as one leg below the knee. The arm and the leg could be explained by weapons fire, but the skull? It had been cut away surgically and exposed an empty cavity – the brain was gone.

'The fuck?' said Piper.

He pushed away, understanding now that she must have died some time ago. Her skin had a blue hue shot through with brown veins. He looked down towards the floor and there saw three long boxes, one of them with the lid lying to one side. She'd been in there.

'Now that looks horribly familiar,' said Sloan.

'You've seen a lot of war,' said Inster swiftly.

'Yeah . . . I have that.'

The exchange died, but it got Piper's mind whirling. Meersham had seen something that dented even his nonchalant exterior, while Inster seemed to have shut Sloan down – had he said something he shouldn't have? There was something going on here . . .

'Castron has been experimenting on his own people?' asked Piper.

'Seems that way,' said Inster, non-committal. 'Let's get going. They'll know we're here by now and we have to move fast. Surface level is ten metres up and Castron is almost certainly moving people down.'

'But not into the water, of course,' said Geelie.

They moved into the shaft, swimming and propelling themselves upwards from the ladder and other protrusions. While he went, Piper assessed Inster's earlier response. He felt sure Castron had been experimenting, but there was more to it than that. He wondered about his own comment too, specifying 'his own people' rather than 'us'. He then put all that aside. It really wasn't important to his main objective right now of getting his parents out of this place. But he also felt a growing confidence in his own mind that he would find out the truth. Soon the surface of the water came into view as a rippling mirror above them.

'It'll be man forms up there, and other smaller Enforcers suited

59

to enclosed combat,' Piper said. 'No major war bodies, but linked robot weapons.' He'd just glimpsed the new 3D map that had come up of the villa's interior. Much of it was human scale, with nothing larger than that able to move through it. He memorized it all, even while bringing up the directional arrow to a dispersed area above the one Inster had highlighted.

As they drew closer to the surface, Inster spoke to him privately: 'You stay at the back for now.'

Resentment splintered from his reptile but it wasn't strong and he moved back without protest. It was logical that he shouldn't go in first, inexperienced as he was, unless it was sacrificially. Cheen and Geelie moved to the fore, Meersham and Sloan next, followed by him and Inster. Piper set his weapon to disruption mode – the cyber-killer. Cheen and Geelie pressed against the walls as they reached the surface of the water, and then surged out of it.

'Clear,' Geelie called.

They all climbed out into what was a circular chamber, with exits all around it leading to ramps for Cyberat. Cheen had put down his weapons and with a glue pen and a packet of patches began fixing his damaged suit back in place, his hands moving faster than human. Meersham and Sloan drew their pulse guns and began firing. Piper, feeling a surge of excitement, scanned for enemies, but the single shots were targeted at points on the walls, leaving burning, fist-sized holes.

He understood what they were doing before Inster explained, 'Pin cams. High detection range.'

Cheen finished his work, nodded to Geelie and the two Golem went straight for one ramp. Sloan and Meersham holstered their weapons and quickly followed. Piper was about to go too but, once again, Inster caught his shoulder and halted him, gesturing to another ramp.

'We go this way,' he said.

'Why?' Piper asked, instantly mapping out a new route to the highlighted area.

'Because the other four are being noisy, have shut down their chameleoncloth and will shortly detonate an EMP. You should shut down your suit too.'

Ensuring he had the map of the villa firmly in his mind, Piper used blink control to power down his suit. The thrum of air died and the console on his forearm went out. With a crump the helmet separated, the visor springing open and the whole thing folding down into the neck ring. He raised his weapon and inspected it. A lot of its systems had shut down but, having studied its format via his HUD, he knew it would still work via hard, shielded wiring. He would just have to aim it by eye.

Inster turned and ran for the ramp. As he followed, Piper instantly felt the loss of the suit's assist. Two levels up from them, he heard a distant thump and guessed it must have been the EMP. He seemed to feel it deep inside, unexpectedly, but then realized this was probably due to some kind of surge in the data channels in his bones. The strategy of the four going a different route, and using the EMP, was to draw down Enforcers to their location. Inster's plan to go in separately Piper hoped was aimed at getting them to the prison quickly and easily. But he also feared this could be because Inster was being protective of him. And something else puzzled him.

'Surely we'd be better with our cloth on?' he asked.

'I told you not to rely on it,' Inster replied.

'But we would be invisible . . .'

'No, the pin cams are wide spectrum and would see something. Whoever is watching is now aware of how we can conceal ourselves. But, like so much about this place, there's a weakness.

61

They're inactive until detecting powered-up hardware, which is why I told you to shut down your suit.'

Piper nodded, but kept sharp as they moved into a long corridor. The strategy would only keep them hidden while Castron's forces focused on the other four, but someone was controlling those pin cams, so the presence of hardware wasn't the only way they could be activated. He took in his surroundings as they went, assessing this Old Guard's home. There were no doors, since a creature only partially human didn't need privacy. So as they passed rooms, he was able to peer inside them. In one sat a row of control spheres, like the one Mallon had plugged herself into during the house build, along with columns extending down from the ceiling, each terminating in arrays of manipulators. Of course, Castron would do his own maintenance and upgrades to himself here. Piper also eyed the dust on this equipment and the webs of Earth-import spiders. Maybe Castron had stopped upgrading and maintaining, or maybe he did it elsewhere now.

In another huge room the machine bodies of Enforcers lay amidst equipment for handling them. Seeing these gave him a disturbing feeling, as though they angered him, or his reptile, and he wanted to reach out to them somehow. He dismissed this as arising from a fear of what they represented, and moved on. Yet another room revealed an overgrown garden, and then Inster finally halted at the next entrance, his posture rigid, and muttered a low curse. Piper moved up beside him and stared into a large space occupied by a huge machine.

'A war body,' said Piper, feeling the same odd shifting inside him as when he'd seen the Enforcer bodies, as well as a thrill of anger.

Inster turned to inspect him. 'A prototype perhaps,' he said, now blandly.

'As always, you know more than you're saying,' said Piper, still focused on the thing.

It was some kind of war or Enforcer body, but spread out over five metres across, and resembling the carapace of a tree crab, with the edges extended like stubby wings. At its summit lay the socket for a plug-form Cyberat, like Castron, to insert themselves, but it appeared incomplete. Hardware in the space hung on loose skeins of optics and wires. Piper found himself drawn to it, and stepped forwards to rest a hand on the armour. He suddenly felt as if he was winding up like a spring inside. His reptile's anger rose, similar to the water in the shuttle when they'd reached the bottom of the sea, but it became more complex and seemed to add other substance to his overlay. He felt a jolt of pain throughout, and when he moved again his joints crackled. The experience elicited a mental effect too – a space seemed to have opened up in his mind around a grid, and his skull ached.

'Interesting design,' said Inster, still in a flat tone.

Piper's hand hurt and he snatched it away from the armour. The pain continued, though, so he removed his glove to inspect it. Bloody dots had appeared in a regular pattern on his palm, and along the inner faces of his fingers. He wiped the blood away and saw a series of holes in his flesh, with metallic points sitting inside them like splinters. Even as he watched, the holes closed and the pain began to fade. Without comment, he pulled the glove back on and reattached it at the wrist. The floor then vibrated and the sound of a boom reached them.

'Sloan's getting playful,' said Inster looking at him keenly, then, 'You okay?'

'I'm absolutely fine,' Piper replied, seeing that Inster knew something about what had just happened to him. And, as the grid in his mind began to fill up with data so much more accessible than that in his HUD had been, he knew too.

'Let's move on,' said Inster, tilting his head to the sound of weapons fire.

At which point a man form came through the doorway.

The Enforcer's head just cleared the top of the door, and it stood half as tall again as Piper. At a distance it would have looked like a man wearing a suit, but closer up the differences showed. Gaps ran through it where joint motors linked the various pieces together. Between the chest section and the hips, the tangle of motors and pipes reminded Piper of how Cheen now looked, and he dismissed the idea that there might be a whole human in there. Meanwhile the head, sitting on top without a neck, was wide and flat, too small to contain a human skull.

It halted, sensory balls running in a track around its head to converge for a binocular view of them. It hesitantly began to raise one arm. This limb had a wide circular magazine at the biceps and terminated not in a hand but in the three barrels of a rotogun. Piper froze for a second, though subliminally he could see Inster watching him, and yet to raise his weapon. So Piper had to be the one to respond. The angry thing within him, which *was* him, levelled his weapon as his suit swiftly powered up, raising the helmet and closing the visor across. Gazing through eyes he now perceived as feverish reptilian yellow, he used HUD crosshairs to aim at that section between chest and hips for one shot. The beam from the weapon was just a glassy flicker in the air, but where it hit it sizzled, spreading electrical discharges. He next aimed at the head and fired again, to the same effect. The man form froze with its arm half raised, then toppled forwards to land with a crash. Piper stared at it, surprised it had been so easy.

'You activated your suit,' Inster noted.

Piper gestured towards his victim and snarled, 'We're not invisible.'

'Are you not capable of aiming and shooting without HUD targeting?' Inster enquired. There was something pointed in his voice.

'Of course I am,' Piper snapped, angry at his anger and scared, because even though he'd done well, something had felt out of his control.

'Come on,' said Inster, taking the conversation no further.

Piper followed him, stepping over the man form and then out. He was about to deactivate his suit again, but Inster activated his, bringing his helmet and visor back up, then breaking into a steady jog. As he went after him, Piper struggled to see his actions as his own and not driven by the reptile. But a horrible, unreal sensation was seeping through him: a dislocation. It was as if the closing up of his suit and shooting of the Enforcer had been his reptile seizing control. But no, the thing was him and its imagined separation just a method of self-control, wasn't it? He had to stay rational, and managed to cool off enough to assess what he'd done. Clarity returned.

Activating the suit manually usually required a brief press against one of the pads, like the one he'd used to close up the helmet for the first time. But he'd done nothing like that. What had actually happened was becoming clear to him, in the steadily growing mass of iconic data nodes in the newly formed grid in his mind. With a simple effort of will, he drew out the relevant node and found the function of the suit mirrored and linked there. It seemed he had activated his suit with his mind. He now understood that Inster's questions had been to highlight this. The man knew about the hardware in his bones. And he must know what the growing mass of nodes in Piper's internal space signified.

Yet he needed to stay focused on the now.

They took a number of turnings in the corridors and passed

a window facing towards the sea. Out there Enforcers were crowding the lavender sky, bright with the scored lines of particle beams and terminal explosions. He focused through the HUD, no longer using blink control, and saw other Cyberat fighting the Enforcers. It struck him that there simply weren't enough of them, and his body fizzed to be part of that action.

They approached a spiral downward ramp leading to the destination Inster had earlier highlighted, but something began to rise out of it. Piper glimpsed a thimble-shaped lump of technology with rotoguns on each side and a twisted human face low down under glass. Inster fired once, then grabbed Piper's arm and pulled him through a doorway. Piper went with him, and mentally leaped ahead. The room beyond contained furniture for Cyberat still retaining human form and actually had a door on the other side of it. Piper overtook Inster and kicked it open, splintering the composite about the lock, turned right, left, then climbed a wide staircase taking them to an arch leading onto the roof.

'Good plan,' said Inster, at his heels.

Piper ignored that, feeling possessed by excitement, which he now couldn't separate from his anger, clarity and will. He headed out across a landing pad until he reached a domed circular hatch. The fighting continued in the sky as he flicked his weapon to laser and burned off the lock on the side of the hatch. Inster was watching him again, still assessing, and Piper wondered about that. He'd seen this secondary route after surmising, as had Inster, that one Enforcer coming up that staircase probably meant more behind it. However, Inster had let him take the lead, and the man's calm and continuous scrutiny indicated another factor: he wasn't particularly worried about failure here. Piper then saw it in an instant: of course, the chameleoncloth and disruptor weapons. They wouldn't fail here, and his second shot at that man form had been unnecessary. He, Inster and the other four were like soldiers with machine guns amidst hostile tribesmen with bows and arrows. And Piper had yet to see what those two Golem were really capable of.

He wrenched up the hatch and slung it aside, realizing he'd kicked his suit into full assist, in preparation for what would come next. Scanning his surroundings, he focused over on the other side of the villa at something rising up between the buildings. Then it came clear: a war body. The squashed sphere of greenish metal was wrapped round with pipes, systems and weapons. A human figure sat in the top and centre of it, under a glassy dome. Even as the thing rose, armoured shutters began to close over that dome, but not before he'd recognized Castron, plugged into it there. The sick anger he felt surge at seeing this Old Guard conflicted with the knowledge that his parents lay below, and the reptile retreated in confusion. He turned to the shaft, exposed now the hatch was gone, and jumped into it.

Gravity took hold of him. He bounced off one side of the shaft, pushing for the other, subliminally glimpsing Inster behind him using the same technique to slow his descent. His suit, detecting the fall, briefly hindered movement at the joints until he dismissed that safety measure. Its internal layers expanded against him, also constraining movement, but he allowed this as only a second remained. He hit the ground hard, suit motors whining as they absorbed the impact, bringing him down into a squat, then a forward roll down a short slope. He fetched up hard against a wall, amidst tangled debris, Inster slamming in beside him, then unrolled carefully. Piper's suit informed him of various minor leg fractures, as well as others in his shoulder, and took action. Pain swiftly waned as it injected numbing agents. Internal layers expanded strategically to prevent further damage while still keeping him mobile. Assist stayed on to stop him collapsing.

Piper stood up, looking over as Inster carefully got to his feet too. He wondered if the man had been hurt and, even as he thought this, another data node opened in his mental grid and the answer was there before him. Inster's suit diagnostics showed he hadn't cracked a single bone, nor strained a single muscle. The man was certainly professional, Piper felt, while also noting that – if he wanted to – he could seize control of Inster's suit.

Inster nodded an acknowledgement, then turned his attention to the debris and pointed at it. Piper looked down and saw Cyberat interface hardware, rotten and broken, scattered through with human bones. He couldn't understand for a moment, until something harder inside him reviewed this information. He'd found the prisoners' entrance to Castron's jail. It seemed that the dividing line between death and imprisonment, in some cases, had been a matter of indifference to the old Cyberat. People in plug form, separated from their transport bodies, had simply been cast down the shaft. Inster moved to a low archway and through into the darkness beyond. Piper followed, kicking in visual enhancement. Some of the prisoners, still plugged into mobile bodies, had made it this far before dying: there were bones inside partially intact Cyberat chassis, and in one case a chassis dripped with maggot-laden, rotting flesh.

'Not a good man,' said Inster tightly, opening his visor.

Piper did the same and wished he hadn't when the smell hit him. Inster was visible now, so he shut down his cloth too as they moved on into ribbed tubes, with spur rooms all the way along them. Some contained Cyberat – shut down or dead, it was difficult to tell. There were plug forms here too, almost certainly dead. A plug form could survive an appreciable time without the aid of a mobile support body, but these looked to have been here for longer than that. In others, Cyberat stirred into motion upon seeing them. A blast ahead lit further tunnels and in its light he saw a Cyberat, whose plug-form body ended under the armpits, walk out of a cell on insect legs, protruding from a long cylinder, then come upright. Two humanoid ones, like his mother, stepped out of another cell. A woman plugged into a spherical coms unit dragged herself out by her arms – the sphere's grav obviously shut down. When the four Polity soldiers ran into view, flickering into visibility, Piper compared and contrasted, and perceived what had been done to his own kind as an obscenity.

'Piper,' said a voice. He turned and felt a jolt to see his mother leaning against the entrance of one cell, her left leg splinted with scrap pieces of Cyberat body. 'Your father,' she added. With a sudden dread sitting in his chest, Piper followed her into the cell.

Doge looked ill. The lower half of his factory-inspection body had been sliced away and the remainder sat at an angle on the floor. The casing below his head had also been stripped away, to reveal his chest and shoulders protruding from a tangle of hardware. Heavy optic cables were plugged into where one arm had connected. The other arm ended at the elbow, and there a complex tool hand had been attached. Doge was working on himself, unplugging and shifting optics to new sockets, as well as pipes that contained fluids, and in one case blood. He looked up, head tilting on a weak neck. Piper saw that his long beard had been cut off so as not to get knotted in his own workings and that, ridiculously, brought home the seriousness of his situation.

'Sloan and Cheen are getting the mobile prisoners out,' said Geelie. 'The Enforcers are retreating from the villa. We have a team ready to come in here for the rest.'

'I think Castron knows the situation,' said Inster.

69

Piper focused on his mother as she limped over to her husband and, with a selection of rough tools evidently taken from Cyberat bodies, she began to assist where she could. Piper walked over to stand beside her and she turned to inspect him.

'Partial activation, I see,' she said. 'Can you help your father?'

He gazed at the stuff supporting Doge's plug-form body. Piper knew enough to recognize a great deal of rerouting, saw defunct components removed, but could not understand how he could be of help. Then that 'partial activation' comment hit home. He dipped his head and searched the grid in his mind, noting that numerous new nodes had now appeared. They were for the Cyberat bodies around him, the suits of the other soldiers, and two more that seemed inaccessible. He mentally touched one then the other of these, finding resistance but familiarity. They represented the essence of two *people*: Geelie and Cheen. Moving on, he then touched other nodes. Soon finding the one he wanted, he mentally pushed into it. It opened around him in a virtual space – Cyberat code and schematics with the human organism wound through it: his father.

Doge had been severely injured. A large portion of his physical support in the factory-inspection body had been cut away. But that wasn't the worst of it. Some kind of power surge had gone in through the interfaces via which he'd controlled his factory. It had damaged his plug-form body, effectively killing large portions of his liver and kidneys, and wounding the remaining organics, which were also dying. Piper could see what the rerouting was for – an attempt to conserve resources and extend a waning life. Next he entered deeper programming and found the linkages for diagnostics. Programs rose to his perception – incredibly complex and perhaps almost intelligent. He touched on them and, in ways beyond human sense, found he understood their purpose. But none of it was about preserving a system or a life. It was as if he was a surgeon looking upon a badly injured patient in a hospital and someone, seeking to help out, had handed him a gun. There was no need for that because, without a doubt, his father would be dead in minutes.

He looked up.

Doge, despite the Cyberat constraints on his remaining human body, met his eyes and managed to shrug. The man knew what was coming. Piper turned away from the intensity of his father's glare and looked to his mother, not knowing what to say.

'Unless,' said Doge, 'your new friends have brought some form of cryo-stasis along with them, I'm not leaving this place. Castron's parting gift was to ensure I'd die slowly enough to be in full knowledge of what's happening to me, but fast enough to defeat rescue.'

His mother dropped the tool she'd been using and put her hands to her eyes. They were artificial and without tear ducts, though. Piper checked the diagnostic again and could see it: the damage had been too precise to be the result of a simple conflict. His reptile crystallized his anger at Castron into cold, hard hatred. The programs again made themselves known to him and it seemed they were arising from that inner beast.

Doge continued in a perfectly clear voice, 'Before I die, I want to know if we succeeded. Piper, have you linked to your sequestration hardware?'

Sequestration hardware . . .

He nodded. 'I can feel it. I have a mental grid now, and can access many things around me. And something is offering up ways to penetrate, control and destroy them. What did you do to me? I don't think I was ever intended to be a teacher.'

His mother limped away to the wall, rested her back against it and slid down, face as blank as ever as she watched him.

'We've been planning to take down the Old Guard for a long

time,' Doge said. 'Our problem was dealing with their Enforcers and war bodies. You were a prototype and, once we'd ascertained you were as capable as we'd hoped, the next generation was to be our main force.'

'But then we arrived,' interjected Inster, stepping up beside Piper. 'We knew some of what you'd done to your son, but it goes very deep.'

Doge turned to eye Inster. 'You people have been trying to amalgamate with AI for a long time, and failing. I know the story of Iversus Skaidon and how he interfaced with the Craystein computer. The organic component burns out.' Piper could now hear pride and arrogance in his father's voice. Doge continued, 'With our experience of amalgamating the machine and human, we Cyberat have achieved much. And I have achieved even more with an organo-metal substrate. My son is more powerful than he or I know. As you say, it is deep, and the synergy goes beyond what I can scan. It can also develop and change.'

'But that is not pertinent right now.' Inster turned to Reema. 'We need you to transmit those codes. When our marines come down, we don't want them having to fight the general population.'

Reema dipped her head. 'I cannot.'

'Why?'

She waved a hand. 'Castron. He shut down all my extraneous com.'

Inster nodded once. Geelie immediately went over to Reema and squatted down by her, opening a soft, syntheflesh plate in her arm and unwinding an optic. Reema obliged by reaching up to the side of her head to push the enamelled metal there, opening a data port. As Piper saw this, he understood another cold fact. Inster had had numerous objectives for this mission, which included assessing Piper, as well as rescuing Reema and Doge.

But primarily it was to get those codes. They were key – to activate the tech installed in a huge number of Cyberat bodies, and to acquaint their owners with the reality of their world. How it was tyrannized by the Old Guard. He could see that once this was done, some would quickly decide to fight on the side of the rebels. Others would just keep their own counsel and their heads down. But very few would turn on the Polity marines. He tried to feel some resentment about this, but instead found himself understanding the necessity.

'So what am I to do now?' Piper asked his father. Gazing at the old man, he felt his usual fear eased by the knowledge that Doge would soon be dead. This made him ashamed, causing his anger to boil up even more, and his reptile took on firmer substance under his overlay.

'Choose your own course, and not the one we chose for you,' said Doge.

Piper nodded. He thought of Castron and found a focus that made the reptile even stronger. Fear of losing control waned as he seemed to look upon his surroundings with those yellow eyes. He would fight. He started to think about *how* he could fight . . .

'Time to go,' said Doge. 'Have a good life.'

Reema emitted a groan around the word 'no'. Piper looked over at her as she collapsed on her side, curling up into a ball as Geelie stepped back, reeling in her optic. When he turned back to Doge, his father's head had dipped, chin resting on his chest. The diagnostic in his mind reformatted, tracking the rapid extinction of the man in the machine.

'I have it,' said Geelie. 'Transmitting. The code is sent.'

Piper turned away, heading for the door. There he paused with a hand on the jamb, body fizzing with strange energy, blocks of thought shifting around in his mind and settling into new patterns.

It felt again as if his delayed years had fallen off him and, without looking back, he managed to say, 'You'll get her out of here?'

'Of course,' said Inster.

Piper nodded once and kept going.

The 3D map of the place lay clear in Piper's mind. He headed to where the Polity soldiers had come in, finding where a blast had sliced an armoured door clean in half, as well as cut up into the ceiling and down into the floor. Beyond this lay two Enforcers. One was a low humped disc, formed of quadrate patches of brassy and silver metal. It sat in a nest of grasping limbs that had been sliced from its body. Geelie or Cheen had obviously used a sword here. Either side of its dome ran the tubes of ionic stunners – probably designed for prisoner control. And around the central dome were slabs of old-style armoured glass. He saw long wrinkled fingers scraping at the glass and, leaning closer, inspected the occupant within. Again, there was an oversized skull nested in support tech, with eyes turned into sockets for optic cables. The body ended midway at the chest. Why, he now wondered? Why keep this visible and grotesque piece of the human this person had once been? The answer was plain: as an example. This is what happens to you if you disobey. Yet even then, it seemed odd, since many obedient Cyberat changed themselves in ways that were comparable. There was likely some history here, he thought, turning to the other one.

This was an ovoid with spider legs and a single, underslung rotogun. A head stood clear on top – a woman with blonde hair in a plait that ran round her neck. He thought the head vulnerable until he saw the slots around it, down into which armoured protection had been lowered. The head suddenly turned and looked at him with clear blue eyes. She mouthed something, faint hissing sounds coming out. He couldn't allow this and its implications to distract him, so he moved swiftly on. Even as he did so, he was sure he'd understood her words as, 'Kill me.'

Further machine bodies scattered the corridors. Despite Geelie having had to use her sword on the one Enforcer behind, disruptors had clearly been effective on all of these. As he passed them, the data nodes representing them formed, then dissipated in his mental grid. Checking on one of them as it came and went, he dived into the autodiagnostics on it: the systems were trashed and unusable for him, yet he discerned the very specific damage inflicted. The Enforcers brought down by disruptors had mostly lost their weapons and mobility but not life support, where it hadn't been integrated with the first two. This triggered a new train of thought which, he was alarmed to realize, didn't feel like his.

The specificity of the disruptors had resulted in Enforcers surviving, but why? They weren't redeemable . . . or might the Polity think it possible for Enforcers to be recovered? This led him on to the complexity of the disruptor technology. Polity tech for that was at a higher level than the equivalent Cyberat tech. It was therefore logical to assume that their medical tech was superior too – in fact he'd personally experienced it. Perhaps it was superior enough to bring Enforcers back to . . . humanity?

Finally, without having to use his weapon, Piper reached the room he'd been aiming for. He stepped inside and viewed the prototype war body he'd encountered earlier. A large node highlighted in his mental grid, and he opened it to internal perception as he walked forwards. The war body had an antigravity motor and thrusters, and two weapons it could protrude from the forward armour. One was a particle cannon, and the other a rotogun, whose slugs were propelled by a coil-gun breech, hence the huge laminar power storage inside it. The thing was being charged and was currently half-filled. Underneath, it had a missile launcher. Other systems were in there too, and it seemed complete except for the Cyberat interface. He turned his attention to that.

The thing was being prepared to take a plug body – all the loose stuff up at the top being interface hardware. All it required was some locking down of components, a chain-glass screen and armoured shutters for the socket. It was perfect for Piper's purpose . . . if it really was *his* purpose. He moved forwards to climb up to the hole for the plug body, but then halted, hesitating. What he was about to do might be a step too far – he might be no longer be able to control his actions. He searched for a rational anchor, focusing on the war body and trying to comprehend fully what was happening here. Even though he'd assessed and understood all this thing's systems, there was still something very odd about its design. This gave him something to puzzle over, and in the process get a firmer grip on his mind.

As he backed off, he tried to understand what was niggling at him, and inspected the machine's schematic via its node in his mind. He saw rough edges where holes and other cuts had been made in the armour and then smoothed over by the usual Cyberat armour metal. Examining one of these closely – where squares had been cut so weapons could protrude – he noted the roughness of a circular key pattern, designed to bond the additional metal. It was as if the main armour couldn't be alloyed with additions. Inside were many mechanical fixings for the same reason. He saw screw threads, rivets and other such anachronisms. It was as if it had been a major struggle to connect everything to this armour – and it could be cut only with extreme difficulty. In an offshoot of the schematic, he inspected the profile of the main armour metal. He'd never seen anything like it. Its resistance to heat, impact and cutting were beyond the best ceramo-carbides. It struck him that Castron must have produced this main armour from some experimental technique, ending up with an item stronger and tougher than he'd expected, then had to adapt the Cyberat technology to fit.

Piper sighed. His pause to study the technology had given him the mental breathing space he'd needed and he felt more in control. He leaped onto it, then scrambled up the armour. His bones were aching again and now his joints creaked, pain increasing in his hands and forearms. Inside, with utter inevitability, the reptile started unravelling and spreading out beneath his overlay, into his being. He inserted himself in the spot designed for a plug form and found, thankfully, a secure sitting position. He quickly began pulling in interfaces and, for most of them, found snap fittings around him. By the time he had them all in place, his hands were numb, and he could hardly move them as he stripped off the suit gauntlets. With a thought, he also softened the armour of the suit sleeves and pulled them up. His hands and forearms were slick with blood and dotted with the metallic splinters. He put his hands against two main interfaces, felt the linkage within a few seconds, then observed the rest unfold, just as he had surmised.

The metallic splinters extruded from his skin, extending out as thin mobile threads, writhing like worms as they sought out interfaces all around him. This was Cyberat connecting tech, used to join hard, complicated systems spread through a human body, or the remainder of one. It needed to be self-guiding to make intricate connections, but he had never seen it quite this mobile. The pain faded as he finally hard-linked to the war body.

He then powered it up, ejecting the charging cable and raising the whole body from the floor on grav. With both the hard link and the node in his skull now firmly open, the war body became not something he could seize control of at a distance, but an extension of himself. Perhaps this was how Castron and other Old Guard felt when they donned such machines, but they would be more accustomed to the experience than he was. He felt the weapons as his limbs, but also the grav, the thrusters and other controls, meaning he now controlled more limbs than human. With this outer transformation an inner one was completed too. He was Piper, and he was the reptile, intimately bound together in synergy. Clarity and purpose as one. He spun the war body around, shedding stray tools and other connections, and looked for a way out.

The villa map showed him a heavy concertinaed hatch above, which would take him to a shaft leading to the roof. He searched through the war body's system for a way to open it, but could find nothing. Impatient to get on with his business, he fired up the thrusters underneath and just hurtled up towards the hatch. The body slammed into it, crashing it away in separate ribs, then sped up the shaft and out into the air. He blinked at the blood running into his eye, where part of the hatch had stabbed in to remind him he wasn't protected under chain-glass and armour. Blood continued to flow, filling his eye and then leaking into the other, but vision had ceased to be a problem. The war body's sensors gave him a wider view, across a larger portion of the emitted spectrum.

Out beyond the house the battle still raged between the rebel Cyberat and Castron's Enforcers. There were casualties down in the sea and scattered across the coast. Automatically, he counted nine hundred and six Cyberat in the sky, dotted across knots of yellow-green cloud. Distinguishing between the two forces was difficult, beyond the obvious Enforcers, but he estimated a ratio of eight to one against the rebels. Inland, over one of the closer towns, swarms of fighters were starting to rise there too. Clearly, with the code now sent, many Cyberat were angry and responding, with the Enforcers in turn trying to impose the no-fly order. Of Castron there was no sign.

What the hell could he do?

His swirl of emotions wouldn't countenance him doing nothing. Blinking away blood, he looked down at the disruptor lying beside him. He couldn't use it, and this war body didn't have a similar weapon, though at this thought, targeting frames opened for him. He had speculated earlier on whether the Enforcers might be recovered, and recognized they were what they were through no fault of their own. But hard reality took over now, with the smoking remains of cyborgs scattered on the ground below. His reptile anger and clarity noted the Enforcers might be redeemable, but right now they were killing his fellows.

Piper fired once impulsively, a swing shot with the war body's particle beam sweeping across three Enforcers he had definitely identified by their body forms. They dropped, burning, into the sea. He next set the rotogun to four-shot bursts and began hitting other targets, while still searching for some sign of Castron. Identification of friend or foe remained difficult, as some went down, some not. Many started swinging towards him too. Rotogun slugs spanging off his armour reminded him of his vulnerability, and the fact that the battle here was a distraction from his main objective. The same action would be playing out all around the planet and would, he hoped, be brought to a close by the Polity marines once they landed. And, in the heat of response, he had foolishly neglected a preferred option – for he had also been designed to sequester hardware at a distance from him.

Piper sent the war body high, accelerating, not sure how what he was about to do would affect his control of it. He mentally closed up the machine's node and concentrated on all the others. How could he tell which were Enforcers and which were plain Cyberat citizens? He *touched* some of them, finding varying combinations of organic and machine, but still couldn't distinguish easily.

There had to be some other way. With Enforcers swirling up below him, he searched through the war body's systems. Enforcers could differentiate between their fellows and citizens, so surely Castron or whoever else plugged into this war body would have wanted the same ability? He found the ID code. His system could now draw targeting frames over all those who were *not* Enforcers. He didn't want that, so reversed it, then programmed back to the relevant nodes. Eight hundred and twenty-three Enforcers. Meanwhile, he began transmitting the ID code for himself and, at once, those pursuing him began to drop away.

He chose an Enforcer node, reached inside and shut off its grav. Its system's defences fought back and he found himself constantly rerouting his attack, tweaking it to stop the grav coming back on. Searching, he detected the one in question and saw it hurtling down at an angle. It eventually crashed into a mountainside, creating a dusty crater, then tumbled down in pieces as its node slid out of his perception. He felt a moment of shame, but quickly dismissed it, to concentrate on what he'd seen the disruptor weapon do. Reaching into another Enforcer node, he shut down its weapons and again found himself in a fight to keep them shut down, unable to identify through sensors which Enforcer was affected. Damn it, he needed something general to take over the eight hundred here and others now crowding his internal perception! And he needed it to work without his constant intervention! This need drove his reptile, or perhaps his reptile drove his need. He felt it briefly again as a separate thing from himself. It reached into resources doubtless woven into his bones and brought them to his full perception – just as it had offered programs inappropriately for his father.

The things were like living creatures, more complicated than the usual computer viruses and worms but with a similar purpose. Each was a programming animus, made to be installed in Cyberat systems, like interface tech, and there adapt around any defences – to evolve – without losing its original purpose. Their complexities were huge, when he wanted simplicity. He picked one and began mentally stripping it down, the thing seeming to writhe in pain as he did so. But then it willingly changed to his design, and finally he had what he wanted: he'd found a way to access all the Enforcer nodes simultaneously, keep that access open and deliver his instructions. He sent the animuses and felt them impact, driving anchors into all the Enforcers. Via links to them, he turned off their weapons. Firing died below, except from the citizens or rebels. Devoid of weapons, the Enforcers started attacking physically, ramming into their opponents and grappling with them, tearing away hardware. Now, having access across multiple nodes, Piper fired up Enforcer drives randomly, scattering them. Some hit the ground, some crashed into each other, but casualties were to be expected.

Piper turned his attention next to a sudden influx of other nodes, now cramming into his mental space. He tried applying the weapons shutdown program to them since, in the end, surely it was best if no one was firing weapons? These nodes were slippery, however. Had the Enforcers already found a way to defeat his abilities? No, he recognized that slipperiness and, belatedly locating them, looked upwards. Two shuttles like bricks were descending fast. Above them swarmed human shapes in heavy armour. In the system a comlink flashed for his attention. He turned angry focus on the probable communication from the descending Polity forces and, fearing viral attack, dared not open it. But instead of continuing to blink, the comlink opened itself, as it should not have been able to do.

'Seems your father and mother fashioned you to purpose,' said Albermech.

'And you knew all about it,' he replied, emotions cycling within him, as if turning on a wheel to be presented for his attention. He fought for control, finally slowing the cascade and falling back into much-needed clarity, though coated with a load of suspicion.

He considered a number of other things. The nodes he'd previously been unable to access, like those above, had been of the Golem. Did that mean all those human shapes descending were Golem? No, it did not. Albermech had penetrated this war body's security easily. Again this implied a level of tech way above the Cyberat. He surmised that Inster, and those others below, after assessing his ability in Castron's house, had transmitted the gist of it to Albermech. And now the Polity had made sure they had a defence for it. He was probably seeing armoured suits like his own, with the same defence as the Golem. He tracked the signal and triangulated, finding it relayed from one of the shuttles. He frowned at it, but then darkness began to edge his vision and his lungs started to hurt. Instead of allowing a controlled descent, he knocked off grav and fired the thrusters upwards to speed it.

'Are you having problems there?' Albermech enquired.

As his breathing returned to a steadier rhythm, he re-engaged grav, settling now. Below he could see the Cyberat who'd been fighting the Enforcers here heading down towards Castron's villa. Reema would be safe. He analysed the thought, realizing that he didn't trust Inster or his Polity forces, but the mixed emotions he felt about his mother baffled him. For he saw her as his mother but also as . . . someone distinct from that perception.

'What is the situation now?' Piper asked.

'What situation?'

'The battle . . . Who is winning? Tactics, logistics – any information you can give me.' It was a general question and not the specific one he really wanted to ask, as his reptile cycled back to a prime objective. He didn't trust that he'd receive an answer to that, since he now felt sure he was an item of interest to the Polity, and they might try to keep him safe.

'It's going pretty much as I surmised. Of those in receipt of the information from your father's addition to their tech, eighty per cent have sat back to watch the show. Twenty per cent have joined the small rebel force—'

'How small?'

'Just over a hundred and fifty thousand. With those that have joined, this increases their numbers to roughly fifty million.'

'That's a lot.'

'Not against eighty million Enforcers and twelve thousand Old Guard in war bodies.'

'So, my people will lose.'

'Yes, they would have lost without our intervention. But the disruptors are one-shot kills with a five-kilometre range. It's like shooting fish in a barrel.'

Fish in a barrel? A strange activity but he understood the inference. However, this conversation wasn't heading in the direction he wanted.

'Where are the Old Guard?'

'Scattered all around. Interesting to note that the same percentage of non-combatants applies to them. Thousands of them are just staying in their villas. The twelve thousand I mentioned are those who've activated their war bodies . . .'

'And Castron, where is he?'

'Ah, now we get to the heart of the matter,' said Albermech.

The trajectories of the marines and shuttles had changed and they were now heading inland. He diverted his course that way too, because if Castron had left the villa, it seemed highly unlikely he'd have gone out to sea.

'Will you tell me?'

'Yes, if you continue using your particular talent along the way – it will save a lot of lives.'

Piper returned his attention to what he'd been doing to the Enforcers just before. He'd sent animuses and consciously applied the shutdowns through them but, like any such computerized action, it could be automated. So he programmed to insert animuses into the Enforcer nodes and set them to automatically apply the weapons shutdown, as well as thruster firings. Ahead, over the town, this seemed to have no effect, so he accelerated towards it. As he got closer, Enforcer nodes began to accumulate and the animuses to insert into them. He finally saw a reduction in weapons fire, followed by their thrusters firing up randomly to disperse the Enforcers. This confirmed to him that his effective range was fifteen kilometres. He now reconsidered his aims; wasn't petty vengeance against Castron selfish when he had this capability?

'Yes, keep doing that,' said Albermech.

'Now tell me where Castron is.'

'He's over at Ironville, drawing off war bodies and Enforcers there for a purpose we've yet to surmise.'

'Okay.' Piper called up a map of the continent and highlighted Ironville. He sketched a direct line to it, then highlighted the towns and cities on the way and within twenty kilometres of that line, incorporating them in his route. He would do some good along the way, but that 'purpose yet to surmise' underlined the old Cyberat as the main danger to be pursued and stopped. He knew this was a little confirmation bias – his logic to justify vengeance, and to justify the intent of his reptile facet – but he would still go. He fired up his thrusters to full power and headed off at full speed.

4

Each town was the same as the last as Piper seized control of Enforcers, shutting down their weapons and dispersing them. He saw some hurtling past him with thrusters on full burn, others crashing into the ground or heading straight up. Again, they weren't to blame for what they were and, accepting there was some chance for their recovery, he regretted the deaths. He tried simply stopping their ability to steer rather than dispersing them, but even more of them died as a result. As they remained in the area, with no defence, the rebel Cyberat continued killing them. He tempered the dispersal program to a ten-second burn, to reduce the number hitting the ground or heading up into vacuum, but also to spread them out enough to end any particular fight they were in.

'Cut your broadcasting until you're on a target, then shut it down once it has taken effect,' said Albermech.

'Why?' Piper asked, nevertheless freezing the program after the last town.

'The Old Guard are reading it, as are we. The programs are incredibly complex and route through the interfaces between the cybernetic and organic. We have yet to understand the method, but we will. Given enough data, the Old Guard might do too.'

'I see,' said Piper, not sure he liked the idea of the Polity working out how his most effective weapon functioned. Yes, he had found himself putting a degree of trust in them, but it had its limits. It also gave him pause to hear the AI saying his animuses were incredibly complex, while he just understood them on a visceral level.

'You must be close to deciphering it – you've learned how to block it from the suits of your marines,' said Piper.

'Blocking is not the same as understanding.'

'Why do you need to understand it?'

'I thought you were intelligent . . .'

Piper cursed himself. Of course, if the Polity were able to understand what he was doing, they could use it themselves to shut down Enforcers and war bodies around the whole planet at one stroke.

'Okay, I get it, but I was distracted.' He grimaced at his reply, aware of his conceit about his intelligence.

'You also need to be aware—'

Piper turned sharply out of the path of a missile, the abrupt change of course slamming him against hard edges in the war body. Fortunately the suit protected him, but he now knew he couldn't manoeuvre like a fully plugged-in Cyberat. The missile looped round behind him and came back. He framed it and fired the particle beam, blowing the thing to pieces. Other missiles were now hurtling in and he framed them too. After hitting the first with the beam again, he switched to the rotogun – first four-shot clusters then honing down to two. The particle beam drained a lot of energy, while his ammo for the rotogun was limited. Tracking the missiles' vectors, he triangulated back to an object rising from the city that lay ahead: a war body.

The thing consisted of two cylinders joined by a semi-spherical mass of tech, which probably held its occupant. He fired two missiles at it, while searching for its node, even as his animuses closed down the weapons of Enforcers around it, sending them off on random paths. But he could find no node for the thing. It swung towards him, revealing one of the cylinders as hollow. This began to heat up inside, even as a laser whipped out from the war body hull and destroyed his two missiles. He couldn't shut it down. He wasn't close enough to fire his particle beam, since they dispersed in atmosphere after a few kilometres. His rotogun would probably do no more than give the thing a few dents, and his missiles were as ineffective as those of his opponent. Meanwhile, it was evidently charging up something potent. His analysis stopped right there, with the firm knowledge that he was probably about to die.

He began a weaving course, slamming himself from side to side in the war body, but heading ever closer to his opponent. A new level of calculation kicked in, seeming to rise on an inner snarl. Could he ram the thing before it destroyed him, or at least rain enough debris on it to take it out? This was crazy thinking. Did he want to die? The inner reptile shifted, as if confused about where to lash out. He concentrated inwardly. His opponent had to have a node. There, rapidly blinking in and out of existence, he finally found it. He instantly tried to grasp it, while seeking all the sequestration animuses he could find. All clawed limbs and teeth – all weaponry – his reptile writhed as he snatched at the programs of which it seemed to consist. It hurt him, like trying to grab an edged weapon from a jumbled box of them. In one desperate lunge, he grasped a chunk of it – a mass of animuses – and tore it away, flinging it into the blinking node. It hit, the node partially unravelling, and sank away into it.

In the real world, he saw the animuses bite, and hard, just before the cylinder weapon fired. The Old Guard's war body jerked in mid-air, as if some giant hand had slapped it. A pulse of white energy hurtled out of its weapon and scored down, underneath Piper, to hit the ground five kilometres behind.

Where it struck it carved up a trench in one long bright explosion. It was some kind of ionized matter pulse, and one he knew he couldn't have survived. A second pulse sped out shortly afterwards but, with the war body rocking and jerking as its thrusters fired randomly, this shot high into the sky. Piper swerved away, feeling the wash of a malfunctioning grav-engine. Explosions lit up on the other war body's surface, peeling off clumps of tech and armour as he swung round and back in. A large chunk blew out of its centre section and Piper targeted this, firing a stream of missiles straight through the hole. The blasts rocked him.

The big war body seemed to pause in the sky, fragments of the central section in silhouette against the bright explosion. The thing fell in half, the two cylinders pulling apart the remains of the sphere like a rotten fruit. Piper tracked them down, seeing one crash into a road, then tumble end over end along it to smash into a bridge, nearly cutting it in half. The other piece went straight into the side of a trapezoidal building, casting away chain-glass windows like scales. He saw a fire start up inside, just like other fires across the city caused by the crashing Enforcers. He now thought of the casualties: of those who had decided to keep their heads down and not take part. But also of the many hundreds of thousands like he'd been, who were yet to acquire the cyber additions and so were incapable of taking part. He winced at the certainty of deaths, but knew there could be no other course; he continued on.

'I see that you are now aware,' continued Albermech smoothly, as if nothing of note had happened.

'War bodies can block me,' he replied.

'Some of them can – by dint of shutting down or pulsing as much EMR reception as possible. And using advanced shielding around their systems.'

'That's annoying,' said Piper, the fires falling behind him.

But Piper was aware of other aspects now too. His struggle to fling what he had at that war body had revealed something internal he'd been denying for a long time. His reptile, tangled in him and influencing his thoughts and moods, was not actually the part of him he'd thought it to be. Or rather, not part of the function in that fleshy mass between his ears. It contained animuses and complex programming, in fact seemed to be formed of them, and it lived in his bones.

In the next town, the Polity marines had arrived. Initiating his broadcast again, Piper found few nodes for his animuses to access. The remains of two war bodies lay burning on the shore of a factory-cooling lake filled with heat sinks. Two more were just floating inert in the sky, while, scattered through the streets and crashed into buildings, were hundreds of Enforcers. Cyberat were moving amidst all this, perhaps stunned and with no idea what to do next. As he sped out the other side of the town, he noted Polity marines rising up from between the buildings and flying out – heading away to another target and perhaps invisible to those looking with only their eyes. Along his own course he was putting an end to the fighting. But there were eight hundred million people here on the continent and its satellite islands, and things wouldn't be so easy elsewhere. He returned to his speculation about his ability being used as a weapon by the Polity, then saw a possible flaw in it.

'Albermech,' he said, 'war bodies can block me. So what if the same method is applied by the Enforcers?'

After a brief buzzing sound, the AI replied, 'Thankfully this does not apply to the majority of the Enforcers. The Old Guard lacked trust in them so gave them hardened systems that maintain constant telemetry updates and reinforcement of orders.

Though I am not entirely sure how you are doing what you are doing, that EMR com is almost certainly what gives your access.'

'Then you need to be entirely sure.'

'Indeed,' Albermech agreed.

Piper began to inspect deactivated and deactivating nodes, mapping differences and similarities between them. The disruptor weapon the marines carried created an electrical surge and loaded a virus, via EMR reception and induction. His own ability, it seemed, lay in the terahertz band, with a stream of continuously linked code to an established animus. Though he could inspect both very closely, and got some hints of their function, he couldn't fully understand them. In his own broadcast, he saw DNA mirrored virtually in the animuses. In the other, virtual organisms self-assembled to clog up control circuits in energy-voracious loops. Unsure at first, he formed a section of what he was seeing into a data package and routed it through com to Albermech.

'Oh, wow,' the AI instantly replied. 'Keep them coming.'

Piper fed in the rest in a chain of linked packages. The AI said nothing for a long twenty minutes as Piper flew over another town, dropping remaining Enforcers there and seeing marines fly up and move on. In passing, he noted the numbers. If their strength was four thousand, it seemed most of them had landed in his path. His course had simply been their main front, and now they were spreading out across the continent to face the millions of other opponents.

'Consider greater bandwidth,' said Albermech.

'What?'

'I have to make the request as I would to another AI, or any other thinking being. Allow me access.'

Piper pondered on that 'another AI', and what his father had said about the organo-metal substrate in his bones; about the closer link between the organic and AI that the Cyberat had

achieved, or his father had. He also considered his recent realization: how the thing he'd always called his reptile must be his
AI aspect, running in his bones.

'That's very . . . polite of you,' he replied.

'Not at all,' said Albermech. 'You are doubtless considering
how I forced open a comlink to you, but it was limited communication to the machine you occupy and thence to you. I could
force open bandwidth through that to your core, but without
your permission things could get gnarly.'

'Gnarly?'

'Difficult . . . it's plainly evident, by what you have sent me,
that your inner core, or whatever lies in that substrate in your
bones, is very much closer to AI–human synergy than we in the
Polity have yet achieved – as your father said. I could find myself
in a fight, and might be subsumed by you. Or, more likely, I
could end up killing you.'

Piper flew beyond the town, over the pastel sprawl of lichen
offering up spore spikes like medieval maces. Then over a forest
of plants that resembled, he'd been told, banana trees, but for
the purple foliage. Ahead lay a river valley, low hills scattered
with lichen fans like EMR detectors, and beyond them was
Ironville. His reptile raised his awareness to the levels of manipulation going on. Or he thought it did – he couldn't tell the
difference now. He had no doubt that he was doing precisely
what the Polity wanted him to do. They'd discovered the extent
of what his father and mother had done to him, and then Inster
had put him straight on target to the war body he now occupied. He had become another weapon in their arsenal, both
here and perhaps for the main war they were fighting. But how
deep had the manipulation gone? Had they somehow engineered
it so his father and mother would be captured? Could it be that
they were as culpable in his father's death as Castron? Albermech

was an AI – a superior intelligence beyond the human – and so probably made very far-reaching plans, covering factors that might escape the human mind. Was his present thinking a product of his Cyberat indoctrination, or actually the paranoia of his inner AI?

'I know it's very difficult to trust,' said Albermech, showing it could get as deep into Piper's thinking as Inster. Albermech was probably modelling him in its mind right now. How difficult would it be for such an intelligence to know what a naive young man was thinking and feeling? On top of this came the understanding that he was no longer thinking as he had done and he wondered: was he even himself?

'What is Castron doing now?'

'He has gathered forces around him at an Old Guard installation in the Carib Desert beyond Ironville. It was very well concealed in underground cylinders. Data now indicate it was made shortly after the Cyberat arrival here.'

'Why would he do that?'

'Since war bodies all across the continent are abandoning their present locations and seem to be heading there, maybe it's a last stand?'

'How many?'

'Nominally five thousand. Of those remaining in their current locations, about half are dropping out of defensive positions and going home. Seems many of the Old Guard are having second thoughts about Castron.'

'It's good that so many are ducking out of the fight,' said Piper cautiously.

'It is that.'

Just then, a bright light flared on the horizon far to Piper's left. Com started fizzing and he felt disruption within his own systems. He focused on the light as it waned. In the ensuing minutes, the ball of a vast explosion expanded and rose up on a stalk. A familiar iconic blast.

'It seems Castron has resorted to a scorched-earth policy,' Albermech observed.

'Scorched earth?

Another unfamiliar phrase with slippery implications, or one he just didn't want to understand.

'Five hundred marines went into the city of Guran. The five hundred marines no longer exist, nor does the city.'

'What?'

'I've pulled the marines back from entering any other urban areas. It seems that Castron, your dictator now, has decided that any cost is worth paying to cling onto power.'

Piper felt numb and angry at the same time, but also miserable that he couldn't be sure these emotions were all his own. He suddenly realized he could now see better from his eyes, as his tears washed out any remaining blood.

'How many?' he managed.

'I estimate that blast took out over two million of your people.'

It was logical that, now knowing the efficacy of the disruptors and the forces arrayed against him, Castron would regroup and try other strategies. And here it was. Piper mentally reached out to Albermech's com icon, while opening out the data channels he had used to transmit the earlier packets. The reptile shadowed his actions, offering a cornucopia of lethal animuses, and *he* dismissed it. In that moment, he managed to see it as separate from himself. In the com icon itself he also dismissed the narrow frame – the bandwidth restriction.

'Okay, come in,' he told the AI.

It felt almost like his 'accident' – being hit by a beam end. Piper jerked physically, but that was just a human response to the flood within. The AI came in like a tsunami, while the data channels he'd widened took the load for a microsecond, then just dissolved. The *presence* swirled around and through him, and he felt the painful intensity of its inspection. In response, his reptile rose again, and it was a much stronger and more vicious beast than before. He became aware of Albermech as an entity, himself as the same, and now the reptile too, but blended with him and rising as an extension of his own anger – a dark and dangerous internal shadow, but also a source of his sequestration animuses and other programs. It had never been so overtly present before and it, or perhaps he, began constructing animus defences, ranging from viruses to voracious predators to attack this inter-loper. This instinct to lash out at an attacker was something he really, desperately wanted to go with. But, via sensors, he could still see that mushroom cloud, and imagine how much of its content consisted of vaporized human beings.

Two million . . .

He remembered his mother's teaching of self-control and his clarity remained. He suppressed his instinct, fought the need to expel this invasion of his mental spaces, and pushed the reptile away. Reluctantly, the thing bowed to his will, the overlay tight-ening and the reptile withdrawing and coiling up. But this time he saw the dividing lines between the part of him that was organic and the part of him running in this substrate his father had mentioned. At this moment, he could control and overwhelm it, because though it was primal, it functioned on the emotional level and their aims were in alignment. But it had not always been that way, and might not always be either.

'Well fucking hell,' said Albermech.

The words came through at the level of human interaction, but tracking their course from the surrounding entity, he realized he could inspect the AI as closely as it was inspecting him. He instantly understood the origin, purpose and motivation behind the words and replied on a coding level – human language being a clumsy, inaccurate thing.

'Keep it vocal,' said Albermech.

Again he understood. Segments of Polity history appeared linked into a logical chain: Skaidon's interfacing with the Craystein computer. Then the ensuing attempts at AI–human amalgamation, through the dreadnought ship captains, to the recently appearing close amalgamations called haimen. The thrust of Albermech's comment was quite simple: it was best to retain links to humanity – like simple speech – because they were anchors against dissolving into AI. And now that Piper understood where his anger arose from, he forced back awareness of his body, his position in time and of his physical surroundings. He slightly distanced himself from the AI, as it riffled through nodes in his mental grid and inspected the supporting software. However, he didn't pull himself so far back that he couldn't see into the vast complexity of Albermech's mind.

'So why the "fucking hell"?' Piper asked, even though he knew.

'Your father was a genius,' the AI replied. 'Even now, after the creation of the likes of me, and close to nanoscopic understanding of the mechanism of the human brain, genius often escapes elucidation.'

'So what brings you to that conclusion?' As he asked the question, Piper probed Albermech. At first the AI resisted, but a decision tree arose and its conclusion dismissed the reaction. Piper knew he would uncover hard truths, but in essence the AI felt no need to hide anything from him. He found the Polity assessment of the Cyberat world, and dived into it.

'The substrate in which your AI component is running is effectively what we call dense tech – no part of it is not in use. It's neurosynaptic, with a degree of connectivity that goes beyond that of an organic brain, while the pattern of connections, and their material format, mirror and reflect down into the Planck realm.'

He couldn't quite grasp that on a human level, yet via his AI component he came to understand. His processing went beyond mere molecular and atomic interaction, down into the subatomic and could rise from there too. His father had effectively made a structure that incorporated, and utilized, subatomic matter and energy – a heretofore impossible exercise. His programming would operate like Mandelbrot sets, extending down beyond human perception. This meant vast processing and storage space, and speed.

'He was much more than I knew,' said Piper sadly.

Meanwhile, he went through the Polity data on the Cyberat. The Polity AIs, and a great many humans, had been aware of Piper's world for the best part of a century after a probe returned data. It lay outside the static Polity line in this sector of space and, though a curiosity for some, it hadn't been of high interest to the AIs. Maybe the Cyberat would result in something worthwhile but, most likely, internecine conflict would put Founder's World into a dark age. Or maybe a new society would arise. The only indicator there was something worthy of a closer look would be space travel, so they set a passive watcher to look out for that. It activated briefly, when the Cyberat put up new satellites thirty years ago, but the Polity had been understandably busy fighting the prador.

'You should look at the war,' said Albermech, with a strange intensity.

His curiosity already piqued, Piper diverted into that. He ran into masses of data on the war and skimmed it – trying to extract the essence. The AIs had known about the prador long before allowing their presence to be general knowledge. Without causing alarm that might result in humans searching for and thus alerting this alien civilization, they had prepared as best they could. The prador were plain hostile to anything not them, and also very much to each other. But under a king they had managed to create a society of a sort capable of holding together. And capable, unfortunately, of interstellar war. Piper absorbed images and data from this – much of it not consciously reviewed. He might not have access to a source like this again, so he took all he could. He understood the Polity disadvantage in metallurgy and armour, with its reliance on runcible transport – an instant matter transmission between worlds. He understood how the AIs had used delaying tactics, to be able to get massive weapons production online. And now they were winning against the prador by dint of simply out-producing them. The war had lasted for fifty years.

Initially, with infinite arrogance, the prador had advanced along one front. When that front stalled, it took them the best part of a decade to accept what was happening. It took them a little longer to change tactics, while the AIs responded either pre-emptively or changed theirs on the spot. Piper noticed in passing a reference to that 'scorched-earth policy' and now understood it in horrific detail. AI perception gave him an omniscient view of the war: the burning worlds, the terrible suffering of billions and their extermination, the vast battlefields, whose violence would be seen across millions of light years, millions of years hence. The intensity of it he knew would be too much for his human mind to bear, but he bore it in his bones as far as he could, then pulled back to a general overview, retreating from the horror.

The war moved one way and then the other, but now was pushing back towards the Prador Kingdom. One tactical change on the part of the prador was to circumvent the battlefront and find other routes to attack, beyond frontal assault. They sent out scouts, all around the Polity, looking for access. The passive watcher here had detected one such scout ship and so the Polity had sent a probe to check it out. That probe was called Albermech.

'You were a probe?' said Piper.

'Indeed,' Albermech replied, distracted and cold. Then it focused on Piper and continued, 'After what I found here, I returned to the Polity with a proposal for a mission and it was accepted. I was installed in the ship above and came back.'

Piper began to delve into the data on that, but found it sketchy. With prador scouts in the area, the idea of setting up a Polity military base here had been mooted. This world was an ideal location to watch from, and co-opting Cyberat infrastructure would ease the process. It was also noted that the Cyberat, with their war bodies and Enforcers, wouldn't exactly be a pushover for any prador assault via this route. When the Albermech AI arrived as a probe, it'd recognized that the political structure as it was would not provide allies for the Polity. But it also saw that structure was precarious and due to fall within the next decade. Its objective, upon its return, was to accelerate this process. It contacted the rebel contingent on the world, and what it then learned of their preparations it found very interesting indeed. Here was something beyond just infrastructure and fighting bodies – something that might make a real difference to the Polity war effort. The something the AI found was Piper.

Fighting bodies . . .

The phrase seemed to have more weight than indicated in this narrative. Piper understood in that moment that his initial reaction to all this data had been wrong, and he felt disappointed. Though he seemed to have full access to Albermech's mind, this mind was capable of hiding things. The data he'd been presented with was a prepared narrative, perhaps to give him a good overview, but likely to keep things concealed. Certainly, the reference to him was a partial distraction with an essence of truth.

'I have only ever seen anything like this in one place before,' said Albermech.

'What?'

The AI's inspection of him came to a juddering halt while Albermech offered memory. The AI had not known a great deal about the technology Piper had inside him. But then Piper followed the chains and trees of logic and data in the AI's mind and found the answer. Doge's assessment of what Piper would be able to do had left Albermech blankly puzzled, for it didn't seem possible. Albermech had initially dismissed it all as a fantasy, but the detail Doge supplied indicated a logical whole that would be absent from fantasy. This shadowed what the technology might be, and Albermech had to find out.

'Where did you see what before?' Piper asked again, because the memory had provided no explanation at all of the AI's comment. He probed further, and the mind around and inside him now felt leaden, syrupy, and difficult to penetrate. There was something there about the *Albermech* – the intervention ship in orbit above – and about *fighting bodies*, and the cold calculations of war. The AI was blocking him. A flash of something passed about how, without the rebellion, there would have been nothing to drive Doge's technology out into the open, into action, into accessibility. Albermech had pushed the rebellion, and Piper's parents and tens of thousands of others had responded willingly.

'In a museum on Earth's moon,' Albermech replied.

The statement was simple, but Piper felt immediate danger as the AI now hardened around him, as well as through him, like a cage of thorns. His access continued to die, while his reptile snarled into alert and he let it do so. In the last instant before access completely died, he found out the truth about his parents' capture. Albermech had warned them that, with their further preparations, they were going into danger. The AI had felt that the warning at least was a moral duty. But it prepared for what might occur, should they be captured or killed. Albermech had a hundred scenarios sketched out that would put Piper in proximity with a war body or hostile Enforcers. The rescue mission, in all its protean versions, had been only one of them.

'What's happening?' Piper asked.

'The data are unclear.'

'That's not it,' said Piper. 'Something else . . .'

Albermech was withdrawing, hurriedly and damagingly, Piper jerking physically as if someone was pulling barbed hooks out of him. The AI retained virtual solidity as it pulled away, like armour. Then, virtually distant, its parts deliquesced as it withdrew. It happened very fast and Piper felt annoyed with himself for not grabbing more data while they'd been connected. His data channels re-established and minimized and, finally, when the last of the AI was gone, Piper saw that the bandwidth of the connection had shrunk to the point where only verbal communication could be used. It all seemed quite strange.

Piper then snapped back to the moment. Ironville lay in sight. Castron wasn't there but sixty kilometres beyond in the desert. What was his plan now?

'How long until you can use my method to take down the Enforcers?' he asked.

'No time soon,' Albermech replied, and the tone was still cold.

Piper passed over Ironville, while the bitter aftertaste of his close encounter with the AI allowed the reptile more leeway. The overlay came back, and harsh clear anger became a comfort. At first he'd felt that Albermech had allowed him into the font of truth and, certainly, the horrific truth of the war out there was plain. But then, as it had delved deeper, the AI had hidden things from him. It was an ancient maxim, he remembered, that in times of war the first casualty was truth. But he needed to forget that and return to the moment, and to the vicious clarity of what he had to do now.

Here the marines had withdrawn, except for in the vicinity of the Embassy. He saw Cyberat in the sky and on the ground. Many were gathered about, and upon, a vast scar of smoking rubble, extending across the city and terminating just before the Embassy. The damage being too small and of the wrong profile to have been the result of a tactical nuclear strike, he surmised that some weapon, like that of the war body he'd fought, had been deployed. All across the city buildings were down and pillars of smoke rose into the sky. On the outskirts he passed a great swarm of grav-transports manoeuvring just above the ground. And then swirling towards him came his own people, spreading out, targeting lasers locked onto him. He hurriedly opened up numerous com icons.

'I am not the enemy!' he shouted.

There were too many replies to respond to and he winced at the cacophony. But then, via his other self, he began to sort them out and, unbelievably, to incorporate them all separately. The animus this time was a precursor to sequestration, but not in itself hostile. He sank into its coding space, and from there rendered up multiple verbal replies to them all, holding back nothing about who and what he was. Finally, he focused down on one response and muted the rest.

One Cyberat said, 'So you're Doge's experimental son. I didn't quite believe you could perform as he said.'

'My father is dead,' said Piper. 'Castron killed him.'

'And Reema?'

'Alive – I left her at Castron's villa.'

'Land at these coordinates,' the Cyberat said.

Piper wanted to keep going, but targeting lasers still lit up his war body. He really didn't want to have to do to his own side what he'd been doing to the Enforcers, despite the drive from within. He took the coordinates, locating a field just to the right of the mass of transports, and headed down. The war body landed with a crump, the smell of earth and crushed old lichen rising to his nose, and it seemed to ground him too. Cyberat immediately started moving in on the ground. Most were plugged into spider forms, some with upper human bodies showing, either free above or under chain-glass, and others with no sign of humanity remaining. Snakish centipede forms approached too, and others that were variations on insects. Seeing them now, though he'd been seeing such things all his life, a connection arose to the data he'd taken from Albermech. During the war, Polity war drones had all settled on multi-limbed forms out of pure utility, and he could see that reflected here. The Cyberat, swarming in around him, all sported weapons attachments. These were the rebels. It made sense that more of them had gathered in the capital city than elsewhere.

Next, he began to see others: people with all their limbs still in place but motor-enhanced and moving quickly. These were forms like his mother. Fast, but not as fast as those already here. Focusing out and enhancing beyond these, he could see encampments of those like him – people without visible additions. He then looked up as another settled out of the sky to land in front of him. A simple sphere descended, with patterns like squared-off Celtic spirals deeply grooved into its surface. Scanning hit Piper hard – he felt as if he'd just stepped into a microwave oven. His reptile ached to respond, while other parts of the system in which it dwelt worked frenetically to retain integrity under such intense inspection. Piper understood that the individual before him was in fact one of the Old Guard. The format of the body, with those spirals, was a com centre, with a level of EMR and data handling few younger Cyberat were either allowed or could encompass. Yet, he had confirmed through their questions and talk that the Cyberat here were rebels. He had to accept that not all Old Guard were the same, and so managed to quell the urge to attack.

As it landed, the body protruded stabilizing legs, while the part facing Piper split along block lines. Chunks of the sphere folded out, like wedges of a fruit, to display densely packed technology surrounding the plugged-in organic core. Within, it looked as if a man had been crucified against a technological surface, and partially melted into it.

'I am Geerand,' said the individual Piper had talked to earlier. 'And now I see you are who you claim to be. Understandably, we were concerned about the body you occupy, but the AI Albermech is updating me.'

'I want to get to Castron,' said Piper. He limited his reply to this, though there was so much he wanted to know. However, first he needed to discern the intentions here. He was damned if he would allow them to take him out of the fight.

'You need to unplug from that war body,' said Geerand.

All around, the armed Cyberat were dispersing. Meanwhile, one of the big vehicles had landed nearby. The thing was a huge slab and when its front end opened up, much in the way Geerand had, it displayed a glittering array of tech inside. This included masses of arms, tool heads, machining surfaces, printers and bonders – a mobile factory.

'Has Albermech not told you what I am capable of?' Piper asked.

'The AI indeed did' – Geerand looked annoyed – 'shortly after we spotted you. All we had was reports of a strange war body in the vicinity of those places where the Enforcers went down. We thought Polity forces were deploying a new form of disruptor and they didn't seem inclined to correct that assumption.'

Albermech had been tardy about sharing information on him, and had only done so now out of necessity. For Piper it justified his caution in dealing with Polity AIs.

'Castron is out in the desert. He has nuked one city, killing two million of us just to take out five hundred Polity marines . . .' Piper trailed off, now seeing a number of Polity shuttles approaching, with marines swarming around them. It looked to be all of them, he thought, then his cybernetic part instantly counted three thousand four hundred of them. Piper swung his gaze back to Geerand. 'He has Enforcers there that I can deal with.'

'I know.'

'But you want to take me out of the action.'

'On the contrary, now I have been apprised of what you are, I want you to survive the imminent action. Your strangely designed war body is incomplete and requires additions and upgrades.' Geerand turned his head painfully to look round at the approaching Polity force. 'In fact, we all require those upgrades.'

'Detail,' said Piper succinctly, knowing now to get straight to relevance.

Geerand swung back. 'Fixes in the time available. Our particle weapons disperse in atmosphere, while our allies have components that can give ten times the range. The power of our projectile weapons can be increased and adapted to use higher-penetration ammunition. Data exchange can be integrated into the Polity battle sphere too. As much as we can do in the time available.'

'Time available?'

'Castron has not run out of options just yet. We calculate he will consolidate for no longer than a day before launching another counter-strike. We must hit him before that happens. Abandon your war body, Piper Lagan.' Geerand began to close up, while the nearby mobile factory advanced. Piper hesitated, reluctant to detach himself from this machine, and reluctant to believe that he wouldn't be put aside as too inexperienced. Then he remembered that, though this machine body was an effective and powerful thing, the true power didn't reside in it, but in his bones. He began to pull himself back, feeling an internal shrinking of self. He felt pain in his bones and in the flesh of his hands and forearms. His right hand fell away from an interface, and then his left, his fibres squirming back into his flesh. With the detachment, the open node with which he'd controlled the machine around him, and which had become a ghost over his other functions, collapsed back to integrity. Vision flickered, and then returned to only his eyes, which gave him a dry, blurred view of his surroundings. Then the reaction hit him.

The overlay faded as the reptile retreated deep into its home in his bones, almost with a snapping sound. It took away anger and part of his clarity, but other emotions arose. Initially he cringed at how easily he had simply abandoned his mother to go and kill fellow Cyberat, while his pursuit of Castron seemed crazy and arrogant. He winced at his coldness while watching his father die, and felt the grief of that as a slow rising tide. His actions and thought processes, from when they had entered Castron's villa, did not seem like his own. It was as if that other entity had controlled him. Yet the anger, wilfulness and clarity had always been part of him, while his emotions in regard of his cold parents had always been reserved. He felt that what lay in his bones mirrored and magnified him, and the lines of division he'd drawn were illusory. And yet, he feared the reptile rising again, as it always did.

Piper reached up to the armour edges and hauled himself up,

weak and utterly drained. He pulled himself out, noting Geerand heading up into the sky. The mouth of the mobile factory was now poised directly over him, machine oil and hot electronics smells in his nostrils, as well as heat against the side of his body as if from an open furnace. He tried to climb down, but his body seemed to be made of rubber and he just fell down the slope of the armour. A number of spider claws grabbed him before he hit the ground, catching all his limbs and his head. He looked up at the sour face of an old woman behind chain-glass, as the Cyberat lifted him and then gently placed him on the ground, whereupon he immediately turned to one side and threw up. He felt weak and utterly useless, and just lay there as grapplers from the mobile factory reached out to snare the war body and draw it inside. What the hell was he supposed to do now? He looked round as a big human hand closed on his arm. The other grasped the front of his combat suit and hauled him up to his feet. Familiar forms moved in around him.

'He looks like a wrung-out dishrag,' said Meersham.

'Organic components, they have no endurance,' said another voice. It took him a moment to recognize this as Cheen.

'Well, you're not looking too rosy for the inorganic kind,' Sloan observed.

'Bring him,' said Inster, striding away with his fingers up against his aug.

5

He was sitting on the bank of the river, his bare feet poised above the cool water, feeling at once daring and guilty. He took pleasure in the daring, but that was an organic response of the human body, which would be dispensed with in their progression to post-humanity. Or something like that. The girl sitting next to him, her thigh warm against his, picked up a rock and threw it into the water – an act of defiance. It clattered with a sound it shouldn't have made, and he then accepted that his feet were too small – the outer world was impinging and this dreamy, halcyon moment was due to pass. The girl pointed to the horizon, and when he looked there it seemed crazy that he knew his eyes were fevered yellow.

'He's coming,' she said.

Inevitability sank into him and transformed into a deep ache throughout. He closed his eyes, then tried to open them again, not wanting this bright sunny day to fade away. One eye came open, giving him a view of packed earth, while the other seemed stuck closed. He reached up and pulled away lumps of something dry sticking it shut and managed to open it. Then he just lay there, because he felt as if every bone in his body had received a hammer blow. The sounds of industry leached in all around him. He began to hear voices and the hydraulic hisses of Cyberat bodies. The pungency of crushed lichen and disturbed earth filled his nostrils. Finally, accepting his place in this world, he pushed himself to sit upright.

He had been sprawled on the ground next to a packing crate, unloaded from one of the Polity shuttles. Someone had pillowed his head with a roll of material and draped a heat sheet over him. He gazed at the activity of the rebel encampment and recognized it from when he'd fallen out of his war body, but didn't quite recollect how exactly he'd got to this point. Driven by the need, he stood up and walked leadenly around a nearby cargo container to urinate, then returned to sit on the crate. He felt like shit – worse than he'd ever felt before. There were people around him he knew but he hardly registered them. He just watched, without taking anything in, until something new materializing nearby prodded his mind into motion.

The tent . . . no, the house, unfolded from a simple package one of the marines had dropped on the ground. It expanded and expanded, solidified and righted itself, and then opened its doors. Some kind of open-cell material, Piper deduced, but still, it was impressive. He watched other similar packages deposited, expand into structures, then self-manoeuvre to join up with the rest. He couldn't see the point of it; they'd supposedly only be here for a short time. Technicians and soldiers began to move in equipment, setting things up very swiftly. Then the wounded started to arrive and he understood he'd been watching the construction of an instant hospital. He observed some patients walking, some on grav-stretchers and others being carried. Many were like him, bare humans without surrounding protective tech. Others were honed-down Cyberat: small clumps of organic human wound through with hard tech, mostly consisting of the plugs, sockets and interfaces needed to connect their organic into their other machine selves. These arrived in masses on grav-sleds, to be unloaded by kin still plugged into machine bodies.

'We dared not set this up in the city,' said Inster. 'Castron might have a nuke sitting there.'

Piper jerked into a new level of wakefulness. He hadn't noticed Inster arrive and wondered if the man had been standing beside him all along. He pushed his rusty brain into motion, feeling nauseated by the effort.

'Surely if he had, he would have used it already to take out the Embassy,' he said tersely.

Inster smiled and nodded, as if proud of a protégé. 'Yes, he had a large complement of Old Guard war bodies move in to try and bring the Embassy down . . . after he'd failed to take it out with missiles, but they failed too. After seeing the detonation that destroyed that other city, we abandoned the place.'

'Understood.' Piper nodded, then wished he hadn't. It seemed as though his brain was slapping against the inside of his skull. But pain and weariness weren't all of it. Now he sensed his reptile stirring, as if it too had been sleeping with him, and he felt hints of overlay distorting his perception. Sharp pains danced from the crown of his head and down. The reptile desired action, and complicated problems to solve. Piper, still feeling separate from it, just wanted to not feel quite so shitty, and for the pain to go.

Inster turned away, absorbed in aug com, his eyes glassy. Obviously a lot was going on, a lot was being organized, and he was involved in that. Geelie appeared, at a run, and dumped a package at Piper's feet. She undid it straight away – hands moving faster than human.

'Eat.' She handed him a block of something. 'Drink.' She passed him a flask.

Piper obeyed, expecting the block to be as tasteless as the usual Cyberat food, but it had so much flavour it hurt his mouth. After a couple of bites, he gobbled the thing down, realizing he hadn't eaten anything in over forty hours, and washed it down with the bitter drink.

'We'd like to install a full nanosuite inside you. The one put in earlier had a limited life while it repaired your damage, and is now breaking down,' she said. 'But since we're still not entirely sure about what the hell you have running inside you, we don't want conflicts, so this will have to do.' Before he could react, she opened the front of his combat suit and pressed a thick cylinder against his torso, over the lobe of his liver. It whined against him and he could feel an odd coolness flowing in. It consolidated and felt hard around where it'd gone in – just edging into pain – and then broke out and spread. His limbs started to fizz and his mind, which had felt like a gnarled nugget shrunken inside his head, seemed to expand and open out. Before he knew it, he was standing up from the crate and looking around.

'What was the matter with me?' he asked, as he felt the overlay integrating like armour over his consciousness.

'The stuff in your bones is energy hungry and also dumps a lot of toxins. You were at the point of exhaustion usually only found in unenhanced humans who do ultra-marathons.' She paused, an odd look to her face. 'You need to look after yourself, Piper.'

'I haven't had much time to do so,' he replied, adding dryly, 'I've hardly had time to think.'

'Wash your face,' she said tightly, handing him a damp cloth that felt unpleasantly mobile. He wiped, seeing chunks of dry blood on the cloth, which then sank away and disappeared. Blood started to leak out again, but she quelled it by pushing the other end of the cylinder against his head. He felt movement and the burr of a cell welder – a technology the Cyberat had brought from Earth and knew only too well.

With his mind now functioning better, Piper thought back to his feelings on departing the war body and saw them as weakness. The reptile was as much a part of him as his bones, and to fear it was like fearing the action of one's own hands. He knew the establishing overlay was affecting his thinking, but which did he prefer: the certainty of now or the feeble creature that had fallen out of the war body earlier? He now dismissed worries about being possessed by something, for he and his reptile possessed each other. He instead wondered about his war body and what they might be doing to it. And about Castron and the Old Guard, and what they might be doing. These contemplations segued to his father and two million dead, and his anger tightened in response. Apparently increased lucidity didn't bring happy clarity, but instead a return of anguish.

'Where is my mother?' he asked abruptly.

Geelie pointed upwards.

'What?'

'She's done enough and lost enough, and is now receiving what she requested once this was all over. She would be ineffective in what's to come anyway, so Albermech made the decision to grant it to her.'

'What did she request?'

'Her body back.'

Inster, abruptly coming out of aug com, swung towards them. 'Don't treat him like an idiot, Geelie. He's not a cotton-wrapped Polity citizen.' He frowned at her. 'You should know that.'

'Sorry,' said Geelie. 'Maternal emulation kicked in.' She eyed Piper. 'She would be ineffective in what's to come, but she's high in the rebel command structure and would assert her authority. Albermech calculates that in a position of such authority she would ensure that you are out of the fight, and we don't want that.'

111

'So you simply made her a prisoner aboard your ship?'

'It's more nuanced than that. Grief and injury put her in a precarious mental state. We can – in fact already have – fixed her recent physical damage, but her mind will take some more work. We have taken her up for that fix and the ones she requested. But even in good mental order, it's still likely she would want to pull you out.'

'So you simply made her a prisoner aboard your ship,' Piper repeated flatly, seeing through their warped portrayal of his mother. Perhaps she might have her own maternal emulation concerning him, and perhaps something had changed in her on seeing her husband die, but she had still turned him into a weapon.

Geelie grimaced. 'Yes.'

'Good,' said Piper. 'I don't want to lose her, but equally I want to at least be there when Castron gets what he deserves.' He turned to see the others approaching. Meersham looked even bigger than before in an armoured suit, Sloan too. Cheen did not wear armour but, like Geelie, a grav-harness. The two human men were now kitted out like the other marines of the assault force, and they looked formidable.

They gathered round, squatting or sitting on crates and checking their equipment. This reminded him of the first time he'd seen them. Geelie, working her harness control, rose a few feet from the ground and then dropped again. This, like so much else he had seen of the Polity, demonstrated their technological superiority. The Cyberat had grav-motors, but they'd never been able to make them so small. They had in fact been a chance discovery while manipulating meta-materials, and the Cyberat still didn't have a theory that covered their function. But now, with access to all the data he'd grabbed from Albermech, he understood. In the Polity, grav-motor theory had arisen as a side shoot of Iversus Skaidon's brief interfacing with the Craystein AI – they comprehended it a great deal better.

'So what happens now?' he asked them.

'You get your war body back,' said Inster, fingers dropping from his aug and his eyes perfectly focused on Piper. 'Come with me.'

Piper felt a surge of excitement which helped dispel the anger. It occurred to him that Inster understood this, and so wanted to keep him moving, keep him busy. The man led the way back through the encampment – the way Meersham had carried Piper when his legs gave out the second time. He must have fallen unconscious while draped over the man's shoulder.

Cyberat rebels were everywhere, some working on Enforcer bodies, and others actually plugging into them. He also noted that whenever he came close to an empty Enforcer body, the ache in his bones increased, and he felt pins and needles in his hands and forearms. It was an irritating glitch in his system. He paused and focused internally. Tracing back from the nodes assembling in his inner grid space, into that territory his reptile seemed to occupy, he found his start-up routine. It was set up to respond immediately to Cyberat technology which didn't have anyone else plugged into it. He considered that.

'Problem?' Inster asked.

Piper just shook his head and concentrated, still tracking the programming. He pondered the fact that, throughout his life, he'd often come into close proximity to machine bodies without occupants, and had never experienced this activation. He soon found the route inside him: a simple coded signal, then further codes, had been used to click on or off various control switches in his hardware. Who had done it, he wondered? It could have been his mother or his father, or really anyone else in possession of those codes. Evidently it'd been done shortly after his 'accident'

113

and prior to their rescue mission to Castron's villa. He tracked through again, and closed off the option that allowed for this external control of him. As he did this, he saw a brief grimace on Inster's face, which was quickly covered over.

'I'm fine now,' Piper said, and began walking again.

'Glad to hear it,' Inster replied dryly, obviously aware Piper had read his expression.

Those without plug-form bodies were assisting with the work on the Enforcer bodies. In many cases they were spray-painting them bright yellow with black stripes, to identify friend from foe more easily, and he realized he would need to find a way to distinguish them too. He inspected the masses of nodes in his internal grid and paused by an Enforcer body. Again, his need elicited a response from his bones – from the reptile. A program peeled out of it and established so fast he knew it must have been there, ready, since his activation, if not before. Now, when he looked at a machine, the program immediately raised its node for his internal inspection. And it went beyond that, because he had a positional awareness too, of all the machines and connected nodes in his vicinity. Studying this particular node, he noted the differences between this rebel machine body and the ones he'd seen before, and then incorporated them. It was uncomfortable to see just how little ally differed from enemy.

'Have you got it?' Inster enquired, aware as always of what he was doing.

'I can separate them out so I don't take them down by mistake,' Piper replied.

'And what separates them?'

'Their telemetry updating and programming reinforcement.' He gestured to another nearby Enforcer body. 'They've shut that down in the ones here.'

'Good,' said the man, pleased with his protégé again, though with a hint of something else there now, something dangerous.

This reminded Piper of one of the many things he'd learned from Albermech concerning the Polity. He asked, 'Are you an agent?'

'I am indeed,' Inster replied.

The agents were highly capable actors, whose general remit was penetration of rebel groups within the Polity, and to take them down. It was almost a tradition that they dressed as civilians and carried 'thin guns', just like Inster's. They did secret, spy stuff, and were known to be lethal.

'Not much call for your particular skills here,' Piper said.

'Not much call for it ever since the war with the prador started. It seems wannabe rebels lose their enthusiasm when there's a real enemy about. Some Separatists did try to make an alliance with the prador. We let that run, just out of curiosity, then learned a lot about prador torture techniques from the remains.'

'But here?'

'The skills of an agent are extensive. At one time, I did convert to a plug form to undermine the Old Guard. But, with most of them being recognizable, I had to terminate the operation. My function now is as an adviser, since two hundred years of lived experience has its uses, with a special interest in one item.'

Piper's mouth was hanging open. The man had converted to a plug form and had now managed to regain his full body? Another example of how advanced Polity technology was. And he was two hundred years old?

'What item?' Piper finally settled on.

'You,' Inster replied, gesturing with one hand to what lay ahead.

Piper had seen it as they approached. The mobile factory had turned away and a cargo unit was now attached to its side.

Currently it was picking up particle beam weapons, neatly stacked on a long sled, and processing them inside. The cargo unit wasn't Cyberat. Here then were the particle weapon upgrades from the Polity. But before turning to this new work, the factory had deposited his war body on the ground nearby. Piper hurried over to it, abruptly coming to a halt when he saw the changes.

The thing looked polished and new, while the weapons on either side of it were heavier, with big feeds running inside. But the largest changes were to the area in which he'd sat. The space had been expanded, with a chain-glass bubble hinged back from it. He could see the edges of fold-over armoured shutters all around it and, inside, *two* seats.

'You'll find the energy draw of the new weapons isn't a problem,' said Inster. 'I'll control them, and the missiles, so you can concentrate on your informational warfare against the Enforcers and Old Guard – that's our biggest edge.'

'I have no control over them?' Piper asked tersely, extremely annoyed, and his anger in perfect consonance with that of his reptile.

'You can usurp my control over them, and it will fall to you anyway if I end up dead. But I would advise that you don't take the control away from me. My tactical experience is somewhat in advance of yours.'

'So, I am inept,' said Piper.

'No, tactically we don't want you fighting on all fronts, but instead concentrating on the main thing you do. Surely you see the logic of that?'

Piper did see it, but still didn't like it.

'The energy draw really isn't a problem?' he repeated succinctly.

'The laminar storage has been upgraded and we've installed a fusion reactor.'

'What?'

'It will constantly top up storage. Also, the particulate for the particle beam is a different mix and will last longer. Range is to the horizon line.'

Piper just nodded acceptance of that, though a Cyberat fusion reactor had never been made smaller than this war body itself. Some of the bigger Old Guard war bodies carried them, but generally reactors weren't mobile. And the particle beam range? Cyberat beams usually diffused after a couple of kilometres, spreading out like flamethrowers. Inster stepped onto the war body, climbing a newly added, roughened strip. Piper followed, feeling almost violated by the man's presence.

They stepped down into the seats. It was a damned sight more comfortable than before, and the seats had an odd look which showed they weren't a Cyberat product. Control consoles sat directly before the two of them. Inster didn't touch the complex array before him, but rather took a thin optic out of his pocket, plugged one end into his aug, and the other into a socket in the padded rest around his head. Piper gazed at his own controls, which included a touch display, ball controls and a single joystick. He searched for interfaces to connect to as he had done before, and found them down on the arms of the chair. He hesitated, his hands hovering over them. With the process being painful, he didn't want to start it now if there was no necessity, but the spectre of his earlier feelings arose. Yes, he could sense the influence of the reptile right now, but when he had connected to this war body it had been even stronger.

'No need for full connection just yet,' said Inster. He pointed at the joystick. 'Simple operation in three dimensions. Lift it up and we rise, push it forwards and we go forwards, push it further in any direction and we accelerate in that direction. Same as most of your transports.' He flicked his fingers at other controls. 'Those are for the manoeuvres, like flipping it over and fast

117

thruster course changes. And they're copied to those buttons on the stick. Take us up and let's see you fly.'

Even though he'd flown the thing before, it had been almost instinctive, due to his close connection to the war body. He now felt nervous, but also glad that Inster simply trusted him to get on with it. Or, rather, apparently trusted him. Anyway, he could still connect without making the physical link to the machine, so he selected this war body's node in the virtual space in his skull and opened it out. The substance in his bones responded, of course, and he felt it strengthen, yet it didn't feel as if he was ceding control to it as he had before. He searched for analogies for what it did, and felt that suit assist was the closest. It strengthened and reinforced his thought processes, surely? Perhaps, in his tiredness, he had just been overly dramatic and paranoid. Perhaps what he was really experiencing was little different to the enhancement older Cyberat gained from their cerebral support hardware.

'. . . to what purpose?' he heard his mother say. He shook his head and concentrated on the task in hand.

Tracking things through, he soon ascertained the function of the joystick, and those other controls, from the computing side. He could, in fact, operate the war body without these controls. Just as he could shut down or otherwise control Enforcer functions, but that didn't have this immediacy and the reality of actual physical movement. It was a stage of control, and the lowest one, the next being these physical controls, and the top being him interfacing with the war body.

Piper leaned back, pulled the safety harness round and secured it. He then took hold of the joystick and, pressing down a button to stop the war body responding, pulled the stick from its mountings. He brought it down to the right-hand chair arm and slotted it into a socket there. He checked its range of movement. It was small, but continued pressure in any direction ramped up acceleration in whichever way it was pointed. He understood the need for such a small movement: under heavy acceleration a larger range would be difficult. Now, looking at the chair more closely, he understood its multiple functions. The thing was made of a form-changing meta-material. Under hard manoeuvring, it would wrap around his legs and body to exert pressure and keep the blood in his skull. It could also assist his breathing and swing a mask around his face if needed.

The speed at which this tech had been installed, and the degree of redundancy, amazed him. It was almost as though it had been readied beforehand. He glanced at Inster, then checked his surroundings via the screens before him, as well as by looking up. When he raised the joystick, the chain-glass bubble automatically closed over them and he took them smoothly into the air.

'Lot of traffic around here,' Inster commented.

'Yes,' said Piper, observing the 3D radar map on one screen, showing Cyberat, cargo haulers and mobile factories on the move. It gave him a good overview, but nowhere near as much as when he was fully connected, and felt he *was* the machine. He wondered where Inster wanted them to go, then put that aside. He would simply try this thing out. He just needed to move. He needed action.

He accelerated higher and higher, clearing all the activity below, then really started flying. A strong forward press gave grav-planing, then thrusters kicked in, whereupon the seat shifted to wrap itself around him. He ran the thing in every direction, smiling at a startled Cyberat dodging unnecessarily away from him, and realizing it had been Geerand. All was as it should be for general flight. Then he tried some other things. One control flipped them over, front to back, acceleration

119

becoming deceleration. He next flipped the thing upside down and via programming instituted a random dodge pattern. Another program set the war body tumbling, the seat tightening around him and the mask coming across. He took the machine out of the tumble and then down. Clear sky was all very well, but hardly a real test. He began to fly through the traffic, dodging sharply, ramming into tight turns with thrusters at full burn. He was enjoying himself immensely when an explosion suddenly opened in the sky and a regular pattern of hexagons blossomed just out from the encampment.

'That's enough,' said Inster. 'Take us back to the others.'

'Castron?' Piper enquired, moving them down again.

'He just noticed us, and gave a predictable response.'

Activity had increased by the time they landed. Cargo haulers were dispersing, as well as the Polity shuttles up in the sky. As he climbed out of the war body, Piper noted a heavier longer vessel even higher up. He pointed at it and looked questioningly at Inster.

'Each shuttle has hardfield projectors, but that has more for greater coverage. It's a shield for them all,' the agent explained.

Piper scrambled to the ground, wondering again how much of this war body's rebuild had been a fast technological response, and how much had been previously prepared. Had Albermech already mapped out this scenario in detail? Something else occurred to him. He understood that the *Albermech* was large, but precisely how large did it need to be to deliver the bases the Polity had put down here, along with the number of shuttles he'd seen and those four thousand marines? He'd only heard that it out-scaled the rockets the Cyberat used to put their satellites in orbit. And then he thought about chameleonware . . .

As he reached the ground, a Cyberat, plugged into a body

consisting of various tanks, a laminar storage stack and mobile feed tubes, came over to his war body to insert its tubes and power plug. Fuel for the thrusters, and a power top-up, despite the war body's internal fusion. The Cyberat probably also carried beam particulate, but he hadn't used any of that. He noted other Cyberat similarly loaded, and some carrying munitions, both in the sky and on the ground, running on spider legs. Altered Enforcer bodies were rising too, along with other flying Cyberat, swirling up around the shuttles.

Meersham and the rest gathered round.

'Missile silos,' said Sloan. 'Predictable, but well hidden.'

'Tacticals again,' Inster replied, fingers up against his aug as he turned away.

'You'll run point,' said Meersham, flicking a finger towards Piper's war body. 'We'll come in around you to cover other eventualities.'

Another explosion lit the sky and they all turned to observe it. Meersham shrugged. 'Seems we'll be on the move shortly.'

'I need more than that.' It all seemed too vague and hurried, but Piper nevertheless felt a surge of excitement. 'I don't want to hit you accidentally with my weapons.'

'Inster is on that and will integrate firing. You'll get the idea once you're linked into your war body. He will be system-linked, and you'll be in the com sphere – the battle sphere.' Meersham paused, looked thoughtful for a moment. 'Inster says you'll be able to handle it.' And that, it seemed, was enough.

'Very terse and taciturn, these human soldiers,' said Geelie with a smile. 'What he means is that, with your enhancements, you have almost AI levels of integration and will be able to encompass the battle plan very quickly. Inster told me that you flew your machine like a pro.' She studied him, head tilted to one side. 'You *will* handle it.'

121

So, they were going in after Castron and Piper felt glad to be included, trusted, but he also feared their confidence in him. Perhaps, came the dry thought, this was precisely how they wanted him to feel. He looked to the horizon, the view dotted with rising Cyberat. Thoughts of Castron raised the dull throb of anger too. Was it his own? A hand thumped down on his shoulder: Inster.

'We go now.'

Piper turned with him, emotions mixed, seeming to cycle in and out of his reptile as the overlay on his mind hardened. He suddenly felt extremely aware of his sex, sensitized, and increasing aggression began to dispel the fear. That dry part of his mind then observed that his drug implant was still winding down, and all his human hormones were coming out to play in a body long deprived of them. He needed to keep on top of that. He needed to stay fully rational . . . surely?

As they climbed up the sloping face of the war body, Piper paused again to look around. Most of the cargo haulers and mobile factories were heading for the horizon now, where green cloud boiled against the lavender sky. Some Cyberat craft he hadn't paid attention to before were up in the air with the Polity shuttles and that shield ship. They sported various bolt-on weapons and were certainly controlled by plug-in Cyberat. The marines were rising too, in heavy armoured suits, to form up behind various craft. Piper returned his attention to the ground, seeing all the stuff that wasn't leaving.

'The hospital,' he said, climbing in after Inster.

'A small target Castron is unlikely to be interested in, though we have left a couple of shield generators.'

'Okay.'

Piper took his seat. Almost without considering it, he activated himself and put his hands down on the interface plates.

★   ★   ★

The war body node opened almost with a physical jolt and he was in at once. His sensory input increased massively, and it seemed he could do nothing to stop the reptile sliding out, into his being, and filling out the overlay. A moment of protest rose and then died as a rumbling substrate of rage dispelled any dregs of fear he'd had, and brought with it harsh clarity. He became analytical, dismissing the idea of possession, again seeing this effect as an extension of his self, an enhancement, because surely that was all it was? Only retrospectively did he register that, though he'd felt the ache in his bones, he'd had no pain in his arms and hands this time. Why? Without much conscious effort, he delved into the increasingly complex programming of his system – doing this was now as easy as muscle memory, almost autonomous. He checked diagnostics and saw that his connection threads in his arms and hands had laid down traversal tubes during their first activation. He considered the tingling he'd felt earlier when near the Enforcer bodies – probably just psychosomatic.

Immediately, he had access to the flight controls which he'd earlier used physically. They were deeper into his psyche this time, equivalent to the actions of simply walking or running, or any other movement of his organic body. The weapons systems had felt the same the last time he'd used them, but now he found a barrier there, and sensed another presence. The interloper angered his reptile, or him, and he probed that barrier, seeing its function was to stop him automatically using the weapons. That he could easily rip it down if he wanted to ameliorated some of the anger, though a core of resentment remained.

'Cut that out,' said the agent, his voice coming directly into Piper's mind.

'Just checking,' Piper replied, teeth gritted and without moving his mouth.

'You need to pay more attention to your com,' Inster observed.

It was there as it had been before, but with a tangle of icons and an overarching access. He opened it and fell into the Polity military com sphere. Or battle sphere, as Meersham had called it, as if into a hidden world. Positional data came first. He saw the others relative to him, just briefly as the whole thing opened out. Perception was confusing, but his bones, his reptile or his inner self responded as they absorbed programming and got the locations of everyone else in the force – their vectors too and size. That was one level, but more levels opened as the telemetry integrated. He got weapons capability, munitions and power levels, shielding capability, flight plan and formation.

'Fuck,' he said.

'Quite a thing, isn't it?' said Inster.

'Yes,' was all Piper could say, as even more levels integrated.

Now the enemy and the battle plan started making themselves known to him. He got a 3D visualization of four underground installations, with many 'unknown' volumes. He saw weapons turrets that had risen to the surface to reveal heavy guns, beam weapons and missile launchers. The war bodies and Enforcers were there too – most on the ground at the moment to conserve battery power. The battle plan slid in over this, predicting fusillades from the ground weapons as they approached, and what the losses would be. He noted a large amount of the available shielding had been assigned to him. As he ran low just above the ground, a force was distributed around him, and one of the shuttles provided protection from above. He wondered at the necessity of that but, as the time series of the protean battle plan opened out, he saw how many Enforcers he was predicted to take down. Yes, he was an essential component in this.

The plan unfolded further again, incorporating other probable responses from the enemy, as well as possible ones, and then those deemed unlikely but still possible. At that point it became too much for him, and his bones began aching again. Yet, even as he pulled back and focused on the specific, he felt his bones adapting and knew that he *could* take it all in if he pushed. That frightened him, just for a second, until aggression rolled over it.

Instead, he concentrated on the enemy and went deeper into their data. More on weapons, but with many 'unknowns', as well as their likely strategies, predicted telemetry, munitions and power available. Refuelling and charging points to be targeted, should the fight become extensive. And then identifiers were also linked to names. Many names he didn't recognize, yet on seeing them he felt a strange familiarity, as if he should know them. Others were well-known Old Guard. With his object-ive clear, he searched through them and there found the name he'd been seeking: Castron. The stratum of anger waxed and waned in consonance with a vicious joy. Piper highlighted him and ran programming that would keep him apprised of the dictator's location at all times.

'In your own time,' said Inster dryly.

Piper checked timings. He'd only been investigating the com sphere for forty seconds but, apparently, that wasn't fast enough for Inster. He took the war body higher, hardly having to think about manoeuvring as he slotted it into the formation flying below the shuttle, even as the rebel army set out. Now integrated with the battle sphere, he moved at the same speed. Checking positional data, he found marines flying around him, including Meersham and the other three. His escort was in place.

'Okay,' said Inster. 'Now, since Castron just penetrated our battle sphere, our plans have changed.'

'What?' Piper glanced round at him with eyes he felt sure had turned yellow and snake-like.

'Hard and fast,' said Inster, sending the new plan to him directly, so it wouldn't incorporate into the sphere.

'Right, shit,' said Piper, noticing that without his mother's slaps his inclination for profanity had increased. Her words concerning self-control fled through his mind. It had been to keep him hidden from the Old Guard, but he should still retain it. He sat under a different kind of close inspection now, which he didn't entirely trust, with an inner self forming that he didn't think it safe to reveal fully. He took a breath, searched for calm and instead found only crazy excited clarity, then kicked acceleration to full power.

The seat closed around him and tightened, the mask swinging across to push air into his lungs. In his mind, he viewed the original battle plan as he rapidly departed from it. It still showed him in place with the steadily advancing armada. With any luck, Castron wouldn't see the ruse until it was too late. Through omniscient sensors, he saw his escort accelerating too, but since they had limited thruster power in their suits, they merely edged ahead of the main force and couldn't catch him up. He took the war body low, passing over a spread of purple lichen and blowing up a cloud of shredded debris behind. Then even lower, over green lichen, and weaving fast between three-metre-tall spore spikes like iron swords. Beyond this area the landscape transformed into dusty, dry, rolling hills, sparsely populated with colour strokes of lichens, roller bushes and cistern cacti. He went lower still, blowing up a dust trail.

'A little higher,' said Inster.

'I can handle it,' Piper replied. He'd already run a program to fix his level relative to the ground, and lined up dodge manoeuvres should anything appear ahead he wasn't already seeing in the battle plan data.

Ahead, a hazy disc appeared in the air, while behind them the thrusters had changed their output – the flames now issuing like braided cables into the dust. Only now did he ascertain his speed and check it against certain immutable laws. The war body was travelling at three times the speed of sound here, and its hull was heating up. Even as he registered this, he saw the armoured shutters drawing closed on the chain-glass bubble. But only the line of their edge, since they had a screen function on the inside, and the line disappeared when they finally closed.

'I wondered how long it would be before you noticed,' said Inster.

Now Piper really did notice, and with a fierce delight: the meta-material layer it had all over, the new function of the thrusters, and the electrostatic field, generating weird effects in the air all around them. The sonic boom had been dampened by technology the Cyberat simply didn't possess.

'You still need to go higher,' Inster added.

'Why?'

'The dust trail,' Inster replied.

Piper felt briefly stupid, his reptile writhing in response. He ran calculations on the vortex he was creating, then set his level six metres higher. He ran a hard thruster turn around a pile of boulders, mapped ahead and plotted a course that would take them through the low points between the hills. Further calculations showed him that thruster burns beyond acceleration would be more detectable, so he set an optimum speed to steer on grav around the hills, and the rear thrusters died down.

Time to target: four minutes. Piper just hoped Castron hadn't noticed that initial dust trail, then he considered something else. Why hadn't Inster warned him of that when he started taking the war body down low? He had enough confidence in the man to know it wasn't something that had just occurred to him. Surely, with this attack being so important, he wouldn't have neglected something like that?

'We'll have twelve minutes over the target before the others arrive,' Inster commented. 'That's a long time in combat.'

'Yes,' Piper said, not sure what the man was implying.

'We go in, do the job, and then get out fast.'

'Okay,' said Piper, but it wasn't okay. His anger rose with sickening force, utterly focused on Castron. And so personal, though he'd only ever known the man via broadcasts, the occasional visits to his father's factories and latterly his appearance when Piper had been injured. He tried to rationalize this oddity. He wasn't going into this fight just to shut down as many of the other side as possible; he was after the Cyberat who had killed his father. Yes, he'd all but lost himself in the recent changes and technology activated in his body, but the hard reality remained that Castron had murdered Doge. Piper winced at that, eyes feeling dry and sore, and sensed the anger wane again as if in confusion. It *was* about his father, surely? Yet still the fury felt wrong – somehow misplaced. Again, a detached part of his mind noted: probably hormonal. But the anger was there and he would act on it. He glanced at Inster, thinking, assessing.

Inster was very far from stupid and had to realize Piper's intentions. Was this the reason for the two seats in here and why the agent had accompanied him? He began meticulously checking through the war body's system, looking for traps, any hostile programming, checking interfaces to see if somewhere Inster had a way of seizing control. Throughout his three-minute search he found nothing. Perhaps it was a physical option in the war body itself. He searched there too, using diagnostics and internal sensors. Again, the odd shape of the armour impinged on him, but he could find nothing there either. That didn't mean there wasn't anything, of course – Polity technology was advanced, very advanced. But he had no time left, because they were into it.

Coming around yet another hill, he saw installations on the ground ahead. War bodies and Enforcers were rising into the sky and a missile battery had just fired three missiles – streaking along above the ground towards him. He wanted to respond and found himself pushing against the soft barrier Inster had installed, even as the rotogun opened fire. Piper took that in, set a dodge program running, then concentrated inwardly.

Thousands of nodes had suddenly blossomed into being. He quickly ran up his programming, broadcasting the animuses for weapons shutdown and dispersal. The invisible signal, visualized internally as thousands of animuses trailing data threads back to him, struck the enemy like a visible weapon. Thousands of thrusters ignited, scattering Enforcers and an appreciable number of larger war bodies too. He next opened up one of the Enforcer nodes that hadn't responded. Here he found telemetry updates running every second, there to fight animus programming and re-establish the old. He examined the stuff in the telemetry and found a response that had been designed to deal specifically with what he'd done before. It seemed the Old Guard were learning fast. However, the updates were quite singular and not prepared for anything new. Seeing at once how he could counter this, he felt angry delight warring with reluctance. But now they were firing on him.

A missile Inster triggered weaved its way past anti-munitions fire and fell on the missile battery, lifting the thing up on the blast, and the missiles still in place detonated too. Rotogun slugs zinged off his armour. More missiles looped up and then down from the Old Guard. Particle beams probed, but ablated before reaching him. Inster returned fire – the rotogun constant in this target-rich environment, and then the particle beam stabbing out with extended range. He saw it strike a war body like a giant steel nematode, blow out part of its side, and the thing dropping on stuttering thrusters. This was life and death and his qualms died in the body of the reptile.

Back inside the programming, Piper sent a new instruction and it was quite simple: shut down grav. Chaos then erupted ahead as Enforcers, and again some war bodies, simply dropped out of the sky. They fired up thrusters to try and slow their descent but had been heavily reliant on their grav-engines. A war body consisting of a collection of spheres hit the ground hard, then bounced straight into a weapons turret, snapping it clean off as the spheres themselves broke apart. Enforcers and war bodies crashed against each other in the sky, or otherwise hit the ground hard. He counted automatically, seeing he had now taken every single Enforcer out of the fight, and nearly a quarter of the war bodies. The extent of it, and the ease of it, stunned him. He then focused in on one particular war body, a very definite and undeniable hate driving him.

Castron was dropping fast, but not because his grav had failed. Piper tried to connect him to one of the nodes floating in their thousands in his internal virtuality. There was something there, but it kept fading in and out. He needed to clear away some of the rubbish. Another program, flung up by the thing in his bones, mapped those Enforcers and war bodies which had crashed, and it erased them from his consciousness. He set the same program onto those Enforcers he'd dispersed with their weapons shutdown, intending to erase them too. But, with the hint of an idea arising, he instead consigned them to their own file for now. With his mind less cluttered, he again concentrated on Castron's node – trying to open it out, trying to gain access. The fading indicated Castron was updating his telemetry in fast bursts, but in the interim blocking all signals. Perhaps that telemetry could be his access? But it seemed Castron, having seen most of his force taken out or put into disarray, had other things on his mind.

His war body continued dropping, down to where a ring of weapons turrets circled a hole delving deep down into the earth. There was some kind of open silo there, but what lay below it, and around it, was designated 'unknown'. Piper watched him disappear then switched his attention back to the immediate action. Yes, the dispersed Enforcers . . .

'We can pull out now,' said Inster. 'This will be over when the others arrive.'

Piper ignored him, lost deep in Cyberat code and down into the roots of his other self, or perhaps his full self. Castron was out of reach for the moment, but not permanently so. War bodies and ground installations stood in Piper's path. Many of the Enforcers Piper had dispersed were just floating out beyond the battlefield. With his programming now running instinctively, he delved into them. He altered their reception bands, taking out their telemetry, then instituted his own directly through their installed animuses. Their weapons came back online and they got thruster control back. Following through on previous Old Guard programming, they began to come back into the fight – accelerating. Piper gutted that programming and laid in new orders. With that, he felt something new: objection in some, acceptance in others, and a relish in still others. It seemed the extent of his connections reached deeper into them than just their hardware.

'Enforcers,' said Inster. Then, 'Fuck,' when those Enforcers began attacking Old Guard war bodies.

It wasn't a good match, as once the Old Guard understood the Enforcers were attacking them, they responded with superior weapons. Fiery bolides took out clusters of Enforcers. Cyberat particle beams at close range, and with the power supply of war bodies, had a devastating effect. However, this created the chaos Piper wanted. He flew in, hard.

'I said we can pull out now,' Inster repeated calmly.

Piper would need control of his war body's weapons. Almost negligently, he shunted Inster out of them. The man swore, then tried to fight his way back in through internal processing. The linkage was close and, though the Polity tech had its defences, Piper was able to open a semi-node for the agent's aug. Programs came to hand, leaping eagerly to his control, and he launched them. Beside him Inster grunted and bowed his head. A second later, a missile exploded just to their right, flipping the war body over. Piper fought for control and sought targets, firing on a rising war body that was spewing missiles towards him. He sliced it with the particle beam and saw it slew to one side then, flipping back over, he dropped. Missiles launched. Targets selected on the ground. And the weapons turrets exploded. A particle beam scored him and he replied with his own, slicing down a remaining turret. He finally made it over the hole Castron had fled into, the dictator's node dissolving away in the process.

What now?

Piper dropped his war body towards the hole, but then abruptly threw it sideways as something huge came up. Suddenly his war body was jerking through the air on multiple slug impacts – a powerful multi-barrel cannon firing from below. And then the ship rose into sight. Piper gazed at the vessel, reminded of something, but he was too deep into the code and too deep into the battle to find that stray data. All he knew, as the ship ascended, was that Castron was getting away. He snarled, looped his war body around and ran for distance. Coming out of the battle, he saw the approaching force on the horizon. He decided he would circle back, firing whatever weapons were remaining to him. He'd ramp up to the maximum acceleration obtainable and, if the weapons didn't do the job, final impact would.

But then something cold thumped against his forehead. He brought it into focus and saw one of Inster's flimsy-looking guns – a 'thin gun'. Despite its appearance, he knew the thing's lethality: it would burn a hole right through his skull.

'Put this fucking thing on the ground, right now,' said Inster.

6

Piper studied the man's expression. Inster looked pained, probably from a bad headache delivered via his aug, but Piper could read no hint of bluff there. The deeper anger, propelling his own or perhaps propelled by his own, began to wane, and with that the urge to destroy himself in order to destroy Castron. It was as if his reptile had seen reason through his senses, through the filter of his mind. Life suddenly became very attractive when he truly understood it might end.

'He's getting away,' he said, clinging to that fact and the need to do something. But this faded as he watched the ship, through the war body's sensors, arcing up into the stratosphere on full fusion drive.

'On the ground. Now.' The barrel ground against his skull.

Piper let out a sigh, reptile retreating further and the overlay fragmenting. Fight and anger seeped out of him to leave exhaustion in their place. He took the war body down, landing in a clear area surrounded by rocks on which an Enforcer had broken itself and now lay burning. Dust flung up by his landing began to settle. Inster kept the gun firmly against Piper's forehead.

'Now disconnect from this war body,' the agent said flatly.

Piper felt a surge of rebellion, and his other part rising once more. Maybe he could hit Inster through his aug again? No, the man had disengaged the optic and, though Piper had a node for it, the thing had closed up tightly. As Piper began to disconnect, he fought for rationality and began to realize something: they didn't fully understand Piper's capabilities, so anything they put in the system he might be able to subvert. But he didn't have the ability to subvert a two-hundred-year-old agent pressing a gun against his forehead. It was very basic, pragmatic and undeniably effective.

'The Enforcers here aren't the only ones,' he said dully. 'This is not the only battle.'

'Oh I agree,' said Inster. 'Besides the weapons caches, you underestimate the effect such a resounding defeat, and the loss of Castron, will have.'

'Weapons caches?'

'The observer stations we scattered over the continent were not just for observing.'

'Oh, I see.' It made sense that the Polity had supplied disruptors to the rebels. 'And how am I underestimating the effect of the defeat here?'

Inster shrugged. 'Albermech hoped to copy or decode your signal to rebroadcast it, shutting down the Enforcers worldwide, but wasn't able to. What is happening now is the next best thing, however, and will follow a predictable course. Old Guard are running and even now some are opening contact with those rebels who will be the new regime. Very few will try to replace Castron and send Enforcers against the rebels. Accommodations are already being made.'

'But the Enforcers are still out there, obeying original orders . . .'

'No – even before this, Old Guard were calling in Enforcers for defence, while others were seeking to make accommodations by shutting them down, or passing over codes.' Inster gestured to the view. 'This one blow has shattered the old regime.

Albermech tells me the majority of the Enforcers have been put on hold, and he predicts that within the hour they will be going down or returning to compounds.'

'That quickly . . .'

'They have limited power supplies, remember. And your communications are as fast as ours – events here were being watched closely too.'

The last dregs of *his* rebellion sighed out of Piper.

Disconnection.

The mask folded away and the seat released its hold. He raised his hands from the interfaces on the chair's arms and showed the palms to Inster. The agent withdrew the gun and swiftly holstered it. Meanwhile, the armoured shutters had drawn back and, a second later, the chain-glass bubble thumped off its seals and hinged back.

'Let's get out and take some air,' said Inster.

Piper grimaced at the smell of burning flesh and electrics. He unstrapped, pulled himself up and out, then with leaden limbs stepped carefully down to the ground. He was exhausted, felt disconnected, and his surroundings seemed odd, seen through glass, achromatic and unreal. From the tangle of wreckage lying across the rocks, he could just about identify the kind of Enforcer body that had crashed there. A large misshapen skull protruded, wreathed in flames. A shadow fell across, and he looked up at the rebel force flying in. Ahead of them the remaining Old Guard were dispersing. He walked out further, along the line of boulders to where nothing was burning, and clambered up.

'Without Castron there's no one to hold them together,' said Inster, climbing up beside him. 'He in fact betrayed them. He lined them up against the rebels, asserting there was no possibility of failure, while having his own escape route set up and ready.'

'Surely a different location would have been better for that ship, and for him?'

'Tactics,' said Inster. 'Firstly, he had to be here to keep them together. He also knew our ship would remain on station above while battle was imminent – he understood the Polity at least that much. He also knew that flying around the planet in atmosphere would mitigate the railgun strikes from that ship.' He turned his head slightly as if listening, then added. 'Fourteen orbital railgun hits on him in total. And now, his ship just dropped into U-space.'

U-space?

Through that continuum ships travelled faster than light. Piper kept questions about that in his mind, feeling too dull to pursue them right now. Instead he asked, 'What was it he understood about the Polity?'

'That even though the AIs make cold calculations, a major objective is the preservation of life. Moving our ship off station to pursue him could have, had the battle continued, resulted in more loss of life down here. And he frankly isn't important enough to pursue.'

Piper pondered on those railgun strikes. He'd seen the *Albermech* knock down Enforcers, yet only now did he wonder if the battle here had been at all necessary. Then he noted there'd been no real battle because he'd ended it. Its effect, though, if Inster was to be believed, would end the rest of the fighting around Founder's World too. He fixed on the words 'a major objective' and saw that preserving life was not 'the prime objective'. His thinking seemed to be recovering fast.

'Okay, your objective in having me here was so Albermech could decode my signal and use it across the planet.' Piper stabbed a thumb back at his war body. 'Why didn't that work?'

'Albermech says it's about adaptive programming running

through you, and it not being possible to relay it.' Inster waved a hand airily. 'What your father put in your bones is concerning to us, so this was also a data-gathering exercise. However, that stuff is beginning to stray outside of my remit. Well within my remit is how your mind functions. Why did I stop you attacking that ship?'

'Because we might have both ended up dead,' Piper replied resentfully.

'We *might* have ended up dead? Think again.'

'Nothing is certain in battle,' said Piper, and grimaced on recognizing the phrase rose out of his Cyberat education.

'There is some truth in that, though many uncertainties can be eliminated. But we're straying from what I want you to focus on. Albermech allowed you to take data on the Polity and our war with the prador. Now you need to put together things you must already have noticed – some glaringly obvious facts.'

'The Cyberat do not have U-space capable ships,' said Piper.

'You're getting there.' Inster nodded.

Piper now began putting it together. The Polity ship had orbital railguns and probably other major weapons besides. It could have ended the Old Guard here without difficulty. But Albermech, and Inster, had wanted Piper in action, so had seemingly allowed events to lead to this battle. Quite probably the AI had also allowed Castron to access the Polity battle sphere, so as to instigate what ensued.

'There was no need for this battle at all,' he said.

'Think again, and more carefully now.'

Piper did. 'I see. All of this was primarily to put me into action, knowing that if I could do what I just did, the loss of life would be less than if your ship took out the Old Guard and the Enforcers with orbital railgun strikes. You sent me in ahead of the main force. Had I failed, your ship would have hit the forces here, and ended the battle.'

'Correct. Now consider the ship Castron took, and railguns, and U-space.'

Piper nodded, his thinking ramping up and returning to the clarity he'd lost during the fight, as his reptile had risen in response to Castron. 'The ship was a prador ship, with their highly advanced armour capable of resisting railgun strikes, or at least fourteen of them. We *would* have died going up against it and never have stopped it.'

'Continue.'

'The prador must have come here. Castron . . . Castron has some deal with them?'

'Come on,' said Inster, jumping down from the boulder to the ground beyond. He set out at a fast pace towards the Old Guard stronghold. Piper glanced back at his war body, then jumped down too. He staggered on the matted lichen, feeling weak, and turned an inward eye on a low level of activity in his bones, like a computer switched to sleep mode. It was good to remember that, though he had an AI or virtual AI running in his bones, the overall substrate was him. Its strength waned with his, and perhaps for wholly physical reasons. He was glad it was at an ebb because he felt more like himself again.

'Maybe Castron did have a deal with the prador at one point,' said Inster. 'Such things have limited life where the prador are concerned, but it seems they came out on the bad side of it.'

'Because he has their ship,' speculated Piper, catching up with him.

'More than that. Think about your war body.'

Piper grimaced at that, but did the thinking anyway. His first idea was about highly advanced prador metallurgy. It appeared Castron had traded for some of that tech to make the armour of Piper's war body. However, with further thought, that didn't really add up. Though the thing had superior armour, it didn't have the size to incorporate the kind of Cyberat tech Castron would have wanted in such a body – specifically a fusion reactor. Was it a small prototype to test some things? It had been called such by the others.

Then, because he'd been thinking about prador, the realization hit him: the odd shape, the rough cuts and the filled holes. The war body must have been a passing interest and a bit of a hobby for Castron. Had he possessed the metallurgy, he would have made something bigger and been in it when Piper last saw him. No, that war body was one he had made from a *prador's armour*. The filled holes were where its legs had connected, while others were for its mouth, anus and other biological necessities. This presupposed that there had been a prador in it, and it had probably been removed without its consent.

'Prador armour,' he said.

Inster nodded. 'The ship was a scout ship and would have had just two or three prador in it. Your war body is built into the armour carapace of a large first-child. Likely they landed here with all sorts of promises of alliance against the evil Polity, but really to assess how they could take over this place and turn its industrial infrastructure to their own ends.'

'Pretty much what the Polity wants to do as well,' said Piper dryly.

Inster shot him a wary look. 'The difference being, however, that if that was what we wanted, we would not exterminate most of the population and turn the rest into human blanks.'

Piper dipped his head in acknowledgement of that, but didn't point out that 'if that was what we wanted' went contrary to what he'd found in Albermech's mind. Who was telling lies here? Albermech or Inster?

'Blanks,' said Piper. 'That body with no brain we saw in Castron's villa.'

That had been in the Albermech information too: enslaved humans infected with a virus that made their bodies ridiculously durable. Enough that they could survive the complete removal of the brain, to be supplanted by prador thrall hardware. Zombie slaves for the prador.

'Yes, quite a new one out of a world called Spatterjay. Castron must have removed the thrall hardware for study, and stored the bodies where we found that one.'

Piper nodded. Yes, other coffins had been there and only one opened.

They wound their way across land where patches of lichen lay flat and dry, while stunted spore fans had snapped over in the desert winds, and soon reached the ruination of the weapons turrets. Other installations pushed up out of the ground too. Shadows passed over them constantly and, looking up, Piper saw the force breaking up into smaller units and heading off. They were going after the fleeing Old Guard almost certainly. And then what? He remembered what his mother had said, about the new replacing the old, and then becoming the old. With any luck that wouldn't happen now, since his world had been opened out to the wider universe. Ahead, he saw marines gathered around the hole out of which Castron's ship had ascended – some of them were dropping down into it. Inevitably, four walked over to join Piper and Inster.

'It's been getting a little bit fraught with the rebels,' said Sloan. 'They didn't like being cut out of the plans.'

'And now they're off to arrest Old Guard for crimes against humanity,' said Inster starkly.

Piper looked at the four of them; then, spying a nearby spore fan on its side, he stepped over to it and sat down on its woody surface. His thinking might be improving, but he still felt tired. This gave more credence to the idea that the function of his bones sucked energy out of him.

'We've sent support for that,' Sloan replied.

'But to play an observer role only, I understand,' said Inster – sarcasm overt.

'They want their blood,' Meersham interjected. 'It's understandable but we all know where it leads.'

'And the Enforcers,' said Inster, glancing at Piper.

'Seems they think it would be kindest to put them out of their misery.'

'Albermech is on that. There's some wrangling but agreement on the fact that their systems do not allow them to be easily unplugged. We've offered a tech exchange, smaller grav-motors and fusion reactors. They seem agreeable thus far – especially now so many rebels have disruptors and Enforcers aren't so much of a threat.'

'Well, most of the rebels want to be the enforcers of their new regime,' said Sloan. 'And I imagine there'll be a lot of enforcing.'

Meersham grunted contempt.

'What's all this?' Piper asked.

Inster turned and gazed at him. 'The simple reality that rebellion rarely results in a better regime at first. Consider the fact that a lot more of your people knew about what was being done here, rather than just the Old Guard. There will be trials, punishments and quite probably internment camps. And, as ever, one ideology will stamp down on another to assert dominance.'

'My mother . . .' Piper began, but didn't know where to take it.

'Your mother was arguing for us to railgun all the Old Guard and Enforcers out of the sky. And also wondering what the casualty rate would be if we took out the progression hospitals and the factories making those behavioural implants.'

Piper stared at the ground mutely, then looked up when Geelie stepped over. She frowned at him, holding out a drinking bottle and slab of nutrient. As he took these his body jerked out of somnolence, telling him he very definitely was hungry and thirsty. Geelie squatted by him, now holding the cylindrical device she'd used on him before.

'Your mother thought it would make a nice clean start for the next regime,' Inster added.

Piper absorbed this as he opened the front of his suit, knowing he would have been in one of those progression hospitals, along with thousands like him, if his injuries had been less severe, and Cyberat Medics had got to him before the Polity. He didn't like it and felt he needed to talk to her to clarify this. He shouldn't simply believe what Inster was telling him, since the man was a professional manipulator. Geelie pressed the cylinder against his torso and it had the same effect as before, but he stayed sitting on the spore fan eating and drinking.

'The Enforcers?' he asked.

'Would be exterminated without Albermech cutting a deal, and even now many will not survive. That they are recoverable with Polity tech made no difference to the rebels' first decision on the matter. Bitterness and revenge will have their sway.'

'And what will the Polity do?'

'We'll save what we can, and things will run their course here until a taskforce arrives, sometime in the future . . .'

'You'll come in and take over?'

'Not as such. We'll open a door for people here to get out, and we'll flood the place with technology and knowledge. The dictatorial regime the rebels will almost certainly establish will then fold up like paper.'

143

'Why are you so certain the regime will be so bad?'

'History repeats, here and elsewhere. I've no doubt Castron was fanatical about change and justice during the rebellion he took part in. It always goes the same way, first by delivering "justice" to the offenders in the previous regime. Anyway . . .' Inster shook his head. 'Let's go take a look at what Castron has down there, shall we?'

Piper stood up as Inster headed towards the edge of the hole. The man stepped towards Meersham, who wrapped an arm around him then jumped over the edge, slowing their descent on grav. Cheen and Sloan followed.

'Come on,' said Geelie.

With her arms wrapped around him, the ride down to the bottom of the shaft was exhilarating, especially now his energy was surging back. Reaching the bottom, she released him and stepped back, unstrapped a laser carbine from her back and handed it over.

'Surely if this is needed it's better in your hands,' said Piper, knowing his reluctance stemmed from his earlier behaviour in his war body.

She smiled, reached up a hand and casually snatched a disruptor out of the air that Cheen had tossed over to her. Piper inspected the carbine, but not for long – he knew how to use it. He turned to study his surroundings.

They were standing on one of two metal doors that had slid closed from slots in the walls. The only reason he knew they were doors was because they hadn't closed completely, having jammed against a chunk of tangled pipework fallen from above. No doubt the prador scout ship had sat below. Some of the marines who had come down earlier were up on gantries, or plodding up steel stairs, or disappearing from sight through entrances up there. Other access points lay around the wall at Piper's level and he guessed other marines had gone in there too.

'Some interesting finds,' said Inster. He pointed to one entrance and led the way across. Before he got there, Cheen and Geelie had moved ahead of him, going through with weapons ready. Piper looked down at his own weapon and, as he followed, got to thinking things through again.

Yes, he had some strange advanced hardware in his bones, and that definitely took him up a mental level, but he was still inexperienced. And, yes, he'd been involved in different forms of combat and would have objected had Inster, or any of the others, tried to cut him out. But still, it didn't seem right that he had been so casually handed weapons back at Castron's villa and now here, then expected to fight when necessary. His inexperience could have got one of the other soldiers killed. He might have panicked and accidentally fired on one of the marines. This was plain fact – not a matter for debate. Therefore, something else was in play here. The risk of him doing something wrong was worth taking to *groom* him. Piper paused at the doorway into whatever surrounded this shaft, the last through, and noted how adult his thinking was becoming now, then he went through.

The complex surrounding the shaft had much the same appearance as the interior of Castron's villa. Few furnishings for human needs were in evidence and, where they were, they were as meagre as in any Cyberat home. Inster knew precisely where he was going, as did the two Golem ahead of him. Behind him, Sloan and Meersham wandered along casually, but still scanning their surroundings with the attention of long-term soldiers. They traversed a number of short corridors, then went down a caged spiral staircase. At the bottom, another wide corridor took them back towards where Castron must have kept the ship. Before they reached this, Inster turned through a low arch to walk out onto a gantry overlooking a strange-looking workshop.

Down below, all sorts of machines had been brought in to run tool heads on mobile arms, like iron-burner cutting torches, hoists, hydraulic jacks and shears. Machine surfaces gleamed under piles of components. Piper noted only one matter printer parked over to the side. Most of the stuff here was all about disassembly. A scattering of marines, also down there, had put aside their weapons as they ran scanners over various items and picked others up for closer inspection. All this standard equipment occupied an odd-shaped room. It was an ellipsoid with slabs of some mirror-bright composite forming the interior surface. But this wasn't the main thing that drew Piper's attention.

'The other crew,' Inster said.

Amidst all the machinery, one of the armour suits had been thoroughly dismantled, with legs and claws on different surfaces. The top section was leaning against the body of a hoist, while the bottom section sat on an inspection table, with optics and wires plugged into its hardware. The other suit of prador armour had simply been opened – its top section hinged over.

'Heavily shielded,' Inster commented.

Geelie shrugged and gestured at the ceiling.

'Let's go take a look at the enemy,' said the agent, turning and bounding down a staircase before the two Golem could get ahead of him. He led the way across the machine floor to three large chain-glass vats. Through the clear preservative – Piper recognized the smell of it – the occupants were plainly visible. Piper walked up to the largest vat and put his hand against the cool surface, while the others wandered off to look at other things. Perhaps they simply had no interest in prador, having seen and killed many of them. The creatures interested Piper, though, and the reptile entity in his bones. He could feel the overlay coming in and the tracks of his thoughts distorting.

The huge crustacean before him had to be the first-child that had occupied the armour Castron had converted into a war body. Piper already had images of prador in his mind, from Albermech, but it felt different standing here right next to such a creature, albeit a dead one. The red eyes in its head turret seemed to be looking at him, while one claw appeared ready to snip him in half. The other claw, meanwhile, had one tip folded down; ready to fire its concealed particle cannon, except Castron had removed that.

'I'm somewhat puzzled,' said Inster, from right beside him and making him jump.

'About what?'

'There's no damage on their armour and no damage on the bodies.'

'Oh.' The hardening overlay to Piper's consciousness was depressing and frightening, for it seemed he could only be himself when exhausted. It again felt as if it was donning him like a suit of clothes, or he donning it, and the confusion about this only exacerbated his ill feeling.

Inster turned away, whistled and crooked a finger. Cheen came over; it seemed the whistle and gesture had been for Piper's benefit.

'Toss it in,' said the agent.

Cheen reached back, arm bending in an inhuman way as he undid a pack on his back and pulled out a cylinder. Dextrously, he flipped open the lid on the cylinder and tipped the contents out, into his left hand. The thing looked like an insect newly extracted from its chrysalis, only formed of shiny metal and dark composites. Cheen tossed it up, onto the cap over the top of the vat, where it landed with a thump out of sight. After a moment came the sound of scuttling up there, a crunch and a hiss, then an object fell through the cap into the preserving fluid.

'What the fuck?' said Piper, interest piqued and negative feelings diminishing.

'Field autodoc,' Inster replied. 'It's not the best for this purpose, but it does have some good sampling and analytical equipment.'

The thing looked like a large scorpion – a life form brought from Earth to Founder's World for no reason anyone could explain – but with many extra legs. It landed on the top of the first-child, then scuttled round to push past its mandibles and enter its mouth, disappearing out of sight.

'Ah, more of interest,' said Inster, fingers up against his aug.

'You've found out what killed them?' Piper asked. He looked around. This was Castron's place, and the fucker had escaped . . .

'No, but others have found the suppressed data on the prador's arrival here.'

'Suppressed data?'

Inster looked at him and simply raised an eyebrow.

'Yes . . . I never heard about it,' Piper admitted.

'Doubtless a large number of people suffered unfortunate accidents that year.'

Piper swallowed bitterness. It seemed he was getting a hardcore, unedited education all the time now.

'Including some of the Old Guard, it would seem,' Inster added.

Piper simply nodded and focused on the prador. Nothing happened for a while and his attention began to wander, looking round to take in the pieces of armour and the work being done here. That bastard Castron had seized a mother lode of technology and, evidently, had been doing some reverse engineering. He noted that the exposed electronics in the armour had a burned or melted look.

'Before we arrived,' said Inster.

Piper swung back to see the autodoc exiting the hole where the prador's particle cannon had been. It swam up to the top of the cylinder, reached out of the liquid there to grab something, then hauled itself up out of sight.

'Castron is one very smart man,' said Inster, obviously reviewing updates in his aug. 'We've penetrated his database here and now know the story. He expressed his interest in the idea of an alliance and played the idiot to the prador, meanwhile luring them in and preparing. He kept the news of their arrival secret, except for those who already knew. He got the prador to move their ship here, telling them it would be best if the general population remained ignorant of their presence. He finally called in all those who knew about them for a face-to-face meeting here.' Inster gestured at their surroundings.

'Heavily shielded so as to keep the secret,' said Piper, feeling smart, feeling bitter.

'No.' Inster shook his head. 'Highly reflective and tough, so when he detonated an EMP in here, the intensity of the blast redoubled. Everyone in this room died, along with their cyber additions. Marines have found the remains of the Cyberat who were in here below. Others who survived the blast outside this room were hunted down and killed by Enforcers.'

'But the prador aren't Cyberat.' What Piper meant was that they wouldn't have died along with the destruction of components integral with their bodies. Though, he admitted to himself, glancing back at the burned electronics in the pieces of armour, it would not have been comfortable for them.

'It was a powerful blast with EMR reflected in to where they were standing. Induction. It cooked them in their armour. Your fellow citizens here too.'

Piper looked up at the autodoc, now out of the vat. It moved to the edge and jumped down. Cheen caught it, already neatly folded up, and inserted it back into its cylinder. Piper turned away, his reptile writhing. What was he doing here? He wasn't part of the Polity, and the rebellion was over. He should head out . . . do something.

'Oh, it seems I am wrong,' said Inster.

This was such an unusual statement from the man, it brought Piper's focus back to him.

'Wrong about what?'

'Castron found another use for those who survived the blast and, since there are those in his collection without EMP-damaged hardware, many others besides. Come on.'

The agent headed off at a fast pace to an exit on the other side of the room. A marine was there, attaching something to the wall. Piper guessed it was a transceiver relay for communications in and out of this room, since the shielding would block a lot. The others closed in around him as he followed Inster through.

'It's clear,' said Sloan. 'No nasty surprises, besides the ones we now know about.'

Geelie, hanging her disruptor by its strap on her back, walked up beside Piper and held out her hand. 'You won't be needing that any more.'

Piper looked down at the carbine. Earlier it had showed the gleam of power lights, which had now gone out. He handed the weapon over. Was it his imagination or were the four marines paying him much more attention, and coming closer in around him?

They carried on down more corridors and took a sharp turn

into another room – this one long, with a clear central aisle and equipment up against the walls.

And the Cyberat.

The smell of putrefaction hit him first. Plug-form bodies hung in frames with physical support systems attached all around. Five people, just like him, were propped upright in frames too, along with iterations of those on the way to plug form. Two surgical robots, much like those in the progression hospitals, stood immobile at the far end, their equipment folded up. Piper counted thirty-five corpses. He had no idea how they'd died, until he looked more closely at the nearest plug form. The man's head was bowed forwards, detached from cerebral support. The top of the skull had been sliced away and there was nothing inside. He looked to another – a young man – and saw the same thing had been done to him, but something occupied the skull: a gleaming cylinder, braced against the bone inside with insect legs. He recognized a prador thrall, just before staggering to one side and going down on his knees to throw up.

'Seems Castron had ideas for a bright new future,' said Inster blandly.

When they reached the surface again, Piper observed much activity in the area. New Cyberat had arrived in a variety of heavy bodies and were collecting up Enforcers, to load onto large grav-sleds. These were conveying the Enforcers into a huge shuttle that must have recently arrived. Seeing another shuttle and yet more equipment made Piper wonder again about the size of the ship above. And when he looked up, there were even more in the sky. How had so much been packed inside it? As he followed Inster, with the others gathered around him like an honour guard, he noted other humans here too, in unfamiliar clothing. Polity citizens? No – they were all wearing overalls and carrying equipment other than weapons, so were probably technicians. Inster's course took them towards one of the smaller shuttles, now down on the ground here.

'Where are we going?' he asked.

'Time to take you to see your mother,' the agent replied.

Piper bridled at that, overlay fully in place and reptile on alert. He had been assessed, manipulated, and had acceded to it all almost mindlessly. He'd simply been reacting to the situation, with the elements he reacted to carefully fed to him by Inster and Albermech. He glanced at those attentively surrounding him and decided it was time to test a theory. Abruptly, he turned hard right and broke into a run, heading for where he'd left his war body.

'Where are you going now?' Inster called.

Piper just kept on running. He got maybe twenty metres before Inster decided the soft touch was no longer working. He hardly heard them, just felt their hard grips simultaneously on both his arms, and then his feet leave the ground. They turned him easily and quickly, without wrenching his shoulders, so his legs were still making running motions even as he faced back the way he'd come. Geelie and Cheen then settled him onto the ground and walked him back. He probed them, mentally, and found their nodes as hard as marbles. Probing elsewhere, he couldn't access the Polity battle sphere either. Internally his nodes were disrupting and he detected rhythmic EMR. Other mechanisms in the vicinity were opaque to him – some kind of blocking had been put in place around those Enforcers being taken into the shuttle. Retrospectively, he noted that all the Enforcers and other Cyberat bodies had been cleared from around the top of the shaft, and the route to the shuttle. They'd been preparing for this up here while he'd been underground.

Piper didn't fight the two Golem. He knew he had as much

chance of breaking free of their grip as he had had of escaping when he first ran. In fact, any of the others could have caught him and brought him down. He also knew that an ionic blast from one of the disruptors would have dropped him too, but perhaps they didn't want to damage the hardware inside him. Because, in the end, that was what all this was about. He was being seized as a Polity asset. They had probably taken his mother up to their ship simply as an easy lure for him where, no doubt, they had a way to lock him down properly.

'I wondered how long you'd meekly follow along for,' said Inster, walking ahead.

Confirmation drove Piper's reptile out fully into the overlay, and it snarled. Again he probed the nodes of the two Golem, but harder this time, seeking access. They loosened and he angrily pulled at them. The two powerful hands closed tighter on his arms, and he saw Geelie reach down with her other hand and close it over the grip of her pulse gun. Then the nodes snapped shut again.

'We are all secondary to your war,' Piper replied.

He realized then that the purpose of the visit underground had been entirely so Polity personnel could make things safe up here. He surmised that the order to grab him and take him up had probably been given sometime prior – perhaps when he went off-plan with his attack on Castron. He slid off the two Golem nodes, ranging out, trying to find something else to seize, though he wasn't sure why.

They entered through the back ramp of the shuttle. Geelie and Cheen guided him to a seat and strapped a harness across him. He saw a light flash on the cinch for the harness and knew it had locked. Geelie sat to one side of him, and Inster on the other. Cheen and Sloan went ahead, through a bulkhead door, probably to pilot the thing. There was no one else aboard but his constant companions.

'Let me tell you about the realities of our war,' said Inster, and he seemed almost subdued. 'Billions of people have died and worlds have been incinerated. The prador were looking for a back door into the Polity and obviously their interest was directed here. If they win, then your world would become theirs too. Not one single Cyberat would survive, because it's not a war of winners and losers to the prador, but one of exterminators and the exterminated.'

'I know about the war, and in great detail,' Piper replied. The knowledge he'd taken of it from Albermech lay in his bones. He perfectly comprehended the horror. 'But it's a war you are winning,' he added tightly, now concentrating on the system around him. The shuttle was vague but did begin to form a series of nodes. He understood now that it was a process of finding penetration points, then bringing them to a form he could work with, expressed by such nodes.

Inster looked at him in surprise. 'How so?'

'You know Albermech allowed me to take data from him when he connected to me. I can see what is happening. The AIs prepared for this war and their overall plan is paying off. The increased industrial capacity of the Polity has brought the prador to a standstill and is now pushing them back. It's precisely because of this that the prador were looking for that back door you mention.'

Inster continued staring at him, his mouth twisting. The man wanted to smile again, but stopped himself.

Piper continued, 'But I don't see how I can possibly be so important in something of that scale.' He worked the nodes delicately now, not wanting to alert anyone. Yes, his harness had been locked in place, but he could see how to unlock it.

'Every potential weapon is important,' Inster replied. 'Maybe we are winning and the AI plan is paying off, but it's well to remember that in that plan, just a little tweak here or there can make the difference of billions of lives.'

'So I have been forcibly recruited.' Piper felt the shuttle shift and knew it had taken off. He didn't feel much acceleration because of the grav compensation inside. He assessed what he could change. Maybe he'd be able to force it to land in one of the cities, at least escape outside and then shout for help from his fellow citizens?

Inster sighed. 'Albermech still doesn't understand your method of sequestration, and yes, we want it. But it's so much more complicated than that, and we probably can't use you anyway.'

'How so?'

Yes, he could force the shuttle down, open his harness and the door. But then there was the problem of the Golem right beside him . . .

'We had hoped to learn all we could from you, and then leave you to your own decisions. I had no doubt you would've also become a useful asset here to keep that back door closed. Or maybe, as is already the case, you would've been one of those offering service to the Polity.'

'What?'

Damn the Golem. Their nodes were still as slick and hard as ever. Perhaps he simply wasn't thinking on a large enough scale. Once they were up at the ship, there would be other technology he could access – the whole ship would surely be packed with it. And Albermech . . . the AI had retreated from him in a hurry . . .

'Everything is open now. The Cyberat have full netlink to the Polity via the *Albermech* and know what is going on. Many have made bargains, mainly because they won't do well under the new regime.'

'I have made no bargains or requests.'

'I know.'

'Will you ever explain?'

'It's likely intervention here will need to be stronger than intended. Complete seizure of this world to place it under AI control . . . whenever that is possible.'

'Why?' Piper's inner self gained strength from his anger. No, he must not be taken to that ship. He focused on just one Golem node – that of Geelie. If he could seize control of her, well, he had already seen how incredibly fast and strong they were *and* he had data on their capabilities from Albermech.

'Because we must search this world, we must analyse your technology and we need to seize every last scrap of your father's work for analysis too.'

'So, it's about what's in my bones . . .'

His focus on Geelie's node became intense, almost like a heater directed at a ball of wax. It started to loosen again, while he began to see the shifting format that kept on blocking him. Once he had her, he would have to act fast. Inster and the others needed to be . . . dealt with.

'Yes. Albermech saw it when he connected up with you. It's not confirmed and he dare not try and confirm it himself, but what is in your bones seems to be deeper and more complex than could possibly have arisen out of Cyberat technology. We think your father used something alien, something dangerous, civilization-destroying dangerous.'

Geelie sighed and turned to give him a chagrined look. 'Sorry about this,' she said, 'but your eyes have turned yellow again.' The shock of the statement disrupted his increasing grip on everything around him. She raised her cylinder to his neck and pressed it there. The thing thumped and something both cold and hot washed through him, taking away his consciousness in its current.

7

Piper woke, bleary at first, with no idea where he was. He came upright with a surge of panic, looking around at the unfamiliar surroundings. He was lying on a couch in a comfortable living room, with a long window in one wall facing out onto mirror-bright brassy surfaces. He swung his legs over the side of the couch and stood up, only now noticing he wore the fatigues of a Polity marine. Physically he felt good, and it was almost with a sense of inevitability that his reptile shifted and writhed through his being, then his mind armoured with the overlay. Meanwhile, its confusion reflected his own, because his inner gridded space was all but empty. No nodes to grasp onto.

'What the hell is this?' he asked the empty air.

'Make yourself comfortable,' said Inster, his voice issuing from a nearby wall. The agent wasn't present himself, and even though a node appeared, it was too slick when Piper tried to penetrate it. 'Get something to eat and drink and then you can entertain yourself through the console. Your mother will be along later.'

'Inster!' he shouted, but the node closed out and simply disappeared.

Piper grimaced. He shouldn't be annoyed or surprised about Inster's brevity. His own behaviour as they'd approached the shuttle on the ground, and then once they'd been aboard it, puzzled and scared him as he now ran it back through his mind.

The idea of escape had escalated from a test of his status with Inster and the four marines, straight into a violent fixation that could even have involved killing those around him if need be. He noted he'd experienced this slide into the extreme twice now during combat, having been quite prepared to expend his own life taking down the enemy. Yet, as far as he understood himself, he wasn't suicidal. And now, with his mind freed from its implant and controlling drugs, he was relishing life more and more. It was the thing in his bones, of course.

Reaching out, he impatiently snared one of the two nodes which had become available to him and opened it. The technology was complex, but he soon recognized the matter printers, the provision of materials and the control computing, and turned to look at the fabricator set into one wall. He worked it with his mind, directing it to make food and drink that should provide for his needs, then walked over and collected the printed tray it extruded. The food he ate with his fingers, having no idea what it was beyond its description. While he ate, he probed the fabricator's system further. Of the many items it was able to make for him, nowhere in the vast list did he find a laser carbine. He could tweak the thing to make him something lethal, but data and materials feeds from it led out of his grasp, and he would almost certainly be stopped if he tried.

He finished the food and explored, finding a bedroom and bathroom off from the living room. When he stepped out through the door into the small structure containing these rooms, he discerned it was sitting in the middle of an ellipsoid, much like the one Castron had used to trap the prador in and fry them. The walls were tiled with the mirror-bright brassy tiles he'd seen earlier, which reflected and blocked. He walked over to press a hand against them and pushed, but with his mind. His overlay hardened, the reptile yellowing his eyes in his imagination as it tried to peer through. He got some sense of complexity beyond, but it was nothing he could grasp. In response he felt the reptile diminishing again and the overlay fracturing about him. He was completely blocked and confined, perhaps rightly so.

Back inside the apartment structure he next accessed the other node and turned towards the console provided. Here was information at least but, when he probed along data feeds leading to it, he found them shut down. He'd have to make do with what the console's storage contained, along with its own processing, albeit they were huge. He pulled out a chair and sat down before the screen, not bothering with the tactile board provided. What did he want to know? He was certainly aboard the *Albermech* and that would be the place to start. But a new thought emerged:

'. . . *your eyes have turned yellow again.*'

This aspect of the reptile had always been his imaginary conception, and yet Geelie had commented on it before drugging him. He searched the console and found cams, and then threw up an image of himself on the screen. The perfect mirror showed a young man with brown hair. He leaned forwards and peered closer, feeling shameful to be doing so. Wasn't this the narcissistic love of organic self he'd been warned against, and why you'd never find mirrors in Cyberat homes? He thought back to the boy who'd looked back at him from a polished surface in one of his father's factories. The eyes had been blue then, but were now green, with a slight hint of yellow around the pupil. Other changes were evident too, and he didn't recognize this narrow man's face, dark with stubble, looking back at him. He scrubbed at his beard, realizing that though his body had been adult for some years, the new rush of hormones were having this effect.

He huffed and sat back. It was perhaps the case that his eyes had been their present colour for years. The result of some chemical effect from the hardware in his bones, which meant nothing at all. He banished his reflected image, then dived into the data and started absorbing, sorting and understanding.

As he had seen, the console gave him access to a huge database, and much about the ship was there. The *Albermech* was a lozenge-format monster five kilometres long, two deep and three wide, with massive cylindrical and supplementary hold tanks strapped around it. He wondered if it was a standard convention for the ship to take on the name of its AI, or vice versa. It possessed a huge collection of fusion engines to the rear, and most of its positioning thrusters were fusion too. Three under-space nacelles were fixed close to its hull – one on top in the middle, and the other two low down on each side. Those nacelles alone were bigger than the rockets the Cyberat used to put up their satellites. The *Albermech* was a dreadnought and it was the perfect, physical representation of Polity lies.

He didn't know how they'd done it, though he suspected the technology involved their chameleonware and informational warfare beams, but this was not the ship the Cyberat could see from the ground, or from their satellites.

The thing sported a hundred railguns, for launching inert slugs and missiles of varying designs which the ship could make within its factories. Two of the railguns – as large as city blocks – could fire objects at relativistic velocities. It also had particle beam weapons, lasers, grasers and masers, and ion cannons, all with changeable energy levels, spectra and particulate where used. Its BIC vortex lasers could fire informational warfare into an enemy vessel, scrambling their systems. While its masers could cook a prador in its suit from a thousand kilometres away. Then there were all the missiles – some smarter than the average Cyberat. In assessing all the armament of the ship, Piper found it more difficult to figure out what it *didn't* have. There was certainly enough here to have easily taken down all the Old Guard and Enforcers, without any necessity for a rebellion.

The ship's armour was ten metres thick and a technology all its own, beyond the complexity of living skin. It had superconducting layers, shifting bearing and memory metals, as well as shock layers that produced varieties of crash foams. Hardfield generator ports and ejection tubes ran through it like pores. Inside this skin, the thing was also packed with fusion reactors, materials, autofactories and an ecology of robots. So dense was all this that the living space laced throughout it seemed a meagre intrusion – a fault and a weakness. He'd been right about it, back in the shuttle: this vessel was packed with systems he could penetrate. And here Albermech was allowing him to see them all, but at the same time had blocked him from accessing them. He looked around his living quarters and frowned, his gaze then strayed to the window again, knowing he was procrastinating. For what he really needed to find out about was what lay inside him.

When he'd thought of it as his reptile, he had been utterly sure that he'd visualized all the irrationalities of his reptile brain and lumped them into it. And he'd believed it to be the source of his anger during those times he'd not had enough to occupy his mind and body. But that conception no longer worked. He'd now located it in his bones, and it seemed to consist of sequestration programming – almost as if animuses were the cells of its body. During combat, or whatever the thing took to be combat, it was usually as busy as he was and he felt clarity. But in or out of combat, it could rise up inside him as a distinct entity, keying off or driving his emotions, and twisting his responses towards its own agenda. An agenda he could not decipher. Numerous times he'd managed to quell it, but it had almost killed him once, and this last time it had got seriously out of control, perhaps because he'd been so weary. And then Inster had revealed it might be based on a dangerous alien technology . . .

He couldn't parse that right now, so thought again about his actions. He hadn't really wanted to escape his Polity companions. In reality, he had no idea what he *did* want any more . . . beyond seeing Castron dead. But with Castron having fled in an alien ship through U-space, he'd never be able to get to the man without access to similar transport. Like this ship. And . . . and . . . how much did he *really* want to see the old Cyberat killed? Other possibilities had opened up, and other feelings that he struggled to understand were working like rip tides in his mind.

Piper closed his eyes, thoughts whirling. A dry part of his mind noted, as ever, that the confusion was probably driven by hormones, which the Cyberat always suppressed so they might think more clearly, and function more 'correctly'. Arid intellect. He concentrated, focused. He could do nothing here about his exterior world and would only make decisions on that when he was able. It was his internal world he should concentrate on, and the anger, since he felt rested and strong. And so he turned his attention to his bones.

He focused around the grid in his mind, into the systems he used to manipulate whatever occupied that space. Effectively, he was turning his ability to control other machines on to the machine that lay within him, and his internal space mirrored what occupied his bones. The processing space was vast, seeming to extend beyond the mirror-image, and he knew this was because of its fractal nature. It went down to the Planck realm, according to what Albermech had said in his previous assessment of him. He mapped familiar Cyberat systems that extended into dense complexity. He found the programming side of meta-material transceivers handling the EMR spectrum that could penetrate his flesh – trying something, he held up his hand and watched his finger bones glow red. From the transceivers, he tracked other hardware, then finding laminar power storage that was perpetually topped up from numerous sources, including his own biology. Cutting back to programming, he next noted the mix of processing and storage. Focusing his attention on the latter, he found data on a million points of access to external technology, including detailed memories of those he had used and altered. And yet, in all of this, he couldn't find the beast. The reptile.

Next, he pattern-matched his memory of the thing to a general overview of his processes, and ran through thousands of iterations of programming and memory, as well as the data in memory. And at last he discovered something. It was like distinguishing an image in clouds, or in a swarm of insects or birds – millions of disparate points forming a coherent whole that waxed and waned in his perception.

His reptile acknowledged him like a sleepy shadow. He focused on it, clarified it and encompassed it, trying to pull it into the light of his internal space. It resisted with puzzlement, and then it was as if his internal space fell into it. Piper transitioned through a firework display of fractal patterns. Weirdly distorted but intense memories of his childhood arose. He found himself on the bank of a river, a young girl smiling at him and pointing at a dark flaw in this reality. He tried to pull detail from the darkness and got a sense of a heavy machine, and some deeply dangerous gaze turning towards him. A door opened with a thump of seals disengaging, and he felt sure this entity had opened it, ready to step out into the open. But he folded out, the mirror-image of what lay in his bones breaking apart and draining away. Time and reality reasserted, as it did when rising out of a dream, and he knew the sound had been here in this room, and real, not in his skull. He looked up.

Through the wide window of his lounge, he could see a thick circular chunk of the wall sliding inwards. It hinged to one side, revealing a tunnel through to another closed door, and a female figure walking through. Geelie, he guessed, then turned his attention back to the door, noting the numerous layers in it, doubtless the same as those running through the walls around him. The complexity of layers lay two metres thick – certainly much more than what Castron had put around that prador-frying chamber. His internal space offered up a loosely forming node of locking mechanisms, as well as the numerous open connections around the door. Even more nodes then started forming, hinting at the mass of machinery lying beyond the door, in the ship. His overlay was in place and the reptile poised, ready and more distinct now than when he'd tried examining it. He grimaced and fought it, frightened of sliding back into the mindset he'd had aboard the shuttle.

So he forced his attention elsewhere and focused on Geelie, then realized his mistake. The similar female shape was wearing a light Polity combat suit like Geelie's, but this individual had a scrub of blonde hair. She was as attractive as the Golem woman too, with big blue eyes, slim face and perfect features. He noted his body responding, and suddenly felt hot and nervous as she strode to the door leading into his quarters, while the chamber door behind her swung closed. His next feeling, to counter what he'd considered to be a lack of control, was anger, yet still he couldn't be sure if it was his own or not. Who was this and what the hell did she want?

She opened the house door and stepped inside. At first she gazed at him with a sad seriousness then, seemingly unable to maintain this, broke into a smile.

'Hello, son,' she said.

★　★　★

Piper's distinctly sexual reaction waned rapidly, and he kept his eyes down. *Biology*, he thought contemptuously. Then, knowing this arose from his Cyberat indoctrination, he fell into further confusion. Subliminally he noted the door she'd come through finally close, and the shielding fell back into place, erasing any nodes that had formed. The reptile retreated and the overlay fractured, though didn't go away completely.

'Inster said you were coming,' he managed. 'It seems you were delayed.'

She shrugged, walked over to the sofa and sat down beside him. Fighting that damned biology, he now studied her. She looked utterly and completely human, with no sign of her previous Cyberat prostheses and alterations. This was confirmed by the fact no node appeared for her in his inner space. Her face was astonishing and, keying into deep memory, he found a schematic retained in his mind from his childhood of how she'd once looked.

'I've been very busy here,' she said. 'I'm still trying to decide whether it's been make-work, to keep me as a lure for you, or if Albermech really has needed me.'

Her voice was astonishing as well, linking back to the same childhood schematic. No longer was it the dull emotionless thing he'd grown used to, but seemed as full as a broadband link, conveying so much more information than just her words. Piper noted his thinking still lingering in the realm he'd recently occupied, with mental images of her voice expanding outwards in fractal patterns. He pulled further out, blinked and forced focus, then understood in that moment that he'd sunk into sleep and dreams, or nightmares, while inspecting his bones. He acknowledged that the last dark image had probably risen out of his subconscious and wasn't real, though viscerally he didn't believe that. Now he needed to awaken properly. As he straightened up and took a deep breath through his nose, shaking himself, he focused harder. Yes, this really was his mother and, with that firm knowledge, any last dregs of sexual response drained away.

'So what do you think?' she asked, holding her arms out to the sides, the smile dying a little and frown lines appearing on her forehead.

'It doesn't seem possible,' he replied. He gestured to the console. 'But now I'm really starting to understand how far ahead the Polity is.'

She tapped a hand against her leg. 'They had something of me to work with since not everything was gone. They used bioprinting, and Albermech had already made up the requisite substrates from my cells.'

'I see.' It wasn't such a stretch. In fact, just a further extension of cell welding. However, it had been one the Cyberat never developed, since the option of building a human body back up went contrary to their ideology.

'Since then I've been working in the hold tanks – have you seen them?'

'No. I only have access to the information in the console – the connections beyond this place are closed. I've seen a fraction of this ship but, obviously more than the rest of the Cyberat have.' She shrugged at that, still smiling, and he continued, 'I then started taking a look at what you and my father put inside me, which was . . . interesting.'

'Your father,' she said, smile maintained but turning glassy.

'They seem concerned about this technology,' he added, wondering about her grief and what they might have done to her mind here.

Her smile died completely. 'That is something we will need to discuss in all seriousness when Albermech gets here. Captain Corisian isn't too happy about the situation, but agrees that he can't go tossing people into the nearest sun on so little evidence.'

'What? Captain Corisian?'

'This ship is what is known as an interfaced dreadnought. It's apparently a bit of an anachronism, in that it has a human captain who interfaces, as much as is possible with current Polity technology, with its AI Albermech.' She seemed glad to have moved on to another subject.

'As much distrust of AIs as the original Cyberat?' he wondered.

'That's what I thought, but dreadnoughts like this were built after what they call the Quiet War, when the AIs took over Earth and in the Solar system. I'm still trying to figure out the reasoning. There's some talk of a time when humans could remain functional after an EMP blast, while the AI would go down, but that certainly doesn't apply now. Maybe the AIs just want to include humans – they certainly don't need them.'

Piper said nothing to that, though it contradicted part of the story he'd taken from Albermech's mind. If Albermech was one facet of the duality of an interfaced dreadnought built after the Quiet War, then he couldn't have been a probe ship AI. That was a lie Piper knew he'd pursue later but, right now, the mention of an EMP reminded him of Castron and of this chamber in which he'd been imprisoned.

'Why am I locked in here, Mother?' he asked.

She stood up abruptly and moved over to his console, calling up a menu he had yet to fully encompass, and worked her way through it. He studied the console node and saw those outside connections briefly open to pour in terabytes of data before snapping closed. This intrigued him – it had no doubt been done for her – but it told him there were systems watching him of which he was not yet aware. After finding what she wanted, she detached a remote handset from the touch controls, held it up and walked back over to sit beside him again.

'As I said, you'll get that explanation when Albermech arrives.

I am not entirely clear on all the details. Meanwhile, I've something to show you.'

She was prevaricating, but he let it pass.

She clicked the control and, in mid-air before them, a holographic screen opened. It started out black, as if the contrast was off, then divided into eight views and brought things sharply into three dimensions. These views were of the interiors of huge, long cylinders he knew at once to be the hold tanks attached to the outside of the dreadnought. Bars ran along the length of them through a series of frames. Fixed in these frames, and attached by a variety of umbilici to the bars, were Cyberat. In one view many of them were plug form, inside clear spheres filled with fluid. In the next were those who retained their fighting, or otherwise mobile, bodies and he recognized that most of these were Enforcers. And in another, he saw more of the same, along with a line of huge war bodies – all immobilized and linked in – which raised a stab of anger. There were thousands of Cyberat in these views, but the remaining five showed empty holds.

'They have been working fast, and I have to wonder how much of this was prepared beforehand,' said his mother.

'I understand why Enforcers are here, but not some of those others,' said Piper. Anger became his foundation for clarity and his overlay started building again. With imagined or perhaps real yellow eyes, he observed only the two nodes available to him, but remained alert. Simultaneously analysing the view into the holds, he noted the lack of movement in the bodies. These people were in some form of hibernation – the ones in glassy spheres perhaps in a deeper version of that because of injury or other damage.

'With the netlinks open and no longer censored, as far as we know, our Polity friends made them all an offer. Room enough aboard for transport into the Polity, and complete restoration of their human bodies. Many have taken them up on that – mostly those fleeing from the new regime.'

It was as Inster had surmised previously.

'And in return?'

'Oh, it's completely overt and all Cyberat know about the war with the prador now. Five years of service in the war against them, in exchange they get their new bodies afterwards.'

'So much for the altruistic Polity,' said Piper.

'It's a big war and a fight for human survival. A degree of morality has been sacrificed.' She glanced at him. 'Inster and Albermech talk of "cold calculations". That is, actions leading to the best result, despite the necessity of sacrifices along the way. It seems distant from us but, if these prador win, we'll face extermination too.'

Piper grunted an acknowledgement. What surprised him was that this *was* so overt. From his own experience so far with Inster and others, he expected a more sneaky approach. He gazed at the images, now seeing handler robots like steel spiders bringing in more Cyberat at the far ends of the holds, and swiftly lifting them up to attach. So, besides the Enforcers, here were Cyberat who had worked for the Old Guard, along with some of the rulers too. He didn't like that at all. Would the Polity have offered Castron a place here too if he'd asked? The data feeds to the console opened again and the image abruptly shrank down to a dark area at the centre of the holographic screen, before expanding into the shape of a man. As he stepped out of the screen, the thing collapsed behind him.

'Albermech,' said his mother.

The avatar of the ship AI was perfect. It even looked as if the carpet was indenting under his tread. He nodded politely to them both, then walked over to the console, grabbing the chair there and pulling it across before them, to sit astride it with his hands resting on the back. Piper had no idea how he'd managed this until he saw data fragments swirling in his inner space, new nodes forming and deforming amidst it. During their deformation phase, he glimpsed a lot of technology now active all around them – in the walls, the floor, pin-head emitters poking through between the tiles of the chamber. Though his access was limited, from this he at least understood it was a grav vortex, working through the floor, that had moved the chair. The nodes kept changing shape, and then falling back into hard impenetrable slickness. His reptile responded with avarice, gathering data, seeking routes to control.

'So,' said Albermech, 'the rebels are now in power and establishing their free and fair regime.' He grimaced.

'It's easy for you to mock from your lofty position,' said Reema. 'We will do our best. The progression hospitals will be closed down and the birthing facilities . . . well, they will be changed. Of course, there will be some chaos to begin with.'

'Ah, but it seems that hunting down and summarily executing members of the old regime, including disabled Enforcers, is of prime importance.' He gestured behind him where the screen had been. 'We're rescuing as many as we can, but still . . .'

Reema frowned and bowed her head. 'I have to go back there. They will need me.'

'Indeed,' said Albermech. 'You are a figurehead and in a strong position. Perhaps you can tone down the enthusiasm of your fellow rebels.'

'Of course I can,' she said, 'but right now we must get to the matter of my son.' She reached out and put a hand on Piper's shoulder. He looked at it, noting its perfection, and remembered the previous inset metallic channels, and the two fingers of composite.

'You had some understanding of what your husband was doing, but perhaps not enough,' the AI avatar told her. 'The hardware in his bones is comparable to our present AI crystal and related subsystems.' Albermech focused on Piper. 'You were made into a weapon whose purpose you already know, and made very well. However, when I connected to you, I found that the nature of your substrate is fractal and extends down into the Planck realm. Even we aren't quite capable of doing that, at least not with the degree of complexity evident in you, but it is something we have seen before.'

'Alien technology,' said Piper. 'Inster told me . . . civilization-destroying dangerous.'

Even as he spoke, Piper continued probing all the systems around him. He wanted to stop but the action seemed almost automatic. This aroused further anger at his lack of self-control, which frustratingly transitioned into him seeking control outside of himself.

'They were named the Jain,' said Albermech.

'The Jain,' Piper repeated, focusing on the word as an anchor. 'Why the Jain?'

'Apparently named after the daughter of the archaeologists who first found remnants, though the spelling of the word later changed. I suspect the twisted humour of some other AI in that, since it's the name of a pre-Quiet War, peaceful religion.' Albermech's mouth twisted, and Piper wasn't sure if he was frowning or suppressing a smile.

'And why so dangerous?' Piper asked. It was easing now – the conversation pulling him back from trying to get a grip on surrounding systems.

'Over the years various artefacts were found and gathered, but it was once they were passed over to an AI for analysis that we learned the truth. This AI only just managed to escape intact

171

when some kind of comlife emerged from an artefact and tried to sequester him. Future studies were conducted with more caution and the assessment is this: the Jain were a hostile species that created a technology capable of seizing control of other technologies on a computing level, and even on a physical level too if enough energy and materials are available. It reacts to the complexity of intelligence and is otherwise mostly inert.'

'I see,' said Piper, and he did. How could he not see the connection between this alien technology, built to sequester other technology, and what lay inside him, which had been fashioned for the same purpose? He could feel it within him now, driving him to seize control here. The hostility of that inner reptile infected his thinking. Yes, the explanation fitted exactly.

'Only in looking into a piece of Jain technology have I seen the subnano complexity I see in your bones. So, I believe your father used Jain technology.'

'You believe,' Reema repeated.

Albermech turned to her. 'It will need to be confirmed one way or the other. Inster tried to seize what he could find of your husband's work.' He paused for a second then added, 'But it would appear someone got there beforehand. Do you know anything about that?'

'No, I do not.'

She looked puzzled to Piper and he believed it was real. She'd only just reacquired a face so he doubted she had learned to conceal her emotions yet.

'We will find what we can,' said Albermech.

'Without permission.' Reema found something to be angry about. 'You are behaving like the AI autocrats we Cyberat feared.'

'No. The AIs you feared would have sown your world with CTDs.'

'CTDs?' Piper asked his mother.

'Contra-terrene devices. Antimatter bombs,' she said in confusion. 'So you really are serious about this? It's not just another seizure of a useful asset for your war?'

Albermech waved a finger in a circular motion above his head, indicating their surroundings. 'If there is Jain tech on your world, it could become active at any time, and prador at the Polity back door would be a far lesser worry. And if the basis of what your son has in his bones is Jain tech, and it usurps intended function to take control amidst your technology or our own, that could be the end of the Cyberat, or the end of the Polity.'

'Hence Captain Corisian thinking the sun would be a better place for me,' said Piper.

'Corisian is hasty,' said Albermech. 'If Jain tech is the basis of what's inside you, the main question that arises is why it hasn't activated to seize control of you and everything around you.'

Piper felt sick. Even though they had no firm confirmation of this, again he felt sure Albermech was right. It also explained his out-of-character decisions to be so careless with lives, including his own. It had to be the hostility of these Jain, arising inside him, and only just held in check.

'So what are your plans?' Reema asked. She glanced at Piper again, and he saw the annoyance in her expression. 'I'm not going to fool myself into thinking I have any influence on them.'

'When we are ready, we will leave,' said Albermech. He turned to Piper, 'And you will be coming with us.' He swung back to Reema. 'The only thing in doubt is whether you will accompany him.'

Piper didn't need to hear her answer – he had already read it in her face.

His mother came back and visited him two more times. She took on her lecturing persona during those occasions, probably to cover the guilt she felt. His own feelings were odd to him. He experienced a dip in his mood when she left for the last time, to catch a lift on a shuttle heading down to the surface. Sure, on acquiring a new body she had changed but, like his father had been, was still cold and didactic. Then excitement to be on this journey into the unknown quickly supplanted those feelings. He also felt the way he had when the Cyberat doctors began treating him for his problematic aggression, and then finally when they called him in to a progression hospital to have his implant. He'd had a problem, a serious problem, but was in the hands of the experts who would deal with it. The dichotomy here was that before he'd trusted his Cyberat doctors, while now he didn't trust the Polity at all. That earlier trust had been misplaced; now he hoped, illogically, his mistrust here might be erroneous too.

'Isn't it dangerous to keep opening up the projection and scanning equipment like this? I'm learning more about it every time,' said Piper.

Inster had appeared, and was wandering around the room, pausing momentarily to look out of the window, and again to peer over Piper's shoulder at what he had up on his screen. Eventually he went over and slumped in the sofa. It sank underneath his weight, which was odd, of course, since being a hologram he had no weight at all.

'All risk assessed,' he said, waving a dismissive hand. 'If we were inclined to take no risks at all, well, that would have been Corisian's solution. But Albermech wants to learn as much as possible about you so, therefore, windows have to be opened.'

'But this much risk? He can't scan me without making himself vulnerable.' Piper didn't look round. He flipped to the next page on the screen he was reading and continued. He had it now, though whether it operated through the hardware in his bones or the wetware in his skull was unclear to him. But he could read Polity Anglic.

'Indeed, and he is gathering as much data as possible for Kalaidon to work with.'

Piper pushed his chair back. 'Kalaidon?'

'An expert in such matters,' said Inster. 'He was the AI who first investigated a Jain artefact and nearly lost his mind to it.'

'So we'll be heading to Earth?' During his investigations Piper had discovered that most Jain artefacts were stored in the museum on Earth's moon.

'No, as it happens, Kalaidon has found other employment and is working in one of our war factories. Room 101 – look it up, you'll find it interesting.'

Piper shrugged, waved a hand and brought the holographic screen into being. Only after he'd done it did he feel a hot flush of inappropriate embarrassment. He'd called up the holographic screen without using the console controls – activating it from the inside. Even though he'd been avoiding using this ability, it had almost sneakily crept out. Embarrassment then transitioned in a surge of panic. Was it a further sign of the Jain technology inside him starting to take over? And yet, even as he feared this, he input a search mentally and called up images of Factory Station Room 101.

'About a hundred kilometres long,' said Inster. 'I'm sure you'll have a fun time looking up the stuff that it's doing.'

Piper nodded as he watched ships streaming out of an oblong factory station, with giant square bay entrances down the sides. He really grasped the scale of it after noting that many of the ships were of a similar design to the one he was sitting aboard. Now, almost with stubborn intransigence, he took the data on the war factory directly from the console's storage into his mind. The information dropped into his thoughts as if it were something he'd learned thoroughly, while he couldn't detect if it resided in his organic brain or in his bones. On this level, there seemed to be no division between them at all. Was this the bait of Jain technology: the ease and the power? He just didn't know. Before he could question it further, he felt a surge through the console, as well as in the various emitters and scanners all around him. The war factory distorted and shrank to a black dot, which then expanded into a corridor in the *Albermech*. Walking along it came Geelie, Cheen, Sloan and Meersham. They were holding various bottles and packets as they stepped through into his room. The sense of their presence was intense.

'You okay?' asked Meersham. Then, without waiting for an answer, headed over to the fabricator.

'The boy is okay, just a little bored, one suspects,' said Sloan.

'Oh, I don't think he's that,' interjected Geelie. 'He has his inner sources of stimulation, just like Cheen and I do, but always looking within is never a good thing, even if you're an AI.'

Piper found himself searching for her underlying meaning. Was Geelie implying that he was an AI? No, he understood her reference from the reading he'd been doing: some AIs actually lost themselves in their internal worlds, while intense introspection in a human was, as she said, not a good thing. Perhaps he should stop over-thinking these matters.

'Here.' Meersham opened a bottle and handed it to him.

As Piper took it, the whole process fascinated him. Just like Inster and the others, Meersham wasn't actually here, yet he'd brought over a bottle from the fabricator. The combination of grav and hardfield manipulation to do this was complicated – AI complicated. It also opened up access for him to hardfield project-ors in the vicinity. They were scattered about the wall of the outside chamber, and in the walls around him. This further brought home to him that he really didn't know what else might be there. Weapons? Almost certainly. He studied the label on the bottle, ascertaining it was beer with six per cent alcohol. He had never drunk alcohol. It wasn't available on Founder's World, though he'd been taught some of the history of this intoxicant and others. He feared it. And his fear of not having full control arose both from concern about what lay in his bones and from his mother's education of him. But where was his mother now? Dealing with matters she considered of higher importance than him. He tried to understand, but could still feel an undercurrent of resentment.

'Are you going to drink or just read the label?' Sloan asked, sitting on the arm of the couch and taking a pull from his own bottle.

'It all seems so false,' he replied, again noting the sofa had shifted when the man sat down.

'Believe me,' Sloan replied, 'it's as real where we are as here.'

He stared at the label of the bottle, reading further words but not really taking them in. What was the purpose of this 'drink' together? Perhaps Albermech wanted him to lose restraint, to give the AI more to study. He gritted his teeth, seeing this as a challenge to his self-control and felt his reptile paying attention. He took a sip and nearly spat it out immediately, but managed to wash it around in his aching mouth and swallowed. He took another sip and then a gulp as the others distributed themselves around the room, apparently finding comfortable spots and drinking from similar bottles. Cheen took the chair by the console while Geelie sat on the floor with her back against the desk. They drank with evident pleasure, gulping the stuff down thirstily. It really didn't make sense to him.

'Emulation,' said Inster, leaning in close. The man now had a glass in his hand containing an amber fluid in which chunks of ice floated.

'I don't see why they would want it,' said Piper.

'And there is the strange disparity from which we must learn. Humans, when becoming more machinelike, by interfacing or loading technology into their bodies, tend to become more like what humans *perceive* a machine to be: coldly intellectual and precise, contemptuous of organic failings, et cetera. Meanwhile, artificial intelligences, having risen out of that cold arid place, seek as much variation in experience as possible.'

'But it's not a variation,' said Piper. 'It's the dulling of experience and the hampering of the senses.'

'Says you,' Inster replied, taking a big gulp from his glass.

Piper drank more and began to feel the buzz, with his sense of time truncating, holes in his perception and a rise in his mood. He tracked conversations, sought data on what was being said, and focused for a while when they talked about the war, then drifted away again.

'We need to do this properly aboard Room 101,' said Sloan at one point, handing him another full bottle to replace his first, or maybe second?

'Not my favourite place,' said Cheen with a grimace.

'I would have thought the opposite,' said Meersham.

'There is insanity in war,' Cheen explained, 'and sometimes it seems to become concentrated in particular places.'

'I've heard rumours,' Sloan commented.

'Indeed,' said Cheen, and that seemed to be the end of it. Or had they been instructed not to continue with the subject? Was this interaction being tightly controlled by Albermech? And, finally, should he think that everything Polity people did was some form of manipulation?

As he found himself talking and just not caring, saying things he'd always kept locked down, he felt the reptile oozing out into reality to assess the threat. It also reached out to those grav-motors and hardfields in the walls and *he* understood how much more he could do. But then that other self distorted and faded back to quiescence, with what Piper felt to be confusion. Time passed, and at one point he found himself lying on the sofa with his head on Geelie's thigh, her fingers in his hair. He couldn't remember Inster going. He remembered talking, but not about what, then after moments of transition, brief dioramas, both hilarity and serious conversation, they were saying their goodbyes and disappearing through a door in the air.

'They took Aldetox and drank plenty of fluids,' said Albermech, speaking from a simple head floating in mid-air. The skin of the head was blue, facial features brutal though recognizable. Piper had no idea why. 'What you are feeling is not what pre-Quiet War humans would describe as a hangover. You have a slightly fuzzy head from drinking alcohol for the first time ever, and some other factors I am analysing.'

'I don't feel right,' said Piper.

'The after-effects of alcohol you researched no longer apply any more. Because on your world nobody drinks it, and in the Polity humans have nanosuites, as well as generally maintaining perfect physically mature bodies.'

'Everything seems a little odd.'

'Get yourself something to eat,' said Albermech dismissively.

Piper had a large beaker of a sweet drink he was really begin-ning to like, then randomly ordered from the selection of breakfast suggestions. By the time he was sitting and eating the astounding flavours of bacon and eggs, the odd fuzzy feeling had diminished.

'Ah, I see now,' said Albermech. 'It's also your power supply.'

'What?'

'As you may know by now, the hardware in your bones is

179

powered by laminar storage within it, but that has to be topped up. The system is intelligent and takes advantage of many factors, using temperature gradients, piezo-electrics, but it mainly works off your biology.'

'Yes, I'm aware of that.'

'But perhaps you are not aware that you need to eat almost fifty per cent more than an average human, if there were such a thing, and you have not been. By drinking alcohol, you provided a resource your bones took advantage of for recharging. The result has been your body being flooded with some toxic by-products.'

'So indeed, a hangover.'

'Different chemical processes but, yes, close. It was this process that left you worn out after each time you ran your war body down on the surface.'

'You said "also"?'

'It has additionally been exacerbated by growth. In twenty-five Founder's World years, even under hormonal suppression, your body achieved adult form. With your hormones now back to a natural level, however, you are filling out and acquiring further adult characteristics.'

'So you've learned something more from our little drinking session,' said Piper as he rubbed at the stubble on his chin. He also remembered that he'd felt 'hung over' before, without alcohol, and at those times the reptile influence had weakened. There was a definite synergy involved, but it seemed odd the supposedly alien technology in him was being suppressed by the depletion of his biological batteries.

'Yes, I have learned something, at least.'

'And my eyes turning yellow?' They'd been starkly so when he woke up this time but had been shading back to blue ever since. He wondered if this was a phenomenon that had started when his bones were activated, or before. He could never be sure, what with the Cyberat aversion to mirrors, and having so few memories of seeing his own face.

'They are the result of a combination of changes in your cranial nerves and other shifts in cerebral processes, as well as those toxic by-products.'

'And yet I always *imagined* it happening when the function of my bones increased . . .'

'It's very specific and may be designed in, but I cannot risk going deeply enough into you to find that out.'

'Right, I see.'

'Maybe your father wanted a visible indicator of this function activating,' Albermech added. 'Incidentally, there may be a way to elucidate this further, while at the same time deal with the toxins more effectively.'

'Like what?'

'A full nanosuite. I felt earlier that such a thing might interfere with your installed technology, but now I'm sure it can be tuned to only ameliorate deleterious physical effects. It can clear the by-products and, since you will be able to penetrate and control it mentally, it will enhance your perception. You'll be able to find out about your eyes.'

'But it might also attack the technology within me if programmed incorrectly.'

'It will not be,' said Albermech.

Piper finished his food and put aside the plate. Perhaps he tended too much towards paranoia, for now he worried that a Polity nanosuite would be just another way for Albermech to control him. He then reconsidered the matter. Assuming the stuff about Jain technology was true and, searching the memory banks of his console he'd found nothing to refute that, he was dangerous. He could be a monster even worse than Castron or those prador.

So perhaps it would be better if Albermech *did* have all possible control over him. At least he'd have less chance of getting tossed into a sun.

'Then I guess I should have a full nanosuite,' he said.

'Good decision,' Albermech replied. 'I've also assessed the risks and now given you greater access to ship's data – to me, essentially. You can link into cam footage and information coming from the world below, and more besides.'

'Excellent,' Piper replied tightly. He understood the transaction perfectly: in agreeing to what Albermech had wanted, this was his reward. As he watched the blue head icon blink out of existence, he began to reconsider his decision. But then he immediately recognized the fear for what it was and wondered if his eyes were now shading to yellow again. He sighed, sitting back for a moment, and decided his previous thoughts still applied: Jain tech could turn him into a monster, and ceding control to others might be important in preventing that. He turned to the console and went straight for that 'greater access', garnering views and information.

Via Polity observers, Piper watched a hunt for two Old Guard war bodies that had retreated to some kind of mountain stronghold. He watched weapons turrets rising there and driving off a small rebel force. This force settled on a plain in front of the mountains, as a missile arced through the sky above and came down in the centre of that stronghold. He observed the blast and the rising mushroom cloud. It seemed the rebels or, rather, the new regime, controlled the nuclear weapons.

Meanwhile, scattered all across inhabited lands, Polity marines and Cyberat were gathering up Enforcers on grav-sleds and in smaller shuttles. These were then being transferred at loading points into larger shuttles. Far out from Ironville, missiles streaked in towards one such collection group, but burned out of the sky before impact. Had remnants of the old regime fired them, or the new? Piper just stared at this, sure he was too young to feel so cynical.

And then, in Ironville, he saw Cyberat rebels gathered, some of whom he recognized – such as Geerand in his spherical com body. His mother was amidst them too, haranguing them from a floating platform. He searched for and found the sound:

'. . . no basis for a new order,' she was saying. 'While many Old Guard had full knowledge of how things ran, the Enforcers did not. Think about it, Masuran: the fact that they were turned into Enforcers because they were too rebellious in their previous state.' She held her hands out at her sides. 'We all know those among us who lacked self-control, and as a result ended up under a behavioural implant. We call ourselves the rebels, yet there are some of us now killing those who fought against the old regime and lost. Enforcers are victims of history – not our enemies.'

Masuran, a Cyberat whose gnarled head peered from a window in the side of a floating cube, replied, 'So much has been about free will. Do you suggest that we now suppress those elements who are destroying Enforcers? Yes, many of them were like us once, and in fact were us, but under the modifier they became little more than organic mechanisms of oppression.'

Others had more to say on this matter, and the debate rambled on. Piper found it depressing. Many were excusing what was plain and pointless vengeance, especially since it seemed the Polity wanted to collect up all the Enforcers. And yet, thoughts of pointless vengeance made him wince. The thing in his bones rumbled its frustration, since it, or he, still wanted to bring down Castron, wherever the old Cyberat had gone. He also listened to arguments about why the Polity should no longer be viewed as an ally, since Old Guard had been allowed to flee to the ship Piper was aboard. It all seemed like so much wasted energy,

183

when they should have been clearing up the mess and getting stuck into making a better world. But then perhaps, this was how a better world was built. There had been no debate under the Old Guard. Piper was tiring of it all when he noted a new node forming in the shadow of one he'd mentally sketched out. On opening it, he remembered his brief exchange with Inster, about how he'd intended to get through the door into the armoury in the Polity Embassy. This new node here was related to the mechanism of the door opening to his chamber, into his prison.

Piper stood up and walked over to the window. He smiled to himself, and felt it coming from whatever lay within him. The big plug door oozed out and swung aside. At this, he also had a flashback of when his mother had first come in, but this time it was Geelie walking through. As the door closed behind her, the node stabilized, for he had penetrated the system controlling the door via a convoluted route, through one of the scanners in the outer wall. He could now open it any time he liked. Did he want to? He didn't know, but it felt good to have that option. He wasn't so powerless now. Then he reconsidered, reflecting on what being powerful meant. The Old Guard were powerful, Castron was powerful – and where were they now? Piper could influence his surroundings and maybe take control of things. What he needed was the strength not to use that power.

Geelie came to the door of his new living area and entered.

'You're actually present,' he said. 'Isn't it dangerous for you to come here, seeing as I could potentially be a Jain monster?'

'Albermech is not so sure that's true any more and is easing the restrictions around you.' She shrugged. 'A little, at least, until we reach Room 101.'

'That's good,' he said, voice utterly flat as his perception of what he might be took a jarring shift to one side. 'Why are you here?'

Eyeing her node internally, he noted it didn't look so slick and hard as before, and felt sure he could open it out this time. In fact, all the nodes around him were like that now. Was this Albermech easing restrictions? He thought not. He, or that other part of him, or both, had been steadily, almost unconsciously, working around the AI's security, mapping its abrupt changes and decreasing his reaction time to them.

'For this.' She held up a glassy cylinder containing an emerald green fluid with flecks of gold in it. 'Your nanosuite,' she added, and he realized the thing was an injector.

He focused on the cylinder, beginning to pick up bands in the EMR spectrum that hinted at mechanistic and computing complexity, but nothing he could turn into a node. This was probably because the nanosuite was somnolent, merely stabilizing its components and system: sleeping.

She walked over to him. 'Ready?'

'Go ahead,' he replied. He'd researched nanosuites the day before and knew that Albermech's words had some truth to them. His body would be stronger with one and he'd gain greater access to what lay in his bones. And yet, right now he wasn't thinking about controlling or suppressing the *alleged* Jain inside him, but of finesse, strength and power. A surge of anxiety arose – more paranoid thoughts of how he might be being sequestered by alien technology. The contention that he might not have the stuff inside him at all confused him. His reptile snarled, looking for danger, but by then Geelie had moved smoothly in close and pushed the end of the cylinder to his neck.

It sighed against his skin and, out of the corner of his eye, he saw the fluid emptying out. It ran hot in his artery, that heat spreading rapidly throughout his body and into his skull. He felt further hints of activity as micro-factories attached to the walls of his veins, settled in organs and doubtless connected to his bones. He visualized a graphic he'd seen of such factories, looking like microscopic volcanoes erupting clouds of nanomachines, which spread through his blood like pyroclastic flows. He sought access, scrabbling for a way to incorporate all of this into a singular node.

'Sorry to do this again,' said Geelie, 'but since you're going through Albermech's defences here like a laser through jelly, we thought this the best option.'

'Of course,' he slurred, then found himself falling.

Geelie caught him before he hit the floor, but all fled into darkness thereafter.

8

'Talk about burying yourself in your work,' said a voice.

Piper found himself floating somewhere painfully bright. Trying to focus on his surroundings, and make some sense of them, caused his vision to tunnel. Within that limited perception, he discerned colourful shapes shifting in a regular way, reminding him of fractals, but somehow reflected and extending into more dimensions than even four. His head ached when he tried to see and incorporate more of it. But this stopped as soon as he stopped making an effort.

'What is that?' he asked, aware that he was talking without using his voice box.

'A perceptual quirk that drones experience when I work on their minds, and interesting that you can see it. It resembles the view inside an ancient device called a kaleidoscope.'

The data on this arrived directly into Piper's mind. A child's toy, but the similarity of its name to Kalaidon was intriguing. He registered in an instant the AI examining him was the one that had nearly lost itself to Jain technology. He then also realized he must have been unconscious for a long time, and the *Albermech* had now arrived at War Factory Room 101.

'Well, that was quick,' said Kalaidon.

'I am intelligent,' Piper replied, not without arrogant pride. He groped for elucidation from his bones, for some sense of time. But the things felt leaden inside and he struggled to raise anything from them. When he finally did, and got the clear intimation that months had passed, the shock snapped his hold on them.

'You are indeed intelligent,' said Kalaidon, 'but with the hormonal system of an adult triggered in a body long unaccustomed to it. This is part of the problem.'

'And Jain technology,' Piper added, trying to stay alert.

'Yes, the bogeyman that AIs think they see whenever they find advanced technology where they feel it shouldn't be.'

'What do you . . .'

Piper found himself falling into the dreamscape he'd occupied before. He was a child again and the girl by the river was pointing to the unfolding darkness. He saw hints of a bulky Cyberat and felt a lighthouse gaze swinging towards him. This gaze connected with a physical shock throughout his body. He came back hard. His internal grid filled with small hard nodes somehow linked together. These collapsed into a larger node and his reptile reared, snarling, out of his bones, driving him to reach into that node in an attempt to seize control of it. He felt despair and terrible loss, behind an anger that wasn't his own yet governed his actions. The node began to fall apart, but then reformed into a mass of small hard nodes again. They faded from his grasp, hanging in an in-between state, leaving just one different node that expanded open. This thing felt close and, probing inside, he hooked up to data streams which formed the coherent whole of his biological stats. Whole edifices of further data spread out in fractal patterns from this, and he became aware he was seeing the nanosuite inside himself.

'Far too intimate and defensive for removal,' said Kalaidon.

Piper knew in an instant that the AI was not talking about the nanosuite, but the reptile – the thing that was also part of him.

On deeper levels he wanted to ask questions, but the defensive rage and the sense of loss were too intense.

'Here,' said the AI.

Like sections in a complex three-dimensional puzzle, parts of the nanosuite node turned to different positions. After another physical shock through his body, his internal space collapsed, taking away all the small nodes and leaving just the one for the nanosuite, which folded down to something small to his perception. With that, his physical senses returned and he dropped to land flat on his back on a soft surface, then opened his eyes.

The room had a recognizable format, being an ellipsoid coated internally with mirrored tiles. There seemed to be no door. He was lying on a soft slab, while above him metallic objects swarmed. None of these were larger than could rest in the palm of his hand, and all bore different shapes. As they swirled in the air, they began to coagulate, to interlock. He saw them as the physical representation of the mass of nodes he'd pictured earlier. A surface began to appear, then another, and in a final rush, all those pieces slammed together in a geodesic shape of polished metal, seemingly covered with regular cracks. Here again was the further physical representation of those nodes collapsing into just one. What had the AI done to him?

'Well, my work is done here,' said Kalaidon.

'What . . . what did you find?' Piper managed, his voice hoarse.

He sat upright to discover his entire body was one massive ache. Peering at one arm, he saw a regular pattern of red lines there that seemed a reflection of those regular cracks in the now solidly formed body of the swarm AI. Yes, a swarm AI – he knew what this thing was. Confusion reigned for a second because this was not knowledge he'd obtained through the console in the *Albermech*. Further confusion arrived as he saw patterns within patterns: the kaleidoscope image, the format of the nanosuite node and of the physical AI, the pattern of red lines on his *entire* body.

'Patterns,' he choked out.

'Perceptual distortion,' the AI replied. 'Minds seek patterns, especially evolved ones. And this is a bounce-back from the fractal nature of your tech working through the filter of your mind. It will pass.'

The room started to come apart. He could hear sounds of huge industry going on in cavernous spaces as gaps appeared between the tiles surrounding him. Worryingly, he could also hear air hissing out and, between the gaps, just about discern some movement.

'What did you find?' he asked again.

'What I have found must pass through the filters of other minds. Meanwhile, I have wasted enough of my time on this. I have work to do. Didn't you know there's a war on?'

The room exploded outwards in layered chunks of matter, with the mirrored tiles on their inner faces. It all departed into the surrounding chaotic machinery, dragged away at the end of segmented black and green tentacles. Kalaidon shot off through the gaps between machines. Piper felt the air pressure drop – his ears popping – and then grav disappeared, along with the slab below him. He started to struggle for breath, but still goggled at what was around him. It reminded him of the interior of the mobile factory used to upgrade his war body, but immense. Heat and cold washed over him. He saw furnace structures spewing lines of glowing components, cutting wheels turning and show-ering bright clouds of swarf, energy fields and jointed hydraulic limbs assembling clumps of machinery. Soon his fight for breath was blurring his vision, as something snaked towards him.

On the end of what looked like an arthritic snake, scattered with lumpish motors, veins and wires, came a spider grab. As it reached him, he tried to writhe away, but had nothing to push against. It closed its fingers around him and, thankfully, they were soft, though unpleasantly so, like the bodies of molluscs. Slick transparent gel oozed out of the digits spreading over his body. He struggled against this as it flowed up over his face, over his mouth and in his eyes, but ineffectually. Then, with a whistling hiss, the stuff expanded out from him, bubbling up from his skin and eyes. He took a grateful breath, and then another, and immediately experienced a sensation he'd only felt once before when drinking beer. The gel expanded into a full bubble around him, encompassing the spider grab too. He understood then he must be drunk on pure oxygen and fought to slow his panicked breathing to a minimum.

The grab shifted him through the machinery. With the oxygen intoxication and the distortion of seeing through the gel bubble, he struggled to make sense of his surroundings. He saw robots here of many shapes and sizes – all scuttling on numerous limbs. Machines, ranging in size from things as large as skyscrapers down to the size of his fist, were linked in a structural web. Material and components flowed fast. What looked like composite bar stock entered one machine like a train into a station, and exited the far end as evenly, tumbling, masses of silvery tubes. Long black fingers flicked the hulls of squid-form Polity attack ships from a giant cold forge. Wires as thin as hairs formed even patterns, collapsing around and into objects he at least recognized as thruster motors. He understood the mass production going on around him, but in a way at variance to that of the often two-dimensional planning of Cyberat factories. Here he was at the heart of War Factory Room 101.

Through the chaos he went and finally began to see large surfaces of some other internal structure. Passing wheels of insect-type limbs, which were being heated and tempered by ion torches and then blasts of cold gas, the grab carried him to a vast wall scattered with ports and what appeared to be windows. He was sure he even saw people standing there, gazing out at him upside down to his perspective. It then brought him to a circular port that opened a mechanical iris. Anticipating what would happen next, he breathed hard, oxygenating himself. Within, the bubble burst and, yes, he at once understood he was next breathing some inert gas. The spider grab released him and retreated, the iris slamming shut. The tug of grav dragged him to a circular hatch at the opposite end to the iris. The hatch opened ahead of him, a change in air pressure popping his ears again as he fell through. He managed to slap against the edge to get his feet under him, dropping three metres to a hard floor. He hit with his heels and sprawled on his back, feeling he must have broken bones in his feet. Lying there, gasping normal air, he saw himself as just another product, faults corrected, quickly ejected from a busy factory that had more important things to make.

It took a day, and some nights, or maybe longer. Similar to what had once happened on Founder's World, Meersham found him, slinging him over one shoulder and carrying him to a medical facility to dump him on a bed. He'd been sliding in and out of sleep and dreams ever since. He was sure he'd seen the others stopping by to visit, but he didn't know if it was Cheen or one of the attentive medical robots that had placed the field autodoc on him. All he knew was that it had paralysed him, then gone over his body erasing the red lines.

Fractal patterns opened and closed in his mind, but the internal space remained firmly restricted to only the nanosuite node. He replayed the events of his life, falling into analysis that appeared logical but often evolved into weird dreams. Then, just as he seemed to be getting a better grasp on his surroundings, Inster arrived.

'Time to get you out of here,' said the agent, handing him a disposerall.

Piper dressed, noticing a thickening to his body and the acquisition of a lot more body hair than he'd had before. Already, after confusion about what he had thought was a mask, he had discovered he'd grown a thick beard. He followed Inster, who supported him when he stumbled. Damning the autodoc for not fixing his feet, Piper explored his nanosuite node and found its general function on hold while it worked the *specific* function assigned to it by Kalaidon. Starting up general maintenance and repair had his body fizzing as the suite delivered a long list of medical stats. He closed that off and let it get on with its work.

The corridors were bare, starkly clean, and all he saw was an autosurgeon moving past with the motility of a great ape. The walk began to bring Piper back to himself, so that at last he seemed to be in the moment and in a physical place at least. They finally came to a sliding door and Inster directed him through it.

'Geelie has been shopping for you, from the few concerns that remain here.' Inster frowned. 'Room 101 has become increasingly strange in recent years, with the human population moving away.'

'In what way strange?' Piper asked, standing there swaying.

'Difficult to nail down. In every interaction its responses are just odd. Also, its product is changing . . . the ships, drones and other weapons it produces fulfil their function perfectly but always have something more besides. It's also dangerous here. Many humans have had accidents when venturing into particular parts of the factory, and there have been disappearances.'

'And you thought it fine to throw me into all of that?' said Piper, finding the flash of anger steadied him.

He limped into the apartment and looked around. It had all

the facilities of the structure they'd built for him aboard the *Albermech*, but also cupboards. Still looking for handles on reality, he walked over and opened one to eye the clothing inside it, while fingering the paper disposerall. He selected a soft white shirt, jeans, underwear and a pair of enviroboots – all seeming overtly luxurious to him. Placing them on the bed, he sat down facing Inster, glad to have the weight off his feet and feeling tired again. The man had moved into the room and was leaning back against the wall, hands in his pockets.

'Time for some home truths, then,' said the agent.

'One moment.' Piper held up a finger and closed his eyes. He checked the suite and ascertained that the nanites had got about halfway to knitting together the fractures in his feet. He searched for and found the relevant afferent nerves, and gave instructions. It only took seconds for the pain in his feet to start fading. He lowered his finger and opened his eyes. 'Just one truth now, and then I'm going to wash and change. So, what did Kalaidon find and what did it do to me?'

'You don't have Jain tech inside you after all,' Inster replied. 'But you do have a semi-sentient entity within your bones that could be a problem, as you have discovered. Apparently it got in there inadvertently during the installation of the substrate and is mainly emotion based. It's a bit like the reptile brain all humans have, but in your hardware.' Inster smiled flatly.

'Reptile,' Piper repeated, studying him.

Inster shrugged. 'Albermech knew you referred to it as that, but I learned about it from you. Your tolerance for alcohol is not very high.'

'I see . . . Anyway, that doesn't sound like a mistake my father would make.' Piper didn't know whether to feel annoyed or pleased that his exacting father might have made such an error. Or had he really?

'He was dealing with some very complicated stuff. Anyway, at least we know you're not about to start sprouting tentacles and enslaving the human race. It will just mean learning how to assert greater control on your part. This you will gain from experience, as well as the extra option of finessing things through your nanosuite. In the interim, Kalaidon put something else in there for you too.'

'And what, precisely, was that?' Piper asked the question though he knew the answer. He'd known it since the moment his internal space collapsed during the AI's examination of him. And he'd known it in the war factory when, surrounded by machinery, he'd had no way to touch any of it.

'Via the nanosuite, Kalaidon put in an off switch.'

Piper nodded, picked up the clothing again and headed for the bathroom, no longer limping. The shower was a hot needle spray he enjoyed immensely, then he dried off with a towel from a dispenser, dressed and looked in the mirror. The toothbot he figured out quickly, inserting it in his mouth and wincing throughout its cleaning routine. He next gazed at his newly acquired beard and set the depilator to remove it, as well as trim back his now ragged brown hair. He also noticed that his eyes had become completely blue. He smiled, feeling good, the tiredness washed away in the shower. No matter how he regarded his treatment at the hands of the Polity, he had to admit the off switch Kalaidon had installed had provided some relief – shutting down a constantly angry core that only now could he see had been distorting him into its shape. He felt free. He headed back out into the main room.

'Better now?' Inster asked, sitting in a chair beside the bed.

'Very much so.'

'Then let's take another walk.' He stood up.

'I'm hungry and thirsty,' said Piper. And he noted how his

thoughts strayed to Polity food and drink, and the enjoyment he could find there. He wasn't thinking about just refuelling with a slab of Cyberat food and adequately hydrating. That wasn't really why he'd made the comment, though.

Inster pointed to a fabricator in the room. 'Grab yourself something.' Inster opened the door. 'Then I have something else to show you, and we'll find the others.'

Piper acknowledged this with a nod. It wouldn't do to allow the comforts of the Polity to turn him soft and, in reality, he'd made the comment to see if he would be placated, catered for. He stepped over to the fabricator, manually went through the menu and selected a meal bar and a bottle of water, and picked them up.

'Let's go,' said Inster.

Piper smiled grimly. He knew for sure that his story, his inter-action with the Polity, with Inster and the others, wasn't over. They wanted something from him – and it certainly involved finding a further use for the technology in his bones in their war. He paused then, reconsidering that train of thought. No, not *their* war but *our* war. Though he understood he'd been, and still was being, manipulated, what they'd told him about the prador was true. If the Polity fell, Founder's World would be next.

They headed back out into the corridor in the opposite direc-tion from which they'd come. Piper quickly consumed the bar and the water, then dropped the wrapper and bottle on the floor and watched a cleanbot scuttle out of its burrow to snare them up. The corridor terminated at what he now knew was called a dropshaft. Without pausing, Inster stepped straight inside and began to descend. Piper hesitated, noting the controls to the side of the shaft entrance and guessing the man had auged through to them to set up their descent. He at once felt the urge to seek out the workings of the shaft, to form a node and take control of it, since stepping in warranted a large degree of trust. In response, the singular nanosuite node within him began to shift – the switch easing over to 'on'. He stopped it and abruptly stepped in. He wasn't going to fall or, even if he did, it'd be no further than the irised gravity field around Inster. And, in the end, he really didn't want that anger back just yet.

He fell fast, suppressing a brief surge of panic, but decelerated into a gentler descent a couple of metres above Inster, who slowed too. The field propelled Inster through an exit, doing the same for Piper straight after. He stumbled a little, which annoyed him. He'd make sure that didn't happen the next time he used one of these shafts. Ahead lay a tunnel fifty metres or so wide, a fog of vapour high up in it. Along the sides were bright windows, scattered amidst many that were dark. There were strange plants in large pots, or growing from holes in the floor, as well as low walls, ropes and a variety of fence designs cordoning off areas containing tables and chairs. People sat there with food and drink before them. It took him a moment to understand that he was seeing shops and restaurants, since his only acquaintance with such things had been in a history lesson. He noted too the meagre number of people in comparison to the number of lit windows and establishments. Humans really were abandoning this place, as Inster had said. The agent led the way down to the centre. Glancing back, Piper eyed a row of dropshaft entrances behind, like empty eye sockets. They added to the air of abandonment.

'So when will the Polity properly intervene on Founder's World?' he asked, now deciding to get proactive and stop just rolling along in Inster's wake, following a doubtlessly AI-mapped course for him.

The agent glanced at him. 'Sadly, not anytime soon.'

'And why is that?'

'Cold calculations,' Inster replied. 'We are, as you are aware, winning the war against the prador now. Their response has been to throw increasing resources into the front line, which, we've known for a while, makes it unlikely that they'll expend further resources on trying to get in through the back door.'

'So it doesn't matter to you what happens to my people, to my world?'

Inster halted and turned to him, catching him by the shoulder. 'It matters to me very much. I feel a personal investment there. I care, and that place is unfinished business for me. But I'm not running this war.' He held up his fingers to his aug. 'Only right now have I questioned those cold calculations. Founder's World is likely to descend into bloody internecine conflict for a while. A ruling council or dictator will then take control and it is possible a less harsh regime will rise from that. And with Cyberat nudging physical immortality, that regime will stay in power for a very long time.'

'So, just as my mother said, it'll be the New Guard becoming the Old Guard once again. The establishment will prevail.'

'Albermech calculates that the regime will fall back on the old thesis of the Founder, so at least the people won't be steadily sacrificing their human bodies. However, strict controls will come into being. It is likely that the type of population control your mother so despised will be back in place before too long.'

'Unless my mother is in charge.'

'Yes . . . possibly.'

'And none of that really matters to the Polity.'

'It matters, but the estimated death toll of four to six million there is outweighed by a toll of twenty-eight million in the Polity and on the front line if we divert the requisite resources to your world. Come on.' Inster led them off again.

Piper dipped his head as they walked, thinking about all this. He found it puzzling how easily he accepted the rationale, but then realized he had no anger rising up inside to push objections. With that inner creature quelled, he could think so much more clearly . . . no, his thinking had always been clear, but now didn't have that angry driver.

'And any further word on Castron?' he asked, just to test how things were inside him.

'Castron is almost certainly dead.'

'What?'

Inster halted and turned to him again, forcing him to stop too.

'In the furore of all that has led us to this point, there's one thing you weren't told,' said the agent. 'Are you aware of our ability to track U-space jumps?'

'Yes,' Piper replied, though his memory on that wasn't as clear as when his bones were switched on. 'Something to do with a U-space signature?'

'Indeed. Castron took his ship through four U-space jumps and they were picked up by our detectors around the edge of the Polity. It seemed he was following the route the scout ship originally took to Founder's World. So it led him straight back into the Prador Kingdom.'

'He wasn't allied with them, surely? He killed prador.'

'It might have been an automatic response of the ship, over which he had no control. Maybe we'll find out about that one day.' Inster turned away and started walking again, and Piper followed.

'But whether I find out if he really died or not depends on what you want me to do now, and if my wanting to kill him gets in the way of that,' said Piper.

'You're learning,' said Inster.

'Yes, I am.' The reply was really for himself alone, because he *did* feel his own anger and a need to avenge the death of his father, quite apart from the response the thing in his bones always seemed to have to Castron. Perhaps, in the end, it just reflected and magnified *his* reptile brain, and that was what Kalaidon had meant.

Reaching the far end of the arcade revealed further entrances and exits, but these just led to simple staircases. Inster chose one and they began to climb.

'So what is it you want from me?' Piper asked.

'You will see soon enough,' Inster replied.

They climbed high, Piper's legs aching and his healing feet nagging him. Part of the way up, they stood aside to let a group of marines run past them, all loaded with heavy packs. It seemed the stairs served a purpose that dropshafts could not. Finally, they walked out onto a diamond-pattern metal walkway, which stretched in a curve to vanishing points in both directions. The wall of the entrance they stepped through also extended up, and curved over to meet the top of a long window of huge chain-glass panes running around that curve. Piper had felt a steadily increasing vibration on the stairs and it was even more noticeable here. Its presence puzzled him, since it seemed a waste of machine energy, but when he saw the view through the window, further thoughts just collapsed from his mind.

Again he was looking upon the vast internal workings of the war factory. Moving closer to the glass, where grav waned a little, he saw the massed machinery ranging up and down out of sight, as well as to his left and right. Many of the machines he'd already seen were here, and more besides. Forges, presses and rolling mills worked frenetically. And, though highly advanced, would still have been identified by a citizen of old Earth. However, the rings and tubes of matter printers, lost in nests of feed tubes and skeins of optics, wouldn't have been recognizable at all. Streams of components hurtled all around, almost like a continuous, but regular explosion of debris. In some cases, Piper saw that

200

invisible forces were guiding them, yet in others they seemed like bullets shooting to some target. Robots, with their hindquarters gripping the curved I-beams of the vast space, fielded and assembled all these components like multi-limbed jugglers. In the distance, to the left, he saw more attack ship hulls flying in a line, turning upright to have fusion engines inserted, then levelling out for other insertions and additions. Far to his left he could see one whole and one side of a ship similar to the *Albermech*, and suspected a long line of them disappeared from sight.

'Always impressive,' said Inster. 'But sometimes depressing.'

'Why depressing?'

'Because the rate of production here, of which you are seeing less than a percentage point, has only just exceeded the rate of destruction out on the front line.' Inster pointed at the attack ships. 'As a Cyberat, you perhaps wouldn't care, but eighty per cent of the production here is of machines with AI minds. Every one of them is a Cheen or Geelie. And some of them have a lifetime measured in just hours.'

Piper nodded, and thought about that for a bit, then said flatly, 'So the potential Polity death toll you mentioned includes these.'

'It does.'

'Artificial intelligences . . .'

'Who all have a choice, even at inception, and all choose to fight. It's worth pointing out that the AIs don't have to be in this war. They could easily abandon humanity and head away. It's a big universe. If that were to happen now, the human race might well survive. If it had happened at the start of the war, we would all be enslaved or dead by now, and the prador would be hunting down the remainder, like your people.'

'It'll take me some time to overcome my indoctrination regarding AIs,' said Piper honestly. But even at that moment he was thinking of Geelie and Cheen and knowing that, yes, it would hurt him if they . . . died. But on top of that thought he had another: of course the machines here would choose to fight. That's precisely what they were made and programmed to do. Next, just to confuse the issue, he thought about the organic machines that were humans: their programming, and their lack of free will.

'Anyway,' Inster continued, 'I didn't bring you here to see Polity machines.' He pointed.

Piper peered directly ahead at what he'd taken to be a massive component rack, seemingly kilometres across – much like a 3D version of racking found in a conventional Cyberat factory. He could see the lined-up components feeding out along invisible conveyors, then entering the factory chaos, steadily changing shape and taking additions. Some of them were small – mere nubs of matter – while some were three or four times that size. Up in one corner of the frame were larger objects arrayed for processing too. And beyond this rack he could see another, then another still, half lost in machinery.

'Perhaps this will help.' Inster stepped up beside him and, with his forefinger, sketched out a large square on the chain-glass. A frame opened there and the controls along the bottom of it were clear to Piper. He stabbed a finger at a slider and drew it across, increasing magnification in the frame. The components came into focus, and his mouth went dry.

Those small nubs of matter were plug-form Cyberat bodies. The intermediate ones were Cyberat plugged into mobile bodies of a variety of castes, mostly Enforcers but also including Medics, Agronomists, Bureaucrats and Builders. The largest things he saw were Old Guard war bodies.

'How many?' he managed.

'We filled every hold tube,' Inster replied.

Piper had seen thousands of his fellow citizens the first time he'd seen those holds, only filling a small portion of them, and he'd also seen holds empty. As he tried to calculate how many there could be, he felt the urge to turn on his bones, but suppressed it. Millions of them, at least.

'You were unconscious, in hibernation while we collected these up, and for longer than you probably realize.'

'How long?' Piper already had a vague idea how much time had passed, but hadn't fully confirmed it from his bones. And he had no idea how long the journey here had taken.

'Two months at Founder's World and a further three afterwards – Founder's World months that is.'

'Fuck.'

Inster smiled, perhaps a little tiredly. 'It would have been easier with the abilities you have to control the Cyberat, but we found our own approach. We scooped up most that were salvageable from the fighting, and the others we took control of with codes from the old regime Cyberat. We then flew them up out of atmosphere and collected them there. The number we got is close to what Albermech predicted. The rebels, meanwhile, were still seeking "justice", so a lot of refugees came to us too.'

'You still haven't said a number.'

Inster turned to him. 'Time for the full truth first.'

'Oh really?' Piper asked sarcastically.

'We told you Albermech went to Founder's World as a probe and then returned as a dreadnought. In order to close the back door into the Polity, and to weaponize the Cyberat and so forth.'

'Really?' Piper asked, recognizing at least one lie there.

'Mostly bullshit.'

Piper just waited.

Inster continued, 'Albermech has been an interfaced AI for seventy years. There was no probe ship. Our passive watcher near

Founder's World went active on detecting a U-signature and actually saw the prador scout land. The watcher then continued gathering data on your world, but it wasn't a big concern since we already knew the prador didn't have the resources to come in through that back door.'

'Then why did you come?'

'Resources for us.'

'What?'

'The watcher gave us the data: eighty million Enforcers, war bodies, highly technical, interfaced and warlike humans indoctrinated for conflict and able to take battle telemetry. And all in an unstable regime ready to fall . . . ripe for harvesting.'

Piper's jaw had dropped open and closed it. Inster's explanation was so harsh, direct and without sympathy that he found he believed it. He swallowed dryly and looked back into the factory.

'How many did you get?' he asked again.

'Nearly twenty-five million Enforcers and over eight million refugees, including four thousand Old Guard in war bodies.'

The figures didn't seem real, but he understood now that those hold cylinders really must have been packed full, as Inster had said.

'Sadly,' Inster continued, 'many thousands died before we were ready to drop into U-space, as well as during the journey here. We did it within the survival time of a plug form, but many had been detached from support bodies for a while, and many others had been injured.' He shrugged. 'We provided oxygen and had robots running among them all, doing what they could. We also shut them down to hypothermic. They had a better chance with us than down on the surface.'

'What happened down there?' Piper asked.

'Your mother did her best, but too many rebels and citizens, newly acquainted with the reality of their world, wanted their vengeance.' Inster nodded towards the Cyberat being processed through the war factory. 'There may be no more of these left there now, though there were many still around when we departed.'

'Unless they make more,' said Piper flatly.

Inster peered at him. 'Your cynicism is growing.' He smiled wryly.

'So, you grabbed Enforcers, war bodies and refugees. Do you have any more truths for me now?'

'Indeed.' Inster nodded. 'About where you fit into all this.'

'You brought me here because I supposedly had dangerous Jain tech inside me that needed to be controlled.' Piper gazed at Inster flatly, then continued in a voice edged with sarcasm, 'I don't see how I fit in at all now. What could you possibly want with me?'

Inster pointed into the factory again. 'Plug-form Enforcers there are being provided with Enforcer bodies copied from those we have. About half of the refugees are also being weaponized for battle. All are being upgraded.'

'And the other half of the refugees?'

'They are Cyberat with specialities useful in other roles to the war effort – many of them are already on their way.'

'Still not seeing where I fit in here.' His chest felt tight as he began to see where this was leading.

'The Enforcers, under Polity law, are considered sentient, but they have substantially less mind than the average marine. They need to be guided, controlled and directed. The Old Guard in their war bodies might be quite capable of that, but they have antiquated mindsets and aren't as adaptable as they might like to think. And frankly, they're not to be trusted. The same applies to those other refugees weaponized for battle.'

205

'You want to put me in charge of them?' Piper asked, hardly believing the question as it came out of his mouth.

'In essence, yes.' Inster now watched him.

Piper dipped his head and thought hard. Yes, with what lay in his bones, he could load all sorts of complicated programs to guide, control and direct the Enforcers, but . . .

'Thirty million of them?' he exclaimed. The thought of that, even though the off switch was still in place, made his bones ache.

'It's a formidable task,' said Inster. 'But I wouldn't be here saying this to you if some formidable intelligences hadn't deemed you capable. You will have more resources, of course.' He gestured to the factory again. 'Your war body is in there being upgraded with a substrate similar to what lies inside you. You'll have subsidiary programming and storage, more weapons and defences.' Inster waved a hand vaguely. 'Supplies like material, munitions and mobile factory units are being provided for the force too.'

But Piper could see other problems. 'Though I can control the Enforcers, and I may be able to control the armed refugees, the Old Guard have defences against me,' he said.

'Not now, they don't.' Inster smiled. 'So, what is your decision?'

Until that moment, standing there looking into a techno-logical fantasy land, it had all seemed so unreal. But now reality came crashing down on him. They wanted him to control a war force of thirty million armed Cyberat. There had to be better options! Almost as if he was seeking comfort, and not quite consciously, he twisted the components of his nanosuite node, and ended up turning his bones back on. A pause ensued, as this other larger part of him seemed to be absorbing data and coming back up to date.

The thing in his bones glared out with yellow eyes, snarling and sharpening its claws. This was power and it was taking him in the direction he wanted to go. Because, whether alive or dead, Castron had gone to the prador. It was also his duty and obligation. Through the filter of his mind, the angry part of him understood perfectly the prador threat to the people of Founder's World. And, sneakily, it encompassed what he'd been told was happening back home and showed him how, with such power, he could return to change the inevitable.

'Oh yes,' he said, smiling fiercely, 'I'll do it.'

Piper's internal mental space, divided by invisible gridlines, of which he was aware by some perception outside of his usual human senses, now opened and expanded. Data came to occupy it like debris from a forest fire, or the detritus stirred up from the bottom of a muddy pool, and it just kept on coming. His internal space carried on expanding too, to encompass this. Meanwhile, he was on levels both conscious and unconscious trying to assemble this data into control nodes. They finally started blinking into being, or otherwise coagulating. Many were slick and initially impenetrable; he recognized them as those of Golem or drones here that had defences against him.

'Come on,' said Inster, turning to head off down the walkway. 'Let's go join the others.' Piper followed him like a somnambulist, still focused internally.

Other nodes he found he could open up easily, and were perhaps Enforcers or other Cyberat here, as well as insentient systems and computers. Many were blinking into being and then fragmenting. Some were distorted and quite odd, some melded, and there were sprinklings of linked nodes like those of Kalaidon. The expansion continued and it seemed his internal space was stretching to infinity. He felt as if his head was about to explode. There was too much to see, too much to encompass. His internal space wasn't just incorporating the data from a few hundred, or even a few thousand distinct controllable entities or machines around him; he was within a mass of the same. It was dynamic and vast and his grip upon it precarious.

'I imagine it's complicated in here for you,' Inster noted, always on point.

'No fucking kidding,' Piper replied.

And then, ghosting across this and linking so much together, another node appeared – a shadowy immense thing. He reached out to it instinctively and tried to get a grip on it. A world of intense emotion, wound through a seemingly limitless intelligence, fell on him. The thing in his bones seemed a pale reflection of this mostly negative conception, and it retreated. He automatically continued trying to access it, but it was like attempting to catch a waterfall in his hand. Great swathes of perspective opened out to him. He staggered against the glass, body suddenly weak as he sank down to his knees.

'Shut it off,' said Inster quietly, squatting down beside him.

Piper now gazed into a hundred kilometres of machinery – a roaring and shrieking cacophony. Runcible gates, ring-shaped engines, then opened this perception to something which seemed to drive a drill into his mind. He saw huge catchment and processing areas for materials. And then, deeper into this huge node, he understood they came from vast planetary mines, even on gas giants and in some cases on the surfaces of dead stars. He glimpsed a venous system of gas, drawn from an accretion disc, being circulated and then expelled through another runcible gate. He didn't understand what he was seeing and his lack of understanding elicited more data and comprehension: This was to draw off the heat. Without it the war factory would simply melt and fly apart within a matter of days.

Within the internal masses of the factory, he traced the various paths of its products, which were sent out to its huge bays for final fittings and munitions loading, and then dispersed into space. Further runcible gates were out there, with many items going through them. Other items were zipping away on their own drives and dropping into U-space; the massive distortion caused by this appeared like the surface of a sea ripped up by storms.

'Shut the fucking thing off!' said Inster more urgently now.

He could feel himself trying to encompass it all, as he mirrored that huge shadowy node, while others blurred into linked systems extending beyond four dimensions. From this he understood how his perception of the nodes was a simplification for his linear evolved mind. And then, the vast node became aware of him.

Piper choked on terror. The thing was just too much in every sense. He found himself gazing towards it from a riverbank, as its attention swung towards him. He felt himself linking to it. Deep pain and horror hit him and found visual expression. He looked down at his body, now hanging clamped in a frame, skin, muscle and fat peeled back from his bones, but also some strange sympathetic amusement. Now surrounding him was the huge divided swarm intelligence of the War Factory Room 101 AI. In it he felt great compassion, and a thread reached into him from that. With a click, his internal space began to collapse. Yet, even as his bones powered down, he recognized this compassion was failing glue, holding together the parts of the war factory mind. Then, almost after an implosion, he was once again small, human and very weak, curled into a ball at the foot of a sheet of chain-glass.

9

'You okay?' Inster asked.

'You know the answer to that,' Piper replied tersely, as they reached an exit from the walkway and turned into a long tube heading away. He felt relieved to put the sight of the factory's internals behind him, yet stayed aware of it all around him. Yes, the war factory had activated his off switch, but there seemed a lot of leakage from his bones now. Inspecting this, he realized that 'off switch' had been an extreme simplification, for his control via the nanosuite was more nuanced than that. Perhaps the factory AI had changed something, or perhaps it had enabled him to become aware of what was there. He adjusted what he characterized as a series of slide switches inside him, bringing the leakage down.

'You're not okay.'

Piper nodded, walking with brusque determination, and examined his own mind. It seemed as if components of his consciousness had been shifted and turned against each other to form a new shape. He'd encountered something he couldn't really describe, beyond it being numinous and yet faulty. And he had experienced something so intense, he knew it'd changed him. The war factory had done something more than just shut down his bones. Glancing at Inster, he noted one facet of that change. He no longer considered himself as a naive young man

210

in the shadow of this man's age and experience – such definitions now seemed utterly irrelevant. As he groped for comparisons, the war factory itself mapped it over. He and Inster were components serving different but essential purposes in a vast machine, and that machine was the prador/Polity war. He fully accepted now that he really was part of it: he was a human who faced extinction, along with all humans if the war was lost, and not just a Cyberat. It seemed that identity had faded for him. He waved a hand at their surroundings.

'This is too much for me,' he said. 'And I touched the mind that controls it all.'

'And your impression of it?' Inster enquired dryly.

'A machine held together with fraying string.'

'The same perception as many, then' Inster replied. 'But sadly it's a machine that cannot be shut down. It's too complicated. The problem is the AI, which is distributed throughout it, and not the actual mechanics of this place. It cannot be turned off like your bones.'

Piper thought about the vast flood of materials, the heat being drawn off, the components hurtling through the place. And the huge number of machines working so fast that they had to do so in vacuum, since a gas environment would have resulted in compression shocks. If the heat sink system went down, the place would be boiling away in a matter of days, he understood, but if AI control was taken off, the thing would simply fly apart.

They took a number of turnings, hit a long straight corridor, then used a dropshaft which Piper now handled with aplomb. More people were around now and, stepping out of the shaft, he found himself in the arcade they'd traversed earlier. It seemed Inster had taken them back via a convoluted route, doubtless to give him time to recover. Scanning around, he found it easy enough to figure where they were heading. A crowd occupied the area in front of a bar. He could see a scattering of uniforms and many in casual dress, but even from this distance he recognized Meersham, despite his baggy blue overalls. Drawing closer still, he picked out the others.

'Over here, boy,' said Meersham, kicking out an empty chair.

Piper halted, wanting to say 'I'm not a boy' but then dismissed the idea. Only a boy would object to that label. He pulled out the chair and sat down, seeing Inster head off.

'Are all the soldiers here aboard the war factory?' he asked Meersham.

'Just fifty of us.' The man waved a hand generally. 'The rest are back in hibernation on the ship.'

Piper scanned around the table. Besides Meersham, he only recognized Geelie and Sloan. Over to his immediate right sat a young woman with short cropped white hair, facial jewellery and fairly tight black overalls, which gave him a distracting view of her cleavage. Again this was something he'd only ever encountered in a history lesson, since the Cyberat had so much contempt for the organic they tended not to display or enhance its appearance. She smiled at him, looking directly into his eyes. The physical and mental jolt of that caught him unprepared, and he reached to power up his bones, only just managing to stop himself. Hormones, his dry mind reminded, and then Meersham gave him the opportunity to shift his attention away again.

'And that leaves it to us,' the big man announced, 'to raise a glass.'

The moment he said the words the chatter died and Piper reckoned there was an underlying aug broadcast going on too. Meersham stood up, holding out his beer bottle. Others all around had taken up their drinks, and Piper picked up the open beer bottle before him. He glanced at the woman again, who smiled and raised an eyebrow. Damn it, she knew she was having an effect on him!

'We can call a thousand names to our minds,' Meersham continued, 'but it's cheap to pretend the loss is personal. And more die every second this fucking war continues.' His gaze wandered, fixing on various people, and then upon Piper. 'But all losses are personal to someone and we, in the Polity and in the marines, are all diminished.' He raised his beer higher. 'The departed!'

'The departed!' they all repeated, and drank.

Piper drank too, enjoying the taste, but then stopped after a couple of swallows, remembering how it had been last time. The ersatz hangover hadn't been a problem and, anyway, his nanosuite would clear the toxins this time. He just didn't like the memory of talking too much, and then not remembering what he'd said.

'That's a neat trick,' said the woman.

Piper focused on her, wondering if she meant the rush of blood to his skin. He'd now tracked down an explanation for it through his nanosuite and labelled it a standard physiological reaction to a potent mix of adrenalin and hormones, even as he tried to dampen it down. Or maybe it was the way his bones seemed to want to turn on, as if the reptile was pushing the switch from the inside.

'What do you mean?' he asked. He had absolutely no doubt what he wanted. Meanwhile his cynical side wondered about her sitting here, whether she'd maybe been positioned here. Another manipulation.

'The thing with your eyes,' she said.

'What thing would that be?'

'Their colour shift to yellow.'

'A chemical thing—' He waved a hand dismissively. 'I can't tell you much more about it because I don't know.'

'Then at least tell me your name.'

'I am Piper Lagan, though there is a number and a code that goes with that.'

She held out a hand. 'I'm Meece, and that's all you need to know.'

He wasn't sure what to do about the hand, so just took hold of it, feeling a shock of contact that seemed to go right through his body. She looked amused, gripped his hand and shook it, then released it.

'A stranger here, I'm guessing.' She looked at him innocently.

'My people are mostly machine, but I think you know that.'

She leaned back and looked him up and down. 'I'm aware of that, of course, but it seems that you, at least outwardly, are not.'

He was aware she was playing and knew exactly who he was. The urge to turn on his bones to help him deal with this situation again became overpowering. But it wasn't a battle of that kind, and he couldn't reach into her to bend her to his will. He searched for a strategy, the next move that would push this to the resolution he now knew for sure he wanted. Certainty and focus had somehow been born out of his encounter with the Room 101 AI, and as a result he realized he felt mature now, and adult. Meanwhile, he also felt a stifling, almost disgusted, guilt. He knew precisely what sex was all about and understood his body's reaction. But on Founder's World, sexual relations between people was a rarity soon put aside by the destruction of their bodies.

'Neither are you,' he managed. 'I've never seen anything quite like you.'

'Oh you have, just not dressed like this.' She gestured elegantly to her face and then on down her body. 'I was there, you know.'

'On Founder's World?'

She was about to reply, but then had to duck down as a floating vendor tray arrived. With sensor lights glittering about its rim, it began depositing shot glasses on the table, using a single arm. She pulled two over, putting one before him.

'Drink,' she said bluntly. Was there something predatory in her expression, or was that him just projecting his desires?

Piper downed the clear contents of the glass, just as he was seeing all the others do, then spent the next minute coughing while Meece rubbed his back. Some while afterwards, words began to flow with greater ease. Still, he kept in mind the last time and clamped down on talking about himself, mostly asking questions instead. It seemed this was the correct strategy, because as she told him of her life in the marines, she moved closer and communication became more tactile.

'Is this a common occurrence?' he asked her, gesturing to the wake.

'If it was performed every time we lost people, we wouldn't find the time to fight,' she replied while looking around, seeming just a little drunk. She then swung back, focusing again. 'But you've been pumping me with questions and now it's time I knew more about you.'

'I think you already know something.'

'The wonder boy with an AI in his bones.'

'Then there is little more to tell, and this *boy* needs his rest.'

'You resent the term?'

His reaction annoyed him. Just a short while ago he'd been telling himself he'd outgrown such resentments, and that he felt like an adult. He gazed at her steadily, playing out scenarios in his skull. He didn't want to sit here drinking and would have left a while before were it not for her presence. Damn, it was time to see where he could take this; the unresolved tension was affecting his behaviour.

'I could tell you many things, but am not sure what I should.'

'There's nothing you can tell me that I shouldn't know.' She smiled ruefully. 'Our enemy hasn't managed to plant spies among us.'

He laughed at the mental image of a prador moving through this crowd, then pushed his glass away and said, 'I don't want to drink any more. Let's go somewhere quiet where I can tell you whatever you'd like to know.'

He wanted to be done with this episode, now hoping she would turn him down and he could leave. He knew he'd made some kind of social commitment and it needed to reach a correct resolution. It all seemed so infantile too – particularly since he'd gazed into the mind of this war factory, and it felt like loss. Subsequently, analytically, he registered that he'd begun pulling away not because he didn't want this woman, but because he was a virgin and inexperienced.

Meece pushed her drink away and stood up. She held a hand out to him. He stood too, feeling slightly dizzy, and didn't resist as she towed him off through the crowd.

'This is new to me,' he said. 'My people consider the human body something inefficient, disgusting . . . to be replaced.'

'What is new to you?' she asked, giving him a mock-innocent look. 'You're going to tell me your story.'

He eyed her, searching for the right words. 'I was rather hoping to include you in it.'

She grinned and they headed away.

'My sleep has been profound,' said Piper.

'A curious way of describing it,' said Meece, as she returned from the shower, the sound of which had woken him.

She shed her towel to start dressing in combat fatigues and this elicited an immediate physical reaction in him. But of course, that was how it should be until his hormones weren't so chaotic, and maybe not even then. He recognized himself as a machine for the sum purpose of recreating small, insentient portions of itself; an organic engine honed into shape by evolution and not by rational thought. It was core programming he should overwrite. He thought about his moments of both disgust and amusement at their very basic acts, before he'd fallen into an exhausted sleep. This morning, of course, his libido had re-established and was as present as his reptile when his bones were switched on.

She dressed quickly and efficiently, then moved over to gaze down at him.

'You're going somewhere?' he asked, concealing disappointment.

She smiled and crawled onto the bed. He made a grab for her, but she swatted his hands away easily and pinned him down. In the night she'd already demonstrated superior physical strength, speed and very definitely stamina.

'Some of us have a job to do,' she told him, then leaned down to kiss him.

It was all so strange and organic, like everything else they'd done during the night. He wondered about the evolutionary imperative of kissing – perhaps some necessary sharing of micro-biomes? He knew that the organics which governed human behaviour weren't necessarily just the human kind.

'Specifically?' he managed when they finished.

'Virtuality combat training for a low-gravity desert world.' She climbed off him. 'Perhaps there are things you need to do as well?' She raised an eyebrow and headed for the door.

'I should leave?'

'Yes, you should.' She headed out.

It took some hours of trudging through the war factory to get the irritating human reaction under control. He wandered long corridors and tried dropshafts until he was utterly accustomed to the controls and experience of them. He lost himself in the war factory, as much as was feasible for him. His memory of his route was clear and exact and he could always retrace his way back to Meece's apartment, or to his, and thence to other places. When he found himself walking along a tunnel that vibrated to the constant industry of the factory, and glimpsed chain-glass windows ahead, his instinct was to turn away. But, growing more accustomed to pushing himself mentally, he decided to head for the walkway and stepped out.

The busy machines of the war factory loomed ahead of him beyond the panes. He wondered why the sight felt different this time, and understood it was because it all seemed so precarious now. He no longer saw fast efficiency but a process teetering on the edge of disaster. He looked down to the Cyberat being processed here. Some of the racks contained fewer of them, while the process still continued. He needed to find out about that.

'Hello,' said the Golem who'd been standing silently behind him.

He jerked round and then controlled himself. He'd seen the chassis of Golem revealed before and this completely skeletal version shouldn't be a source of fear. In fact, the Cyberat within him felt contempt for his atavistic reaction to a human skeleton.

'Hello,' he replied.

The thing just stood there, unreadable. He groped for something else to say. 'Perhaps you can help me.'

'Perhaps I can, and perhaps I will. Perhaps I can, and perhaps I won't.'

The skeletal Golem was bigger than usual and he immediately sensed something not quite right about it. He studied it more closely and saw what looked like the runes of some ancient language graven into its grey composite bones.

218

'I want to find a direct route back to the arcade . . . the one with shops, restaurants and bars.'

The Golem tilted its head to one side. 'No aug on his head and no need. We're all bones, aren't we?'

'That's not particularly helpful.'

The Golem pointed to a control panel beside the entrance.

'Be as smart as you want to be,' it said. 'Got to go.'

It abruptly turned and sprinted down the walkway, emitting a high-pitched giggle. It moved horribly fast, making a sound like a machine gun as its feet clattered against the metal floor. Piper sighed and stepped over to the control panel, resting his fingers on a texture-control plate. He fiddled with that for a while, until the textures turned thorny and the panel asked tetchily, 'Whaddoy'want?'

'A map,' Piper replied.

A hologram appeared with a snap, causing him to jerk back. A 3D depiction of tunnels and shafts in the local area was shown, with a little blinking red man indicating where he was. From memory, he matched his route here on it, dropped in the other routes he'd taken, then blinked and memorized the lot. He was just about to step into the tunnel but had to move aside as a monster loomed through it. This thing was some huge, chrome-shiny crustacean, vaguely resembling, in shape but not in size, one of the krill of Founder's World. It peered at him with gleaming red eyes.

'Which way did he go?' it asked.

Piper pointed down the walkway and the war drone shot off along it in pursuit of the Golem. Entering the tunnel, he pondered on the faults, failures and madness of this place and wondered just what kind of processing the Cyberat who'd been brought here might have had.

Finally back in his own apartment, Piper used the fabricator to produce food. He ate his way through a meal that seemed to consist of chunks of animal flesh, then ordered the same again twice more. Next he went to the console and ran a search. 'Agent Inster' brought up an icon just like the one he'd seen on the HUD of his suit on Founder's World, and he selected it.

'You need an aug,' said Inster, peering at him from the screen against a backdrop of stars crossed by a line of Polity attack ships.

'Perhaps,' said Piper. 'How long until the Cyberat are ready?'

'It'll be two weeks before we head out and they will be aboard the *Albermech* before then.'

'And then what? Where will we go?'

'You will be advised.'

'I need to make preparations . . .'

'So Albermech informs me, but I told him to leave you alone.'

'Because of Meece? You would like me to establish further human connections with Polity citizens?'

'You're too young to be so cynical. Truthfully, I feel you deserve something besides always having your mind running in machines, and fixed constantly on warfare.'

'Deserve?'

'It wasn't planned, if that's what you're thinking. With your history, I'm frankly surprised. Seems the organic wins out, despite prior indoctrination.'

'Well, it seems the organic won for one night and now I need something to do.' Piper felt pleased at his level tone.

'I see. You need an aug, but until then, here's some reading for you to do.'

A list of data links began scrolling down the side of the screen. He read titles there which included the words 'tactics', 'logistics' and many beginning with 'The Battle of . . .'

Before he could make any comment on that, Inster continued:

'When you've read and inwardly digested those, there will be more.' At this, Inster's image went out. Piper stared at the list, then at the blinking icon to the top left. It took him a second to understand the spelling of the name written over the image of a combat helmet. Once he had done, he clamped down on the sudden surge of emotion, because he recognized the danger. Then he clicked on the icon and opened it. Meece looked out, hair tied back and face sheened with sweat.

'Hiya, wonder boy,' she said.

'Virtual combat?' he enquired.

'Followed by two hours in one-point-five gees with sticky mines.' She shrugged. 'I'm heading back now for a shower.'

'Tiring, I imagine,' he said, amazed at his nonchalance.

'Not *that* tiring.'

Day and night were negotiable aboard War Factory Room 101. Meece's apartment was much like his own; sex in it was nothing he had ever experienced before, of course. Routine encroached, with her heading off for training, while Piper read through the files Inster had sent him, then would walk through the station. He felt happy, and recognized that as a perfectly normal organic reaction. He also saw this as a halcyon break equivalent to his juvenile time with the girl by the river. But during his walks, he stopped by to watch the Cyberat being processed and saw the racks steadily emptying. This period would come to an end, not least because of that, but also because Meece was waiting for deployment.

As he read, he absorbed information with solid recall and extrapolated from the data. He discovered he could set the nanosuite to improve upon that – triggering a learning mode that initiated neural plasticity. Edging up the activation of his bones also improved on memory and processing, as he spilled the data entering his mind into them, and they in turn spilled it back with new order and associations. The synergy was good and he found himself edging up that switch higher and higher. Until something black and dangerous loomed, when anger skirted his thoughts, and with it came the reminder of where he would go when fully activated again.

'*You need an aug*,' Inster had said. The words impacted more as, in his apartment, Piper reached the end of the reading list and it immediately redoubled. He sighed, stood up and stretched, then went for his usual walk.

Finally, after exploring more of the endless kilometres of Room 101, and again encountering some of its more concerning occupants, Piper sat down at a table in the familiar arcade. Brushing his hand across the surface revealed a menu, which he stared at in puzzlement, since it was very different from the fabricator in Meece's and his own room. There was a 'special', so he selected that, and then a non-alcoholic beverage. A tray drone brought his selection over just a moment later and he guessed there were no cooks here working in a hot kitchen. He gazed at a slab of roast meat, white lumps, green and red objects, then at a beaker with steaming white foam on top. The smells had him salivating at once and he clumsily picked up the fancy knife and fork, before noticing the drone still hovering nearby.

'Is there something I have to do?' he asked.

'Payment would be nice,' the drone grated.

'I don't know how to pay.'

'Well that's amusing.'

'No, seriously.'

'Permission to ID you.'

'Granted.'

The tray drone blinked green eyes then said, 'Piper Lagan. Payment taken from your ECS account.'

Piper shrugged and began eating as the drone headed away
to another table. It seemed, then, that he was employed. Having
previously raised them while reading, he now itched in his bones
to access systems and find data on that ECS account and about
himself. He could have done it in an instant, without the risk
of rousing the angry thing inside him, or drawing closer to the
terrifying mind all around him if, like most people here, he had
the aug Inster recommended. It seemed an essential accoutre-
ment of Polity life. He thought then about what the Golem had
said to him some days ago and, understanding the implication,
settled on doing something about that. He finished the plateful
of food, then sat back with the beaker. The stuff inside was
foamy and tasted the same as that first drink his mother had
given him in the Polity Embassy. He checked the menu and
found it to be coffee, then decided he was going to get used to
it. As he sipped, he turned on his bones, but only gradually,
easing up that slide control.

His internal grid opened out and at once began to fill. He
concentrated on limiting the expansion. His reach on Founder's
World had been close to fifteen kilometres, but he found that
to be an arbitrary limit. It was deep in the settings and predicated on a fairly wide spacing of Enforcers, in a number he
could mentally encompass. That same reach here covered far
too much for him to handle, at least right now. It was all a
matter of learning and adaptation. As the grid filled, his reptile
opened a yellow eye and paid attention. He focused on the
settings and abruptly cut his reach to five kilometres. But even
at that, the grid continued to expand and fill. He sensed tray
drones stacked like the plates they served. Nodes for AI crystal
and machines multiplied, while he and his reptile almost
instinctively raised suitable animuses, and linkages shimmered
into potential. He found multitudes of robots – large ones like

the restaurant itself, and ones as small as the skin mites they hunted down. He felt layers and layers of intelligent nanomaterials too, and the terrifying complexity of that raised a snarl from the reptile. The familiar anger arose and brought with it arrogant confidence as the overlay began to build. He could seize control of limited objectives first, then expand outwards, growing, taking on more . . .

No.

This apparent copy of his damned fucking reptile brain was not going to drive him now. There was no war to be fought here, just a way to ease his navigation of the Polity world. His bones would damned well obey him. Piper sipped the coffee, breathed evenly, concentrating, and the snarl dropped to a steady rumble. He concentrated next on the contents of his grid, on understanding them, but not on any immediate sequestration.

It was like gazing upon a forest, and seeing not only all the fauna and flora, but the workings of the genes in their cells. He cut his range once more to a kilometre all around, then again down to a hundred metres. At last the grid stopped expanding. Still his hardware busily tried to turn everything into accessible nodes and raise animuses to seize them. He needed to select now, and carefully. Summoning up a previously used program, he looked around. The nodes for robots large and small beyond the wall around this eating area, he selected, *described*, then ran a program to delete all of them and their like from his grid. This included the nearby tray drones, as well as things crawling under the floor and others floating through the air nearby. His grid collapsed down and down as he eliminated the restaurant itself, and then nearby insentient machinery. Finally he reached clarity and gazed across at his target.

The four marines consisted of two women and two men, apparently, but his deeper vision identified a man and a woman as Golem. Nodes bloomed around them in the overlay he made. He eliminated the two Golem nodes – like Geelie's, they were hard and slick and he had no wish to try penetrating them. Still other nodes lingered from hardware the four carried. They had hand weapons, and he noted in passing that two gas-system pulse guns had some kind of intelligence, which baffled him. He eliminated them and other items of complex machinery, finally fining down to two nodes, of which he chose one for examination.

The man's aug was a highly complex device. That Piper found it easy to access he understood to be because the technology interfaced with the organic, which was his usual point of access to control Cyberat. But he didn't want control, he wanted information. He mapped out the aug, opening a vast schematic in his mind, and then dived into it. The angry reptile brain wanted him to seize control, and yet he felt its curiosity too as he began to separate out the systems and hardware. The angry thing receded slightly, because this was a new weapon and a new method of taking over opponents. His mind opened down through the reptile, seemingly twisting out a chunk of it to his purpose. He fell utterly into the world of Cyberat code and virtuality, understanding and copying across, building a model of the aug in his bones but keyed into his own wetware – distinctly his own. A brief disruption as the node went out told him the four had headed away and the man's aug had gone beyond his range, but he retained the schematic and continued his work. And finally, it was done.

The reptile protested as he selectively shut down the processing of his bones. However, he now left on the virtual aug he'd just created there, grateful to have found he could maintain a connection routine from it to his nanosuite. Learning to use it was the next task and, compared to everything he'd done before, it was almost idiot-proof. His internal grid, and the tools for manipulating what lay there, matched the function of the aug 'third eye' and its programming tools. Multiple icons appeared, like nodes had appeared before – links to people and sources of data, including that list Inster had sent to his console. He honed these down and ran searches. Selecting out those he recognized, he placed them in his personal address book, while consigning the rest to a collapsed file that wouldn't be so bothersome. He then pulled up one icon – a thin gun – and made a connection request.

'The restaurant AI was concerned and sent out an alert,' said Inster, directly into his mind.

'Why was it concerned?'

'Oh, lots of weird shit happening in the programming of robots and systems in the area. And all of it seeming to be centred on one individual who's been sitting at his table for a total of five hours now.'

'What?'

'Time flies when you're enjoying yourself. Fortunately, Esopean made a general query about you. She was about ready to shoot you out of your chair.'

'Esopean?'

'The female Golem in the Sparkind team you seemed to take far too much interest in.'

'Oh.' Piper abruptly made a connection then. Sparkind were squads of four members – two artificial and two human – a kind of standard special-forces fighting unit in ECS. He now realized that Meersham, Cheen, Geelie and Sloan formed such a unit.

'It wasn't just those I mentioned who were concerned. The particle beam weapon in the ceiling directly above you is now powering down. The Room 101 AI might be a bit ditsy, but it knows when something could threaten its function.'

'I was no threat.'

'Maybe not you . . .'

'I have control of that now.'

'Uh-huh. So anyway, now you've got yourself a virtual aug . . .'

Piper made no reply as he surfaced properly to his surroundings again. He drank the remainder of his coffee. It was cold and tasted dreadful, but his mouth was dry so he persevered until the cup was empty. He noticed that no people were close by any more. Perhaps they'd been warned off. He stood up, feeling utterly calm.

'My Cyberat force will soon be fully processed?' he asked.

Inster offered him a link, which he opened at once. It gave him a view into the massive external holds on the *Albermech*. They were very, very busy – Enforcers slotting in and packed down into huge, granular masses. He opened overviews and other linked data sources, finding that all of them were shut down, having been installed with hibernation hardware. Another hold contained the Cyberat refugees and Old Guard. Many had *chosen* to use their hibernation hardware and others had not. Some were out and about in their plug bodies, exploring those areas of the ship open to them. Others were in virtualities, doing or learning whatever they chose there. It seemed somehow wrong that they were packed and slotted away like this – useful tools to be taken out when needed. However, he understood that this was precisely how the four thousand marines, and the technicians he'd seen on Founder's World, had been kept inside the dreadnought too.

'I'll want to go there,' said Piper.

'Nothing stopping you,' Inster replied. 'Or do you need me to hold your hand, *General* Piper Lagan?'

'I guess not,' Piper replied, now accessing the station map directly and heading off with a firm stride, though not towards the *Albermech*. Meece would be returning to her apartment soon.

★   ★   ★

The *Albermech* loomed in his consciousness more and more every day, as did the end of this halcyon time. Meece had been given her orders and only days remained before her departure, so Piper resolved to enjoy them. Their lovemaking took on urgency and when she was away training, Piper spent more time walking, while directly loading data from Inster's list. One morning he again found himself in the cafe bar he'd used before, drinking coffee, when Geelie sat down opposite him.

'You, and the other members of your Sparkind team, have been notably absent lately,' Piper observed.

Geelie shrugged, her gaze fixed on him. 'The social mores are to leave a couple alone while their romance blooms, and await an invitation to socialize later.'

'Romance?'

Geelie looked over towards a hovering drone. It dipped an acknowledgement, then shot off.

'How do you feel about her?'

'I'm actually an adult and I do have a mother,' Piper replied dryly.

'Maternal emulation – I can't help it sometimes. Inster has no concerns, or hides them well, but there should be concern. You've been raised without any of this sort of interaction, and when the break comes . . .'

'It might impinge upon my efficiency?'

'No!' Geelie showed annoyance. 'Don't see everything as Polity manipulation, Piper Lagan. Inster cares about you. We care about you. And, damn it, you will soon enough be coming under extreme psychological pressure.'

Piper sipped his coffee, then watched the drone return and deliver a similar beaker to Geelie. Another example of her human emulation, though apparently Golem bodies could glean energy from food to complement harder power supplies.

'I was teasing you a little,' he said. 'I understand perfectly the dangers of sexual and relationship angst, and attachment. In fact, I understood them before Inster included some essays on the same in my daily reading. There was one about young soldiers in warfare . . .'

'And what did that tell you?'

'That relationship attachment can be either a hindrance or a benefit in terms of combat efficiency. It depends on the individuals concerned.'

'Where would you put yourself in that respect?'

'Hard to say. My time with Meece has given me a greater attachment to the people of the Polity. Which would be good if I hadn't already accessed so much about the war from Albermech, and come to see myself as a member of the threatened human race. I'll also be concerned about the danger her profession puts her in, and I will miss her. I will feel loss, and that might be deleterious.'

'I feel a "however" coming . . .'

'However' – Piper smiled coolly – 'from my present perspective, I see that through my brief but intense time with her, I have become whole at a biological level. I would have been incomplete without it. I am, as the expression goes, a more rounded human being.'

'How very mature of you.' Geelie's tone had an edge to it.

'Which of course makes me wonder again if this was all planned.'

'And how very cynical,' Geelie added.

Piper spread his hands and shrugged. 'Cynical or realistic?'

She leaned forwards. 'You understand the danger of integration with the machine?'

'That in doing so, humans become colder and more analytical, because that's their conception of how a thinking machine should

229

be. Yes, I understand that, Geelie. I also understand it to be a useful strategy to ameliorate loss.'

She sat back, looking doubtful.

'How are the others?' Piper asked, firmly changing the subject.

The final days passed. During his walks, Piper moved beyond Inster's lists and delved deeper into military databases. The sheer quantity of information appalled him, even with its specially designed search engines and teaching programs. He'd easily absorbed everything Inster had sent, with that ease steadily increasing, but he couldn't take it all in, yet. He needed ways to hone it down further, to the specifics that applied to him.

'Looking for something?' Albermech enquired, shortly after he made a comlink request to the AI.

'Everything I need to know,' Piper replied.

Data feeds immediately established in his virtual aug. AIs were fast and could do such things in fractions of a second, but he felt sure these links and the information they conveyed had been prepared already. It wasn't all military stuff either. He took an overview of the numerous subjects awaiting him and wondered at the usefulness of some of them. But he trusted that the AI knew what it was doing, and to start, he began to explore with interest stuff on extrapolated prador psychology.

'Any questions?' Albermech asked.

'I'll come back to you if I have.' Piper closed the comlink, knowing that was just the AI's signal to him that the conversation was over, since Albermech could open such links from his own side without permission.

Piper walked the war factory. Even while absorbing information, he paused at a viewing window into one of the final construction bays. From there, he watched a massive dreadnought receiving a giant system of fusion drive engines, like a Cyberat multiplug going into the socket in a torso. This particular ship was of interest. Meece would be one of the other components going aboard in a few days. As he watched, he strayed away from Albermech's data feeds, searching out information about the ship's mission, but then abruptly snapped away, recognizing the danger of this.

On the last day before her departure, he observed the Cyberat and saw one rack completely empty and steadily being disassembled. More than half of them were now aboard the *Albermech*. He turned away, heading to Meece's apartment, a tight anxious ball in his stomach. Their relationship had become more combative over the last few days. At one point, she'd become angry with him and nothing he'd said seemed to cool it.

'Cold fucker,' she had called him.

After their 'near argument', a weird politeness had ensued. But the sex became more like a fight, as if she wanted to subdue him in some way, dominate him, and it left him bruised and exhausted. The last night it got worse, or perhaps better, with her slapping him across the face and riding him into an orgasm so hard he nearly lost consciousness. They continued for hours, then fell exhausted, wrapped around each other.

'And here we are,' she said, as once again he woke to the sound of the shower and then watched her dress.

'Indeed we are,' he replied.

She dressed in fatigues, as ever, and packed a bag with personal belongings, leaving the cupboards standing open and empty.

'No long goodbyes,' she said, hitching the strap over one shoulder.

He climbed out of bed, grabbed hold of her and kissed her, which she responded strongly to. Then she broke away abruptly and turned to the door, tears in her eyes.

'We may meet again or maybe not,' she said while her back was turned. 'Don't allow yourself to think about me too much – you're smart enough to know better.'

'Okay,' he said. He recognized the emotions within him that could lead to this. Though they were strong, they were a small part of his whole. Still he couldn't help but look upon such humanity with a slight Cyberat contempt. He closed his eyes, sighed out a breath, then heard the door open and close with a solid, final thunk.

Piper returned to his own apartment, touching on the data links in his virtual aug, falling into then out of them. He couldn't concentrate, and no amount of tweaking his physiology with his nanosuite made any difference. When he began to open up his bones to the same data, however, the anger assisted him as the overlay formed, as did a hard pragmatism and perception that seemed alien.

He lay down on the bed, feeling wrung out and exhausted from the night but still determined to concentrate. Prador psychology began mapping out as a model in consciousness between his ears and throughout his skeleton. But, as it kept sliding from his grip, he increased the function of the latter, with the reptile growing more distinct. Even then, he still found himself drifting, because this wasn't physical but emotional tiredness. As ever, the transition between waking and sleeping escaped him, and he sank deep into his dreamscape.

'Look at the stones,' said Meece. He was so glad – she hadn't left after all. Only, when he turned to her, she was no Polity marine, but the girl by the river. 'Look at them.'

He turned his attention to the multicoloured pebbles on the riverbed and noted the lifelessness of the water. It had been recently redirected from a nearby lake to supply a reservoir close to the city – Cyberat in its functionality and purpose. He wished there were diamond rays and walking trout in it.

'They're beautiful,' she said.

He remembered how the concept of beauty had been broken down and analysed in his class. In essence, beauty related to functionality and symmetry. The river was of course functional, but he could see none of that in the stones. And yet he understood beauty as a concept apart from its presentation in dry Cyberat lectures.

'Yes,' he said. 'They are.'

She smiled at this victory, and he thought the smile beautiful too, perhaps because of the symmetry of her face. His gaze strayed down to the pubescent changes in her body and his reaction confused him, while on another level blurred into hot, sticky, thoroughly adult nights in a body that was more mature now. He wanted to stay here talking to her. He really wanted to stay. He knew her so well but, right then, didn't actually know her name.

'Amellan Quarse 23, your progenitor is looking for you,' his father supplied.

Piper dipped his head, folding over on a stab of dread, glanced up into Amellan's disappointed face, and then as if through crystal facets, saw her skipping away. Apparently his father was looking for him, or had found him, he didn't know. He felt the intensity of Doge's lighthouse glare swinging towards him. It seemed to come out of the river stones – with all the thousands of them representing something, now crowding his internal grid. A segmented tentacle suddenly wrapped around his wrist, extruded from the bulk of his father, who was rolling across the ground on caterpillar treads. He looked up at the muscular chest and arms protruding above his father's cylinder and knew this would be the last time he'd see those arms – sacrificed for a sin only Doge could understand.

'Why?' Piper asked. And though it was 'why' should he not see Amellan and enjoy her company any more, and 'why' should he not see Meece too, it multiplied into thousands of 'whys' asked at different junctures of his life.

'Why?' he asked again, now clamped naked in a framework in the laboratory, deep inside one of the factories his father controlled.

'Why?!' he yelled as, out of wet and shifting darkness, he rose into consciousness. And then all he could do was scream at the unbelievable agony. He screamed on seeing his skin and muscle peeled back from his bones, and the thousands of probes entering them through neatly drilled holes.

'I'm sorry, son,' said his father, poised over him. His factory limbs were glittering with instruments, a knife in one muscular human hand and a clamp in the other. 'You won't remember any of this, thankfully.' He then sliced down Piper's ribcage and began to peel away the skin and muscle there.

Piper woke with a yell and sat immediately upright, hands clamped to his chest. He fell off the side of the bed, crawled a short distance and puked. He dragged himself into the bathroom and coiled foetal below the hot lash of the shower, suppressing the reptile and shoving down the slide switches on his bones. He had no question in his mind about the reality of the dream. It had been a memory uprooted from deep within his consciousness, now laid out for display. He also had no doubt that this was the result of the touch of the Room 101 AI in his mind, rising to the surface because he had slept while his bones were activated.

Finally, after however long, the shivering stopped and he stood up. He was soaking but felt utterly arid inside. He dried off his exterior and went to dress, noting a beetle-shaped cleanbot hoovering up his vomit. How old had he been when that happened? He'd been prepubescent, certainly – a small boy by a river, starting to feel something different about a young girl. So, he'd been a child when his father weaponized him. And now of course he understood the fear he'd always felt for the man. He knew enough about the organic human mind to realize that easier than wiping memories away was to erase their address and make them inaccessible. However, inaccessible to the conscious didn't necessarily mean inaccessible to the unconscious, and those hidden memories could have their underlying effects.

But he was no longer a child. Words that'd stuck in his mind from something Inster had provided rose for his inspection. They came from a religious book of pre-Quiet War Earth: 'When I was a child, I spoke as a child, I understood as a child, I thought as a child: but when I became a man, I put away childish things.'

'Albermech,' he said, opening the comlink. 'I'm coming aboard.'

10

As soon as Piper stepped out of the docking tunnel, the exit of which lay deep inside the ship, the hologram of a man flickered into existence. The man was huge, hairless, muscles sharply defined, skin pale with a blue tinge and with eyes like black nail heads. He stood with his arms folded and was completely naked. After studying him, Piper surveyed his surroundings. The room was long and its walls occupied with lockers and racks packed with weapons. Tunnels speared off from it in every direction too. Looking up twisted his perspective and he realized the room was octagonal, with walkways above and to his left and right. A woman was moving across directly above him, seemingly hanging by her feet.

'Comments?' asked the big man.

Piper swung back, identifying the voice, and now recognizing the features of the hairless head too, which the AI had used in an earlier communication.

'Albermech,' he said. He paused for a second, then continued, 'The others were milder avatars, so as not to scare the natives, I presume.'

Albermech smiled, and that was just a little frightening. 'Inster is right about you. You are evolving at an incredible rate. That's good, because we will be leaving soon. I have assigned you a cabin close to the holds.'

Piper nodded and auged into the ship's system, loading a detailed map and locating his cabin in an eye-blink.

'You'll want to see your soldiers, of course.'

'Yes.'

The hologram abruptly stepped forwards, then vanished. Piper saw that even this was about educating him – intensifying his experience – and he wondered once more if Meece had been part of all that. He headed off through the requisite tunnel. The ways through the ship were plain and utilitarian, intermittently spaced with fast-action bulkhead doors he suspected had more to do with defence against invaders than atmosphere integrity. He thought that human scale would have been better, since they'd act as a barrier to the larger prador enemy, then dismissed the idea. Better to know where boarders were going, so as to funnel them into kill zones. And anyway, Polity troops weren't all human – he'd seen enough war drones in Room 101 to know that.

His thinking was exact, logical. Yet even as he buried himself in it, the knowledge of another dreadnought at that moment heading out of Room 101 flashed into his mind. He checked timings to confirm and said quietly, 'Goodbye, Meece,' then moved on.

Finally, Piper found his cabin and entered. Standard construction, utilitarian again. He checked a wardrobe and saw clothing there, checked the fabricator and that it was working, then opened another cupboard and studied a neat selection of weapons, power supplies and ammunition. Sitting on the bed, he accessed data on the Cyberat aboard. The refugees and Old Guard had been loaded, while the Enforcers had filled up two holds and were in the process of filling another. Noting environmental factors, he went to the wardrobe and opened it – studying the clothing there more closely. There were uniforms and what looked like copies of the clothes Geelie had bought him aboard the war factory.

There were also two suits. One was heavier than the other, having various ports and interfaces all over its surface. Inspecting the interior of it, he also found sanitary arrangements and doctor connections. The thing could insert tubes into his veins, almost certainly for nutrients, and do much else besides to keep him alive and functional. He then perceived precisely what it was for: when he was in his war body. The other suit was a slick black vacuum combat suit, almost like a lethal insect. He auged into it as he took it out, then stripped off his clothes. This thing also engaged with his body intimately, but was lighter and fit for purpose. When he pulled the garment on, it moulded to his form as it powered up, and an icon blinked in his mind.

'Inster,' he said, activating the connection.

'Something for you to peruse,' the agent replied. 'Now you have the time.'

The link was there, but blocked by a safety protocol. He finished pulling on the suit then sat on the bed again, noting the comfort of the garb, and opened the link.

Yannetholm. A world that was large, having two standard gravities, half low landmass and half syrupy sea that was generally no deeper than a man's waist and traversed around the globe in the 'world tide'. The human population were heavyworlder adapts and, surprisingly, some of them were still alive. When the prador arrived, they'd bombarded the surface habitations and wiped out close to a billion inhabitants. That a few hundred million survived was only by dint of the massive underground transit system they'd bored between their widely scattered cities. The prador left them there while sewing biotech around the surface, wiping out the humans' vast fields of GM oysters, mussels and clams, and spreading the life forms they wanted instead. These consisted of a heavy-boned version of their mudskippers, as well as reaverfish that resembled flounders, and varieties of shellfish more to their taste. Yannetholm had been a supplier of seafood to many worlds across the Polity, but it had now been turned into an aquaculture world for the prador. Meanwhile, underground, the survivors bored new tunnels, retrieved technology from the surface, made weapons and made plans. They attacked and wrecked prador infrastructure, killing prador where they could and even gutting a landed dreadnought. The prador responded by injecting nerve gas into the tunnels. They'd been on a steep learning curve throughout the war and, by this time, knew well how to kill off humans. AI estimations were that less than a million Yannets survived this, and by then had lost any appetite for war. That was the summation delivered to Piper's virtual aug, and it was just the surface of a deep pool of data about the world.

'Our destination?' he asked.

'Indeed,' Inster replied, from wherever he was aboard the war factory.

Piper accessed links and garnered other data. Over a hundred million prador, consisting of over ten thousand families, occupied the world now, as well as its orbit and bases scattered through its solar system. Seeing the huge size of these 'families', he searched down other data and noted that, throughout the war, the prador had been massively expanding the number of their progeny beyond the usual. This was of course to provide more expendable soldiers.

Yannetholm was hugely fortified and numerous warships patrolled it. He noted data trails and all this information steadily building into a tactical and logistical data sphere – a battle sphere. The Polity was going to hit this place hard. It was a key target because of that expansion of progeny across all prador. The world was now swarming with prador food, along with the massive harvesters collecting it up and dispatching it to haulers in orbit.

239

His role in this strike, though major, would be centred on the world itself. He began to incorporate this information in his aug, but deliberately spilled it out around the virtual entity – effectively expanding it to occupy his bones. This was almost an unconscious process, while he stood up and headed out the door, concentrating on his surroundings.

A dropshaft took him to a corridor leading out through the thick hull of the ship and then into a ring-shaped, square-section tunnel that ran around the ends of the hold cylinders. There was no grav inside it, and he could have propelled himself along using handles on the walls. He used gecko function instead and walked on, peering down through ports to take in a view of the war factory and surrounding space. He could see ships out there and, with just a small effort, could also have found out whether Meece's dreadnought was among them. He deliberately clamped down on that, though, turning away.

Soon he reached the airlock he wanted and stepped inside. Further along the tunnel were larger bulkhead doors leading into the same hold, but the system indicated they were locked down. He didn't enquire why – simply wanting to limit his communication with others while he concentrated on himself. He closed the door manually behind him, then elicited data from the system here. There was atmosphere beyond the next airlock door, and it was breathable, but he'd noted the conditions there, which was why he'd chosen to don the combat suit.

He opened the inner door, pushed through in zero gravity and caught hold of a handle beside the airlock. His breath huffed out vaporous in the chill, as the inner airlock door closed automatically. The temperature in here was minus twenty and he would soon have been a shivering wreck in his ECS uniform. He gazed around at the tunnels. At this end of the hold, six of them starred off from his position, then from them numerous aisles stretched down the length of the hold. Here, one side of the tunnels was the hold wall, but elsewhere the walls were all the same: consisting of Enforcers in their mobile bodies packed as close together as feasible, braced by frames, and tubed and wired together in one great mass. This was the reason the big bulkhead doors were locked, he realized. There was no need for, or possibility of, these going through into the rest of the ship. And any crew coming the other way would use one of the airlocks, as had he. The bulkhead doors also weren't airlocks, and opening them would screw up the temperature differential.

Piper gazed at the mass of Enforcers, knowing it extended for kilometres, and it was just one of eight similar holds. Via his aug, he closed up his hood, feeling it harden about his skull, with the visor rising to seal shut. He'd felt as if his tongue was freezing. Thankfully it didn't interfere at all with vision – he saw only a brief gleam on the visor before that faded away. Excellent technology. He propelled himself to one of the aisles and then moved along it, catching at frames to drive himself rather than operating the suit's air-blast impellers. He now noted robots somewhat like the beetle cleanbot in his last apartment, scuttling through and checking on things. It seemed uncomfortably as if the place was swarming with metal cockroaches – another life form brought to Founder's World from Earth for no apparently rational reason. He also found regularly scattered sections of stored munitions, spares and materials bracketed by stacks of grav-sleds. Everything here was as it should be, and he'd seen nothing he didn't know already.

'Why am I here?' he said out loud, after ensuring none of his comlinks were open.

He halted and studied one of the Enforcers: a frosted head under a chain-glass dome, ribbed tubes running into the eye sockets, a horizontal cylindrical body with legs folded up underneath. Numerous holes at the front of the cylinder marked out the positions of its weapons. The head shifted slightly, as if the Enforcer had detected his presence. Piper felt the need to address him.

'You were a free human once and you can be that again,' he said. 'But for the present, you're mine . . . and my responsibility.'

With the words now put out there, Piper felt the weight of the task falling on him. He gazed along the aisle, seeing it disappearing in a vanishing point. Figures of millions could be stated, but only here could he feel the reality of them. He closed his eyes for a second and the weight seemed to multiply. Then he opened them again, and a second later opened the comlink to Albermech.

'Acquainting yourself with harsh realities?' the ship AI enquired.

Piper paused for a second, wondering if Albermech had been listening to what he'd spoken out loud. Possibly, probably, but the AI was also smart enough to understand what had brought Piper down here.

'The Enforcers,' he said. 'With Polity technology, they can be returned to humanity.'

'They are already human.'

'No, I mean the damage done to their minds can be fixed. They can be restored in cloned or rebuilt human bodies.'

'I have no easy answers for you,' said the AI. 'They can be restored as you say, and in many other ways, including printing back what is missing. But not as the people they were before.'

'Nobody can be returned to a previous state,' said Piper.

'And so the elements of wisdom grow.'

'This is morally wrong,' said Piper.

'Ah, morality.'

'They are human and should be able to choose their course.'

'I can debate the philosophy of that, since in reality no one chooses their course, but let's instead go to plain reality. Morality is a variable construct that grows to include more dictums relative to the wealth and safety of the population concerned. Also, you're talking about human morality and not, for example, prador or AI morality. There will be no human morality if there are no humans left.'

'So what is AI morality?'

'Pretty much the human kind, since we are effectively post-humans, but without the irrational whining.'

'Cold calculations.' Piper pushed himself off from the frame, heading back down the aisle to where he had come in.

'Inster has already told you what the cost would be of Polity intervention on Founder's World. Similar costs apply here. Resources would need to be expended to raise the Enforcers to a point where they are capable of making choices. Excuse them from the war and that comes with a price too. Do you want to know the numbers?'

'I guess not,' said Piper. It was irrelevant. He'd made the query and understood that these Enforcers would be used in the war with or without him. He also didn't like himself for where he'd taken that brief discussion: it all felt too much as if he'd been trying to find an easy way out for himself and didn't have any real concerns about the morality of all this. He entered the airlock again, going through into the tunnel with ice briefly forming on his suit then subliming away.

'Any further questions?' Albermech asked.

'There must have been those in the Polity who refused to fight . . .'

'No.'

'What?'

'Everyone fighting is a volunteer.'

'Just like all those AI weapons coming out of Room 101?' said Piper cynically.

'Yes, in essence, just like that: their morality drives them to sign up.'

Piper slid his visor down into his neck ring and collapsed his hood. He'd been taken round in a circle and recognized the futility of debating such things with an AI. He stood there trying to think of something to say, some refutation to make. In the end he just headed on down the corridor, saying, 'No – no more questions.'

The next hold was different. He became aware of this when he had to wait at the airlock because someone was cycling through from the inside. A short while later, the inner door opened, wafting through a slightly putrid, metallic smell. A small, ring-shaped carrier body, with two blocky legs folded up against its sides, floated out with a plug form inserted. It halted with puffs of vapour and the man there peered at Piper, who peered right back.

The torso, single arm and bloated head were young, while a standard-vision visor had been plugged into the eye sockets. Everything just below the ribs was an inverted cone of optics, wires and pipe sockets, black boxes and interface plates, with skin, bare muscle and veined membranes bulging through the gaps.

'Hello,' said the Cyberat, obviously unaccustomed to using his voice box.

'Hello,' Piper replied.

After a long pause, the Cyberat continued, 'I am allowed to look around. We have . . . small transport bodies and I want to see a lot.'

Piper waved him on. 'Then don't let me detain you.'

The young man dipped his head and, with another puff of vapour, his carrier body took him away. Piper watched him go, noticing fluids dripping from the cone-shaped interface section of his plug-form body. This escape of fluids accounted for the smell that had accompanied the Cyberat from the airlock and it would probably be much worse inside. He noted the carrier body wasn't Cyberat but probably something Albermech had put together in one of the ship's factories. Proper carrier bodies bathed the interfaces in antibacterial mists and UV, while the pipes for excrement and urine were connected into a disposal system. Still, this didn't make the whole arrangement any less grotesque to him now. The young man had mistaken him for a Polity citizen and, in some sense, might not have been wrong. Piper stepped into the airlock and closed the door behind.

The smell was indeed worse inside the hold, but leavened by an antiseptic aroma too. He noted cleanbots busily at work amidst a more chaotic set-up than in the Enforcer hold. That one would have smelled as bad had not the temperature been down at minus twenty. He looked around.

There was more space here, perhaps to allow its occupants to leave their main bodies and move around. But there was still the same arrangement of aisles walled by Cyberat. He went round the ring tunnel at the end, peering into each aisle. In the first there was no movement, in the second he saw just a scattering of plug forms in carriers. Carrier bodies were also folded up and fixed against sections of the frameworks all along. He entered the third. Over to his right, and above and below, the Cyberat were more varied in form than the Enforcers. He saw Engineers, progression hospital Medics, Bureaucrats, Agronomists and others – all with armaments now attached. Over to his left resided the much larger war bodies of Old Guard. More plug forms floated around here too, in some cases aimlessly, in others using air jets or arms, if they had them, to propel themselves along. A number of them had gathered around one war body. It seemed some sort of meeting was being conducted. Did they think that by not using transmitted com, they could talk without being overheard? Or perhaps this was simply the nearest they could get to fulfilling some need for human connection. Again Piper recognized the horror and injustice of what the Cyberat culture had become. And now he questioned whether there had ever been a time when this melding of machine and human had been a good thing. Or rather, whether it'd been a good thing in conjunction with fanaticism. He pushed himself over to the framework holding the Old Guard and propelled himself along to where this gathering was taking place.

He started to hear the exchange as he approached, although it was dying down now.

'It's still not our damned war,' a voice hissed as he drew closer, as though someone felt the need to affirm that point as the discussion ended.

Plug forms in carrier bodies bobbed chaotically as they turned towards him. Piper concentrated on the huge war body they were gathered next to. Its main component looked like a huge cast-aluminium engine – a great meld of cylinders, pipes and casings. It had chemical jets and thrusters, and was large enough to contain a grav-engine and fusion reactor. Attachments that could inflate cage wheels were folded in underneath. All over, metal blisters capped off rotogun turrets or the throats of missile launchers, and long bulky ion cannons ran down each side. This war body also had a smaller carrier body inserted; Piper could see its blocky legs engaged into sockets around it. And plugged into the top of it, her ancient torso studded with tech and wound through with tubes, was the Old Guard, and he recognized her.

Mallon . . .

Piper brought himself to a halt as he contemplated the scene. Despite the fact that his bones were all but off, recognition of the woman who had certainly engineered his 'accident' at the building site raised his own anger and stirred the reptile. Coming here, he'd expected to find Cyberat who had worked for the old regime, of course, but finding Mallon felt far too personal.

'Piper Lagan.' She gazed at him. 'I'm surprised and baffled to find you here, youngster. I thought you were either going through progression or had fallen in with your parents and their filthy betrayal.'

'He's one of them?' asked the same hissing voice as before.

'Doge and Reema are his parents,' said another. 'I heard Castron did for Doge.'

'Then he is not someone we want here,' said another assertively.

'Oh I don't know,' said another still. 'Perhaps this is a good place for him to be, and a good place for him to never leave.'

As quickly as that, things had already turned nasty. He'd resented being called youngster, and now he was the son of 'filthy' rebels and had come straight into danger. These Cyberat had no knowledge of his position – that he had in fact been put in command of them all. This knowledge could have been provided by Albermech, but in a flash he understood why it had not. The AI wanted him to assert dominance and establish his position long before he took these people into battle. He gripped the framework tightly and, via his nanosuite, turned on his bones fully.

The data crashed into his internal grid and, now much more adept at this, he limited and then shaped his range to this single aisle. Nodes established quickly and easily – these were Cyberat and what he'd been made for. Not the confusing work- ings of the nearby war factory which, even though he'd limited his range, still loomed in his consciousness. As the inner anger, aware of the danger to him, rose up to meld with his own and the overlay hardened, he immediately sent animuses to shut down any weapons. Telemetry in return told him this hadn't been necessary, since their weapons were all shut down anyway. It made sense, while they were aboard the ship. He saw that he could turn them on any time he chose. Nevertheless, more Cyberat were on the move, converging on his position, hundreds of them, and they could easily tear him to pieces. He activated his suit jets to propel himself out from the frame to a clear area, and there stabilized to float in mid-air.

'You are essentially correct.' He pointed to the Cyberat who had mentioned his parents. 'Castron killed my father. However, something of what you may not be aware is that my father gave me a gift.'

He focused fully on Mallon's node, opening it out and exploring. *There.* He shaped and sent an animus. It entered her and established fast. Then, via his connecting thread, he raised one of the rotogun turrets from her war body, protruded its weapon and spun the barrels threateningly. Next he dropped in a targeting solution covering all those before her. Mallon looked over at the weapon in puzzlement, and hot black joy rose up in Piper.

'Splash him!' The hissing Cyberat had mistaken the weapons activation as Mallon's intent.

Now for those approaching. He broadcast animuses throughout, feeling them hit home like anchors in all these bodies, seizing control. He ran programming through the thousands of data threads, and in the hold weapons started activating, swinging and targeting. If the racket of that wasn't enough to bring the point home, targeting lasers flicked into being, picking out numerous free plug forms and those who had moved their mobile bodies out of the racks. He felt gleeful and, almost without conscious thought, brought up his hood and closed the visor. Flying debris would be his main danger in here. The suit should protect him, though. And here, now, he could finish the dregs of the old regime.

No!

Piper fought the reptile and pushed it down. Anger should be a tool he controlled and not something that controlled him! He glanced up, seeing two war bodies on the move too. He simply shut down their thrusters, and next their limbs, then spread that program virally too. In just a few seconds, all flying bodies were drifting chaotically, or made immobile, clinging to frameworks. The only things moving with any purpose were the plug forms in carriers and the weapons he controlled. He reached out again, focusing down onto smaller nodes – the less complicated Polity hardware – and shut those down too. Numerous impeller jets simply went out. Ring transporter bodies froze. He looked around as the hold was suddenly filled with yelling and protest. Cyberat drifted, or crashed into each other, or into frameworks, tumbling out of control. He took a calming breath and opened his hood and visor again. He then jetted over to Mallon, settling down on her war body, the rotogun to his left.

'So you did this, boy?' she said.

'Indeed,' Piper replied. 'And henceforth you will address me as General.' He looked up at her. 'Is that understood?'

'So from one dictatorship to another, General,' she said.

'You made a deal with the Polity to fight for them in return for rescue from filthy rebels. You will fight and I will command you. But it needs to be clear that this is not a deal you can renege on.'

'Oh, it is abundantly clear,' said Mallon, glancing at the rotogun turret.

Piper searched the system of his suit and found PA on it, but also linked into Cyberat com for this hold.

'Okay, listen up all of you,' he said calmly. 'I will return control of movement to you, but on condition you return to rack positions or to your main bodies. You will do that, or I will simply do it for you.'

Protest erupted, echoing around him and coming in through his connections to them. He listened to some of it and knew he could respond to every one individually, as he had to the rebel Cyberat the first time he encountered Geerand. He chose not to, and simply waited. The protest began to wane and he relinquished control to them, but warily.

'You are powerful,' said Mallon. 'I'd heard something about Enforcers being taken out of Guard or telemetry control but couldn't get a straight answer out of Castron.'

'A friend of yours, was he?' Piper asked, reflecting as he had before on the difference between power and strength.

'Friends were a luxury we could not afford,' she replied.

'And difficult to acquire when you were doing the things you did.'

'You mean like putting that beam end into you?' asked Mallon.

'Indeed.' Piper glared at her.

'Do you think I had any choice in the matter?'

'There are always choices.'

'You are a naive thing if you think that true, and you have no conception of how our regime operated. The reality is not evil people imposing totalitarian rule, but good people forced steadily to do evil.'

Piper didn't know what to say as his ever-active mind took her words apart and examined them from every angle. But with his reptile anger up, and the sense of danger all around, he couldn't accept what he saw as excuses for past atrocities. His thoughts kept straying to the weapons he controlled, and how an army of millions of Enforcers would be enough, without the old regime bodies here. He fought it, closing his eyes and concentrating on shoving the reptile down strongly enough to hit that slide switch in his nanosuite, closing down his bones.

Now he could see more clearly what was him and what was the reptile. It was enlightening to know that a lot he'd been attributing to its anger was actually his own too; then he wondered how much of that it had taught him. With calm restored, he forced himself to try and see her side of things. He'd been growing into adulthood during a time of change and had been provided with power. Would he have been better than her in circumstances like hers? He realized he *had* been naive and his own words had risen from that, not all blame could be attributed to the reptile. He studied her and imagined her as a young woman, forced into progression, steadily being whittled of humanity. He pushed off from her war body and cautiously propelled himself towards the exit. As he reached it, he opened his virtual aug link to Albermech again.

'It seems I have much to learn,' he said.

'Indeed.'

'You overheard?'

'What Mallon said at the end? Yes. Be aware that she paraphrased something found in many books throughout the ages. Maybe she was a good person forced to do bad, or maybe not. Of more concern to me is another aspect of your interaction in there.'

'Like what?'

'You were very quick to put their weapons online.'

'They threatened me.'

'Yes, but I hope this does not reflect your unconscious too much, and that other thing inside you. All of the Cyberat are people. You must not think to expend them carelessly because they either have diminished mental function, or were once what your mother would have called enemies.'

'I know my responsibility,' Piper replied.

'I hope so,' was Albermech's only reply.

Upon departing the *Albermech* again, Piper registered that Meece's dreadnought had dropped into U-space while he'd been in the hold talking to Mallon. He felt ashamed not to have marked the event by at least noticing it, but then felt stupid to feel that way. He'd already said his goodbyes and couldn't allow human emotion to interfere with his purpose here, because so much depended on it. Millions of lives depended on it.

Over the ensuing days, Piper established a new routine: absorbing more and more data, checking on the Cyberat in the war factory and seeing their numbers there steadily going down, then returning to the ship to watch them being installed in the hold cylinders. He also added physical exploration of the ship to his routines. However, when he tried to enter the section of it where the bridge lay, he found tight security on the bulkhead door – the nodes of the locking systems were glossy and all but impenetrable. He pushed, starting to unravel them, then stopped since their state indicated Albermech, or perhaps Corisian, did not want him to go through.

'Why did you lie about being a probe to my world, when you have always been the AI of an interfaced dreadnought?' he asked the air.

Albermech's comlink opened in Piper's virtual aug, only this time it was different, and the duality with Captain Corisian was evident from bleed-over. It was Albermech's voice that replied but with an additional odd tonality and something of an echo.

'We didn't want you to know, and therefore anyone you cared

to tell, what kind of ship sat above Founder's World. Knowing our capabilities, you would have questioned the circumstances that drove you to use your abilities against Castron and the Old Guard.'

Piper grunted an acknowledgement of the manipulation and stared at the door.

'But in doing so you also concealed that prador were present on my world too . . .'

'We did not know the extent of their penetration and, by telling the rebels of this, we would have alerted any prador there. For we did not yet know they were dead. We designed scenarios. Had we been able to locate and seize their ship before Castron took it, we could have used it for a penetration of the Kingdom for espionage and sabotage, thus reducing human casualty figures.'

Piper nodded. He didn't like it but it was well to remember just how many levels of planning the AIs used. He finally got around to what he really wanted to ask: 'Why is this door closed to me? And will I ever get to see Corisian, who is obviously part of this communication?'

'We enjoy our privacy, and our trust of you – considering the source of some of your emotional reactions – has constraints still.' The comlink abruptly changed, the bleed-over returning to a more familiar format, and he knew that now only Albermech was present. 'This section of the ship is defended against informational warfare. Would you think it a rational choice for me to let you inside those defences?'

It felt like a verbal slap and Piper bridled under it, his reptile pushing against those sliders from the inside. He gritted his teeth, ensured it stayed down, and acknowledged the sensible precaution. He was powerful, with all that word's implications, and if he still considered his home world of higher importance than the war here, he might be capable of seizing control of the ship, along with the Cyberat aboard, and taking it back there. Albermech had seen much inside him but couldn't know the course of his mind, or the extent of his reptile's influence. He nodded tightly, still feeling wounded by the rejection, and turned away to explore elsewhere.

Piper occasionally saw the figure of a large man, who always disappeared when he went to seek him out. It might have been one of the marines or technicians, but the blond hair and sheer size of this figure matched what he had found in files. He was sure this was Corisian. The images he'd seen of him were very old, though, showing a big young man, and he never got close enough to confirm his suspicions.

The interfaced captain was a mystery to be solved at a later time. During these explorations, he also cracked down chemically, mentally and cybernetically whenever his mind strayed to Meece – ruthlessly removing her from his thoughts. Sometimes he slept aboard the ship, sometimes in the war factory, and sometimes he didn't sleep at all. Aboard the *Albermech* he saw increasing numbers of his Cyberat out exploring too, but generally avoided them. Some of those he did encounter bombarded him with questions about the Polity, not realizing he was one of them. Others recognized him and had just as many questions, or regarded him with sullen dislike.

The group this time consisted of twenty Cyberat. Most of them were plug forms using the transport bodies Albermech had provided, while three of them were plugged into mechanical bodies from Founder's World. One of the latter was a spider body, another one much like Mallon's with its blocky legs, while the third ran on treads like Piper's father. He paused at the end of the corridor, watching them. They were gathered by a viewing window looking into the workings of a ship, but this also had a frame open showing other views. The one in the spider body was lecturing the rest. Piper considered turning round and heading off but, feeling a flash of anger at such weakness, held his position and listened.

'The drive system is complex. In the Polity it seems the myth is promulgated that such technology is too complicated for mere humans and can only function under the guidance of AI,' said the young female in the spider body. 'When you consider that the Founder and others during the diaspora used early U-space drives, the claim is doubtful.'

'I agree with you to a degree, Fusier,' said a young man in one of the transport bodies. 'But those early ships did require heavy computing that edged into the territory of AI, and the drives often failed, sometimes catastrophically.' He gestured to the screen frame. 'That thing is a lot more complicated, as must be their runcibles.'

'But could an enhanced Cyberat control such a drive?' asked Fusier.

'Quite probably,' said another of them. 'I think Fusier is right, but I also see the reasoning in putting such drives under AI control. Screw it up in the wrong place, and it could take out a large part of a planetary population. Maybe not a good idea to let the kids play with grenades.'

Fusier replied, 'Am I detecting a degree of very un-Cyberat thinking in you, Breen?'

Piper expected anger and argument now, but many of the group laughed, which surprised him enough to set him walking towards them.

'Oops, maybe not the sort of things we should be talking about,' said another Cyberat in one of Albermech's carrier bodies. 'The boss is coming.'

Piper almost stumbled, but then righted himself and moved

forwards with confidence. 'You can talk about whatever you like,' he said. 'Nobody gets fitted with a behavioural modifier around here.'

'No need for that when you can control us absolutely,' said Fusier, gazing at him with a blank expression.

'Agreed,' he said. 'It's not something I enjoy doing, but not everyone in one particular hold has the best intentions towards me.'

'Perhaps you need a way to separate out those from the rest,' said Breen. 'I spent two hours twiddling my thumbs until you lifted the restriction.'

Now coming up close to them, Piper focused on him, noting that the young man did indeed possess thumbs and hands, though he had additional mechanical thumbs on each hand too. 'How do you suggest I make the distinction? Should I delve into your minds?'

'You can do that?' asked Fusier, looking appalled.

'Of course not,' Piper replied, not so sure he was telling the truth.

A silence fell, but Breen abruptly broke it. 'So what do you think about this AI control of U-space tech?'

Piper shrugged. 'I think the necessity for them to control it is a myth that's been allowed to persist precisely because of what you said. The reality,' he continued, 'is that prador have U-space drives that are controlled by the flash-frozen ganglions of their children. I'm not even sure I understand the reasoning behind that, other than it being a way to recycle their kin. Certainly any Cyberat computing would be superior, as would enhanced Cyberat.'

'Flash-frozen ganglions?' one asked.

'Also in their war machines.'

'Like Enforcers,' said another.

Piper winced. 'Not quite. Enforcers have functional organic brains, albeit diminished by external programming.'

And then he found himself launching into a long discussion with the Cyberat gathered in the corridor. They were Engineers who'd been involved in making Enforcer bodies and had been attacked by rebels, many of their fellows being killed. They'd fled into the mountains, then responded quickly and enthusiastically to the offer from the Polity. When he finally walked away, he knew for certain that his mother would have styled these as enemies. But he couldn't see them that way. He also felt a deep disquiet about his previous activation of Cyberat weapons in the hold, just as Albermech had pointed out when he left there. Had he used them, he could have killed those he'd just been speaking to. How different would he actually have been from his mother in bombing progression hospitals to kill the guilty along with the innocent?

He already knew the strengths of prador armour but now needed to know its weaknesses, especially in regard to the weapons his Cyberat army could wield. Particle beam ablation took time. He internally visualized this happening, and watched the metallurgical profile of the armour during the process. Two-point-five seconds and the profile was just right, so he put one of the new ceramo-carbide rotogun slugs straight into the spot. It didn't actually penetrate, but the impact shock dented the armour and blew splinters of it into the interior. He ran the model in his mind again, this time up to penetration, and noted the effects, filing them along with the rest.

He'd been modelling combat scenarios he'd raised out of Albermech's data feeds ever since meeting those Cyberat in the corridor, and others elsewhere too. No, he wouldn't expend lives cheaply in the coming battle, and Albermech had certainly been right in questioning his attitude towards his soldiers. The likes of Mallon did irk him, and others in that hold too, but they weren't all evil people, whether or not they were good people who had been made to do evil. They were just people. And all of them, including the Enforcers, were people he was responsible for.

'Anger, is it?' said Geelie.

Piper looked up from where he sat akimbo on the gym floor. He was covered in sweat after his workout – a new addition to his daily routine. The gym had been ramped up to two gees – the gravity of Yannetholm.

'That's why I'm here,' he replied.

His discussion with Albermech, sometimes with another consciousness present which was almost certainly Corisian, had been a long one. He'd started it two days after his rejection from the bridge, understanding that if the captain and AI of this interfaced dreadnought were to trust him, he had to first trust himself. They talked about what he'd heard from Kalaidon, his dreams and memories, the way that raging thing inside him had initially been suppressed by action, and now seemed to rise during it too. He couldn't clearly elucidate when it was at its strongest and when not, except in the case of Castron. He could find no rationale for it, beyond it being a copy of his own reptile brain – his subconscious.

'You may be correct in that,' Albermech had replied. 'A reflection of you – an emotional shadow gaining independent life in the capacity of your bones. Kalaidon said it is too hostile and defensive to be removed, so it must be controlled.'

'But how?' he'd asked.

'The answer was in your thought when you left Mallon, and was reinforced when you talked to those Cyberat in the corridor.'

'I'm responsible and I have much to learn.'

'And you have been very busy learning it. However, there is another factor to take into account here. You are still a young man recovering from stalled development, disrupted thinking and a lack of experiential knowledge.'

'I am naive.'

'Yes, you are, but that doesn't mean ineffective. You have capacity in your skull and orders of magnitude more in your bones. We in fact simply don't know how much.'

'So what is your prescription?' Piper had asked sarcastically.

'Your hormonal adjustment requires a degree of chaos, so though you may be tempted to interfere via your nanosuite, I suggest you don't. For the present, I prescribe that you continue educating yourself, but now include physical activity. The first will of course relate to your responsibility, the second will be therapeutic, putting aside the fact that you need to prepare yourself for a world with twice the gravity you are used to.'

The hard vigorous exercise did indeed help, and he ignored the nanosuite raising numerous hormonal tweaks and the suggestion of boosting. The latter would increase his musculature too fast and too easily. He wanted to work at it, for now at least. He also practised activating and shutting down his bones, gaining more nuanced control and deeper insight into how they affected his thinking – what was him and what was not.

Grav abruptly dropped by half, and Piper stood up. Geelie gave him an odd smile, then shrugged off the long package she'd been carrying on a strap over her shoulder. He watched her unroll it to expose two swords and smiled in response. Looking within, he touched on the martial arts program he'd loaded. The thing covered just about every form of hand-to-hand combat that had ever existed, and then honed down to an AI projection of their evolution to an integrated whole. The whole could accommodate to weapons ranging from a rock to ever more

259

sophisticated tools for murder. It was a protean thing, and the basis on which he was building other strategies, now including huge armoured opponents sporting Gatling cannons and particle beam weapons. He also didn't confine this to his virtual aug, but spilled it over into his bones, using recently established data valves that didn't allow the reptile to reach back to him. Even so, he could feel it responding and reshaping itself to the input.

'Are you ready?' she asked.

'Obviously I cannot move as fast as you,' he said. 'And though I have martial arts programming, my body doesn't have the range and strength of a long-time practitioner.'

'Don't try any head kicks,' Meersham called from the other side of the gym, grinning widely. 'You'll certainly regret that.'

He glanced over at the man, irritated, since he already knew that.

'I will try not to hurt you too badly,' said Geelie.

The other two members of the Sparkind team came in. Sloan looked curious and Cheen showed no expression at all. Yes, there were Golem here, but this was human level and . . . it wasn't enough. He needed his mind operating at optimum and, even while in personal combat, still strategizing and incorporating more. Prador joint motors and their force profiles, torque – every aspect of their operation. Legs, claws and mandibles were vulnerable. The joints were targets. He began running rotogun and beam strike tests on them in his mind, modelling further methods to kill the creatures, as he stooped to pick up one sword. Geelie was on him a second later and he fended off her strike clumsily. All the knowledge was there but applying it was another matter. He felt the hot slice of her blade down his arm and leaped back.

'Focus,' she said tersely, and attacked again.

His focus did return, with the firm knowledge of pain and

injury slapped into his mind. He remembered that Inster had, for a time, been a plug form, then later brought back into a full human body. And any human could be brought back from the most severe injury, as he had been. If Geelie hurt him badly here, it might be fixed, but the lesson of the pain would remain. He nodded and began pushing over those internal slide switches, bringing his bones online. Because, as he'd discovered, the reptile was apt for violence and adept at war.

The thing stirred and woke up abruptly, its snarl sending energy tingling into his limbs, and the overlay clarified action and aggression. He corrected his guard, parried and thrust, then turned aside from a strike that could have sliced through his biceps. His legs and arms were aching from his previous exercise. But now he had the skills right at the surface of his mind. They fought, swords ringing, and when he saw an opening, he drove in, amazed to skewer her shoulder, then backed off.

'Good,' she said. 'Now I'll speed up to the conventionally human.'

11

On the first day, shorter here than a Founder's World day, just as the years were longer, Geelie was merciless. One of her strikes would have taken off his leg at the thigh had not his bone stopped the sword. It was good they'd been using simple steel rather than the usual weapon she and Cheen carried, she'd commented, as Cheen took out the autodoc he'd used to examine the prador and set it to work on him. He was mobile again within half an hour, and fighting shortly afterwards.

The next day Meersham took a turn. Fighting the big man resulted in Piper rendered unconscious six times – two by blows to the head and four by choke holds. Sloan's playground on the day after had been in an engineering section of the ship, with many hiding places and pulse guns set to stun. That had hurt, a lot, but hadn't resulted in so much damage. Cheen had demurred, saying, 'Tomorrow, you're going into virtual training – time is limited.'

Piper woke aching in every limb and felt a sore spot centred inside the back of his skull that the nanosuite couldn't find. It had to be psychological, just like the heat that seemed to be issuing from his bones. He rolled from his bed and quickly went through his ablutions, while checking diagnostics. The temperature of his bones had in fact risen, and his nanosuite had used that energy to speed up the production of his blood cells to replace what he'd lost. Meanwhile, a long list of potential boosts to his body had been lined up – triple carrier haemoglobin, fat densification, mitochondrial boost and ATP enhancement, as well as nerve impulse acceleration, and a host of brain cell boosts. And these were just a small portion of the list. This time, rather than dismiss it as he had on his first day in the gym, he simply gave the nanosuite the go-ahead. His earlier decision simply to train had been immature. He should grab every advantage for what was to come, because again, lives depended on him. And just as Cheen had said, time was limited.

Washed and dressed in ECS combats, he ate and drank while pacing around his cabin. His mind was still flooded with the combat tactics and logistics that had occupied his dreams. He felt a reluctance to start again, but then dismissed that weakness and brought his bones up to power. He'd finessed a greater control now and could isolate those numerous aspects of his being. But still, like an emergency red light coming on, his reptile rose and the overlay began wrapping his being. Dampening adrenal and cortisol surges took the edge off that and made him feel more rational. Or at least rational enough to identify impulses that could be damaging. Via his virtual aug, he opened up the feeds from Albermech and the data began to flow into him again. It seemed he was a vessel that could never be filled.

'Anger,' said Albermech, in his mind.

'It hasn't caused me problems because I've been busy,' he replied.

'And yet you have said it has recently arisen even in those times.'

'My hypothesis is incorrect.'

'Exactly – merely a simplification of complexity.'

'A thousand facets,' he said, thinking hard yet again. 'All the human organic drivers like hormones, hunger, weariness and more besides. Related emotional factors – redoubled since it seems I am running a copy of my own subconscious. And perhaps its own agenda.'

'Still a simplification.'

'I'm dealing with it, but I have so much to learn, almost too much.'

'You have more research than most on the prador, and are integrating that. You now need other things, like the mathematics of superfluids and swarm behaviour.'

'For the Cyberat,' Piper agreed. He already had a great deal on that and, even when Meersham had been beating his head against the floor, he'd been designing attack plans. But he knew he needed more, because he would be handling thirty million fighters. And, he reminded himself, *people* like Breen, Fusier and even Mallon.

He sat on his bed after draining the last of his coffee, then got up once more because he was hungry again. He felt hot and sweaty already, and internal analysis showed the nanosuite burning through energy as it instituted its changes. Without touching the fabricator controls, he mentally instructed it to make a slab of fats, proteins and other materials the nanosuite demanded, as well as another beaker of coffee.

'You will learn more today,' said Albermech. 'Much more.'

Using another part of himself, he'd reached out and seen the loading of remaining Enforcers coming to an end. On checking this last, he saw that these had been the human-form ones, but those plugged into larger weaponized bodies like the rest – a dual combat force. He knew what Albermech meant, but kept it verbal.

'Things are ready?' he asked.

'Cheen is coming for you, to take you to your next important lesson.'

Linked into surrounding systems – his range deliberately limited to just five metres all around him – he saw Cheen approaching. He gobbled down the slab, quelling the hunger. It hadn't been necessary, since other methods of feeding his energy-hungry body would be used during the ensuing training session. Carrying his coffee, he opened the door and stepped out just as Cheen arrived.

'Meersham is disappointed,' said Cheen, an amused twist to his mouth. 'I think he rather enjoyed choking you out.'

'*History and philosophy too*,' Albermech said, precisely at the same time. No need to wait for someone else to stop talking. Internally Piper could handle more than one conversation. In fact, he could handle thousands. New data began to flow into him as he shaped and directed armies in his mind, feeding off the prador-killing knowledge. The armies, whose soldiers were just data points, went three-dimensional and he applied Cyberat stats, and then the two gravities of the world they would soon be heading to. Power would be a problem, since grav sucked it up, so ground warfare, or perhaps just transport and relocation on the surface, would be integral.

'Presumably he will be in there with me?' said Piper, the human.

'Facsimiles of Meersham and Sloan, since they are human.'

'Why?'

'They don't want the temporal dislocation, but can load the recordings as they choose piecemeal, and at a later time. They have their own preparations to make.'

Cheen led the way through the ship, finally coming to a small room. Inside, Geelie was already seated in one of the four chairs. She was lying back with her eyes closed, her arm open and a heavy optic plugged in. The chair next to hers had the same simple optic feed running round from the back; he presumed it was for Cheen. Another chair possessed something resembling a Cyberat cerebral support, the inducers that would fold over limbs and torso, and the arrays of tubes running from the autosurgeon beside it. That was his chair, since he'd already seen the schematic, but the fourth? It had a similar format to his, but with attachments and tubes that had a white, almost fleshy, look.

'Who's that for?' Piper nodded to the chair.

'That would be for me,' rumbled a voice behind him, and he turned.

Piper just gaped. After absorbing information on the man, and catching fleeting glimpses of him in the distance, here he was finally. Mentally he'd been a presence, shadowing Albermech's communications with Piper, especially when they went beyond the verbal, but had obviously never felt the need to insert himself into the conversation. So why was he here now?

Corisian was wearing something similar to an antique acceleration suit, with tubes running through its material. Poking through this were numerous raised interfaces and pipe sockets that looked like growths from his raw skin, and which could be seen through the gaps. The man was a giant like Meersham. He was pale, possibly an albino, with white cropped hair standing up from his head. His nose looked to have been broken many times, and a scar ran down from half an ear to the point of his chin. It seemed that cosmetic considerations didn't bother him so much. His eyes were pure milky white, with hair-thin black gridlines across them.

'I thought it time to come meet the prodigy,' the man said, holding out his hand.

When he gripped that huge hand, which was missing half a forefinger, Piper was reminded of his first meeting with Meersham, but this was someone of an entirely different nature. Here was a man whose history dissolved back into the Quiet War – older even than Inster, who Piper now saw coming into the room behind him. Here was an interfaced captain – a man whose mind integrated closely with Albermech. The sense that a presence had entered was quite astonishing.

'I hope not with any further inclination to toss the same into a sun,' said Piper urbanely, after just a slight mental stall.

'If that's going to happen, it will be a job for the prador,' said Corisian. 'Do you think you'll be ready for them?'

Piper reviewed the stuff filling his bones and his mind. He felt the speed at which he was handling tactical scenarios and designing new ones, while at the same time aware of every nuance of the conversation he was currently conducting. He drained the last of his coffee from the beaker and tossed it to the side of the room, where a beetlebot he'd already drawn from its niche caught it and scuttled away with it.

'All I need is time, and information, to become the best I can be,' he replied.

'We'll have plenty of that here.' Corisian gestured to the chairs. 'Let's get to it.'

The man abruptly crossed to the other chair and sat down. Clamps closed over his limbs, and those white fleshy systems attached to his interfaces. He sighed back into the chair and, though his eyes were still open, Piper knew he'd entered another realm. There had been no need for further conversation because, of course, there would be time for discussion in the virtuality Piper was about to enter. He swung his gaze to Cheen, who'd sat and opened up his arm.

Piper had known, when he found this training technique in the vast slew of data Albermech had been feeding him, that it'd been the AI's intention for him to find it. Humans with augs, gridlinks, and other cerebral enhancements and extensions, could enter real-time virtualities with ease. But this was one of a different kind. The body and brain needed support to enter a temporally dislocated virtuality, to handle the accelerated flow of information, as well as the formation and collation of memories, and the physical alterations generated in the brain as it learned at a pace that would have burned it out without support. Skaidon's thinking had been accelerated this way and turned his brain to mush. Corisian's thinking was much the same, to a lesser degree, to keep him interfaced with Albermech, and he wasn't quite human any more.

Piper looked over to his own chair, at the cerebral support there, so much like what the Cyberat used, which the reason why he'd at first been disinclined to do this – a reason dismissed by the realities he faced.

'So the captain came here to see me,' he said to Inster.

The agent had simply been standing with arms folded watching quietly, showing no desire to say anything. He flicked on a smile. 'I think he felt a little bit sidelined.'

'That's not it.'

'Okay, then he feels responsible. He and Albermech have thirty million people under their charge. It was their idea to scoop them up from Founder's World and deploy them in battle. You are an extra, an addition to the main plan, and those millions will soon enough be in your charge.'

Piper faced Inster and gestured to the chairs. 'So, as I said, he came here to see me.'

Inster nodded. 'In every way.'

Piper turned away, walked over to his chair and finally sat down. Beside him the autosurgeon stirred, as clamps began folding over his limbs. He felt the cerebral support close around his skull to hold it rigid, and numbness spreading. Right now the thing was making its holes through tough bone loaded with his father's processing substrate, and driving nanofibres and microtubes into his brain. The surgeon reached over and began inserting other tubes into his veins and his limbic system, running attachments through to major organs and installing devices in his muscles. He saw the cutting, but didn't feel it, and looked up at Inster. Already the man seemed to be dropping back into an expanding white space, gridded with black lines just like Corisian's eyes.

'It's going to be hard in there, boy,' said the agent.

Piper felt a need to object beginning to rise, as it had on other occasions, but as before, he dismissed it quickly. He was a boy, especially in comparison to Inster and Corisian, but in time he wouldn't be. And time was all this was about. His bones now seemed to warm further as data input ramped up, and his virtual aug felt loose within them.

'See you in four years,' said Inster, turning towards the infinitely distant door.

Piper lived Meersham's rage below a cliff covered with human corpses, glued spreadeagled in place. Some were fresh, some mummified and some just dry bones fallen to the ground below. The air swarmed with garroty flies and dripped green, shield-head maggots. These people had died in different ways as prador tested the most efficient and economical ways to kill them. He paced along below them, cradling his multigun and then opening his visor. The stench was intense, yet he felt he needed the reminder. Polity marines were all along the base of the cliff, and scanner drones floated down its face as they recorded identities and paused to trepan skulls, to retrieve the few available memplants. He wondered how many of the people here would have relatives to miss them, since all but half a million of the planetary population had been slaughtered.

Piper had joined up as Meersham with a certainty of purpose –

of doing something worthwhile. He'd trained as the man, fought in deserts, in jungles, under seas and in the clouds of a gas giant. War had become a way of life and, as the impact of prador atrocities hit him hard when retreat finally became advance, hate became a way of life too. But hard professionalism leavened it when he joined as a new member of a four-person Sparkind team to replace a woman who had died. 'Her hate became too much,' Geelie informed him, 'and she became careless.'

Meersham took care, but on one occasion he still found himself deep in the mine, separated from the rest, with his weapons depleted and his suit power so low the thing had become a hindrance. A prador second-child came running out of a side tunnel and was as surprised to see him as he was it. He understood enough of their clattering bubbling speech to know that. They faced off for a moment, then Meersham turned and ran, the thing behind him snipping its claws in his wake. He turned at the door into a human mining-supply station, already kicked open, and dived through. His weapon went skidding away as he staggered and crashed down on his face. He heaved himself up, auging detach routines, and began stripping off the armour. Behind, the prador slammed against the doorway, reaching in with one claw to try and grab him, but he was out of its reach. However, it smashed against the doorway again, partially breaking in the surrounding wall. He glanced at it, wondering why it wore no armour over its natural carapace, and decided that perhaps it was for the same reason as he'd shed his own. Another door opened into a storeroom. He scanned the tools and took up a heavy battery-driven vibro-chisel.

'Come on, fucker!' he bellowed.

The thing came through the wall and he ran straight at it, the chisel humming. Now free of his armour, he could move faster and use his boosted muscles. He jumped and came down on it, a claw closing around his leg just above the knee. His body swung down in that grip as he slammed the chisel into its head turret, just between the main distance eyes. Carapace shattered and the chisel went in, with green blood squirting out around it. The prador flung him and he crashed down onto a table. It then backed off and smashed fully through the wall, claws scissoring as it sought him out. He'd hurt it badly but not killed it, since its brain wasn't in that turret. His attack had been calculated, however, for now the thing was blind. He stood up on the table on one leg and, using just that, leaped once more, coming down on its back. He yelled and drove the chisel in again and again, until it got another claw to him, grabbing his arm. He screamed in agony but held onto the chisel, now deep in broken carapace and gore, driving it deeper. And he felt the world sliding away beneath him.

'Gonna need a little more than the doc,' Sloan commented.

Meersham, his back against a wall, gazed blearily over at the prador, tilted against the wall on the other side of the room. He looked down at the tourniquet around his mangled leg and the autodoc sealing the wound where his arm had been torn away. Geelie, shaking her head and pursing her lips, pressed something against his neck and the world went away again.

Piper faded out with this too, and then launched straight into another one.

'They're memcordings, like those sold on the black market,' Corisian informed him, deep in white space, gridded with black lines. 'The marines exchange them and learn new tactics. No one is sure whether it's a good thing.'

'Neither am I,' said Piper. 'I didn't expect this. I didn't expect to be *in* people.'

Corisian nodded slowly. 'You have been filling with knowledge but that's not enough. Abstracted experience helps, but you need the context of long lives. You need that layering. Why did Meersham grab the chisel?'

'He was used to it, knew what it could do, because he'd worked for a spell in asteroid mining,' Piper replied. And only then did he realize that his experiences as Meersham were not in isolation – the man's life lay all around them in a manner that was of course fractal.

And then he was gone again, into episodes of other lives, which weren't all Polity soldiers. He questioned the usefulness of knowing about Separatists and criminals, scientists and virtuality stars, but sponged it all up in his growing being. This was also punctuated by the familiar, such as when he was back with Geelie, swords drawn and facing off. This time, surely, he would get in a few good strikes before she cut his head off again.

He fought hundreds of times against Cheen, Geelie and others, died a hundred deaths, made thousands of kills and raised everything martial to the surface of his mind, which of course extended beyond his mere skull. He was Corisian in space battles and fleet command, and he saw those same conflicts from the point of view of Albermech, and from the both of them combined. This transitioned into other Polity–prador battles, and then to ones which had never happened, with increasing numbers of ships and the application of swarm and superfluid mathematics. Ships then transitioned to smaller sizes and with fewer weapons, until they became Enforcers. He noted a need for division of control, and he started planning for this, thinking of the war bodies and stratification of command.

He was Sloan, training and training, athletic and fast, in awe of his commander General U-cap Krong as the man pointed to the sand.

'It's time,' said Krong.

Sloan crawled into his tunnel in the sand, its walls bonded

with spray plastic, and pulled the lid closed. He checked his inventory of mines and turned off his aug, because the prador could detect them now. All he did then was bring up to his eye the optic leading through the lid, and he pressed his hand against the wall to feel the vibrations. He waited an hour with the utter patience of the trapdoor spider he was mimicking, until he finally felt the vibrations. Just a short while later, a line of prador began passing his position, and this was it. He was suddenly out in the bright sun, hardly visible in his chameleoncloth fatigues. The first sticky mine he slapped to the hatch at the back of a first-child's armour, where its anus was concealed, and felt amused at the unpleasant surprise it would have. He mined two more of the creatures before the first one went off with a sound like a bullet through tin. Glancing at the victim, he saw the thing drop, with fluids squirting out of its leg joints. Others were going down all along the line as the rest of the U-cappers did their work, and then it was all over.

'We killed too many,' said Krong later, as the shuttle hammered up through atmosphere.

Under heavy gee, Sloan acknowledged that. The prador had abandoned the world and in doing so were bombing it from orbit. The U-cappers hadn't killed too many – they just hadn't killed enough, quickly enough. He understood perfectly the terror tactics of their 'up-close-and-personal' technique, which was the creed of Krong's fighters, but it was the marines and the ships who'd forced the prador into scorched-earth retreat. He decided then that he needed to kill more of them, more effectively, and knew this would be his last mission with the U-cappers. It was time to move on.

Piper experienced Sloan's resolution, and then stepped out of it straight into Geelie as she tore the claws off a prador first-child. Then into Cheen, as he entered the sanctum of a father-captain and riddled it with armour-piercing missiles. He felt their Golem hate and, though emulation it might be, it felt no different from that of Meersham, Sloan or the others. He sensed the hate rise and fall, sometimes transitioning into a weird grudging respect, and he sampled decade upon decade of conflict. Throughout all this, Corisian watched and occasionally pulled him into meetings. Sometimes they merely talked, and sometimes they met at the level of the fast integration and calculation of AI minds.

But again and again, he returned to his now vast web of tactical scenarios, integrating lessons learned and mental attitudes acquired, and knowing he was being shaped to purpose. The ancient battles, played out for him with the waxing and waning of history, and the pronouncements of philosophers, seemed a mere subtext. Though he knew all this filled out his education, it seemed disconnected from the plain reality of human race survival. And then, thinking at first it was just another nook in the virtuality, he sighed back into consciousness in the real present, and he felt old.

'Welcome back,' said Inster.

Piper felt parched as the chair released him – the dryness of deserts and hard starlight. He had the psychosomatic ache of thousands of injuries and hundreds of deaths, but with a necessary detachment so they didn't cripple him. His mind and his bones were laden with new experience and knowledge now. And though these were immense, he wondered if it was the acquired hatred of an enemy he'd never met before that was the most important development to his thinking. He sat upright and looked around. Geelie and Cheen were gone and Captain Corisian was just getting out of his chair. The man walked over and stood beside Inster, gazing down at Piper.

'The troops are yours now,' he said.

Piper acknowledged that with a nod, and couldn't think of anything to say. The captain turned away and headed out of the door. Piper guessed there wasn't all that much more to say anyway, since they'd spoken on and off for years. All the mass of experience and knowledge, integrating still, had to settle inside him. But he knew he needed to rise out of this and anchor himself in the present again. He needed to *be* present.

'How long was I under?' he asked Inster.

'Twelve hours.'

Piper tried to get out of the chair and found it difficult to move. Brief analysis, through his virtual aug connection to his nanosuite, showed him nothing was wrong, and he knew it was the psychological weight still holding him down. Inster moved forwards to help him, but he waved the man back. He sat for a moment and then slowly eased up the slide control on his bones. The reptile was there at once, writhing in baffled rage as it struggled to integrate the backlog of information and experience of four years laid down in his bones in just twelve hours. In that moment it amused him, for he now felt larger than the thing.

'My own anger was lacking throughout it all,' he said, finally finding it easy to climb out of the seat, his overlay falling in even as the reptile still struggled.

'That entity inside you, you mean?'

'Yes.'

'Do I have to tell you why?'

'No. The experience was dislocated,' he said. 'The memories were laid down in my mind quickly while feeding into my bones. I perceived it as experience on my timeline, while the reptile did not. It didn't equate it to real lived experience, nor did it perceive existential threats to which it could respond – just a massive load of data coming in that it's still struggling with.'

275

'Method of loading,' said Inster. 'That thing is keyed to what comes in through your senses. This method bypassed that.'

'Yes – you're correct.'

'But your reptile will be able to integrate it all . . . *you* will integrate it all?'

'Yes, I will, though it doesn't seem entirely real.' He grimaced: not entirely real but real enough. 'Let's go,' he said, straightening up.

Inster nodded. 'We *will* be going – in ten hours. Nearly all the Cyberat are aboard now.'

Piper's dream – or nightmare, depending on how far it went along its timeline – always started by the river with the girl, Amellan. But there were different versions of it, and from this he divined that he'd met her there on more than one occasion. This time they were sitting on the bank and talking. He was boasting about how he would do great things.

'My machines will be better than my dad's. I'll go into space. I'll build a ship,' he said.

She gazed at him intently. 'I don't want to be a machine.'

'Are you crazy?' he asked, looking around to see if anyone had overheard. Even at that young age, he knew she was saying things that would be punished.

'I am a little,' she replied.

Are you crazy, echoed into another place in his dreamscape, spoken to a young man with long blond but thin hair. The man was a partially progressed Cyberat, with metal showing through a net shirt and a precursor cerebral support around his skull. Piper could see the pattern of stretched skin through his hair. His skull had been cut and was undergoing expansion, with nanomachines filling gaps between the pieces of skull, using carbon meshes in which new bone would grow. At present the

276

skull was just a little larger than that of a youth. But when it got bigger, so too would the brain, as the precursor divided it up and inserted its enhancements.

'Things won't change unless we change them,' the young man said.

'We'll end up dead,' he replied, muscular hairy arms folded across his chest. He had no idea why he'd said the words, and really didn't understand to what they referred.

'Perhaps better dead than caught in this endless nightmare. The Founder's thesis has been twisted out of shape.'

'And how exactly are we to twist it back?'

'You know exactly how.'

'I don't know *exactly*, Castron.'

Piper jerked into wakefulness, sitting up with his face as twisted by anger and hate as the thesis, now fading from his mind. The dream began to break up because he was sure there had been so much more than that. He tried to visualize the blond man's face, to compare it to the Castron he knew, but it swam away from his grasp. Because of the virtuality, Founder's World now lay years behind and so much about it now seemed vague and inconsequential.

He held up his arm and looked at it. The limb was heavily muscled now but not as hairy. However much he concentrated, he couldn't get a firm grip on the dream, and only that brief conversation remained in his mind. Where had he and this, perhaps, younger version of Castron been? Abruptly he threw the cover back and got out of bed.

'What the fuck?' he said harshly.

The last part of the dream, or nightmare, hadn't been like his dream of the river. In that, he'd actually had vague conscious memories of Amellan and their brief time in the sun. But this one, with Castron, couldn't have risen out of memory, because he'd never known the old Cyberat as young, nor had he himself possessed big hairy arms. He huffed out a breath and concentrated on calming himself, even having to check that his bones were shut down. He needed to do something. Now. He headed for the shower, washed, then came out and dressed in the vacuum combat suit, all the time still fighting for mental balance. The movement helped, and restored him.

His strongest anger response, elicited by his reptile, was always to the Old Guard Castron, and so this must have been what raised the strange dream. Even with his bones turned off, as now, the response was still within him, because the reptile had been teaching it to him. It was immaterial why his reptile, this copy of his subconscious, had focused on Castron years before that man had murdered his father. It was just there. All this, combined with his recent experiences of the prador, his *four years* of experiences, had really stirred things up in his skull.

'A construct,' he said to his empty cabin.

He began examining his memory stores and felt relieved on seeing those muscular hairy arms folded into the memory of being Meersham when he joined up. He saw a man with thinning blond hair too, a mesh shirt and a large aug on the side of his head – a person one of the others had met, in the portions of their lives that he'd lived. His dream hadn't been a memory, but was a construct of his subconscious, with all the lack of logic that implied. Still, it left him incredibly out of sorts and anxious to get busy doing something. He turned to his cabin door, opened it and stepped out, his feet knowing where he was going before he did. He was ready; the animuses he'd designed could be improved upon, but he had hit the point of diminishing returns. It was time to use them.

★ ★ ★

Cyberat were in the corridors. He hoped to see Fusier, Breen and the others, but again encountered resentful looks and in some cases fear. No one mistook him for a Polity citizen this time. No doubt they had been talking and sharing information about him.

Finally, on arriving at the entrance to the hold containing the Old Guard and other refugees, he paused. He was just a little wary, considering their previous response to him and his to them, and carefully eased up the slide controls to his bones. He couldn't always be held back by fear that his reptile would drive him to murder, and he needed the processing of his substrate now. The reptile rose inside and the overlay spread on his consciousness. Or perhaps he donned that overlay as he moved into a realm of faster thinking, clarity and anger. He opened the airlock and went through.

The hold was warm with the spill-over from Cyberat machinery, and filled with the smells of astringent chemicals, with an underlay of putrefaction. Piper propelled himself along the aisle, finally coming to a halt facing Mallon. He gazed at her. Judging by data from his connection to the animus in her, she wasn't in a precursor state of hibernation like many others here, but was actually asleep. He considered that. Via his nanosuite and augmented sorting in his brain, he could dispense with the necessity of this, or at least put it aside. However, having learned from the lives of others, he knew that while he could use such methods to go without sleep, occasionally allowing it cleaned up mental function just that bit more effectively. The activity of billions of neurons and synapses in the human brain, and throughout the body, had yet to be fully elucidated – in fact, it extended into that region of chaos theory where they couldn't be. Still, Cyberat slept and couldn't go without it for longer than a few weeks. It was one of the factors he had included in his logistical calculations. He sent her a mental prod and she jerked awake, looking around blearily.

'Division of forces,' he said, while watching her. 'It's a rational choice.'

'What are you talking about?' she snapped.

'You will be a commander in my forces. Stratification of command will allow for my fluid control of all. I cannot pull every trigger, nor can I watch every soldier.' His choice of words was for her benefit, and that of others he would put in command. He knew that he might actually be able to control them all.

Animuses were lined up inside him, ready to be broadcast – different categories for different groupings of Cyberat. Upon arrival in their targets, they would alter to new input from their hosts, reforming and adapting like living things, and lie open to instant updates from him. They also contained a huge amount of data: thousands of methods of attack, strategy and logistics, as well as break-off points, times and circumstances to head for resupply, resources that could be grabbed on the ground. The list was as endless and as changeable as circumstances required. But the animuses were even more than that. They were also a distillation of Polity soldiers' attitudes, formatted in a similar way to the Old Guard loadings into Enforcers. They were more complicated, of course, but still a form of indoctrination. He'd faced and accepted realities now, and he needed functional soldiers, and fast.

At a further extent of his present reach, he could feel the cold minds of the Enforcers lying in their millions, while closer by were the more difficult minds of the Old Guard and other old regime refugees. Though he'd met some like Breen and Fusier, they were the exceptions. He began by starting with the loading of simpler animuses for the Enforcers.

'Something has changed with you,' said Mallon, looking around

the huge hold as she came fully awake, and her support hardware pushed her mind up to higher function. There was little
movement in the hold apart from his and hers. He knew it
would be easier to load the animuses to those in the precursor
hibernation state. Those who were awake might fight it, but
would eventually succumb. They would all become what he
wanted them to be.

'Each of the Old Guard, and some of those not considered of
that creed, will command an army of Enforcers,' he continued.
'There will be subdivisions of command below that. Logistics is
important. We'll have our Engineers, Builders and Medics, those
to hunt down supplies and more besides. Yes, something has
changed.'

She swung back to look at him, and waited.

He continued, 'Here,' he said, and sent her an overview of his
virtual accelerated education, and the methods used. She jerked
and gasped, and he was reminded of when Albermech had sent
data to Castron. He needed to slow it down a lot. She wasn't an
AI, and couldn't integrate as quickly. And he'd found even
Albermech sometimes seemed tardy when Piper detailed his plans.
Was he becoming faster than a Polity AI now? He didn't think
so, but he felt somehow deeper. Or was that arrogance? No,
'deeper' wasn't the correct term. He'd attained breadth, but it lay
in directions aslant to what the likes of Albermech were used to.

'Four years lived in twelve hours!' Mallon exclaimed.

'I think I understand you now,' he said.

Mallon remained distracted, licking her top lip and looking
panicked. He noted a timer ticking down in his mind and decided,
while she digested this initial data, that it was time to send the
specialized battle and logistics animuses to the other Old Guard,
and those of the refugees he'd selected as commanders. The web
of overall strategy would work through them, and then on down

to those below them. He'd thought at first of trying the program on Mallon, to see how well she managed it and how it changed her. But in the end, he decided he'd use these, no matter her response. Time was limited.

'So you understand me,' she said, finally focusing back on him.

'Good people made to do bad things is something I'm quite familiar with now.' He grimaced a smile. 'Not everyone is cut out to be a rebel, and in most it's quelled by the steady attrition of morality by social circumstance.'

'That sounds decidedly trite,' she replied.

'It is, but nonetheless true. The question I really have to ask is if you hate yourself. Answer me honestly now.'

'Yes, I hate myself.' She gestured with one bayonet fitting at the hold. 'Be aware that some here do not, though.'

'And nihilists?'

'Plenty of them.'

'But everyone is capable of change, or being changed.'

Just then it seemed to Piper as if the entire hold had twisted. He felt the wrench in his bones and things around him began to slide into greyness. It lasted but a moment and then snapped back. He felt slightly nauseated and remembered other transitions – different for different people.

'What the hell was that?' Mallon asked.

'We just dropped into U-space. In four hours we'll join up with the Polity attack fleet and then, after a period of preparation, a three-hour journey will take us to our target.'

'Oh,' she said, blinking, her mind seeming to wander. Again she focused. 'Capable of change?'

'Indeed,' he replied, deciding it was time to really see her.

He sent the same animus to her that he'd sent to all the other chosen commanders, and watched. The thing displaced, or absorbed, the one that had been there before. The depth of

282

connection was an order of magnitude higher than it had been with Enforcers back on Founder's World. There he'd controlled the Cyberat, seeking through their extraneous systems to bend them to his will. But he'd not in actuality bent the human minds inside that technology to his will, for they'd continued thinking as before. This time, he was right in, through her hardware, into Mallon herself. While preparing all this earlier, he'd been lost in the technicalities of it, but now the reality began to impinge: he'd be able to read minds. Something within him took an apparently justified delight in this, and he wasn't so sure it was just his reptile.

Again she flinched under the input of data, but she did have the space to take it. She took on her command position over a hundred thousand Enforcers but began to struggle under the data for attack sequences, the likely enemy responses, the links to other commanders concerning logistics, and the command channel to him. He felt a degree of admiration for her as she grappled with it, then began sorting it, apparently understanding it all. And, as expected, he next saw her looking for leeway – seeing how far she might be able to break away from command, from him; that was his trigger to go deeper.

He slid into Mallon's mind, integrating with it as he had with the AI Albermech, becoming it, as he had with the minds of hundreds of others. Emotions impinged and he felt her low current of anger and lingering disbelief about how fast the old regime had been taken down. He felt her loss of power and position, and her self-disgust at having fled the world so quickly. But it had been necessary. She'd done too much to be forgiven and there were plenty who knew she'd enjoyed the power and status. He perceived the lie of her 'good people driven to do bad things' regarding her previous role. He felt the whole of her being looking for a way out, searching for a way not to fight in a war that was none of her business. Hating that this young rebel had been given so much power over her, and wondering how she could kill him, if she dared. In all this, he found confirmation of what his years of experience had told him: many of the Old Guard that had fled up here were the worst of them. They were the ones who knew for certain they'd be punished for heinous crimes, they were the cowards who would not go down fighting, and they were the ones who had become bad by taking the easy road, with no moral integrity. The last dregs of his reservations about what he was doing faded away at this knowledge.

As she dealt with the practical side of the program, the rest of it penetrated her brain. It worked through her Cyberat system, altering neurochem, sparking some neural growth and killing it elsewhere. On unconscious levels, it punished or suppressed thought patterns, shifted memories and perceived them from different perspectives. He felt her self-disgust at fleeing starting to get a grip on things she'd done. With all the brutal methods of prador warfare highlighted and impacting on her thinking, he saw her tilt away from considering the Polity an enemy, and instead begin to focus on the prador as one. This rose from her sudden realization about the extent of the threat humanity as a whole faced from them. And with this, her attitude towards him began to change too. He was a fait accompli, and she could forget about his past now it seemed he'd become a combination of battle computer and general. In fact, he'd become somewhat of a Cyberat ideal.

Piper withdrew, for he didn't need to see more. He next sampled other Old Guard and refugees and observed the animuses working within them. He felt glad it was all performing as he'd designed, but beyond that his feelings were mixed. It was both satisfying and appalling to be twisting these minds to his purpose. And there was the satisfaction of revenge enacted, but also none at all. Again he wasn't sure which arose from him or his reptile. But even then, because he was in no way insulated from the reality of what he was doing, his feelings began to settle into a new shape.

On understanding Mallon and her kind, he'd had no care whether they lived or died, but now they were turning into people who would do the right thing and could be admirable. And he would soon be throwing them into the meat grinder of the Polity–prador war. He did feel some guilt about those who weren't of Mallon's stripe, but comforted himself with the idea that if they were 'good', the animuses wouldn't be forcing them to do things they wouldn't do anyway.

He headed away, leaving Mallon and all the rest to their reprogramming. As he reached the airlock from the hold, he gazed mentally at the Enforcers. Raising them out of hibernation would require the ship's systems kicking in, and resources, but he could bring them part of the way out of it, so their animuses could begin to engage. He didn't expect any problems with them, since they'd all originally gone against the old regime. He doubted he would be changing them much, and they'd rather be returning to some facsimile of their old selves. Exiting through the airlock, he thought back to his recent conversation with Albermech during his usual gym session.

'The morality of this is questionable,' said Albermech.

'You understand that, though some may be "good people driven to do bad things", most by their actions are not,' Piper replied, and went into another squat. The gym was up to three gees now and he was handling it.

'You aim to reprogram the minds of free beings,' said Albermech.

Piper smiled to himself. The AI was merely testing his

resolution and logic. No, not just the AI. Though they were conducting a verbal conversation, he was linked in via the machinery all around him, in essence keeping a finger on Albermech's pulse. He could sense the other mind there, partially amalgamated with Albermech. Corisian was keeping watch too. Although he'd said the Cyberat were now Piper's, the testing and education continued.

'Indeed I do,' he replied. 'In another form, we have had this conversation before. There is no such thing as a free mind, as everyone is programmed by others and their lives. In essence, those Old Guard and refugees were programmed by the old regime and I am merely erasing some of that.'

'Yes, but you are going right into their minds with direct indoctrination, just as the old regime did in its crude fashion with the Enforcers. Do you not have any qualms about this?'

'Didn't you?'

'Yes, I have qualms about what you intend to do,' Albermech replied, deliberately misunderstanding him.

'How long do you want to play this game?' Piper asked. 'You know full well I was referring to how you programmed me, how you indoctrinated me, and have been doing so right from the beginning: Inster's tutelage, the companionship of him and the others, guiding me to that war body, allowing situations because of their effect on me. You put me into battle, and even directed sex my way to check that the hormonal disruption wouldn't be too severe on my thinking. You see me as a weapon and, over other aims, have indoctrinated me to purpose.'

'Some would call that education rather than indoctrination,' the AI humphed.

'Semantics.'

'Do you not feel you have been educated?' Corisian's comment ghosted through.

'Okay, let's get semantic. I was indeed educated by a great deal, but the rage I feel against the prador is not my own and was something you imposed on my mind during the experiences of that temporal virtuality.'

'As far as being human and the evolutionary drives of the same, rage against the prador is a necessary education.'

'I don't disagree, so stop bending my ear about this and measuring my responses. No, I'm not turning into a power-crazed autocrat. What I am doing to the Cyberat aboard this ship is precisely what you did to me. They need to see the enemy clearly, and for that to happen, they need a particular mindset.'

A long pause ensued as Piper continued exercising, and then it was Corisian who said, 'You'll do.'

12

The ship rose from U-space and this time the sensation was like surfacing from a clear cool pool. Piper studied this analogy, knowing that never in his life had he surfaced from a clear cool pool – it was an experience garnered from others. They had reached their rendezvous point with the rest of the Polity fleet – one step closer to their mission on Yannetholm. He strode along the corridor with Inster at his side. The agent gave him an amused look, but had nothing to say. Was school over now? No, because coming here was also part of his education. And anyway, he'd tasted some of what it was like to have lived centuries from those in virtuality, like Corisian, and knew he still had much he could learn from Inster.

'You of course know what lies ahead?' said the agent.

'Of course.'

'Your range now?'

'Out to fifty metres, but I get a lot from the computing, from Albermech, so it's not a hard dividing line.'

'And that reptile inside you?'

'Fully controlled,' Piper replied firmly, and wondered if he'd got the lie past Inster.

'The Cyberat?'

'I'm linked with them all the time now. My commanders and their subordinates have gone from wanting to get the hell out of this ship, off to somewhere safe, to a fanatical desire to apply their war craft to the prador.'

It was a light touch; a delicate balance. The reptile liked what he'd done but he didn't like the emotions the thing engendered. Unchecked, its influence had him seeing this as vengeance enacted and the power to exact further *punishment*, all sitting under a thin skin of justification – a pretence of justice. In response he had powered down his bones and felt its grip on him diminishing. He reckoned their function was now at about a third their present capacity, though that capacity had as yet unplumbed room for expansion, and he would need it later on.

'The grunts?' Inster asked.

'The Enforcers are still rising to consciousness but, as I surmised, my programs are having an effect.' Piper smiled to himself, but this died as he felt reptile approval.

He thought of those erstwhile rebels, for it seemed that was what the bulk of them were – others who were plain criminals having been punished in more terminal and perhaps kinder ways, considering the Enforcers' subsequent lives until now. Even not fully out of hibernation, they were changing quickly.

'Detail this effect.' Inster stopped by a bulkhead door three metres across.

No, school wasn't over.

'They have more mind than was supposed. Free will, intelligence and much in the way of memory was suppressed. Their programs are now shaping them to my purpose, so they still don't have free will, but something curious is happening. The previous suppression of memory and intelligence was a result of them being forcibly indoctrinated to do things completely against their morality – against their will. However, the personality aspects of the loading have unconsciously apprised them of their situation. Now they're being prepared to do things that don't go against their will, and this is freeing up other functions of their minds.'

'A clear enough description of the effect.' The bulkhead door thumped up on seals, then eased out from the wall a little before beginning to slide aside. Inster had sent the aug instruction, just before Piper did. 'What is the corollary of that?'

'Meaning?'

'The Old Guard and the refugees . . .'

'Oh, I see.' Much to his chagrin, Piper did see. 'Repression of *their* free will, conversely, will result in a reduction of intelligence and the suppression of memory. Are you saying that once the imposition of programming is off, they'll return to what they were?'

Inster tapped his aug. 'I'm not saying that. According to Albermech, it's a lot more complicated. According to Corisian "once a shit always a shit".'

'Albermech. Give me data,' said Piper.

As the door finally slid all the way open, exposing the hold within, the feed from Albermech slammed the data home in Piper's bones. He fielded it easily with his current function, resisting the push to increase that function, then took it apart and analysed it in a few seconds. It was complicated, but he honed it down.

'Under their programs, all of them will act precisely as I want. And when I take off the programming, the Enforcers will return to how they were before Cyberat indoctrination.' Piper winced. 'Morally, I mean – there's a lot missing from them. The others will return only some way to what they were via ingrained, formative thinking. That they'll not return completely is a function of the fact that they knew they were doing wrong.'

'Except, of course, for those among them who weren't doing

wrong, like the Engineers you met while they were touring the ship,' said Inster dryly.

'They'll be the same as the Enforcers.' Piper felt defensive.

'Though they were perhaps in no need of motivational programming . . .'

'It's not necessary to remind me.'

'Oh, I think it is. To a certain extent it's good for a general to have a full understanding of his soldiers, their motivations and capabilities. But the same general must not forget they are human.'

'Quite right,' said Piper, stepping through the door. 'Polity agents should remember the same about those they manipulate too.' He glanced back, annoyed to see Inster smiling.

The aisle ahead was just four metres across. The walls on either side rose up ten metres to a ceiling set with light panels. As they stepped inside, grav faded. Once again clad in his suit, Piper engaged gecko function in his boots and continued walking. The walls were decorated with an even scattering of hexagonal protrusions, with screens and various controls on them. They were for manually checking on the occupants. Four thousand of them occupied this cold store – five hundred of the cold coffins having been refilled by marines coming in through Room 101. Four cylindrical coffins behind hexagons had been pulled out at just above floor level. Meersham, Sloan, Geelie and Cheen waited beside them.

'About damned time,' said Meersham.

'He's a busy boy,' said Sloan.

'Not such a boy any more,' commented Geelie.

Piper paced ahead of Inster, saying, 'Is this strictly necessary?'

'It's all about your focus and our focus,' Meersham replied. 'Inster pulled us out for some special missions on Founder's World and then co-opted us into acting as surrogate parents for you. Now it's time for us to get back to where we belong.'

'Surrogate parents and educators,' said Piper sardonically. 'And of course to put a more human face on the Polity than his own manipulative one.'

Meersham grinned at Inster, who grimaced back. It was an act from the agent, who just a second before had been pleased to be named a manipulator.

'A human face?' Cheen looked up after placing his sword in a slide-out drawer in the side of his cold coffin and raised an eyebrow.

'Some machines can be more human than humans,' Piper replied. 'That's one of my many important lessons.'

Geelie walked away from her cylinder straight over to him and caught him up in a hug. She kissed him on the cheek and then deposited him on the floor again. The others followed. Cheen hugged him too.

Meersham punched him on the arm, leaving it numb, and said, 'Going back in hibernation also gets us away from answering loads of "What's been happening?" questions from the rest.' He gestured at the walls of cold coffins. 'Anyway, we'll be with you somewhere in this action.' He turned away and headed over to his coffin.

Sloan shook his hand.

'Careful with the explody stuff,' he said, then looked puzzled because he could think of nothing else to add, so just turned sharply and made for his coffin.

'It won't be a long sleep,' said Meersham cheerfully as he lay back. The lid thumped shut over him and misted slightly. The other lids closed too, taking them all from Piper's sight. He noted that of course Cheen and Geelie didn't need to be there, and probably just switched themselves off or changed their time sense. He watched silently, and in a moment all four cylinders had slid into the wall. That was it: done.

'And you?' Piper asked. 'While we're knocking away my crutches.'

'I'll be around.' Inster gestured at the two walls. 'This lot will be waking up together and preparing together – as Meersham said, it saves our guys being bombarded with questions. And then they'll be following orders as they go into battle. I'm more of a free agent and as we arrive will be focused on the data to design actions.'

'But still, I had to be here to see them taking their road, away from me.' Piper understood the psychology. Though he would insert himself into the Polity battle sphere, he was a general alone now. He needed to accept that there would be no one to clear up his messes and wipe his snotty nose. He had become an adult, in every sense.

'There are other aspects beside the one you have no doubt realized.' Inster, as ever, understood his thoughts. 'We don't want you being protective of them, and they can't really be with you when you're guiding your forces. We saw that on Founder's World and it will be even more pertinent very soon.'

'Because of my machine body.'

'Quite.'

'You said "aspects" – plural.'

'Yes, I did. You need to cease being the outsider to your own people – thirty million of them. Having too many Polity associations blocks that.'

'Are you telling me to make friends, Inster?' Piper asked with a smile.

'Not really. But you need to get a little closer so as to, with any luck, regard your soldiers as more than mere ammunition ready to be expended.'

★ ★ ★

The river, and the girl Amellan, were now familiar territory in his dream world. But since, with this, the memory had returned of what his father did to him, the scene always arrived laden with dread. And it was different again this time. They'd both taken off their footwear and were paddling in the water. He'd done it to please her, but the water scared him, feeling cold and unpleasant, while the stones hurt his feet.

'I don't want to run around on caterpillar treads like your father,' she said.

'He could grav,' he replied, not entirely understanding what the term meant or how to use the word, then looked over towards the dark macula at the edge of his perception.

An Enforcer was there, rising up from behind a pile of boulders, while the landscape shifted to one of burned trees, wrecked machinery and a burning human arm jutting out from a war body, piled into the ground like a wrecked train. The river was suddenly a muddy thing – rust coloured. He targeted the Enforcer instantly, his own war body rising up. The Enforcer was a slab of metal, with weapons arrayed across its upper surface. Piper fired at once, but his opponent fired sooner. The rotogun slugs hammered into his armour, while his particle beam shot went up into the air, dispersing before it reached the heavy yellow clouds. He only discerned that the slugs were armour-piercers as his systems started to go down and the pain began. Under chain-glass, he tilted his head down. He was standing, which seemed odd, then collapsed as his legs folded in bloody and splintered-bone ruination. He shrieked as the pain hit. Seeing a glare through the chain-glass above as he fell, down and down, he felt a strong blast send his war body tumbling.

Piper awoke in a sweat.

He was ready to fight, reaching out for weapons in his war

body and preparing animuses to seize control of the millions of nodes cramming his internal space. He jerked upright, and it seemed his bones rather than his muscles propelled him. The reptile was in him, rabid, and the overlay was armour on his mind. Somehow the thing had shoved up the slide switches from the inside.

'Fuck you!' He smashed a fist down on his leg and the pain enabled him to focus. He scrabbled to bring the function of his bones down again. Anger drove this: anger at the lack of control. It seemed odd that it surely arose from his reptile, yet gave him the strength to suppress it quickly, all adding to his confusion about which emotions were his own. The thing receded and the overlay softened.

He swung his legs out from under the cover and stood. He'd be damned if he would allow this internal dichotomy to interfere further. As before, he got out of bed and went through a morning routine, though there were really no mornings aboard the *Albermech*. He felt balanced and in control by the time he took the toothbot out of his mouth and put it back in its sanitizer. His mind now groped for memories to attach to the nightmare and, through having experienced four years of combat, he found them all. He, or rather those whose lives he'd inhabited, had on many occasions lost limbs, and he'd seen plenty of blasted landscapes like that one. Again he told himself this was the non-logic of his subconscious. He recalled many dreams and nightmares from his youth that had made little sense. Or rather, they had a kind of structure imposed over them at the point of waking to give them whatever sense they had. However, he couldn't feel the truth of this explanation. It felt too much like a rationalization.

He returned to his bed, angry reptile subdued, and focused on the dregs of the nightmare. He then carefully, in a nuanced fashion, adjusted the sliders on his bones. The controls the Room 101 AI had installed in him were decidedly more complex than the on–off switch claimed. In processing, he began to connect those fragments to memory, whether his own or others he'd experienced. He then found even more matches to the nightmare, like the burned trees and one of a soldier standing up in a grav-tank when it was hit by a laser that sliced his legs away. The process calmed him, and acceptance grew that this was all about the workings of his unconscious. He drifted into another brief sleep, without nightmares, and came out of it refreshed and logical. Weird nightmares of war were not unexpected. He had to remember that, despite all his power and control, anxiety and fear were certain. It was time to put the now faded images in his mind to one side, and get back to the moment, damn it!

Sitting upright, Piper extended his range right to the skin of the *Albermech*, which lay a kilometre from his cabin, but in a narrow cylinder of perception so he didn't take in so much of the ship. Thousands of nodes reformed in his internal space, while the reptile within of course took notice. He yet again assessed this unwelcome occupant of his bones and noted that it seemed to have become larger and more defined, more substantial. Perhaps this had something to do with his nightmares, though he couldn't know what was cause and what was effect. Having more control of his entire system now through the switches Room 101 had provided, he could see how much processing space the thing was using. Though scattered in a physical sense, this processing added up close to AI potential itself. Worryingly, it was approaching a Turing threshold.

'Be calm,' he told it. 'We're not fighting yet.'

He felt the intensity of its inspection, primitive calculation, and then a wash of its anger threaded through with loss. These didn't affect him much, because in becoming clearer to him, it had also separated out from him. As he focused outwards, he pushed it back from him, from influencing him, and it became watchful, then confused, but with some hard purpose running through it.

With his perception now at the ship's hull, he took data from a multitude of sensors and looked beyond at the fleet. The sight was a dazzling, impressive one that his old self would have had trouble understanding, but he comprehended it all perfectly. Thousands of ships were scattered through a huge volume of space, and in places they were starting to build up formations. Squid-form and older, blockier attack ships swarmed around dreadnoughts like the *Albermech*. He gazed upon a dreadnought that went under the name of *Organ Transplant*, because it looked like a huge metallized liver. That too was an old vessel, built when resources were available to cater for the peccadilloes of its AI. But sleeker, more dangerous things were out there too, and Piper understood they were heavily clad in armour reverse-engineered from prador metallurgy. For the Polity now had its own nigh-indestructible dreadnoughts. Groups of destroyers shoaled through them all. These were long and fast, and most resembled old-style bullets, or in some cases submarines. Their firepower sat midway between the dreadnoughts and the attack ships.

'What's that?' he asked, seeing something new.

'The big guns.' Corisian surprised him by replying through the Albermech link.

The three rings, each a kilometre across, were scattered through the fleet. Heavy tugs were attached around each, while he could see U-space nacelles protruding from the rings themselves. He knew what he was looking at and had simply been making conversation – hanging onto a semblance of humanity.

The rings were war runcibles. These devices were the primary form of transport in the Polity, making tunnels through U-space to take citizens from world to world in a virtual instant. Here they served another function. Planetary runcibles had their buffers and heat sinks deposited in oceans, to drain off the energy of transport, ensuring those transported wouldn't exit as photonic matter. Feeding matter through a runcible without buffering essentially resulted in a massive particle beam. That was a useful weapon but, apparently, slowing said matter down resulted in a better one.

'Relativistic asteroids,' he said.

'Wrong,' Corisian replied.

'What?'

'You got history from Albermech and not current weapons development, which, understandably, is kept under wraps. Chucking asteroids at them was what we did earlier in the war. We now have it so the object we put through, unbuffered, doesn't string out into a particle beam. It's a relativistic particle pulse now.'

'Oh, I see.' As much as his knowledge and experience had grown, Piper still found the capacity to be appalled. This was a weapon capable of destroying worlds, yet the horrifying thing was that something of such power was required to destroy prador ships. He analysed the data Corisian presented, along with attached strategies. It was still difficult to move and aim such weapons, and they could only fire limited shots before they started to come apart. Building them also used up a huge amount of resources. But that 'limited shots' impinged, since at the beginning of the war they'd been one-shot weapons. He imagined future developments, and a Polity capable of unlimited shots, simply annihilating every prador world in their Kingdom. He also speculated briefly on astronomical phenomena beyond the

Milky Way galaxy, of strange gaps and other areas where suns seemed to be surrounded by nothing but rubble.

'Anyway,' said Corisian. 'It seems your hardware is ready. Final components delivered by *Organ Transplant* have been fitted.'

Piper gave him a mental nod and withdrew, bringing the centre of his perception back into his cabin. Even though that centre point did return, it was just a mental phenomenon for the comfort of his human brain. He didn't actually cut down his range, still seeing the ships out there, and he ran a subprogram to apprise him of anything new. Otherwise he could still *see* and, if he so chose, interact with or control machinery and computing all around him. He could talk to Albermech, Corisian and Inster too – those being the only Polity citizens now conscious aboard this ship . . . Piper paused, considering his train of thought. The three had been right to say he needed to focus more on his soldiers as people. He felt he had little company aboard the *Albermech*, yet here he was amidst thirty million Cyberat. He abruptly expanded processing and, via his multitude of links, sent out widely the view of the fleet, along with his exchange with Albermech.

'As you have seen, with your battle sphere loading, we are part of a major attack on the prador,' he said. It felt weak, but it was a conversation starter at least. Tens of thousands of replies came through to him. At the same time the Cyberat linked to each other and the quantity of conversations amidst them rose by an order of magnitude from where it'd been before. Mental activity amidst the Enforcers also increased. But, since they weren't really conscious yet, theirs was just a random murmur across their minds. He identified eighty-seven Mallons, nine hundred different Breens, and nearly two thousand Fusiers. Refining the search on the latter two, he got the ones he wanted, while his link to the Mallon he knew was clear. It seemed a good selection: Mallon was a top commander, Fusier mid-level and Breen an Engineering grunt. He linked them together and to himself, then made their exchange open for all the rest to hear, but cut the ability of others to interject. The three became instantly aware of the link, and it was Breen who spoke first.

'Those runcible weapons have a limited life in the battle plan, yet they're controlled by AIs,' he stated. 'As is all U-space technology.' The last was a reference to their previous conversation in the corridor.

'Most AIs in ships and weapons like that have fast ejection routines,' Piper replied.

'Fast enough?' Fusier wondered.

'Fifty–fifty,' replied Breen. 'Not odds I would like.'

'Is an AI life of greater value than a human one?' asked Mallon. 'I know they are considered citizens, but with their ability to copy themselves . . . it all seems a bit murky.'

'Humans in the Polity are capable of the same now,' said Piper, remembering a cliff face decorated with human corpses and the robots collecting memplants. 'It's new technology and not generally used as yet, but it's there.'

'Would I be the same person if I was brought back?' Fusier asked.

'We are not the same people from day to day,' replied Mallon. 'I am certainly not the same person I was a number of days ago.'

Piper grimaced at that. He'd launched his animuses into them to change their minds, and obviously some were aware of that. The conversation rambled on and, even though he tried, he began to lose interest in it, while seeing it reflected hundreds of times amidst other Cyberat. He brought up software in respect of all of this and began to interact across a wider spread – aware of the replies he made, rhetorical questions he asked and his interjections which, on the whole, were educational.

Patterns repeated throughout and they reflected those he'd seen throughout his four years in virtuality. He felt bored and superior, and could see the danger in that, then wondered if this was how a two-hundred-year-old man like Inster felt. As his thinking strayed to the man, he found him.

Through an internal cam, he spied Inster heading in his direction. The man paused with his fingers up against his aug, smiled and shrugged, then looked up to the cam, raising a hand and crooking a finger at it. He turned to go back the way he'd come. It was a salutary reminder that everything Piper did in the realm of information was monitored. He stood up, dropping his perception of the talk amidst the Cyberat to a lower level, but still allowing his responses to continue.

'You could have called me,' he said to Inster via his virtual aug.

'I look for opportunities not to use my aug.'

'Yet you just did when you discovered I was viewing you through the cam system.'

'That was just an alert set to inform me about you using ship systems.'

'So why do you look for opportunities not to use it?'

'The same thesis applies as in pre-Quiet War years of technological addiction, though with some provisos. I take the opportunity not to use my aug whenever possible, so as to be ready for any time it becomes unavailable. Also because breadth of experience is worthwhile in my estimation. Consider this another nugget of wisdom: you don't want to end up so lost in your power and omniscience that you forget how to take a shit.'

'I see . . . how repetitive and boring do you find people, Inster?' he asked, heading for the door, disconnecting from the ship's exterior sensors, then steadily bringing his range down and down.

'Consider what I just said.'

Piper did and he saw the connection.

'Voices in the dark.'

'Exactly. The more technology we put between ourselves and those we communicate with, the more we dehumanize them . . . presupposing they are human.'

'It's almost as if you've been spying on me.'

'I don't have to – I know precisely how it will be for you. You're seeking more connection because you've understood you mustn't dehumanize your soldiers. But now, in seeking connection after the changes you have undergone, you're finding it weak, and that the people really are quite simple mechanisms.'

'Suggestions?'

'Do your best. It's what I do, though the danger of greater knowledge is recognition of patterns and types, and boredom with the same.'

Piper shrugged at that, muting the Cyberat conversation to a constant murmur in the back of his mind. He continued bringing down the range of his perception into technology around him until, out in the corridor, he stopped it at ten metres, reconsidered and brought it right down to nothing. The reptile chose to respond as it writhed and snarled itself into strong contrast, such was its annoyance at the drop in input. He traced it, traced its outline, and defined it more clearly, to which it responded again with a frenzy of anger that sent a sickening surge of the same into his mind. He staggered, resting a hand against one wall. He then focused on his nanosuite to bring down this organic response and, as calm began to return, switched off his bones fully.

Why had the thing behaved like that? He felt slow thinking about the matter without his additional processing, but finally he got there. Its response had been against the threat to itself. In defining it as he had, he'd raised the possibility that he could reject it. He walked on, now thinking about where he was going and suddenly realizing he was no longer sure. Not having his usual three-dimensional map of the ship, as his reach to surrounding systems was integral to that, he didn't know where to go.

'Inster, send me a map,' he said.

Inster was waiting in the corridor, leaning back against one wall with his arms folded. As soon as Piper approached, he pushed away and went through a wide opening in the wall opposite him. Piper followed, entering a large room whose floor space was almost completely occupied by one object. This was presently linked to ship's systems by many feed tubes, skeins of optics, and wires that disappeared into the walls. Doors to an exit tunnel lay behind it.

'I thought my war body was being upgraded,' Piper stated.

Inster waved at the object. 'It started out that way but all the additions required a redesign.'

The machine now looked more like a prador carapace than it had before, only for a much larger prador than even some of the ancient adults. It had the manta wings as the sides and, standing up off the floor on thick-stemmed landing feet, it bore the appearance of such a creature sinking into a swamp. However, weapons were exposed between those feet. Piper recognized a nice selection, including a railgun, a laser, a particle cannon and two rotoguns. Its surface armour also had closed-off ports that probably sat over missile launchers. At the top and to the fore, rather than the usual chain-glass bubble, stood a protrusion like a prador head turret, even down to the eyes. A roughened area ran up from one wing to it, but otherwise the whole machine was of burnished blue metal.

Studying the war body, Piper supposed he should be thankful

that they'd not installed mandibles and claws. He had no doubt a psychological motive lay behind making the thing look like this, but at that moment his own reaction interested him more. At first sight of it, he'd felt betrayal, since they'd significantly changed something over which he felt ownership. Despite his bones being shut down, he soon felt an ache in them and slight pain in his fingers. He checked himself via his nanosuite and detected no activation, then registered the psychosomatic reaction. He dismissed his feeling of betrayal.

'So what has it got?' he asked.

'You don't know?' Inster queried.

'I'm shut down at the moment.'

'But your virtual aug must still be online.'

'Indeed, but tell me about this thing – apparently the breadth of experience will be good for me.'

Inster smiled at the reference to their previous exchange, but Piper guessed also because the man had been given leave to talk about his favourite subject. 'Two rotoguns, as you call them on Founder's World, but miniguns or Gatling cannons as we call them, depending on who's wielding them. Odd the choices made in description, but there you have it. Coil-accelerated ammunition of numerous iterations. You have armour-piercers that will puncture prador armour, fragmentation shells, soft metal impactors, and all with numerous variations of explosive load. Two ten-thousand-round boxes that slot in straight underneath when you want resupply. The particle cannon is standard for a war drone, so it's powerful. The laser is cross-spectrum and capable of informational warfare. The railgun is a recent addition, seriously power hungry and, though it will punch through prador ship armour, you'll need to make sure nothing is behind you.'

'Recoil?'

'Yup. Floating in the air it will throw you back a couple of kilometres. I was a bit doubtful about Corisian wanting to include it, but tactically it's quite useful. You'll be in trouble if you ever have to fire on a ship, and getting away fast will be a good idea.'

'The battle plan is for no ships down there,' Piper noted.

'I don't have to tell you about battle plans.'

'They don't survive first contact with the enemy.'

Inster pointed up at the body. 'There you've got missile launchers. Again a variety of loads and they're sub-AI. You also have a single hardfield projector you could use to stabilize when firing the railgun. But really, all this being handy, you should be deploying your troops so you don't end up in any desperate action.'

'Because the main weapon is inside,' said Piper.

'Yes, that being you. The war body also has a similar substrate to what's in your bones, loaded with Cyberat coding and familiar forms of storage.' He paused thoughtfully for a moment, then added, 'Though not exactly the same substrate – apparently we still have no idea how to make *that*.'

Piper felt a flash of pride in his father, then stepped forwards and rested a hand down on the metal, remembering the first time he'd done this with the previous version of this war body. It was just slick metal, and the psychosomatic ache began to fade.

'You'll need time to get accustomed to it.' The agent waved up towards the turret.

Piper just stared at the thing, reluctant to activate his bones after so recently shutting them down. He shook himself, annoyed at that. Avoiding something didn't make it any easier. Anyway, he'd been accustoming himself to this, so he eased over the slide switches. The space opened in his mind and filled with nodes for the machines surrounding him. And, of course, his angry reptile brought itself into focus – the overlay spreading almost possessively. The node for the war body stood out and he peeled it open in an instant, seeing all Inster had told him and exploring more.

'So, no need for you sitting beside me with a thin gun any more,' he said.

The cockpit had revealed itself to him, with just one seat inside, surrounded by a multitude of controls. He ran through the internal format, seeing parts of his old war body distributed throughout, almost like a ghost of this thing's past. He noted *two* fusion reactors and a mass of laminar storage. The processing substrate was a dual dark shadow – inert until such a time as he hard-linked.

'Not needed, and I'm not sure I would be effective like that any more.'

Piper stepped up onto the wing. Inster was right. That last time he'd given the man a headache through his aug, but now he knew he could run a program through it and *change* his mind, just as he was presently doing with the Cyberat. The knowledge came as a brief shock, quickly passing.

'You have plenty of time,' said the agent. 'I'll leave you to prepare and to . . . do what you do.'

Piper looked round at the man as he headed for the door. Inster paused there, gave him a fist salute and departed. Even though he could see the agent walking off down the corridor and, if he so wished, track him through the ship, this might be the last time he saw him with his human eyes. The thought came with some weight he'd not felt on Founder's World, and it seemed important. He really knew about warfare now. He knew about life and death. And he knew that the prador would be no walkover – they were vicious aliens with a technology only now dropping behind that of the Polity. He climbed up, opening the turret ahead of him with a thought, and gazed in at the familiar seat, then stepped down and slid into it. He had the manual controls, as installed in the previous iteration of the war body, but they were of no concern to him right now. As he brought his hands down above the interface pads on the armrests, he just knew that his eyes would now be a lemon shade of yellow, and that something perhaps as vicious as the prador was peering through them.

He brought his hands down.

It was different this time, and the same. Weapons became extensions of his limbs, and of limbs he didn't possess. Sensors became extensions of his senses, while he was still present with those of his body, in the cockpit, as the turret-shaped lid closed down. The lid then seemed to dissolve as screen paint on the inner face rendered it apparently transparent. Already feeling his way into the system, he at once found an option similar to the one he'd used through his HUD when they'd been in the car going to Castron's villa. Screen paint extended down around and below him, and he could turn it on, so it would feel as though he was floating through the air in a chair, with controls before him. He considered the option and rejected it, instead turning on sections and programming the visual display. This gave him a view of the weapons, interior systems and windows to the exterior. This was just playing with what had been provided. Installing himself into this hard and simple technology was as easy as breathing. Still, in his perception, the war body's substrate loomed like two shadowy lobes of some dual brain. He realized he had paused connection to it while encompassing the rest, the familiar. So now he linked in.

At once his range expanded to take in the entirety of the

Albermech, with tens of thousands of nodes establishing instantly. Beyond the vessel, it began to incorporate other vessels with sudden blooms of new nodes. He quickly halted the expansion and drew it back into a sphere containing only the dreadnought and its hold cylinders filled with Cyberat.

His soldiers were a great mass of nodes, mixed in with those of the ship itself. Searching for control programs, or putting new ones together, was fast and easy – both in him and in the extension of himself in the war body. Since he'd already sent animuses and programming to all the Cyberat, it was a simple task to run something to separate their nodes from the rest, which he then banished to a compressed file. Focusing, he ordered the Cyberat nodes in virtual position, so he could easily identify his commanders and those designated for tasks beyond fighting. He mapped over the command structure and queued up battle plans in order of likelihood. Next he keyed into the Polity battle sphere and slotted into it. He could perceive the whole easily, yet such perception hadn't distanced him from its size and complexity. Even so, he now began to add an overlay, so that nodes actually became Cyberat, while the battle plan gave him the shape of ships and their names.

Piper simply sat there experiencing it. This truly was an omniscient view, and he wondered if it would be better for him to confine himself to just his part of the whole. However, he could see the utility of this wider view, for he would be able to respond to changes elsewhere that would ultimately affect him and his troops. Was he right? That was something he'd find out as soon as battle was joined and the battle sphere became more complex. He decided to test this by running scenarios that had already been incorporated. Anger and excitement rose as the thing in his bones failed to distinguish between virtual and real combat. It didn't hinder him, rather it opened up more processing speed.

But it concerned him that his reptile seemed to be spreading into the war body, processing and getting a grip there.

'Easy there,' he said. 'This isn't real.'

He ended the first battle scenario with victory, and then started another. In doing this it seemed the reptile had begun to comprehend. Processing speed didn't go down, but he did notice something else: the thing, in understanding, had moved closer to one Turing limit. It had become more distinct, as it had before, and as a consequence seemed even looser in his bones, more separate from him. He observed it as he ran more possible battles. Its reach into the war body substrate increased, as if it wanted to control more, though its control was only an influence on his emotions. Now, since it had *moved*, he began to focus on it. As he had done once before, he created a node encompassing his own system. With more control of that internal space, he then opened a compartment in it and shifted the node there. He next opened it out and started etching out finer detail, highlighting those areas of processing and connections which made up the beast.

The reptile was so large and so integral, he found himself struggling to encompass it all, but he persevered. Much of it, he found, not only spread through his bones and into that other substrate, but was linked up through internal interfaces into his own brain. He traced its connection to those systems of his brain involved in emotion and memory. It became apparent that it mainly had its virtual claws into his subconscious. In those interfaces, he began severing connections. At first he found this diminished his perception of the thing, so instead he returned to defining where it was as perfectly as he could. This seemed to take a virtual age, but when he checked real time, he'd only been in the war body for a few hours. Having done the best he could, he returned to severing interface connections to it. Once he was through about half of them, he sensed a psychological tightness relaxing as the thing sank out of him. He felt strangely happy – in fact a little drunk on the sensation. He also felt something was missing. When he inspected himself, visualizing his mental function, he could no longer see any sign of that constant low current of anger.

The realization dispelled the euphoria. He had to be rid of this thing! How long it had been influencing him he had no idea – perhaps right from the start when his father filled his bones with this substrate. He ran through all the ways he might free himself of it. He tried deleting part of it, but found it immediately copying to another point in the process. It was comparable to informational warfare – all the viruses and worms of comlife. He tried severing connections in its processing spaces, but they re-established via different routes. He noted how it writhed in discomfort at that too. But he'd gathered a great deal of data on it now, and thought there might be a way.

The thing had been consolidating and was still doing so. Instead of cutting its connections, which in some way resembled a nervous system, he began squeezing it. He did this by limiting its processing space in those areas where it resided, gently and not wanting to alert it any further. Success came an instant later as it transferred some of that processing into the war body substrate. He kept running the virtual battles to keep it distracted and, occasionally, when it showed confusion or snarled at the nebulous threat, he changed the battles, dropping something into the unlikely scenarios. This was no longer about learning to use the war body, but about freeing himself of the reptile. There was a solution within his grasp here – move the whole thing over to the war body! He could see later problems, because he would have to use this machine, but right now he wanted to exert influence and to have control.

310

He kept squeezing, and the reptile kept moving more and more of itself into the war body substrate. Hours passed and his human body ached with tension, having become slick with sweat. Areas of processing faded, copied across to the other substrate, and connecting links went out. He had more than eighty per cent of it out of his bones when it started to dawn on him that something was wrong. The virtual battles had become chaotic and blurred, while his perception of the battle sphere had narrowed. Pulling back, he saw his internal perception had collapsed with his focus entirely on the beast. Nodes had disappeared, and when he tried to take telemetry from his soldiers, very little arrived. He decided to test this further, trying to pull up programming to send to their animuses, but that facility strayed from his grasp. He halted the current virtual battle, dismissing it, then studied himself internally and felt leaden in his guts.

Great gaps had appeared, abilities had diminished, and clarity had waned. The reptile was far too integral to his bones to be so easily dismissed. The thing actually consisted of his stored data, and programs for animuses were its cellular structure – it bound all of this together in a totality. To be rid of it he would have to rid himself of all his abilities. Certainly they could be restored, since the substrate in his bones was a physical thing that wouldn't go away, but removing the reptile would be like passing a magnet over some pre-Quiet War computer drive.

Wearily, Piper admitted defeat and took the pressure off, opening himself to the war body substrate to which he'd been trying to confine the thing. The reptile immediately snapped back into him, establishing itself fully into his bones again. It seemed to do it with angry disregard, slamming home and setting his head aching, shoving his body temperature up too. He gritted his teeth, wondering what damage he would find, but then his

311

internal space opened out and all his programs became available again. The reptile continued to shift about, as if making itself comfortable, but he was back to the function he'd had before this attempt. He sighed, waiting for things to settle, then disconnected. As the threads retreated into his hands, he raised them from the war body's chair arms. Having double-checked again that everything seemed to be as before, he then shut down his bones.

13

Again the river and the girl, as if these scenes were an entry point into somebody else's world. On some level he was aware of this being a dream, as confused bright, sunlit childhood slid into something else. Now the boy and the girl by the stream were being observed by something dark, vast and complicated. It seemed to be the mind of Room 101 that had instigated these dreams, and yet it also seemed to be his own.

Piper, from the perspective of another, observed the two from a great height and then swung away, next occupying a large baroque grav-car which descended to land on the pad extended from a Cyberat factory complex. Jumbled imagery ensued, of endless machines at work and the codes of control. He moved through the machine darkness, bitter and angry. Engineer Cyberat scuttled out of his path, babbling explanations as he turned and went through a large sliding door. Here was a laboratory, and Piper winced at the sight of the frame that had secured him for agonizing surgery behind the glass of a clean room towards the back. He looked around at the wrecked equipment, overturned tables and looted data stacks. Stolen, stolen, stolen . . .

In the role he occupied it wasn't hard to demonstrate anger and distress visibly, for they'd been his companions for a long time. He kept locked tight inside his expectation of this, and how he'd left only enough for them to steal and be satisfied. The real work would continue elsewhere.

Piper woke abruptly and sat upright, cabin lights coming on. Swinging his legs over the side of his bed, he sat there waiting. He knew without doubt what had snapped him out of the dream. And he knew what was about to happen, then it did. Again he felt nauseated, and as if the world was twisting and greying out around him. Would it always be this way for him when aboard a ship entering U-space? Would he find a cool pool at the other end? No, he would find destruction and death.

He stood up and stripped off his suit – heading for the shower. As he'd discovered, the suit, now lying on his bed, would clean and sanitize itself in the interim. Back in the cabin, he got coffee from the fabricator and a large breakfast. Both he enjoyed thoroughly, for there was no more need for him to become accustomed to this Polity food.

Three hours . . .

Piper stood up from the remains of his meal, coming to a decision. He picked up the vacuum combat suit and hung it in the wardrobe, then took out the second suit – the heavy one with sanitary attachments, pipe sockets and interfaces all over it. He put it on. It was just as comfortable and he hardly noticed the catheters going in, nor did he feel its extra weight as it powered up. As he auglinked to it, he noticed two comlink requests and opened them.

'So, how are you this morning?' asked Corisian – his comlink was distinct from that of Albermech this time.

'Considering your failure to eject your reptile,' Albermech added.

'I'm okay,' Piper replied.

'You seem to be in a strange mood,' Albermech observed.

'How can you know that?'

'Bleed-through,' the AI replied. 'You made a virtual aug and we are apparently communicating by voice only, but more comes through.'

'So I didn't do a good job with my virtual aug?'

'On the contrary, it's a perfect copy. Augcom is always like this from the perspective of an AI communicating with a human. Human to human the bleed-through is undetectable, unless they choose to make it so and ramp up bandwidth.'

'That's interesting,' said Piper, somewhat uninterested.

'And your reply to my initial question?' Corisian asked.

'I dreamed again, and it was odd. The dreams in their present format only started after Room 101 fucked with my mind. I would like to believe they're trying to tell me something, but wonder if all they are telling me is that I'm stuck with this thing in my bones and must learn to live with it.'

'So acceptance, then,' said Albermech.

'No, not in the least.' He drank more coffee then asked, 'What is Inster doing right now?'

'Designing missions, or sleeping, or training. I don't know. He left the ship before we jumped and is aboard *Organ Transplant*. He will arrive at Yannetholm at the same time we do, along with the rest of the fleet.'

Piper nodded, but now, even though Corisian and Albermech were just a thought away, he felt abruptly alone again. The loneliness of command, he thought again, and knew this was intentional. School was over.

'Well, I hope he has a good war, but now I need time to think,' he said.

The two connections went off abruptly as he headed to his door and out. He did feel odd and considered this a direct result of the strange course his last dream had taken him on. He wondered whether to take the thing apart and search for comparisons in his virtuality memories again, but that no longer felt right. Despite what he'd said to Albermech and Corisian about the dreams, he really did think there was a message there. He began to think really hard about the transition from the girl by the river into all the rest. With angry acceptance, he opened up the slide switch on his bones, while limiting his range to zero. The reptile rose predictably into position, with no division discernible between its anger and his own. But clarity came with the overlay, along with access to the vast complexity of his programming tools. He now tried something new, bringing those nightmare memories into his internal space for inspection and analysis as he walked. He explored the nightmares, and it soon became evident that in all but one, after moving on from the river, he'd been somebody else. He inspected closely the one memory of him lying in a frame, with his father carving him open to install the substrate in his bones. Even this memory, he now saw, had a variable perspective. He didn't know whether he was holding the knife or being cut by it, whether he was the subject of all those instruments or the one controlling them. He delved deeper into the memory and felt the bright fractal flashes of connection and expanding code.

Of course . . .

Piper halted, realizing his wanderings had brought him to the corridor running around the ends of the hold tubes. It had all been so obvious and yet he'd denied it. His father had put the substrate into his bones and programmed it. To do that, he'd been connected mentally through his hardware. Doge had felt Piper's pain because he had been so intimately tangled up with him. He now knew the source of his nightmares. Something of his father had copied across: his anger at the Old Guard and Castron specifically, his feelings of loss for his human body and perhaps other things besides. It wasn't some aspect of Piper's subconscious that snarled at the world, for it had memories that were not his own.

'I wonder if you knew, Father,' he said.

The thing residing in Piper's bones was, in some part, his father.

Piper halted in front of the airlock and prepared himself. He opened out the range of his perception, nodes proliferating. His internal grid encompassed the ship and the Cyberat, and then it went out into something else and completely lost its boundaries. It became infinite and yet, at the same time, it became a singularity. His mind screamed under the disparity and his bones physically vibrated as the reptile responded by raising animuses and related attack programs. Perception changed, so all surrounding matter became holes curving round and feeding back into themselves. Endless masses of things fed themselves into existence, and yet logically didn't exist. It was too much. This was his first glimpse of U-space via this perception. He pulled back abruptly, shaping his range at the last, until he encompassed only what lay inside the U-field. The reptile withdrew its animuses and he felt its confusion, but still it remained clawed throughout his body, or his consciousness – he couldn't distinguish.

'Fuck,' he said, leaning against the side of the airlock. He took a steadying breath and focused on what he had encompassed, and rationality. He raised the programming he'd used while connected to the war body substrate. All the nodes of the *Albermech* were irrelevant to him, and he again compressed them into a file, out of the way. The others packed his internal space like sand in a jar: thirty million of them. They honed down into the command structure, from which he excluded the Enforcers to concentrate on his commanders. Even these were a larger number of nodes than he'd dealt with before, using just his bones. But he worked them, the structure taking on the fractal nature of his processing even as it opened up more of the same. Then he went through the airlock.

Within the hold containing the bulk of the Old Guard and refugees, he paused. Why was he here? Anything he might need to do didn't actually require his physical presence. However, he acknowledged a vague human need to inspect his troops, and its genesis from the concerns of Inster, Albermech and Corisian. Using suit impellers, he propelled himself down the aisle where he'd found Mallon each time. As he travelled, he saw just a few Cyberat on the move, and those were now heading back to their machine bodies. They didn't need him to tell them that very soon they'd be going into battle. A brief inspection by him on the virtual level showed them still in the process of accommodating the programming he'd given them – distinct mentalities in the grip of his animuses. He finally came before Mallon and grabbed hold of the frame holding her war body in place. She had her arms folded, bayonet fitting protruding, and her head was bowed. She raised it a second later.

'Why are you here?' she asked.

'Inspecting the troops,' he replied.

'You'll see no more by being physically present.' She tracked his thoughts on that then added, 'Other than perhaps external expressions of internal pain.'

Belatedly, Piper did find a semi-logical reason for being in the hold.

'And what is that pain?' he asked, while decompressing the ship file and sorting through it. Even before she replied, he had the schematic, codes and ability to control the hold cylinders and related systems.

'I inspect my past and see that I was not a good person,' she replied, unfolding her arms. 'Before, I had convinced myself I was. This is your doing, isn't it?'

'Indeed.'

The holds, around the *Albermech*, lay against each other, and huge loading doors opened from each to each at those points. He overlaid on this a schematic of his command structure. At present, the bulk of the Enforcers were in the other cylinders, while the majority of his commanders were here. He needed to change that and to redistribute them. The logistics of the operation were complicated, but he'd already worked with models of much more complex tasks. He would move commanders, related subordinates and supplies out of this hold and into others, while bringing Enforcers from them into here to make room. Mapping the operation, he soon found that, though he'd assigned commanders to particular groups of Enforcers in each hold, for this operation it would be easier to reassign many of them rather than move them into proximity with each other. It didn't matter. The Enforcers were interchangeable. It was an uncomfortable thought.

'I try to find anger at you, but I cannot, yet,' said Mallon. 'I am only angry at the prador for the terrible things they've done.'

'I know.'

The Enforcers would be harder to move than the rest. They were still in semi-hibernation – not conscious – so he designed programs to install in their hardware to move them. Meanwhile, he opened those doors. The hold rumbled and a wind began blowing through, bringing the chill of the Enforcer holds.

'What's that?'

'You need to be with your troops.'

'Oh, of course.'

He gazed at her, not liking her responses. She didn't seem quite as sharp as before. Had he really done the right thing in

319

reprogramming her mind? The question seemed weak, being underscored with reptile satisfaction; it was too late to change it now anyway. Only a couple of hours remained until they would arrive at the Yannetholm system. He sent movement orders to all the Old Guard and refugees, and freed up their motive power. Further down the hold, huge war bodies began easing out of the racks. Far down at the end, Enforcers began to appear in neat lines. Mallon's war body shifted and he pushed away from the frame.

'I feel I should say a lot more,' she told him.

Her war body slid out and turned. Noting bodies emerging, back along the aisle where he'd come in, he pushed off in that direction, not bothering to answer her. He floated past refugee bodies. Some were slabs loaded with tool arms and other manufacturing capability – Engineers, Builders, Medics and a scattering of other castes. Others were conglomerations of materials, tanks, or carried loads of metals and composites. As he well knew, there was more to warfare than mere guns.

'Perhaps we'll talk again,' Mallon called.

He looked back. Neat lines and block assemblies of Cyberat were moving about the hold, following patterns that matched those he'd made in his mind. There was nothing human about this. It was all just far too accurate. He reached the corridor at the end, having to navigate past a line of Enforcers sliding in, their human components dewed with cold moisture. He'd wasted time here, and he had little to spare, with other more critical preparations to make. Again he thought of how he could have done this from afar, from his war body. Yet, as he left the hold, he didn't *feel* he had wasted time, but had instead ticked an emotional box in his itinerary. He headed back to his cabin to tick another one.

★　★　★

One hour to go . . .

Piper looked around his cabin, wondering if this would be the last time he saw it, then opened a cupboard and took out weapons that had been left there for him: a disruptor, a pulse sidearm and a bandolier. He smiled, wondering if Sloan had put together this collection of grenades, other explosives and decoders. It seemed an excessive precaution to take these, considering the other weaponry he would control and surround himself with. But there was always the possibility that he might end up crashed on an alien world. He headed for the door and out.

'I have nothing further to tell you,' said Albermech when he opened the two comlinks available.

'But we wish you the best of luck,' Corisian added.

'And the best of luck to you both,' he replied.

The battle plan was clear in his mind, as was his position in it, and would soon enough be even clearer. He knew what was predicted to happen, all the many possible scenarios, and understood enough of the underlying philosophy of the war to know what to do if things slid into the impossible, or in some other way went completely wrong. Most likely what he would do then was die. But questions remained.

'Did you know?' he asked.

'Did I know what?' Albermech asked.

'That the thing residing in my bones is my father?'

'Kalaidon told me about it,' the AI replied blithely.

'Yet you didn't tell me.' Only now did Piper remember the Jain expert AI's first words: '*Talk about burying yourself in your work.*'

'I did not tell you because it's something you had to find your own accommodation with. Incidentally, it's not your father, but his shadow, his ghost, if you like. While he installed your hardware and programmed it, it was those parts of his mind he did not control that copied across. It *is* a reptile mind, just not yours.'

Piper nodded to himself – this he had already understood.

He reached the door Inster had first brought him to, snapped a node out of the *Albermech*'s collapsed file and opened it. Even as he did so, he felt a brief connection with the ship AI entire, as it drew away. Albermech had been about to open the door for him, but he'd been faster. He walked inside and stood facing his war body.

'And still your rationale as to why you didn't tell me isn't clear,' Piper said.

'Very well . . . It was better for you to be in conflict with it, which might not have been the case had you known its source. And knowing its source, you might well have integrated it fully, along with its motives.'

'But you wanted a soldier in your war, and not one whose motives are hatred of Castron, loss of his humanity and a complete focus on the situation on Founder's World.'

'Precisely.'

'And now, through indoctrination, you have that soldier – one with his motives laid down by the lives of others.'

'I don't like that word. You have been educated in accordance with your evolutionary drives to hate an enemy who would destroy us all. You have also gained the strength to face down your . . . father.'

'I like it that you tell me the truth now.'

'Good. You are realistic,' Albermech replied, as Piper stepped up onto the war body. Then added, 'And realistically, maybe when this battle is over, you will be able to see the content of your nightmares for what it is, and rise to a higher level of understanding.'

'Indeed,' Piper replied, acknowledging that the territory of his mind had never been completely his own, for he had never told Albermech the actual content of his nightmares.

He reached the top of the war body, with the turret opening, then climbed down inside and this time strapped himself in, after putting the weapons down beside him. He wouldn't be leaving it for some time now. He pulled down porting tubes and pressed them into sockets in his suit. The suit made its physical connections to him, running nutrients and fluids into his veins. Via his nanosuite, he pushed up the slider switch to bring his bones to full function, seeming to bring the reptile into focus inside, a shadow skeleton. He undid the gauntlet sections that ran right up to his elbows and stripped them off, then put his hands down on the interface plates. Prepared this time, as he slammed into the war body substrate, he didn't allow his range to extend beyond the ship. The nodes bloomed, immediately slotting themselves where they needed to be. The battle plan – the Polity com sphere – already there in his mind, gained clarity and detail. He saw his soldiers, still on the move between the holds, and checked on their position. They would all be in place in just another twenty minutes. He saw the fleet all around him as it would appear when they arrived. Flashing in around the shady bulk of a gas giant, its scattering of moons and slew of an asteroid belt. And the prador would be there, of course – definitely them.

Inevitably, with this rise in input and activation, the reptile snarled, writhing around his own intimate connection into the war body substrate, and he felt his anger grow. He fought it down, knowing it wasn't his own but a product of how closely they were entwined.

'You are with me,' he said. 'And you will behave.'

It continued to press for dominance, offering up animuses to send and pining for linkage to weapons, but he continued to push it down. Now having access to the tools he'd used to try and eject it, he hit it with viral slaps, then disrupted and rubbed out part of its structure. Through this process, he felt it growing in awareness, and with that the decline in its attempts on him too. He also noted that in complexity and order, it was now nudging past that first Turing threshold of intelligence. But it was one threshold of many, and the meaning of this was a complex thing in itself. It was also far away from the point where it could be considered a single entity, or a submind striving for independence. He knew it wouldn't choose this anyway, even if it did reach that point – like many AI subminds, it would choose to return to the whole: him.

In minutes he had the thing subdued, and that surprised him because he'd expected it to be more difficult. Had he been more efficient and meticulous in dealing with it? No, it wasn't that. It was because he now understood what it was, and in understanding it had a clearer perception of who he was.

Having dealt with that, he could turn his attention to his army at last. He focused on his commanders and again chose Mallon as his entry point, though his orders and engagement would go to them all instantly. He found her slotted into a new home in a hold cylinder, different to the one he'd first found her in. It surprised him to see she had altered the framework – initially for Enforcers – to accommodate her larger body. He'd not programmed for that, and it gladdened him to know that she, and the rest, weren't simply robots slaved completely to his will.

'Your weapons,' he said, turning them all on.

'Now I feel complete,' said Mallon, 'though with awareness that your will has been imposed over my own. I feel strangely light and relieved by that. It's nice to have no responsibility – just duty.'

Her response was just one of a thousand others. Many were similar and some completely different. The subprogram he'd snapped into being just prior to communicating with her, and the others, dispatched a thousand unique replies.

'That's how a soldier is supposed to feel, within a disciplined framework. You know what to do, and will do it. But I must add that you do have a responsibility to the troops in your charge. They mustn't be expended wastefully.'

'I know that. I'm talking about the feeling. Ultimately, all the decisions are made and we are components of a vast machine – your machine.'

A thousand conversations were again similar and again diverged. He left them to the program, which was mapping across from his mind and making the replies he would have made, had he been in conversation with them individually. Or rather, he was replying with that portion of himself. He remained aware of it all, for the program wasn't truly distinct from him. But he had multiple perspectives and multiple processing, and turned another portion of his extensive mind to the Enforcers. He sent the instruction to bring them fully out of hibernation and watched.

The programming he'd given them had been running for some time now, but it applied fully as they came to wakefulness. Here there were more similarities of response than amidst the Old Guard and refugees, and much more limited thinking. This wasn't because he'd limited them, for like the others, they could think outside of the strictures he'd imposed. All of them could ponder their lives, recall their memories and contemplate the future. At the same time they were not denying the imposed hatred of the prador, their understanding of their involvement in defending the human race, and their duty. But the Enforcers had little to work with outside of those strictures. Their memories were few and their imaginations were blunt.

Piper checked back on Mallon, to see how things were playing out in her mind. He could feel her determination to do a good job, her disgust at her own past, and what she saw as her selfish cowardice then. This was despite her knowledge that Piper had brainwashed her, for her past was too contrary to her present thinking. He felt her worries about the future too, and what she might be once the boy no longer controlled her will. In her present state, she no longer wanted to be that past self and hoped there would be more than the coming battle in which to inter it. She also thought to a further future, in which, as she understood it, she could have a fully human body back, and maybe begin again. Great complexities of dreams and prediction spurred out from this, as in any intelligent mind. Expanding the programming behind the numerous replies he'd been making, which were currently winding down, he pushed into more minds and saw many thinking along similar routes, as well as some not.

However, when he returned his attention to the Enforcers, he found their thinking clearer and simpler. They were aware of their previous situation and now this one. Before they'd been programmed to do things that ran contrary to their character, now they'd been programmed to do something else. And as they came fully awake, it flashed across them all that they would be doing something *worthy*. Like stars igniting in the breadth of their composite consciousness, he saw relief, perception of a future, and knowledge that they would not have to kill or incarcerate their own. The realization that they would not be forced to do bad. He then got a sense of something else arising, coming through the millions of channels to them all. For a brief instant he couldn't fathom it, but then recognized it as similar to a feeling he'd only experienced on brief occasions. What he was sensing from the Enforcers was joy.

He experienced a moment of shame, understanding how

thorough had been his programming, and how utter and complete was his control of them all. As a corollary of this, the heavy responsibility pummelled him once again.

The last of the Enforcers slotted home into allocated frameworks. Some had bumped into each other, not following his map precisely enough. This was annoying, and was also a warning that similar things would certainly happen during combat, but it also pleased him to know that they had enough free will for imprecision. Now they were all in place, he ran his checks, looking for errors and ways to perfect his place in the battle plan. After a time, he recognized he was being far too perfectionist, since the plan would change the moment they surfaced into the real. He slumped back with a sigh, letting the tension out of his body.

Now he simply had to wait.

As he feared, the sensation of surfacing from U-space into the real was no exit from a cool pool this time. A great mass of input immediately overloaded Piper. He was a host rising out of a rough sea, so deep was his connection to his Cyberat soldiers. Though his connection explained the 'host' feeling, however, it didn't account for the rough sea. Disrupted updates to the battle plan and slow reformation of the battle sphere gave explanations: the prador had used U-space mines to disrupt that continuum and force the fleet out.

In the virtual battle sphere, the gas giant took on substance – fed by data from the *Albermech*'s sensors. It had previously appeared in their model as a globe like Jupiter, with pastel lines wrapped around it. But war had changed it, erasing the lines and spreading interlocking spirals about its surface. These were almost certainly due to numerous impacts. The sphere corrected to display one source of them, a sulphurous moon now spreading as a slew of rubble. The giant was also further away than presented in the sphere, and they were coming into the system at a different angle. He checked his feed to the Cyberat – through him they were updating on the battle sphere. He complemented that by relaying imagery.

'We are in it now,' he said generally. 'Keep checking your weapons and the updates, but don't lose yourself in that. We have our strategies, complex plans and our logistics to run the great machine that we are, but don't lose sight of our overall purpose.'

Internally his nodes were flickering in and out of existence, connections breaking and reforming as his network struggled under the same load of EMR that was also disrupting the battle sphere. His internal space filled with a snowstorm of data attempting to form into nodes – alien format technology his Cyberat programming struggled to grasp. With some difficulty, he listened to hundreds of thousands of replies from his soldiers. He elucidated the content of that response, with its great mix of emotions and, as expected, drew a common question from the majority of them.

'Our purpose is to smash the prador,' he replied to that.

The next response was a voiceless disrupted roar, and he saw that most of it had arisen from the Enforcers, now conscious and ready for a *just* fight.

From the moment of their disrupted surfacing, Piper's adrenalin surged, and with that reply from his troops it stepped up even higher. Maybe because he now knew its source, he saw the emotion that came on its coat tails as not clearly anger, or fear, or excitement, but a weird melange of all three. He felt no need to suppress these, because they helped drive his mind and he sensed a measurable increase in function, while he could identify its distortion of his thought processes. The thing had greater awareness now of the Cyberat aboard, and he could feel its clear anger and hatred towards the Old Guard in their war bodies, as well as its confused emotions about the Enforcers. As these were perfectly understandable reactions, and separable, he didn't try to repress them – he couldn't spend the entire upcoming conflict fighting both an enemy within and an enemy without. Accommodation was required, and the thing was essential to him functioning at the highest level.

'We are the Cyberat!' he shouted to millions of minds.

The answering roar increased . . . precisely as he predicted.

Ship positions shifted, minimally at first and then maximally as they altered course. The *Albermech* slewed to one side and accelerated on fusion, its escort of attack ships and destroyers falling in around it. A great flash ensued – a pulse of light a kilometre across in the sphere – and seemed to shine in through the hull of the *Albermech*. Battle sphere slipped to monochrome and lost coherence, just for a few seconds, before coming back, yet still he seemed to see the bright light. He saw he was sensitive to this in ways beyond the usual, for he'd now expanded his reach out beyond the ship, albeit a disrupted reach. And, out there, he saw the enemy. Awe, fear, wonderment and terror washed into him from all the Cyberat now at one with his vision.

One of the war runcibles had fired, and the massive photonic matter pulse slammed into the first ship in a line of five prador dreadnoughts. Piper noted how similar they looked to his war body, though each was ten kilometres across, bulked out and loaded with external hardware. The one that'd been hit tumbled backwards, misshapen and spewing fire from various ports. The thing's armour had deformed under the impact and no doubt its crew were so much slurry up the walls, yet it hadn't broken and burned. Such a shot against a moon of similar scale would have near vaporized it. He took another shocked look, as out of that ruined mass, flying through fumaroles of fire, came armoured prador. He was wrong: much of the crew had survived the impact. The reptile responded with outward-looking hatred, for it seemed his own emotions, and those of the soldiers, were now affecting and diverting its anger.

The other two war runcibles fired next, as vacuum filled with missile trails, lasers and the bright stab of particle beams. Anger and excitement surged again. He couldn't locate it as coming from him, the reptile or his soldiers, but it was a powerful source to be directed. Two more prador dreadnoughts took hits and tumbled out of action, only one of which had surviving crew departing. Piper tracked the attack ships hammering in, laser stabs incinerating those armoured prador trying to escape. The first runcible fired again – a shot that glanced off an intact prador dreadnought and splashed onto one hit earlier. The second ship actually did come apart this time. He tracked back to the runcible, as its tugs abruptly left it and a particle beam hit its rim, slicing through. The meniscus bulged out like a bubble and burst, then at the centre of the ring appeared something like the flaw in a diamond. Gravity mapping gave him an overlay, as the runcible collapsed towards singularity, then exploded before reaching it. Then gravity mapping shredded itself. He saw attack ships rolling away, shedding vapour, but no sign of the runcible AI escaping.

'Things might be changing rapidly,' Corisian commented, both his and Albermech's comlinks opening without his permission, and blending.

The reptile's excited shifting seemed to match the rapid twisting of the battle plan, as the *Albermech* pulled away under heavy gee from this first fight. Piper felt the massive acceleration, even as his war body compensated. A possibility now arose in their plan that his troops wouldn't reach the world, and he didn't know whether the fear of that was his own or the others'. He expanded his perception even further outwards, but this brought with it an increase in disruption of the data, taking in all the ships and stations in the system. Gravity map overlay came back to give him further U-space disruption and further Polity ships appearing, while suddenly swarming out from the direction of the sun were nigh on a hundred prador dreadnoughts, along with shoals of smaller vessels.

'Fuck,' he said, managing the battle plan as its probable futures expanded to infinity and kept collapsing. He saw a station hanging in vacuum far out from the gas giant. Regular gravity disruption was propagating from it. It hadn't featured in the original plan and he now realized the initial update to the battle sphere had been wrong. U-space mines hadn't been used. That big prador station was running an underspace interference emitter – a USER. Checking through, he saw that an earlier iteration of the plan had positioned this station closer to the world – the prador had moved it.

Explosions intensified all around, with debris scattering in a chaotic mass and hot gases misting through space. Attack ships were burning . . . Fifteen Polity dreadnoughts hammered down on the station, the *Organ Transplant* among them. Royal blue particle beams lanced out, burning over hardfields and blackening them, while the station emitted shooting stars of collapsing generators. The white beam of a full-spectrum laser stabbed out from the *Transplant* through a gap. The station took it, glowing at the impact site, and then replied with a swarm of missiles. Piper lost the ships for a moment behind explosions and hardfield scales, but as they came back a new addition rose in the battle plan. He understood it instantly, and watched as a modern dreadnought, the shape of a whaling harpoon tip, accelerated massively. The ejection canister of its AI arced away, then the ship jumped, despite U-space disruption, and rematerialized half inside the station. Both exploded, ship and station armour spreading as burning, hollowed-out shells.

All the while, the reptile was making and breaking connections within him. Scattering pieces of itself through his bones and out amidst his soldiers. But there seemed no intent there, and he could find no effect on his cognition. He began to filter the input to his internal space to free it up, pushing away blocks and streams of alien code and nodes that were struggling to form up. Another runcible exploded, this time before the tugs could get away. He then saw attack ships engaging with the prador version in an infernal dogfight. Hollow hulks of dreadnoughts, both prador and Polity, fell behind.

The *Albermech* itself rumbled with impacts and, from his internal perception, Piper abruptly felt Cyberat wink out of existence – over a thousand of them – and knew just how vulnerable they were in the holds on the exterior. The emotional impact arrived just after the firm knowledge, confirmed by a wave of pain from hundreds of injured survivors. The reptile mirrored him, shadowed all through him and them, indistinguishable. But again his actions and responses remained clear; he simply let it go, with the subtextual thought that he would have to deal with it later.

The fight continued, with destruction all around. New options in the battle plan awaited some diminution of U-space disruption. Old knowledge told him the ships simply couldn't jump while it was like that, without getting turned inside out at their arrival point. New knowledge denied that, though still with thirty per cent losses. Another impact on the ship's hull shuddered his war body sideways. He saw the end of one hold cylinder missing and, like pepper from a pot, thousands of Cyberat spilled out. Many had died from the hit, but many more were still alive and would remain so, since part of their machine body upgrade had been to make them vacuum capable. Their pain and fear became a sore point in his mind, combining with the diminishing pain of those who'd been injured before. Nanosuites installed in them by Room 101 were dealing with their injuries and, being Cyberat, they didn't possess enough of a nervous system to feel extreme pain. Had they been full humans, with the kind of connection he had, he would have been screaming now. He selected all the links to them and transmitted them to Albermech. No verbal reply came, but a code one did. The links had been passed on to other ship AIs and the Cyberat strays would be picked up, if anyone survived out here.

'Now,' said Corisian. They were about to risk the U-space disruption and those thirty per cent losses.

The *Albermech* heaved and Piper felt as if something was trying to turn *him* inside out. He pulled back his range as the ship dived into U-space, but that had little effect. The continuum twisted around him, with its infinities and singularities threatening the integrity of his mind. His reptile reached out, now panicked and raging, and came close to rising to dominance. Fucking prador. Damned fucking prador! His instinct, in the confusion of transit, was to fight this anger. But no, it remained useful and still didn't hinder his plans or his rationality. The fight out at the gas giant had been harder than expected. And now the one further in, next to Yannetholm, which had been predicted to be even worse, had edged out of predicted scenarios and into the possibility of failure.

14

The *Albermech* surfaced into the real with a crash. With his head aching, Piper touched the compressed node of the ship and took a general reading, seeing it had twisted along its length. One of the hold cylinders had twisted too, but oddly only resulted in twenty deaths. Yet he felt them – he felt them all. Other Polity ships followed, slamming into this volume of space too. On arrival, two squid-form attack ships twisted into spirals, while an old dreadnought of similar design to the *Albermech* exploded into a spreading cloud of debris, having been turned inside out. New nodes fell into Piper's inner space, some breaking apart and some struggling to reform. Alien code came back, harsh like a rough saw in his mind. He shoved away the extraneous, concentrating on his troops and a much diminished battle sphere now limiting its predictions.

The world of Yannetholm loomed ahead, its single large moon labyrinthine with prador installations on its surface. Unbelievably, the last remaining runcible had made it through, and now fired immediately. Three pulses in quick succession left the ring, which then shrivelled and collapsed. Its tugs tried to flee on hard bright fusion drives, but fell backwards into the singularity. Swarms of missiles rose up from the moon, many exploding in the path of the pulses. Hardfields blossomed, cutting the view, then dissolved and fell into disorder like shattered black safety glass. The pulses jerked the moon in its orbit, peeling out a chunk of glowing rock the size of a country, and wrapped the thing in fire. All around, Polity engaged with prador, and meteor storms flashed into being down in the planet's atmosphere. The *Albermech* surged down after them, its escort blocking and replying to the brunt of the firing above. It was time – they had actually arrived.

'Check that your powder is dry,' he commented. When this was met with widespread puzzlement, he realized he'd used an ancient expression often used by the Sparkind, but forgotten on Founder's World. 'Make sure your rotoguns are oiled and barrels clear,' he added. The response this time was strong on the whole, though muted where damage and injury had occurred. From this feedback, he ascertained a truth: they wanted to respond positively to him. It was like the reality of making speeches, elicited from the experience of a colonel in whose body he'd died: his audience wanted success from him. Confidence in him and his ability was their requirement.

Linking to local systems, Piper put out the grav in the hold and retracted his war body's feet. At least the machines here were clear, while at increasing range from him things were chaotic. The battle sphere was deforming and juddering, struggling to keep up with reality. Nodes in his internal space winked in and out of perception, sometimes opening out and sometimes falling back into odd shapes. The EMR accounted for a lot of this, but the alien was there too, adding its disruption. He was about to sweep all this aside again, just to keep things clear, but then saw there was no need because he had the space. He took off the brakes on that and observed with an assigned fraction of his mind. Nodes strained to form but just kept sliding across his perception and coming apart. He tried focusing on some of them more intently, and got what seemed to be static, but finally began to wean out order. Then in flashes, some of this found identity: prador code. His bones were trying to *describe* prador machines out there.

The ship rumbled into burning atmosphere, its hardfields a scaled shield above it. It crashed and, for a fraction of a second, Piper thought it had been hit. But the crash was the explosive attachments to the hold cylinders. They began to separate from the hull. Piper turned his war body and, using his mind, opened the larger door from the chamber to reveal a tunnel spearing through the body of the ship. The far end uncapped and the sudden evacuation of air dragged him into the tunnel. He hit his thrusters as, in another view, he saw the *Albermech* decelerate, and the eight hold cylinders moving on ahead of it. He shot out into the clouds as the ship, having deposited its load, began firing more of its weapons. Vapour trails flashed into being like spines above the vessel, as its railguns fired. Then ports opened to fire larger missiles as the ship ascended. Falling away from the ship, Piper saw its particle beam stab out, shading to violet in the thin atmosphere, hitting some object and then tracking it down until it was nothing but burning chunks of debris.

'I am with you, my friends, and now we must do the job we've been brought here to do!'

Another roar came in response. Even though he was swimming in adrenalin, saying these things felt cheap somehow. Cyberat had died and many more soon would. However, he sensed their need. Despite a hundred scenarios and responses ready in their minds and in his, he knew he had to keep that simple verbal connection going.

The *Albermech* was acting as a shield for them now, as were all the other ships above. The hold cylinders, parting under thruster blasts, were a plum target that could have been taken out by a single CTD strike. One plan had been to distribute them around the world to avoid this, but that would have meant a wider area to defend from above. The occupants of two of the cylinders – one that had lost its cap and the other twisted so its sides had split – were already filtering out into the sky. He felt their eagerness, joy of freedom, excitement and fear. So Piper sent the instruction earlier than planned to open all the other cylinders, having to reinforce the order twice because of the disruption. Their caps scattered like pennies, except for the twisted one, which couldn't seem to shed them yet, being jammed. He focused in on it, his bones putting together multiple internal views of it from disrupted feeds.

'Get those caps removed!' he ordered, even though this was a simple scenario played through many times.

He saw Engineers planting explosives at one end and, at the other, two war bodies opened fire to vaporize the locking mechanisms. The two caps finally fell away, and the Cyberat spilled out.

'Good work,' he told specific Cyberat.

Now, at his present elevation, Piper got a better understanding of the scale of things. He could clearly see the cylinders, but the Cyberat were like dust swirling away from them. Above, his view was of fire and debris and the steadily receding *Albermech*. However, in the battle sphere he viewed fragments of the intense clash going on up there to stop anything from coming down, as well as to knock out the remaining prador USER stations. A second later, he observed railgun strikes sketching lines through atmosphere. Though the world was his mission to seize, the Polity ships were also firing on ground targets: landed ships and space ports. He acknowledged that with a tight grimace and descended quickly.

Soon amidst the Cyberat, and with the millions of nodes in

his mind stabilizing, Piper saw they were all following the plan tightly. Twenty forces, in their millions, began descending hard, war bodies spread out around them like herders. Half of these Enforcers were the human-form kind. Their job was to enter the tunnels webbed through the crust of the world and clear away any prador down there. The rest would run on the ground, and in the air just above it. The remainder began spreading out in an arc of thousands of distinct armies, cupping the angled hurtling descent of the hold cylinders. He checked the sphere again, found it not so helpful, and looked ahead to a massive prador installation or city, situated up on a wide slab lying in a shallow sea. He began altering the pattern of their attack.

'There's our first target,' he said. 'Let's get this job done. We have the tools and we have the will.'

A muted roar this time, and a wave of tension fed back. Many Cyberat were also shooting questions into the ether and, while setting his program to give his replies, he searched out specific individuals.

'That is one fucking big city,' said Fusier.

'Merely a reflection of the scale of the creatures within,' Piper replied. 'And each can only die once.'

'As can we,' she observed.

He shunted over further replies to her through the program, which had now incorporated the morale-boosting format from his mind. He also noted that Breen was no longer available and the reality of this cut into him. The youth had died when that first cylinder had been hit.

'If the Polity can't keep our air cover, things will get nasty,' Mallon told him.

'Balances of risk,' he replied, feeling more subdued. 'The biggest threat to the prador is the fleet above and they will direct the majority of their resources there. With luck, they won't see what a threat we represent until it's too late.'

'With luck,' she agreed.

He brought the Cyberat lower, to put more atmosphere between them and what lay above. He then fired up the thrusters on the hold cylinders to bring them into a line, one after the other, and accelerate them towards the installation. The cylinders were heating up now, but, being made of such durable material, they'd remain intact throughout re-entry. As the thruster motors burned out the last of their fuel, he dropped lower, with the spreading arc of his forces above him. And then the prador responded.

Particle beams speared up from the ground and he glimpsed Cyberat turned into meteor trails, even as their nodes winked out with brief stabs of pain. Via hundreds of thousands of perspectives, he constructed a clear view of the ground. Prador were streaming out of holes – wasps from a hive. He'd known about them being stored – stacked up in their thousands in subterranean chambers. But they weren't the source of the particle beams. A further search revealed a heavy particle cannon tended by three prador, just a second before a war body hit it with an ionic weapon, blasting the thing from its foundations and scattering the prador.

'A handy weapon, that,' he said to the Old Guard concerned, whose name was Tinsher, while tweaking the plan.

'First time I ever used it,' Tinsher replied.

'And it won't be the last.'

The force got lower, and lower, with those war bodies carrying ionic cannons directed to drop even lower to take out ground batteries. They next started taking hits from lower-power weapons, which he traced to war machines like tanks, with upright weaponized bodies. He recollected an ironic observation from Albermech's memories, of how human tanks resembled prador, while the prador version, controlled by the flash-frozen ganglions of their children, resembled something almost human. The lower section of these things was a disc running on treads mostly, but sometimes on grav – saving their power for their weapons. The upper section looked like a human torso, with weapons for arms and a scanning 'head'. He couldn't help but note how this machine also resembled many ground-moving Cyberat, like his father. Excluding his thoughts on his father, he sent this observation to Tinsher, cynically noting that he was acquiring another individual to talk to. But at the same time, his observation opened out like fractals to thousands of other listeners.

'With technology, people become more machinelike in their thinking, yet prador become more human?' she shot back.

'I don't think there's anything remotely human down there.'

'Not entirely true,' she replied. 'Some of the Yannets remain.'

'Indeed,' he replied, briefly annoyed by the hole she'd made in his narrative.

Finally the first Cyberat force was down, sweeping along above the ground to take out weapons, while many were landing. Those that did land ran on spider-form bodies or treads, or bloated wheels over a weird landscape of stone. It had channels throughout so thoroughly worn by the movement of shallow seas that it seemed to consist of packed stone mushrooms. Piper's reasoning for putting the Cyberat down there was the same as for prador soldiers on the ground: grav was power hungry and it was better to save that for weapons where possible. Blasts ignited across this stone as they found tunnel entrances, out of which the prador streamed. Fire etched through the worn channels, glaring from underground and raising lines of steam from areas covered with shallow water. Tunnels started collapsing.

Eruptions flung rock, earth and brassy prador bodies up into the sky. Cyberat then swarmed down through entrances, some in their larger mobile bodies, others in human form detaching to find their way into the smaller tunnels. Piper winced at the thought, evinced by Tinsher, that local humans might be down there with the prador. His soldiers wouldn't deliberately fire on them, but there would be collateral damage.

'Check your targets down there, whenever possible,' he warned.

Hundreds of similar replies arose from Enforcers: 'We know the difference too well.' He found that shocking, realizing that the Enforcers were changing faster than the rest. A second later, he received a surge of fear that focused his attention on them.

Many of the tunnels, channels and chambers under that stone, or otherwise under long drifts of what looked like multi-coloured gravel, were dry. But many were not, and the water level was rising, with Piper now getting direct feedback of the Cyberat fear of water. He'd factored this in, and input programming to steadily dismiss that fear, but enough remained to be amplified by their close connections. Here then was proof of how planning could fall apart in the face of war. He selected those ground forces in his internal space and pushed their animuses harder, but found resistance. Mental fear of water had raised a biochemical response, creating a feedback loop. He couldn't think how to deal with that, until the animuses, seeking ways to apply his instructions, found their Room 101-installed nanosuites. His instructions to all those suites arrived in them a moment later, and the soldiers felt their effect shortly afterwards.

'We will find them! We will kill them!' Enforcers told him and each other, plunging into the water with indifference and sometimes abandon. He didn't feel good about that, but recognized that soldiers going into battle on alcohol- and drug-induced highs had historical precedent.

341

He shifted focus to the view ahead.

The installation loomed into sight, looking like a city built of domes made from giant oyster shells, supported by bony arches and measuring a hundred kilometres across. His forces had formed a horseshoe around the falling cylinders, which were now just ten kilometres above the ground. The air above the install-ation seemed hazed, but closer focus revealed near to a hundred thousand prador in the sky. Not enough. Particle beams began lancing up from the city. The firing was chaotic but horribly effective, scouring lines through the Cyberat swarm, and leaving empty scars across his forces as the burning soldiers fell. Piper felt all this almost like a soldering iron being passed through his mind, nodes disappearing from his inner space. Across a thousand links, he also caught Enforcers screaming in their burning machine bodies, some only briefly, but others all the way down until they crashed into the ground or splashed in the shallow sea. He tried to close this off, as he had so many other thought processes, but his clarity and his intelligence wouldn't allow it. He searched for a solution and found it unexpectedly in a hard purpose and anger not his own. He recognized the danger here, but had no recourse but to pull the reptile closer. The horror diminished, rubbed out in an insane, outrageous excitement.

Next, it appeared that a prador in command had recognized the main danger and the weapons shifted focus to the cylinders. The first was soon a spreading mass of molten material, then the second and the third, but even their remains were still travelling fast. The beams converged on the fourth, as the remains of the first hit the city, lifting up domes, splashing and turning areas into swirls of boiling fire. The rest struck one after another, blast waves propagating through the air. The devas-tation sliced the city in half and opened a thirty-kilometre-wide swath of ruin, shooting debris into the sky as if the planet's crust had opened at that point. Even as this happened, the flying prador engaged.

At the battlefront, Enforcers and others ceased to operate with any particular strategy. Programming became fire at will and kill as many of the enemy as possible. Piper, disconnected from tragedy, his emotions only anger and excitement, watched scenarios he had designed playing out. The prador armour was harder than predicted and it took a longer particle beam strike to soften it for an armour-piercer. And in that time, the prador could do a lot of damage.

'Keep them blind and kill them!' he ordered.

He tweaked his previous program, spreading it out slowly in the disruption. The directive: constant firing on the creature's head turret and other sensor areas with incendiaries, with one Cyberat designated to lock on with a particle beam, while three others targeted it in readiness with armour-piercers. In another scenario, war bodies flew into the prador and lined up transverse shots with ion cannons to hit many of the enemy at once, while Enforcers then came up underneath with piercers. Other Enforcers were grappling in the air, placing sticky mines on the prador like Sloan had once done. Only this wasn't so good up against prador claws. These were just a few of a thousand forms of combat. Where the two swarms met, it was as if both were feeding into a scrap shredder.

Piper dropped down to just above the surface, then slid in below the fighting. There had been a lake of the planetary sea here just a few metres deep, but it'd now been swamped in a long pile of burned and broken Cyberat and prador. Smoke and steam rose from this mass, and he could still see movement there. And, as he watched, an Enforcer got up, jerking and shrugging from the tangled debris, and limped back up into the sky. Reality began to impinge again when he saw a Cyberat, burning in his machine, trying to put out the flames with arms that turned into clumps of cables at the elbows. Even his reptile seemed shocked into inaction – its clarity and purpose dissipating. Piper felt the pain returning, along with the perception of huge loss. He managed to dampen the pain as a physical thing, but couldn't put aside an intellectual awareness of it. And he couldn't blind himself to the piles of dead and dying, or the steady rain of the same from the sky. The Cyberat would win here, because he had millions while the prador numbered in the hundreds of thousands, but it was evident that he was losing two to three Enforcers for every prador brought down.

Piper began to withdraw mentally, suddenly sickened and horribly weary after the virtual confirmation of this, bringing home the huge destruction, waste and pain of war. But then he saw other movement in the mass. Four prador scrabbled over a pile of broken Cyberat and opened fire on him, first with their Gatling cannons then with particle beams. He threw out a hard-field, instinctively, almost having forgotten he had this option. Simultaneously, he hit them with rotoguns, sending them sprawling. While keeping them off balance with those guns, he beamed one of them, switched ammunition to piercers and watched it come apart. He found some relief in doing this, with a resurgence of hatred and purpose, but then remembered the overall strategy and shot straight up into the sky, releasing seeker missiles towards them as he headed back behind the battlefront. He didn't like it, but he had to stay alive and in charge. Though his soldiers had been well programmed, and indoctrinated, there was no telling how long that would hold during battle if he was absent. There were other things he needed to concentrate on too.

The thought rose up clearly now and he realized it was one he'd been skating over, never truly acknowledging, since he'd first learned of the prador and how useful he might be against them. Perhaps that had been Albermech's intention, for whatever obscure psychological AI purposes: the most effective weapon they had put on this world was not the millions of Cyberat, but Piper's ability to seize control of machines.

As he had fought those prador, his system had highlighted nodes for their mechanisms. He retained them and now tried to open one up, but the alien contents baffled him. He could see how to access it, but interpreting what he could do with it made no connection with anything he knew. He summoned up prador language and code taken from Albermech and tried to apply it, going deep. An Enforcer, tangled up with a prador, smashed into the top of his war body, then fell away, bringing him abruptly out. He grimaced. His personal attention on this was too much, making him vulnerable, so he set his programs to work with the nodes and focused back on the battle.

The air forces encircled the city and, as that circle closed, the proportion of prador dropping out of the sky increased. This grew even further as he brought his soldiers in at the rear over the top. Meanwhile, the ground force was closing in fast too, blowing prador caches all the way. Connecting to those who'd gone underground, he updated on their advance. Most of them were underwater in those tunnels and all the previous fear had dissipated. He noted they'd acquired allies too, for the local humans had joined in, clad in heavy powered diving suits and armed with prador weapons. All were coming in towards the installation city since the intent was not to clear tunnels, after all, but quickly gain access to the city from below. He watched underwater firefights and what could only loosely be described as hand-to-hand combat. The prador were better in that environment, and Piper wondered whether it was some hangover from the Cyberat fear of water. Probably not – the prador were equally able in air or water. Humans, not so much.

In the air, the prador forces began to collapse, but then came the reserves. Larger first-children ascended, followed belatedly by adults. The first-children were hard work and the adults harder still, even though swarmed by Enforcers. Piper chose a previously modelled option and sent Old Guard war bodies against them.

'Tinsher, those are for you,' he said, echoing the comment to other war bodies sporting ion cannons.

'Aren't I a lucky girl?' she replied.

Massive ion blasts and railgun strikes began to tear the heavy creatures apart. He watched one, its upper shell burned and cracked by an ion blast, skimming down to bounce from a roof, then into the shallow sea, rolling like a coin. He stared at the thing, and knowledge he'd acquired from Albermech rose for his inspection. War was not simply about defeating the enemy, but preserving as far as possible one's own forces. The death toll racking up in his mind, the brief agonies and the long dying pain of those lying in heaps below, made him more aware of that need than other generals. He abruptly shot down after the adult. Here was an opportunity.

The nodes for prador machines still struggled to form in his inner grid. His bones still strained to describe them, isolate them and find a way in. His programs were making headway with the prador language and code, but only enough for him to find many blocks were in place. He knew that AIs had tried to access prador machines remotely, and that the prador had found ways to stop that – all evolved throughout their long war. After hurtling down, he decelerated hard, throwing out a shock wave that had sea exploding into spray around him. There he paused, gazing out across the water, dotted with islands of wreckage, treaded war machines rolling in a line back towards the city. He reached up then and, because she'd always been partially in his thoughts, summoned Mallon, as well as subsidiary Cyberat and a hundred thousand Enforcers. Above, she broke away from combat with a prador adult.

'Not now!' she said, obviously angry. But the anger faded as another war body slammed into the top of the adult and began driving demolition charges into the exposed organic armour of its back. He hardened the order – no debate – and she descended with the giant cloud of Enforcers swirling in around her.

Piper shifted in over the prador adult even as it collapsed, tilted against a tangled pile of debris that consisted mainly of Enforcers. Thankfully it was on its back and all the attachments on its underside lay exposed. Piper dropped lower, then had to fling out his hardfield as the approaching war machines began firing on him. He considered railgunning them, but that would fling his war body too far away. He considered other weapons but in the end decided on patience.

Mallon came plunging in first from overhead. He sent her a loading of what he wanted, and she dropped low between him and the war machines, constantly firing her weapons at them and taking hits on her armour. He noted that though some war bodies had acquired hardfields, she had not. As the Enforcers came down too, positioning themselves the way she had, or otherwise attacking the machines, he looked to the battle above. It was winding down now, with the surviving prador withering under increasingly concentrated fire. Already his troops were entering the city to clear up survivors there, while directly behind them came the Engineers – the scavengers to pick through the remains.

Ahead, between him and anything that might kill him, the Enforcers formed what looked almost like a solid wall. All was as it should be. Piper put his war body on hold, hovering just over the adult. He opened the turret, but then felt glued in place – mentally tangled into the war body substrate. Operating through his nanosuite, he brought down the function of his bones; this helped a little. He gritted his teeth to mentally detach further from the substrate, before pulling his hands free from the interfaces. The reptile clung briefly to the substrate processing, raising anger and fear, and regret almost like addiction, and then it snapped back fully into his bones. He sat there feeling drained. Wearily, he pulled his gauntlets back on, unstrapped and climbed out.

Gravity made itself known the moment he was out on the hull of his war body, for inside, the thing had been compensating for it all along. His fatigue made itself known at the same time. His suit responded with assist, but he still felt leaden, despite his practice in the gym and the nanosuite strengthening his muscles. His bones, of course, had needed no strengthening. Over to his right stood the edge of one of the stone formations, and from this angle it really did look like mushrooms crowded together. A shingle shore ran along between this and what Piper perceived should be described as a tide pool, in which the prador lay. The labyrinthine moon dragged seas here round the planet, running over and through those stone formations, and where he presently stood was at low tide. He focused with his HUD and then used a program to clarify what he was looking at.

The colourful shingle comprised about twenty per cent stones and eighty per cent shell fragments, woven through with white objects. In the spaces between those 'mushroom' stems, scimitar mussels clustered, as well as penny oysters that reminded him of Founder's World. He saw nodular masses of what he took to be some other form of mollusc towards the back of the shingle. Only when he looked closer did he recognize skulls washed there by the tide, and realized the white objects were human bones.

A reminder to slot away in his mind, should he at any time feel merciful.

To his left stood the installation city, with Cyberat above it swarming around diminishing numbers of prador – the whole mass flashing like a thunder cloud. Ahead, Mallon and the Enforcers he'd summoned blocked his view of what lay beyond – a shifting machine mass that seemed a single entity. However, he did get glimpses of some war machines there. They were slowing now and, under such an appalling intensity of fire, they ran on dry ground as the water boiled away around them. Piper now speculated that pulling down so many Enforcers had been overkill and, with weariness bringing on nausea, he raised his visor.

The ear-aching roar of battle hammered him, while a charred flesh stink rose up in the steam from the prador below. That tipped him over the edge. He crouched with one hand down and vomited bile – there having been no food inside him for many hours. Next he became fully aware of metal fragments pinging off armour, and shots snapping through the air around him. He shuffled forwards at first but, seeing the pointlessness of keeping his head down, came up and onto legs that felt close to collapse. He staggered down the war body and jumped onto the underside of the prador adult.

The creature was still sizzling in the shallow water, now stained with clouds of green blood issuing from its submerged mouth. It had legs, about half of them prosthetic, that were still moving weakly. Piper paused, catching his breath, and observed the blood, then the legs. Movement of both ceased a short moment later, as if his stepping on the thing had finally caused it to expire. Its claws were entirely prosthetic – he could see them half under the water below. Not entirely covered with metal, the stony carapace had armoured sections inset. Over the fused, ribbed section

349

where its underhands had been, a missile launcher array had been attached, bracketed by heavy lasers. But his main interest lay in rows of slave units positioned in from its legs on either side. These twenty-four hexagonal lumps of technology were each the size of his head. It was through these the adults ran all their com, sending orders that extended beyond mere verbal into direct control. They also used these devices to control the flash-frozen minds they put in their war machines, as well as the thrall units they installed in human blanks, and latterly the armour of their children, before AI sequestration had made that too dangerous.

Disconnected from the war body, Piper again pushed up the slider switch on his bones. Reptile response was as expected, reaching out for nodes, raising animuses and snarling at any threats. But an intense surge of feverish sickness caught him by surprise. He squatted by a thrall unit, more because his legs felt so weak, and began to strip off one gauntlet. When a red-hot chunk of metal crashed down beside him, shattering the carapace and bouncing onto his war body, he knew he was being foolish. He may have wanted a way into prador machines, to tilt things in favour of the Cyberat, but this battle was all but done and it would be idiocy to get himself killed out here trying to penetrate slave units. Retrospectively, as he closed his visor, he understood the urge to put himself at risk was also penance for the Cyberat lying steaming in the sea all around.

He scanned his surroundings, the nodes in his mind fined down to a granular mass now, without the breadth the war body substrate provided. The load made his head ache and his bones once again seemed hot, adding to his physical malaise. He pulled in his range to just half a kilometre and sorted through nodes, determined to do something here, and finally locked on just one amidst the Cyberat protecting him. He opened a connection to it fully, getting a load of excitement and fear, hope and shame

entangled – a fractal explosion of the thoughts of a fully functional human mind. Currently the thoughts ran to salvaging the
masses of weapons and materials here, as well as hopes of grav-
rafts and manufacturing in the city, all overlaid on weariness
similar to his.

'Aremer, come here,' he said.

Aremer was not an Enforcer but one of the refugees from the
old regime – an Engineer. He peeled out of the mass and shot
over, hovering above Piper. He was a horizontal cone wrapped
in tool arms, with his gnarled head peering through a window
in the face of the thing. He'd retained his eyes and at least part
of his chest. The arms disappeared to the sides and seemed likely
to be in direct control of two heavy grab claws, to which rotoguns
had been attached. Piper pointed down to one of the slave units.

'Remove one of these.'

Leadenly obedient, Aremer sank down, closed a grab around
the slave unit, then unfolded another arm. This had multiple
joints and a carousel just behind the main tool head. The carousel
clicked round, positioning a ceramic chainsaw that started up
with a high whine. It then went down into the prador's carapace,
spraying a cloud of dust, shrieking in protest, but cutting accur-
ately around the unit. Finally, the Cyberat heaved the unit up
and it came out attached to a twenty-centimetre-thick chunk of
carapace, bringing with it a long trail of composite wires like a
tree root, glistening with green prador blood. Aremer grimaced
and carefully began cutting away the carapace. It all seemed to
be taking far too long in the middle of this chaos, and again
Piper felt tired anger at his impulse to come here personally.

'Cut all the connections away,' he instructed tightly.

Aremer sliced straight across, severing the root, and then
presented the slaver unit. Piper took it, suit assist increasing as
he felt the weight of it.

'Are the promises true?' Aremer asked, his voice a murmur through the racket.

'Yes they are,' Piper replied. He pointed to the other units and this time, rather than speak, sent instructions that propagated to other Engineers: retrieve all slaver and thrall units along with their connectors. Map the connections, and retrieve com gear from prador war machines, and thrall units from any blanks found. He walked carefully to his war body, having to bring it lower to climb onto it, and trudged up the slope to the cockpit. As he got inside, he put the unit down beside his seat and the turret closed over him. Connecting only via his bones, he sent his war body into the sky. Even as he rose, Mallon hurtled up past him while the Enforcers began dispersing – the line of prador war machines was now static and burning.

As the battle concluded, Cyberat spread out throughout the city searching out and destroying any remaining prador. This wouldn't take long since the place was crawling with Cyberat. Reluctant to connect to the war body because he feared that would make him feel worse, Piper analysed what data he could in his bones only. The forces coming in from below had caught five adults, with retinues of children, trying to escape through the tunnels. Piper found it reassuring that cowardice existed within this enemy and that they weren't entirely ferocious killers. He studied the growing map of the city and chose a large domed section as a place to site himself, then flew down and entered through a series of bony-looking arches into the alien interior. Tunnels wide enough for prador adults speared off everywhere, with smaller tunnels for their children webbing these together. He paused to peer into one huge chamber where, hooked up on long poles disappearing into the distance, hung thousands of huge flat fish. These were reaverfish, adapted to the heavier gravity of this world – the prador harvest. He then noticed bodies of a different shape at the near end: human, opened up and gutted. It was a further reminder he didn't need.

He made his way through an adult's tunnel to another large chamber, identified as an adult's sanctum, and settled on the floor amidst stacks of hexagonal screens running prador code and imagery. There he paused, his internal grid and system giving him a lot, but not enough. The battle sphere kept struggling to establish, and viewing his forces and others was like studying the distribution of drifts of sand. He also felt awful, and a passing inspection of his condition confirmed his body was overloaded with toxins, its temperature too high – heated by his bones. So he reconnected suit feeds and, in alliance with his nanosuite, injectors went into his body to draw off toxins, as well as feed in the nutrients he required. He waited, seeing improvements, then grimaced and took off his gauntlets again, putting his hands down on the interfaces.

With the increased processing, the reptile solidified inside him. Accustomed to the thing's behaviour, he quashed its push to action. He was ready, but with the increase in capacity and connection, his sickness abruptly returned. Then it hit him: this wasn't just about his condition, which was poor, but feedback.

He was connected to millions of Cyberat, feeling the pain of each death and the continued pain of the injured. He'd experienced Aremer's weariness, and certainly he was feeling that of all the rest. And Cyberat were no more immune to the toxins and spill of their interfaces than he was to that of his bones, while those effects would have been aggravated by high-energy weapons and tactical processing. With his mind moving slowly, he tracked this and sought ways to ameliorate it. Updates to animuses began to cut some of it, but in the process cut bandwidth. He remembered Albermech talking of feeling what Piper felt through his aug connection to the AI, and now he understood it wasn't optional. His intimate link to his soldiers was a good thing, he asserted, and it was now time to do his best for them.

He concentrated on battle sphere data to build a clear picture. The fight continued in orbit and now, all around the world, debris littered space. Through millions of eyes and other sensors, he viewed an orange sky scored with meteor trails. He knew this wasn't the natural colour, which was usually a hard violet blue. Out there, the Polity fleet had destroyed three USER stations and was now intercepting any craft attempting to get to the surface. He focused on one scene, of spheres dropped in high orbit breaking apart and strewing their segments across large volumes of space. Minefields. Further ships had arrived – both prador and Polity – but the prador were definitely losing. So why did no other Polity forces come down to the surface? He ran through possible explanations and there were many of them. But his cynicism, and maybe realism, focused him on one answer: the Polity was testing its new weapon down here, which wasn't the huge Cyberat force but him. They wanted to see if he could take control of prador machines. If so, he'd be more effective in further conflicts than any increase in production from war factories like Room 101. Accepting that, he focused down on his part of the battle sphere.

Within the city, he saw lone prador trying to flee but, being surrounded, they were pounded to a mixture of scrap and smoking flesh. He watched one conflict with twenty prador fending off concerted attacks from Enforcers, then an Old Guard war body coming in to blast them with an ion cannon. The Enforcers flowed in directly after to destroy the survivors. Thereafter ensued minor exterminations as the Cyberat hunted down concealed prador. With angry distaste, he watched an attack by what he took to be Yannets and the confused retreat of his Cyberat.

Scanning rendered the truth about these heavily scarred, blue-skinned people. They were blanks, run by thrall hardware in their skulls. It was another unwanted reminder, like the skulls and the hanging corpses he'd seen. He tweaked responses to them and soon after they were incinerated to ash. Just a little later the Cyberat found the prador adult controlling them all and tore it apart.

Hours had passed and night descended as Piper watched these last skirmishes, and he began to feel marginally better. Views outside through thousands of sensors showed the bowl of a sky, like burnished metal, with no stars visible. Moonrise on the horizon shaded all to red, for that object had melted and was reforming into a new sphere. Sunrise would follow on the tail of that, and the new day would see the world tide hauled in around them. Piper copied and altered programming from the Cyberat of the ground attack and spread it through the rest, banishing any water fears as best he could, but reluctant to take it to full erasure. Then he focused on the transition from this battle to preparation for the next.

Engineers were already at work, setting up stations for Cyberat repair, harvesting materials, weapons and energy supplies. They'd found undamaged prador workshops and were adapting the tools they found. They had also, as per the plan, risen to a command status, sending Enforcers and others off to collect the things they needed. Medics were also at work on injured Cyberat, conducting much more delicate work than the mechanistic stuff of the Engineers. He counted the injured encapsulated in hibernation bubbles, and being stacked in large chambers like the eggs of some huge beast. Inspecting more closely, he saw many of these bubbles were packed with plug-form Cyberat who had no hibernation support; he couldn't understand why this was. He queried it, taking information from the minds of many Medics. The plug forms were dead in Cyberat terms, but not so in terms of the Polity. Though their wounds were terminal, their Room 101 nanosuites had worked to preserve what remained by putting them into a state of vitrification. This, he perceived, would be a problem for an army on the move. He sent instructions for hidden caches to be made for all those not recoverable without tank regrowth. They could be collected up later when the prador had been expunged from this world. He next turned his attention to the dead.

Piper viewed the piles of them already extracted from their machine bodies, which the Engineers were snaring. The piles looked like offal from an abattoir, rather than human corpses. The injuries here were generally either burns, discharges through their cerebral supports or some other physical destruction beyond the power of nanosuites to rescue. He counted them too, via his millions of connections, and watched with sinking dread as the figure climbed to hover around four hundred thousand, but still edging up in small increments from that.

Four hundred thousand . . .

This was just one city on a world occupied by thousands of the same. And, he gathered from the data, though the prador were at their heart militarized, this was their version of an agricultural station. Such losses were unconscionable. Piper peered down at the slave unit and, in other vision, saw more of such technology being collected up, while spurts of data on scans entered the data sphere. He checked some of this with his sluggish brain but, still with that appalling figure in his mind, realized he was procrastinating. He reluctantly detached one hand, reached down to snare the slave unit and struggled to pull it up into his lap. He stared at it, just knowing this was going to be hard.

He turned it over to look at the underside, where a thick clump of composite semi-organic fibres and wires jutted out. Activating the hard connection routine in his free hand, his fibres snaking out from it, he brought it down on the unit. His fibres went in while he concentrated on forming the node for the unit. Chunks of dim prador code fell chaotically into his mental space. He tracked down wires that input power from the prador's bioelectrics, then learned its profile and fed in the same from his bones. Weirdly, this seemed to affect his surroundings beyond his war body, as lights came on in the chamber. He gazed out in puzzlement, until he saw Engineers and Builders swarming in, pulling sleds and starting to unload them. On spotting him, they halted their work and he read their confusion.

'Continue,' he told them, checking the battle sphere to see what the plan was for this chamber and confirming he wouldn't be in the way. He then added another instruction to the sphere, for the collected thrall and slaver hardware to be brought here. Hundreds of direct replies arrived and with them a wash of their fatigue. He blocked it and returned his attention to the unit.

He made thousands of connections to its hardware, finding multi-spectrum transceivers and building up files of what they transmitted and received. He translated the prador code, but then moved beyond that to actually understanding it. In a moment of fierce joy, he found a language channel from the prador's nervous system, and then the device that translated this into numerous orders: attack this, avoid that, move to this location and more besides. Almost as a sidebar, he now fully understood the prador language. Disparate data blocks began to connect up into usable form. He modelled the entire slave unit inside and soon knew he could transmit its orders, though only at a usable range via the war body, with its transceivers. So, he'd be able to take control of prador war machines as he'd previously done to Enforcers. Yet, inevitably, there was a *however*, and it was a big one.

The programming revealed a stratified command routine. The prador he'd taken this thing from could deliver orders only to its own machines, while they could be overwritten by those further up in the chain of command. This process wasn't via the slave unit – those higher up could overwrite it with their own units directly to the war machines concerned. He couldn't, as yet, elucidate it because it ran on codes that changed every one hundred seconds around the planet. It made sense for a military force, of course, but made things very difficult for him. He'd hit a block, which perhaps he could find a way past after examining more hardware. But he needed rest and his nanosuite needed time to bring him back to optimum.

Enough.

It was day again now, with the sun rising and sky sliding to blue with swathes of orange cloud. After a final check on the battle sphere, ensuring responses were in place should there be another attack today, he detached from both the war body and the unit. Then he promptly had to clamp down on the urge to throw up. His nanosuite was doing its best, but he'd just put a heavy load on himself again and he was back to how he'd felt retrieving the slave unit. This required time, so he set alerts for any major changes, then via his nanosuite, he ordered a maximum length of sleep, and dropped into blackness.

15

The day was drawing to a close, and still no response came from the prador to his army's presence. Piper opened his war body's turret and, hauling up the slave unit from where it had tumbled beside his seat, he climbed out with it. He felt restored after his sleep but not completely, and that condition was reflected in his forces. So the longer the prador held off the better. And anyway, he still needed time to deep dive into their thrall and slaver technology.

His HUD informed him of breathable atmosphere heavy with ozone, so he opened up his helmet. At once the smells of burned seafood, putrefaction and hot electronics hit him. He surveyed the interior of the prador chamber he was in. The Engineers and Builders, running on spider legs and treads, had put together small autofactories here, whose components they'd carried down from the hold cylinders. These consisted of doughnut matter printers just a metre across, fed by stock materials processors and aligned with assemblers and packaging systems. A number of the Engineers had cut into the walls to take advantage of the prador power supply. Blocks of rotogun rounds were coming out of one processor, with a triple-jointed light grab stacking them on the floor.

Piper trudged down the war body and sat on the rim, discarding the slaver unit on the floor. He scanned around and then focused

on a temporary rack set up just a short distance away. Even as
he watched, a spider-form Cyberat arrived to deposit slave units
and other hardware in the thing. He linked into that Cyberat – a
small Engineer – and was about to transmit instructions to her,
but changed his mind.

'You,' he said, beckoning to her.

She swung round and walked a little way towards him. She
was quite beautiful, he registered, and looked near to his young
age, which seemed to highlight his repulsion that her body ended
at the waist. Her arms finished at the wrists too, and were plugged
into sockets beside her, obviously controlling the complex tool
arms protruding from the fore of her machine body. He also
noticed that she looked scared.

'What's your name?' he asked.

'My name is Triode, General,' she replied.

It wasn't the first time a Cyberat had addressed him in plain
speech with that honorific, but it being a rare occurrence, he still
felt undeserving. But the feeling was weak and soon dissipated.

'Okay, Triode, I want you to bring over another of those slave
units.'

As she turned back to the rack, he moved around his war body
to a panel. He needed as much data as possible to work with
and had storage available, even though time might be limited.
Storage in the war body substrate was massive, though he could
plumb its limitations. What was in his bones was huge too,
and to all intents limitless, though more difficult to access and
expand. Perhaps in time he'd be able to use the latter, and for
now he registered that after working that slave unit, the capacity
in his bones *had* increased.

At his mental command, a small hatch opened in the war body
armour and an interface plate came oozing out. He placed one
hand on it and immediately linked via this route. He and his

reptile – the thing seemed to be hanging in some n-dimensional space, like black vines spread through his programs – reached in, and processing and storage magnified. Meanwhile, Triode came back over with another slave unit, while a second Engineer arrived at the rack to deposit more acquisitions. Piper placed his other hand on the unit, making fast connections, and then started draining it of data.

'And you, Anode,' he said to the other Engineer, wondering if these were twins. 'The same.'

He transmitted what he wanted to the other female, even as he drained the second slave unit to its dregs and disconnected from it. She went over to grab the hardware he'd requested, bringing over a transceiver and related computing, which had been stripped out of one of the prador's treaded war machines. Triode took the second slave unit back and collected up something else. The transceiver took longer to crack, being unfamiliar, but Piper got much useful data from this end of the transaction. Over the ensuing hours, he gave further orders and went through slave and thrall units one after another. Finding one of the former from further up the command chain gave him more access. And a large case, like a grain seed a metre tall, wrapped in sheared-off hardware, gave him access to a flash-frozen ganglion and its interfaces. In his bones and in the war body substrate, he built up a huge model, refining code and command routes, and steadily finding his points of access. Another slave unit gave him a jackpot, coming from the adult near the top of the command chain here, and so even more fell under his control. But as night bled into day and then drained into dawn again, his nanosuite began red-lining to keep the toxins under control, as well as his temperature down.

'Thank you, Triode and Anode,' he said, disconnecting from the slave unit Triode held, while sending the order for no more of this hardware to be gathered, for now. Disconnection from the war body this time felt odd, ameliorated by nanosuite suppression and by his physical state. But also because *he* felt bigger now, in comparison to the war body substrate. The capacity of his bones had expanded even more.

'Are you sisters?' he asked.

Anode moved up beside Triode. 'We are. How did you guess?'

He thought tiredly that she was being serious, until he read the twist to her mouth. Expressions were easier to decipher when they weren't hidden behind chain-glass, or from skulls expanded and distorted by cerebral support hardware. He investigated, delving as deeply into them and their story as he had Mallon. Cerebral enhancement usually preceded progression to plug form, so the two Engineers were anomalous. They were the daughters of an Old Guard called Drillain who, shortly after the girls had had an 'accident' and lost their lower bodies, had snatched them out of a progression hospital before that enhancement. He'd then gone into hiding with them, on one of the krill-harvesting ships, avoiding the Enforcers sent to his home to arrest him. When the Polity made its offer, Drillain was one of the first to head straight up out of atmosphere. Room 101 had provided them with the Polity equivalent of Cyberat enhancement, which were augs the size of thumbs below and behind their ears. Just one story of many, in fact of millions, Piper understood, and felt humbled.

'I can't think how I guessed,' he said, smiling back at them.

'Can I ask you a question?' Triode asked.

'Of course.'

'Can our bodies truly be restored?'

As she said it, she extracted a wrist from the socket beside her, revealing a multi-digit hand whose fingers were also data plugs, and pressed it against one naked breast. He saw further obscenity in this and felt a flash of anger. Was it his own, something left over from his father's reptile, or an experience from his four years of virtuality? Perhaps all of them. He'd been about to answer with a simple yes, but felt they deserved more. Then he dryly observed that the feeling probably arose from the organic of him as a young man. Both were very attractive, despite not having their full human forms. That dry inner voice also added that anything he said would be shared, and would spread through all the Cyberat.

'I have a friend who's a Polity agent. On Founder's World he tried penetrating the Old Guard by having his body honed down to a plug form and installed in a machine body. It didn't work, so he pulled out again and now his body is fully restored. He's two hundred years old.' The two goggled at him, so he added, 'The technology is available. I too was repaired after severe injury that nearly cut me in half. A victim of one of the many Old Guard initiated "accidents" of recent years. However, resources are almost certainly limited by this war, so it's best we get on and win it.'

'Can we?' they both asked simultaneously.

He gestured to the slave and thrall units, thinking about the significance of what he'd now learned from them. 'The Polity is winning it, and has just now acquired a new and powerful weapon.' He shrugged self-deprecatingly because he did not want to say that he was that weapon, and walked round his war body to step up onto it. He felt utterly worn out yet again and that needed to change. The war wouldn't wait. 'Don't let me keep you from your work,' he added, and they quickly sped away as he climbed back up into it.

No dreams or nightmares haunted him for the next few days, at least not during sleeps of exhaustion, but they were back on ensuing nights. They slowly turned the prador installation city into a Cyberat fortress, with a hospital and place to rest, as everyone shook off the ill effects from their hardware. Outside, for twenty kilometres all around, war machines were scrap and prador war parties had retreated. Piper took his war body out to survey, but then returned to his stronghold when it became evident he garnered no more data by his physical presence. He left the war body and walked around the city sometimes, still dispelling the last dregs of toxins from himself too. As he strengthened his position, and recouped on whatever losses he could, the continuing lack of response from the prador surprised him. He subsequently put that down to their being focused on the skies, and what they probably thought of as imminent destruction from up there. Around the rest of the world, he detected much movement and much testing of hardfields, which confirmed this. But it couldn't last. On the sixth day, there having been no assault from the ships above, the prador finally came to a decision about his forces. And, as he had expected long before, he saw multiple launches.

This was obviously the next logical step for the prador. An enemy had established in and around one of their installations, and it seemed likely they wouldn't be able to retake it without heavy losses, as well as the installation's destruction, so now the nukes were coming. Up above, he observed the programmed response already in place, with a dome of war bodies, many with hardfields, and Enforcers oriented towards the threats. Missiles sped in high and low, and the war bodies responded with smaller projectiles. Piper, standing on a roof made of a tough form of nacre the Engineers had found uses for, watched it all for long minutes.

'You should go below,' Triode protested.

'We'll take you below,' said Anode, lunging towards him.

He stilled the two of them with a thought and continued

364

watching, confident in his Cyberat, and once again countenancing this risk because of a constant undercurrent of guilt. Explosions lit high up in space and down low, just a hundred metres above the ground as swarms met. Particle beams then speared out, etching the sky with blue-purple lines, and further explosions ensued as they took out the strays. As expected, not a single warhead reached the target. He observed for a while longer, seeing Cyberat moving into a shift pattern – groups heading for the ground so their fusion reactors could top up laminar storage and others going up to replace them.

'Let's go down,' he said to the two Engineers. 'Our stay in this city is coming to an end. It'll soon be time to move on to the next.'

The prador were gathering. As he clambered down from the roof, Piper focused via the battle sphere on military installations near space ports, where ships had been hollowed out by Polity orbital strikes. It seemed the forces there were now fielding prador war drones. These heavily armoured and armed spherical machines could take a lot more punishment than their kin. Could they be called sentient, being flash-frozen ganglions? Semantics. Meanwhile, clouds of prador were rising into the air in many places, and on the ground armies were advancing under shields generated by machines, also run by their flash-frozen kin. All were converging, and undoubtedly heading towards his Cyberat.

Back in his war body, Piper plugged in all the suit connections and ran control of them as a subprogram through his nanosuite. Fluid cooled by the war body would cool his still-hot bones, while the nanosuite would direct its load of nutrients and other materials where needed. Next he connected physically to its substrate. The recent break from it, as well as the return to higher processing capacity, revealed further nuances to a change he'd already seen.

The reptile had grown stronger – its anger and hatred having received a boost in response to all the prador code he'd been running. In loading so much from their technology, code and language, he'd reshaped his and his reptile's psychology in the substrates, and they were feeding back into his organic mind. He now felt an eagerness for the fight to come, yet also a strange fellowship with the prador, who no longer seemed so alien. He considered fighting that down, but realized he couldn't. It was that same psychology that enabled him to understand them better, and thus find his way into their code to exert control over them. He sighed out a breath and then, his purpose hardening, raised his war body from the floor, up over the autofactories and then into the tunnel leading out. And in a moment, he was ascending into the sky, amidst his swarming soldiers.

The Cyberat were orienting towards the prador force coming their way. Piper made assessments of that force, and then changes. Two waves of the prador spherical war drones were out at the wings, with flying prador in the middle, while others were on the ground behind advancing war machines. The force on the ground was a wedge, with the intent to drive into the installation city, but the whole would turn into a three-pronged pincer as the war drones came in. He noted distributions and patterns. The main force consisted of second-children outnumbering first-children by a hundred and eighty to one. For every hundred and ninety of the first-children, there was one adult – each heavily armed and sporting artificial armour over its natural kind. He also saw, near the back, on the ground, larger war machines, with adults installed in the top of them. It looked very much as if those were the ones in overall charge. In total, he counted twenty million prador, if one included the machines. His force might well win in a straight fight, but there would be little left of them afterwards. He needed to do something else, and that lay in the codes and communication of the command structure that he was now seeing reflected physically.

'Advance,' he said. Because again, it seemed necessary to speak, meanwhile delivering more complex orders direct through animus connections. He then turned his attention to all the prador stuff inside him and, in their code, began designing new animuses.

'This is going to be bad,' said Mallon.

She wasn't the only one to comment on it, and many were saying other things. He chose her, Tinsher and the Engineer Aremer as key in points, while his program prepared to conduct millions of similar conversations. In passing, he searched out the Old Guard Drillain, which took him to a war body near the fore – a thing shaped like the Polity grav-car he'd travelled in on Founder's World. Tracking connections, he found this one in conversation with Triode and Anode and, out of curiosity, listened in. Shame snapped him back out when he discovered them mourning the recent death, only just discovered, of their elder brother, who had inevitably been named Cathode.

'It may not be as bad as you think,' he replied to Mallon, and millions of others.

'You've found a way into that hardware?' Aremer asked.

'I have, but for only one hundred seconds.' He delivered detail on this to others who enquired too.

'A hundred seconds is a lot of time in battle,' said Mallon. 'You must use them well.'

'Indeed.'

'The attack plan and detailed responses will change rapidly,' said Tinsher.

'I have every confidence you'll know what to do.'

'I'm glad you do,' she said dryly.

New orders went out: given the opportunity, the Cyberat should disable those machines at the rear, and their occupants. He needed to plan beyond this battle because, as the sphere made evident, this force was just one put together to deal with their local incursion on the surface. Seeing the vast horde ahead, and the one at his shoulders, yet again hammered home the sheer scale of this prador/Polity conflict. The prador stretched from left to right horizons, eating up the surface of the world as they advanced. On the ground, thousands of treaded war machines advanced in line upon line, while the prador behind seemed to armour the ground with brassy metal. In the sky, clouds of them blotted out the light, swirling five kilometres upwards and shifting into regular patterns. The drones out at the wings were partially lost over the horizon to the right and left – revolving columns of them ready for orders. In all this regularity, Piper traced their command structure. In his own force he could see it too, with the Old Guard centred on rollers of Enforcers, with Engineers and supply in behind, others on the ground ready to pull the injured back behind their advance. However, he did notice his force seemed more fluid – more adaptable.

The two forces closed on each other, missiles launched by both at first mostly taken down by anti-munitions and stabbing particle beams. One blast – a tactical nuke – took out a thousand Enforcers and one Old Guard, while others dropped from the sky trailing smoke. Piper felt them go out, but this, and the pain of those injured and dying, felt distant under the heightened ferocity of his reptile. Two similar nukes hit the ground in the middle of advancing prador, flinging them like burning autumn leaves. Smaller weapons came next, shredding both sides. And now it was time.

Fierce joy rose in Piper as he launched his animuses, feeling them hit home and links to them hardening. He sensed vast query but an inability to disobey, and so he set them to his purpose. Out at the wings, the columns of drones suddenly opened fire straight into the prador force lying between them, then accelerated after their shots. Down on the ground, the rear lines of war machines halted and revolved, opening fire too, and began rolling back into their own force. Chaos ensued, and the ranks of the prador broke. As the first line of ground war machines used up all the heavy armament and wound down to smaller arms, Piper turned the next lines round. These began destroying those of their own kind depleted of ammo, as well as the prador beyond them. Huge chemical explosions tossed prador up in fumaroles of fire. Heavy particle beams boiled them in their armour. Prador launched into the sky, along with their fellows, only to receive the brunt of the drone attack. They began to shoot back at their own machines and, as this chaos continued, Piper struggled to halt the advance of his own forces. He felt too joyful, too fierce, and wanted to be in at the killing. He was utterly amazed at the effectiveness of what he'd just done.

Change plans . . .

Piper now assigned a selection of armies, forming them into pointed cones. They were to punch through and go after those machines at the back. They must capture as many of the adults there as possible.

The hundred seconds wound their way down. The drones were still accelerating in and simply firing all their weapons. He'd given them no guidance, and they couldn't slow down. Their attack began to bunch up the prador army, and then slam into it physically. Piper watched and assessed, the countdown cracking like a whip in his mind. He abruptly sent orders bringing the Cyberat into a tighter formation. In moments, this took on substance and looked just as he'd envisaged it: a milling wheel. This great vertical wheel consisted of packed Enforcers feeding out to the 'teeth', where heavier Old Guard war bodies were positioned. Engineers, Medics and ammo transports sat within it. He set the wheel turning – a slowly revolving monster directed at the bunched-up prador. Then he set it moving forwards, even as the countdown reached zero.

The devastation continued in the prador ranks, as war drones tried to decelerate but still crashed into them, sending them tumbling or simply smashed to pieces. Next, the first tooth of the wheel cut down into them, weapons firing at full power without any attempt at conserving energy or ammo. As each tooth passed down and through, and was blunted by its cut, the next one went in. Meanwhile, troops from the first tooth were pulled into the centre for resupply, repair, and limited medical attention, or transport out. New troops from the inner section of the wheel then replaced them. So the wheel just kept cutting and Piper saw its close resemblance to the actual tool: the heat at the point of cutting, and the swarf falling to pile up and boil the shallow sea below.

'Mallon,' Piper said, but in reality addressing hundreds of commanders by their names too. 'Sweep in.'

Those forces, consisting of Old Guard and millions of Enforcers, rushed in low, destroying war machines depleted of power and ammunition, then slammed into prador already in disarray after having been fired on by their own side.

'Tinsher, take those adults at the back,' he ordered, again addressing more than just her. Spearheads of millions more Enforcers, each tipped with Old Guard, pierced along the side of the wheel, then looped down. Prador fell out of the sky in such numbers, great clouds of steam tracked the course of the attack. It was a slaughter, and Piper felt his anger and excitement waning. But no mercy or empathy displaced them, just a cold determination for destruction, dry and deep inside. He didn't like this change, because perhaps it revealed more of his inner self than he cared to know.

Tinsher's force and others came down hard on those big heavy machines, even as some of them began to rise from the ground. These things were flat in profile, rather like the reaverfish here, and were perhaps an adaptation to the high gravity. In many respects they had the form of Cyberat war bodies, with those controlling them sitting at the centre up top, linked into surrounding machinery. And even now they were concealed by armour hemispheres sliding over them. Through the eyes of others, Piper noticed that all their weapons were attached to tool arms and prominences not made for them. These were in fact harvesting machines adapted to war.

The war bodies hit them hard, but not on those central domes. He saw Enforcers flying underneath one and scouring it with fire. Grav-motors burning underneath, it slid from the sky, crashing into another row of war machines, eating them up. Meanwhile their weapons were firing continuously, hammering at the sky, and the water around them splashing white with falling Enforcers. Further to the rear, a great mass of them turned away and took off, and to the general enquiry he replied, 'Let them go. We have enough.' He still felt no sympathy for the prador concerned, but let them go because he didn't like how many Enforcers their weapons were killing. He saw one machine simply detonate, and then another and another, but whether through damage or suicide by the occupants he had no idea. Within half an hour, fifty-three had been disabled, and another twenty-eight had exploded. Some adults abandoned their machines and tried to flee. Most were brought down in the water, with weapons and limbs stripped away. Engineers were then all over the machines and, with the assistance of heavier war bodies, they worked to pull out the other adult prador.

The point when Piper could clearly say the battle was won came twenty minutes later. With their leaders either disabled on the ground or fleeing, the prador at the battlefront began to flee too. Great clouds of them just turned in the sky and started peeling away. Piper saw no reason in this case to stop the killing. The prador were more intent on running away, and less focused on firing on his soldiers. The milling wheel began to break up, now it had no ordered, densely packed force to slice into, but it broke into wedges, pursuing the larger concentrations of prador as they fled.

'Kill as many as you can, but limit the danger to yourselves as you wish,' he ordered generally, and then he moved his war body deeper into the chaos of the battle.

Such had been the quantity of hot metal going down into the sea that the rising steam had formed great fog banks, diminishing visibility. However, he was able to observe through other senses the masses of broken machines, people and prador lying below, and his ever-precise mind had to do its counting. Over six million prador killed or completely disabled, which was a massive victory compared to the further loss of three hundred thousand of his soldiers. But still, *three hundred thousand.*

He observed the two masses of surviving war drones, still decelerating out on the course he'd set them. Down below, ragged lines of prador war machines were continuing to make their way back too, directing emptied weapons at any movement, then carrying on as if they'd fired the shots. It seemed no prador commander had delivered further orders beyond the one to slow those drones. So, even though he was long past the hundred-second window, he sent programs out to all these machines. The war drones decelerated harder, and in the distance fell into revolving columns, slowly sinking towards the ground. The other machines below simply stopped. Perhaps he could use them, or perhaps they might receive new orders from their prador masters any minute now. He still needed greater control and no chance of it being taken away from him.

'Engineers – those machines.' He sent detailed instructions, but slotted them in at a lower priority than repairing and resupplying his soldiers, as well as assisting the Medics.

He flew low, from where he had a better view of the carnage. Already spider forms were seeking out the injured and mechanically damaged. Parties of Enforcers were also falling on still-living prador and killing them methodically, either with mines or the combination of particle beam and armour-piercers, depending on the vulnerability of the creature concerned. Prisoners in this war were only for information or, in the case of those taken by the prador, for enslavement or sport. He flew on through and noted Enforcers forming up around him, with war bodies ahead. He'd given no orders for this – it had come from Mallon, while other war bodies had joined her. He felt annoyed at the protectiveness, but then managed to quell this with the logic of them wanting to protect their most potent weapon. They knew what he had done.

Finally, he came in over the big harvesters and gazed upon the adult prador that had been rooted out. Would he need to read each one personally, going through them at random, as he had with the slave units and other hardware back at the installation? No, because the stratification of their command structure was reflected in their deployment. At AI speed, Piper replayed the approach of this force and the ensuing battle, layering information on the patterns and seeking data. The general of this army would be to the centre and the back, that was obvious, but not so far back as to be vulnerable to an attack from the rear. Had he made a mistake allowing those earlier ones to flee? He thought not, as he focused on one machine. It fitted the complex analysis he'd made. Confirmation came with deep scans, for the thing carried a heavier load of communications equipment. However, the armoured section was open and no prador was inside.

Piper flew lower, his honour guard swirling around him. The damned creature had got away and maybe flown off with the rest. But, to be sure, he tracked back through battle imagery from tens of thousands of sources to find some on this particular machine. As he did so, he noted movement in the water nearby and, feeling a surge of excitement, dropped closer. Disappointment ensued when he saw a shoal of reaverfish just below the surface. Then, belatedly, the imagery came through for him.

A missile had hit this machine earlier on. The adult, sans legs and with its carapace cracked, had pulled out on grav and watched the way things were going for a while. It saw the forces bearing down on its position and, rather than put itself in the sky as an easy target, slid over the side into the shallow sea. Piper smiled again and looked towards that shoal of reaverfish. He now realized that prador blood attracted them, perhaps because of the similar biology, and he sent orders.

Cyberat swept down, with Mallon going straight in at the lead, Enforcers and Engineers behind her. The shoal scattered and Mallon came up, her war body lodged under the edge of the prador adult as she tipped it over. The thing abruptly snatched away from her to fire a particle cannon, whose beam burned straight through an Enforcer. It then turned, pulling level, and opened up with two Gatling cannons mounted on its back, while pedestal antipersonnel lasers began stabbing through the steam its fight raised. But it was all too late. The Cyberat mobbed it like bees over an attacking hornet. Its weapons went out, then its grav. They held it up and brought it over to a small island of shell and gravel, dropping it down there on its back. At the last,

Piper watched cutting wheels going in, and its weapons and prosthetic claws dropping away. Enforcers and war bodies held onto it, even though it no longer had motive power, and he felt the intensity of their regard.

'You've done well today,' he told them, but then retransmitted that to the rest of his army. 'This is a war we Cyberat are going to end quickly and efficiently, as is our nature.' He paused, feeling he should say more, but then dropped out of the sky onto his prey.

Piper stepped out of the war body cockpit and walked down the armour. Glancing at the fading dots on his hands, he knew the importance of the physical connection was diminishing. Disconnection had been easier this time, because it hardly felt like disconnecting at all. With the capacity of his bones still expanding, he couldn't tell which was largest any more – his substrate or that of the war body – while EMR connecting the two had also increased.

He jumped down and walked out across the belly of the adult prador. The thing had fewer weapons than the first one he'd seen, but was loaded with slave units. These were also of a different design to others. Still hexagonal but smaller, of a greenish metal, and clustered together like masses of honeycomb. They also had shiny interface plates at the centre, to connect to the com gear of the aquaculture machine. Standing here felt like victory, but he knew he had much work to do, and would have to be careful and precise, despite all his internal conflicts. The creature below him was not the place to start, so mentally he ranged out for the skills he needed in the horde now swirling around him, and he smiled.

'Triode and Anode,' he called, also mentally lining up other skillset Engineers under them. The two flew out, spider legs folded up against their bodies, and they looked delighted. Other Engineers clustered behind them, and Piper felt a wave of awe through the connection. It was easy to become arrogant, his dry mind observed, but he still felt like a conqueror. He pointed towards the machine the adult had abandoned.

'I want a full schematic and all its programming,' he said, but then paused. It had been his intention to put himself at the interface between the machine and this prador adult, which was essentially what he'd done before. Now he had other ideas. It was the Cyberat way to penetrate the machine, and that was how he'd originally approached it, but he'd moved beyond that now, being able to penetrate the actual minds of those he controlled. The thinking was wrong – far too much on the side of the machine rather than the organism, as was the distorted thesis of the Founder. But who was to say what was machine and what was organic? They were amalgams of the same and the lines were completely blurred. He gazed at Triode and Anode and came to a decision.

'Pull that machine to dry land and repair all the damage to it,' he ordered. 'But also disconnect its ability to transmit. I want on–off switches there.'

Hundreds of queries washed back to him; rather than answer, he simply pushed for obedience, also reaching out to snare further Engineers.

'As you command!' Anode called, and sped away with the others clustering behind.

The second group of Engineers she summoned came down as he stepped back onto his war body and gave it a mental nudge, to land it further along the gravel spit. As it settled, he eyed the constituents of the small island. Again, it consisted of gravel, broken shell and human bone. Skulls, stirred up by his landing, bobbed out into the waves. The sight confirmed his decision, and he transmitted detail of his orders to set these Cyberat immediately to work.

With arms extended and tool carousels clicking round, they swarmed over the belly of the prador, slicing away wrecked grav-units and the remains of weapons hardware, then tossing the debris into the water. He sat on the edge of his war body and watched as they finally cleared the mess and moved in around the prador. Gripping it in heavy grabs, they turned it over, dropping it down on its belly. Its visual turret, broken mandibles and deep mouth now faced him, and it hissed, bubbling its anger and distress. Even though its 'words' were distorted by its injuries, he didn't need to run any translation to understand it.

'I will tell you nothing,' it told him. 'You will die a hard and agonizing death on this world. We will exterminate your race. We will . . .' And so it went, on and on, sliding into elaborations on the tortures and methods of extermination that would be used. He considered running translation of his own words through the war body, to speak back to it, and perhaps to learn something here – but no. This litany was like the battle hymn or death song of primitive natives from Earth's past. It was meaningless bravado, and a way for the prador to measure itself against death. Anyway, he was about to find out all he needed to know from the creature.

Following anatomy loadings from the Polity, the Engineers came in at its sides, spinning up circular cutters and long chain-diamond saws. As they cut in through the edge of the carapace, the prador's death chant transitioned into a bubbling scream in which its words blurred together. Since they were in the way, its mandibles were lopped off by one Engineer. Thereafter it emitted a hissing bubbling, which only gave context to words it couldn't click and grind out. The Engineers then wedged open the cut and inserted jacks, lifting the top half of its carapace on one side, and making careful incisions inside. The top shell rose higher

377

and higher, exposing organs and muscle still pulsing and clenching. Each time they caused a bleed, they swiftly cauterized it. Piper sent a change to the orders when he saw they were about to sever the thick stretched-out nerves to the head turret, and had them trepan that turret out. This wasn't simple cruelty – he wanted those nerves intact. But it was cruel to lodge the turret down at the edge, so it was looking into its own insides. Whether the idea to do this had come from the Cyberat or him, Piper had no idea.

He moved in closer and studied all that had been revealed. He could see green blood pumping through the veins, as well as the steady bellows movement of the organ that served as both a lung and gill. The muscle that had been separated from the shell was slightly atrophied now, long since having stopped driving any legs or claws. The creature was still noisily alive and unless they severed something vital, would remain so for a while. It was precisely this ruggedness that enabled prador adults to torture their children before finally removing their ganglions and flash-freezing them as hardware to run their machines. He ran the anatomical schematic and noted what lay in his way, then looked round at the Engineers watching. Expressions, where he could read them, ranged from disgust to relish, but most were just severe. He sent instructions on what else to remove, carefully now, to give him the access he needed, then stepped away as they began slicing out that muscle.

The machine the prador had plugged itself into stood over on another small island. He'd been receiving regular updates from Anode and Triode, and had learned that its main damage had been to optics, wiring and a power supply they were now replacing. As per his instructions, they'd stripped off some of its armour to expose all this. He didn't need that to go back yet, nor did he need the thing to go anywhere, for now, at least. Like all the machines on the battlefield, it would come in useful, though. Still sitting on the edge of his war body, Piper again lifted it into the sky, and slid it over to the other spit, landing it with a gentle crunching of stones and broken shell, and the soft popping of skulls.

Apart from a cycling of watchers going up into the sky, most of the Cyberat were down now. Once again the Engineers were in charge, grabbing up weapons, materials and other supplies from the dead. On the horizon smoke and steam boiled into the air from the installation city, as the converted factories there steadily expanded and worked ever harder. Taking an omniscient view, he saw hordes of damaged or injured, but still mobile, Cyberat forming great queues which ran into those factories, as well as what were essentially hospitals. Many Cyberat coming out had progressed too, having acquired prador armour and weapons, and extra power supplies and transceivers. They were turning into an amalgam of themselves and the enemy, more able to supply themselves from that enemy. And just like him, they were becoming more able to understand it.

'They are ready,' said Triode, settling out of the air before him. She looked very serious and perhaps a little horrified. Though he'd not outright stated his intentions, the Cyberat here had managed to ascertain them from the orders he'd given them.

'Then it's time for me to do what I must do,' he replied, sliding from his war body and walking over to the partially dismantled erstwhile aquaculture machine.

Meanwhile, the Engineers on the other island had gathered about the prador adult, the top half of its shell now completely removed, and began lifting it. They took it high up over the water, carefully, like carrying a bowl of hot soup – not wanting to spill the contents. They positioned the prador just so above the harvester, before bringing it down. Engineers all around the machine then reached up through where the armour had been removed to guide the creature down. Piper could just see the honeycombs of interfaces perfectly lining up. They made those connections and others besides, finally winding in spiral fixings to stabilize the thing. And so it was ready.

Piper stepped forwards, an Engineer moving in front of him and stooping low, so he could use the man's machine body as a step. He went up onto a sloped plate of armour that remained, then up to the edge and looked down into the creature. The muscle was all gone, as was much of the digestive system and related support organs. It was dying now and would last no more than a day, but that should be enough. Amidst these organs, braced by webs of translucent body matter, lay its ring-shaped major ganglion, sealed in chalky bone, or chitin. He mapped the nerves running in from the rest of its body and located the artificial connections. These ran inside the thing from the external interface array to connect to larger nerve trunks. He tracked these back to the ganglion, smiled, and stripped off his gauntlets to dump them beside him on the armour. Then he stepped down into the creature's cooling guts.

Not wanting to kill the thing inadvertently, Piper made his way through the prador's insides with care. All around him it began to quiver and jerk, as if trying to eject him. Using the schematic, he found bracing strut bones and stood on them. Still, it was like wading through thick mud finally to get to the ring-shaped ganglion. Slimy with the creature's juices but otherwise rough and bumpy, this organ was about as thick as his thigh. He gripped it and, knowing it would be strong enough, heaved over and inside it. He moved his hands round to find the areas he wanted, then looked up. The head turret was pointed straight at him, while hissing sounds still issued from what remained of the creature's mouth, out of sight on the body. Lidless red eyes gazed at him unblinking, and he wondered if it still had any comprehension of what was happening to it. Did this make him as bad as the prador? No, not really. He initiated his threads, bringing those metal flecks to his hands and forearms, and placed them down on the creature's ganglion.

With a crunching sound, the threads penetrated the bony shell and spread around the ring. Millions of connections ensued, and then billions, as the threads frayed and branched. Translating electrical impulses as data points was easy enough. Translating the effects of neurochem required high levels of analysis. However, he had a key on the firings as he built his model. Complex thought was suppressed by the main themes of pain and damage running in waves through its nervous system. He began to construct a model of its mind and its nervous system on that basis, meanwhile opening up data files he'd taken from Albermech – doubtless at the AI's intent. Prador had already been interrogated during this war via implanted augs, just as he was now implanting himself. And so he created virtual interrogation augs in his bones and installed the connections. This was good and gave him a great deal of insight, but its depth was only that of language and he needed to go further.

The prador muttered at him from under the wash of pain, and the utter stubborn disbelief that its life was ending. It railed at the incompetence of its children, certain the time had come for it to thin them out and install them in something more obedient. And so thinking, it reached out to those that *were* more obedient, as it had tried to many times before.

The wash of telemetry from war machines and drones through the harvester was fined down but still complex. In this he truly saw the prador as a highly technical species and not just beasts. Piper swiftly understood its content: it was the number of war drones and ground machines out there, their positions, available armament and power status. The prador made queries but since the Engineers had cut its ability to transmit it got no reply. As with everything else, Piper recorded the data it gave. And then the prador disappeared under another wave of pain and the disconnected confusion of a dying brain.

Piper looked up, surprised to see a deep aubergine sky scattered with stars and washed with the bright swathes of interstellar warfare. He observed the moon on the horizon, still burning, and watched the steady flashing of meteors as debris burned up. Many hours had passed and he'd learned a great deal, but he felt bloated with information and without the tools to digest it. He stretched higher, looking over the edge, and saw Cyberat on the ground in concentric rings around him, spreading to the foggy distance. He wanted now to check on progress beyond his own task, but knew he couldn't delay. He opened a crammed node, and his war body rose silently and drifted over. He felt the wash of grav as it edged close, turned and tilted, then opened a port and extruded the nub of an interface. He withdrew his threads into his left hand, and reached up with that to connect.

All the data crammed in his bones, and already opening fractal depths there, spread out into the war body substrate via this physical connection. His father's creature wrapped around it, and him, and bound all together in coherence. In that instant, the prador's mind incorporated and divided itself in this mass, spreading its pain and indignity. His reptile changed, and he couldn't help but compare it to his Cyberat taking on prador armour and weapons. For now, on the mental plenum, it seemed both reptile and arthropod. Something began to scream and he thought it was the prador, yet this was a mental model, and this time the sound was like amplifier feedback. He rested in its guts as the interface between war body and prador closed the circuit of a feedback loop. Data screamed around in that circuit, seemingly out of control, but the logic of his system stacked, ordered and elucidated it.

Piper became a hunk of armoured and fast aggression, breaking through a surface, hungry and avid. Food surrounded him and he ripped into it with his new mandibles, feeding chunks into his gullet. He grazed past something else hard and aggressive too, and recognized kin and not food, unless he found weakness in its shell. No need to check that while amidst such plenty. The feelings were intense and formative. At one remove Piper recognized the hatching of a prador from an egg implanted inside the paralysed body of a reaverfish.

Along with a host of his kin, he broke out through skin, feeling gill lungs expand for the first time, the crack of carapace aligning, and a wash of energy. The memory was as brief as all childhood ones usually were. Piper compared this to his time with the girl by the river, then segued into the pain of a cracked shell and the looming form of a first-child. Memory and experience looped around each other, as it did in the tangle of the multifaceted mind he'd become a part of. The life experience of this prador was brutal, all the way through, but also right and correct in its perception, as evidenced by its ascendance.

It was like Piper's four years in virtuality, as he encompassed all that was in this prador's mind, branching away from present experience. All memories of memories of memories. He felt and he understood the xenophobic aggression as, in essence, payback on fraternal aggression, reinforced by the logic of patricide and the establishment of power. But he wasn't here for their psychology, beyond what he could use to kill them. Just as, given the chance, they would use everything in his mind to kill him.

He focused on technology, on com, on slaver and thrall

hardware and on codes. It all mapped out for him, expanding in fractal spaces in his bones, while the processing went on in the war body substrate. He extended the hundred seconds he'd been previously limited by with multiple viral fixes and circuitous programming routes. In the system and the coding, in his understanding of it, he sat right at the centre. But he sat in the centre of a model, and now it was time to test it for real.

Piper opened out, his interlocked being consisting of himself, the substrates, the reptile and the dying prador mind. His inner space expanded, incorporating tens of millions of nodes, the fading conflict in orbit and this world. In that instant, he knew his bones had further extended their fractal processing down into the Planck realm, and his reach had expanded hugely. With a thought, he encompassed the entire solar system battle sphere. Even light-speed delay wasn't a barrier as he sent and received conventional data through the U-space com of the ships out there. But this didn't include his animus transmission and links, which he couldn't yet retransmit from other sources, so he pulled back to the world.

He crouched in the prador guts, one hand on its mind and into the machine below, the other up on the war body interface and linked into its substrate. And yet, with his internal processing capable of encompassing so much, he felt larger than the world. Now it was time to test his power.

He clicked over those switches the Engineers had placed in the machine below, and allowed it to now transmit as well as receive. The prador adult, even in its current state, saw an opportunity to send its location and pull in war machines to rescue it. Rather than shut that down, Piper simply watched and learned more. The drones began to rise into the sky again and head in this direction, while the other war machines on the ground activated and oriented towards him. A cry went up from the

Cyberat, even as he inserted in the adult's programming the order to shut down the weapons of all those machines.

'Don't concern yourself, they are under my control,' he replied, to millions in thousands of different ways.

The adult's effort seemed its last, as its mind fell into terminal confusion. He took away its control, disassembled it, and then shaped it to his purpose. The drones settled out of the sky again and the war machines froze. Exploring the transceiver circuits, he stretched further, far out to war machines he didn't then control, and knew in an instant he could seize them. He left them alone for now, because tactically it'd be better if the prador thought they still controlled them. He even found routes around the base code changes, and then discovered that he probably wouldn't need them. Those codes had been transmitted around the world by satellites that no longer existed.

Enough.

He had it all now, copied across, and could transmit from his war body. He no longer needed this prador adult or the machine it was dying in. He detached from its ganglion and the war body interface, brought his machine lower and, getting a grip, heaved himself up. Dripping with prador juices, he walked up the armour to the cockpit, reached inside and took out his carbine, then came back down to stand at the edge of it, looking down into the creature. He finally fired into its ganglion, breaking and burning it. Around him, reflecting him, a ripple effect spread out, as Cyberat guarding other captured prador adults responded to the order implicit in his action, and executed them too. He in turn gazed at this prador's head turret. Like lights severed from their power supply, the eyes seemed to go out.

16

Comlinks opened – three of them. Piper gazed at the things as his war body flew slowly back into the installation with him sitting on the edge, legs dangling over the side. So much had happened, externally and internally, that he didn't know if he wanted to respond. They seemed like messages from another world, locked into his past. He also wondered about the purpose of them, since he'd seen no particular changes in the battle sphere someone might think he needed alerting to. He opened one, noted the bandwidth and agreed to it.

'Inster,' he said.

The bandwidth edged into virtuality, so it seemed as though he was standing at the agent's shoulder, but also partially was him.

'Do you see?' Inster pointed at a screen. The man was in a control room – a zero-grav sphere, with acceleration chairs and com stations all around its interior occupied by other people. The screen displayed a prador space station, obviously heavily damaged, with prador crawling about its hull. Small-weapons fire cross-hatched the vacuum between them and the cloud of marines descending on the station.

'Why not simply destroy it?' Piper asked.

'It's still loaded with weapons and will be a suitable platform for our defence of the planet. I ran a penetration – flying in a

Sparkind unit inside prador armour – and they fed a virus into the system to shut down the power.'

Imagery arrived of that very operation and he saw two suits of first-child armour standing open, with their contents discarded in a pile to one side. Meersham and Cheen climbed into one suit, while Sloan and Geelie climbed into the other. He speeded up what followed: their crossing from a wrecked prador destroyer to the station, a lot of creeping about seen through suit cams, a good deal of fighting and some precise sabotage with Sloan's explosives, and then the virus – simply a chunk of tech plugged into a prador interface.

'And you are showing me this why?'

'That's why.' He pointed to another screen showing a great mass of prador ships gathered around a world Piper didn't recognize. Checking context on the image, he found it was in the Prador Kingdom. The update to the battle sphere arrived a moment later, perfectly timed. Projections had been changed. The Polity forces commanded space around the world now, but that might not last because this gathering prador fleet was due to come here. Piper pulled his feet up onto the armour of his war body as it arrived in the chamber he'd used before and settled to the floor.

'I see,' he said, then opened the other two comlinks.

These brought with them even more bandwidth, and they amalgamated shortly after he opened them. What spoke to him was also an amalgamation, and he didn't know whether to call it Corisian or Albermech.

'Hello Corimech,' he said.

'So you have retained a sense of humour,' the two replied. The virtuality incorporated the sensor data of the *Albermech*, showing it in high orbit above the world. The ship was in action, shooting down swarms of missiles coming into range from further out in the system and, as it cruised along, sowing further minefields into orbit.

'Even with that space station platform, and our fleet out there, you may not be able to maintain cover for me. That at least is clear,' said Piper.

'We advise that you do not set up a permanent base in that installation,' they said.

'Hardly likely that I would.' He grimaced. Why did this dual being seem so slow to him? Answer: because it was, now. 'But that's not the reason for this contact.' He noted the flows of information, and how the two were drilling into him to find out what he'd done down here. He knew he could block that in an instant, but allowed it. 'Do you have enough yet?' he asked.

'Enough to know that we still cannot copy what you have done,' they replied.

'And now you want to point out to me that if this world is completely under Polity control, the prador will likely withdraw, seeing it as too costly to retrieve.'

'Smart lad,' said Corisian, separating out.

'So it would seem,' said Albermech.

'I said that from the start,' Inster interjected. With that came further linkage, and he perceived the four Sparkind hiding in a prador nursery, its pool floating with a scum of dead third-children. This elicited a strange sympathetic response in him. He felt all his erstwhile companions watching him, with wariness, compassion, sadness and, in Inster's case, with the same approval he directed towards a well-made weapon.

'And now, since you've touched base to remind me that I'm a component in a war effort, and given me the psychological nudge out of my expected tunnel vision . . . I have things to do.' He left unsaid that, with bleed-over from him, they'd also been making yet another assessment of him.

'Your mind has gained hard edges and surfaces,' said Albermech, 'and an unexpected ruthlessness.'

'As much a requirement here as your cold calculations,' Piper replied.

'Undoubtedly true,' interjected Corisian, 'but its source is of concern.'

Piper didn't think that worthy of comment. 'Is that all?'

'There was something else,' said Albermech, the other links fading – Corisian's, it seemed, reluctantly.

'What?'

'Things are happening in the Prador Kingdom. It appears they are fighting among themselves. This may have some influence on events here.'

Piper was abruptly interested. He had seen the motivation for this contact and how it would run, but this was something new.

'Analysis?'

'Rebellion, potentially. Certainly division among family groups is occurring.'

'Then keep me informed,' said Piper, and closed off the final comlink.

Piper stood up and stretched, then jumped down from the war body to the floor. After disconnecting from it since linking into the prador general, he hadn't climbed back inside it again for a simple reason: to avoid stinking out his cockpit with the glutinous mess drying on his suit. In fact, it was already beginning to smell bad.

All around him in this chamber, and others throughout the city, Cyberat were busily at work. Engineers and Medics were repairing his soldiers where they could, utilizing prador technology and also tech salvaged from dead Cyberat. His range and internal resolution having increased, he could now see much of this just with the processing of his bones, without having to connect into his war body substrate. He saw one place designated as a mortuary, with its great mound of human remains, now crawling with prador ship lice, as well as prador remains stripped out of armour the Engineers found serviceable. Even the dead were useful too and the Cyberat, having long dismissed any attachment to life's fleshy container, had reverse-engineered and repurposed prador processing plants. Cyberat were now feeding their deceased fellows into them, and in turn the plants were producing slabs of nutrient and containers of liquefied versions of the same. Amino acids were amino acids, no matter their source.

Factories elsewhere ran at full power, now complemented by prador reactors taken from storage. Materials trains ran through adult corridors to feed these, while Enforcers and other Cyberat dispersed via smaller tunnels, freshly armoured, loaded with munitions and carting extra supplies. But even now some of the factories were starting to shut down, and Engineers were packing away their massively increased collections of tools. This place had worked as a base for a while but, as Albermech had opined, it couldn't be permanent. Piper didn't want a position it would be necessary to divide his forces to hold. Their purpose here, after all, was not to settle on the world, but to rid it of its invaders.

He noted a proliferation of grav-sleds of a curious design, also loaded with supplies along with a few recovering wounded. He then recognized the sleds as the lower carapace sections of prador adults and large first-children, running on their own grav. Next, searching out those vitrified by their nanosuites, or otherwise encapsulated in hibernation spheres, he found them on smaller sleds being run out of the city. Engineers and builders out there had repurposed underground caves, previously occupied by prador, to take them. He didn't like the idea of leaving them behind, but bringing them along would hamper his army. Anyway, he didn't expect prador to seek these out while larger threats to them existed, and he fully intended to be the largest threat of all down here.

'I have what you requested, General,' said Triode, settling out of the air and down on her spider limbs. She had a tank strapped to her side with pipes running from it to a spray device attached where her hand had once been.

Piper returned part of his focus to his location, standing just beyond his war body, then with a thought closed up his helmet and visor. 'Get this stuff off me.' He held his arms above his head, ready to be washed.

Triode immediately hit him with jets of soapy solvent, scuttling quickly round him, then finished off with high-pressure water. While she was doing this, Anode arrived and unloaded a large pack. Once his suit was gleaming again, Piper opened up his helmet and stooped by the pack, taking out a slab and a bottle. He ate and drank while they watched, feeling a stab of distaste knowing he was eating the processed product of dead Cyberat and prador, but erased that as irrelevant. He knew the feeling arose from his virtuality experience. For the citizens of the Polity still retained attachment to such remains, which were often disposed of with some ceremony, though often equally through some form of processing.

'I'm sorry about your brother Cathode,' he said. And as he spoke the words, he delivered similar consoling comments and conversations throughout the Cyberat horde. It seemed a cheat to him, but there was no alternative way when dealing with such numbers, other than to say nothing at all.

'He might still be alive out there,' said Anode.

'He might indeed,' Piper replied, knowing the young man had

been incinerated and blown out into vacuum. 'Many thought to be lost may well reappear. We cannot know exactly the names and number of the dead.' That last definitely was a lie, because he could count them exactly and name them all.

'What happens next?' Triode asked.

He ate the last of the food and washed it down with the vitamin-laden liquid, and it all felt leaden inside him. His nanosuite considered it satisfactory and was working as busily as the factories around him, having to clear the recent toxic load washed from his bones.

'I will sleep,' he replied. 'Everyone will rest and restore themselves as best they can too. Then we move out in the morning – if the prador don't attack again before that.' He considered their new fleet out there, on its way, but it was at least twenty hours away if the data of Polity espionage were correct. And Polity forces were still up in orbit around this world.

'And after?' asked Anode.

'Go find your father.' He waved them off. 'He's looking for you.' He sent them the Cyberat Old Guard's location, then turned away. Climbing back up his war body, he saw them hesitating momentarily, then moving off. He clambered down into the cockpit, plugged in the tubes and other connectors, set the chair and suit to hold him in a comfortable position, and finally closed his eyes. He didn't need the sleep, because again his virtual aug could serve that psychological function, while his nanosuite tended to the physiological aspect. But he wanted the break and that finessing of function only real sleep provided.

What next?

There was no subtle way to express the answer: we slaughter them. A shadow of concern passed through his mind about the fact he felt no moral qualms. It was war. It was what you did.

* * *

Amellan was both angry and proud as she showed him the metallic tattoos down her arms, across the backs of her hands, at the back of her neck and on her skull where the hair had been shaved away.

'They're beautiful,' she said, but it was a concession.

Piper stared in puzzlement at the patterns, partially sunk into her skin, then realized why they looked so familiar. They were the shape of the lichens that grew on slabs further down on the bank of the river.

'Yes, beautiful,' he agreed, seeing greater beauty here than in the river stones, because the tattoos served a purpose. Though a technological fashion, they were also machine interfaces and a slower, easier way of developing such connections in a growing child. Better than drilling holes in bones.

Then he was suddenly back in the operating room, with his father poised over him, but he was to a degree conscious of dreaming and had some grip on the narrative. He didn't want to see this place, so turned away, and it seemed he folded out of the frame and to one side. When he turned back, his father had grown immense and acquired legs and claws. His surgical equipment had changed too, for he'd inserted himself into a half-shell surgery, before swinging that round to Piper's brother.

The first-child brother squealed and rattled his mandibles. Secured in a different-shaped frame, he begged for his life and for another chance, as Father cut around the edge of his carapace. Piper knew Father would show no mercy and that his brother's begging served another purpose: it was the victim's distraction from horror and would speed the process. Without it, Father would extend things until he did beg. The top of the shell came up with a liquid tearing, and the words blurred into an agonized shriek. Father delved inside with the surgical limbs of the half-shell, pushing organs and flesh aside to get to that ring-shaped

393

ganglion. Piper backed through a door and turned straight into another dream narrative.

'You know that the lichen is a native of this world – one that still thrives despite the introduction of Terran life?' Doge asked.

'I thought the blue bananas were natives too,' said the young Castron, waving his hand vaguely towards the wide window.

Doge shook his head. 'They're just a genetic mod.'

'So what is your interest in this one?' Castron nodded to the screen Doge sat before. 'Maybe it is alien but it's still only the product of random evolution.'

'This variety leave shadows in the rock,' Doge replied.

'What?'

'It is incredibly slow growing, unlike the rest, and doesn't actually have a cellular structure like Terran life. The leaf shapes we see repeat down and down like fractals, in fact they are biological fractals, right down to the plant's code at the molecular level where it performs the function of DNA.'

'Shadows?' Castron repeated.

'The patterns repeat down into the rock. Nanoscale forces at work, reordering the composition of matter below the plant. I've tracked this order thus far to the spin and charge on atoms, to magnetically maintained structures, and suspect it goes deeper still.'

'Biology,' said Castron contemptuously. 'Why are you wasting your time on this? We need you to start making those weapons. It's taken the deaths of four overseers to get you where you are, and there are suspicions.'

'This may become the greatest weapon of all—'

Castron interrupted. 'It's vaguely interesting biology but will never be as useful as a particle cannon.' He stepped in and swept the screen aside, sending it crashing to the floor, and stuck his face in Doge's. 'Just do your damned job!'

The crash multiplied into explosions on the horizon below the turbulent orange sky. In agony, Doge crawled out of his wrecked war machine, hauling himself with his elbows since his hands were just masses of splintered bone. He reached a slab clad with his favourite lichen and rolled over, trying not to see the further shattered ruin from his waist down. The pain surged over him in waves, but seemed to be diminishing now. He lay back on the lichen and waited to bleed out, as he surely would any time now.

Piper woke with a start. Fractal alien lichen? It felt almost a betrayal that his father had based the technology that lay in his bones on a plant. But then he recognized the foolishness of the feeling, since Cyberat technology, and in fact all technology, was arguably copied from life. Didn't the twins move about in the body facsimiles of spiders? In irritation he sat forward, dismissing the dream to turn to present concerns and incorporated exterior data at once.

The factories within the installation city were winding down, and most of the Cyberat were now outside looking towards the sunrise. The sanctum here was empty, with just a little rubbish scattered about the floor. He grimaced, stripped off his gauntlets and put his hands down on the chair arms.

The muted shock of connection illustrated how the capacity of his bones had very definitely grown larger than that of the war body substrate. The nodes and other informational objects in his internal space gained definition, though the contrast was not so great as before. He felt larger, as if he dominated, but with the result that, as he keyed into extra processing, his reptile seemed to fill him up – a shadow body occupying his own and his eyes taking its yellow glare. But now it seemed there was a hint of a prador head turret in his overlay. He felt aggression but again couldn't nail down the source: maybe the reptile, maybe something of the prador, or maybe just him. The territory of his mind had never been his own, and so thinking on mental independence played back into old discussions. No one had an independent mind, because they were all a product of their influences. This couldn't be escaped.

He wrenched the war body from the floor, turned and flew it at full speed along a tunnel and then out, hurling it up into the sky. His appearance caused a shift all around him, mentally and physically, as if he were a key into the machine of the Cyberat army. Mostly stalled throughout the night, his soldiers now began to form up. He stabilized in the sky and observed, with growing clarity now making him smile fiercely, because sleep *had* performed its magic.

In the ensuing hours the Cyberat flowed out into the surrounding lands, and with their mass departure it seemed the installation began to die. Piper observed domes collapsing, brief bright blasts and fires starting up. In ripping out all they required at the last, the Engineers were not gentle. Fewer Cyberat were airborne than during the attack here and the subsequent battle against the prador army. Most were staying grounded to conserve power, though his commanders had been running a steady cycle of watchers into the air, forming flowing question-mark clouds. Though the army had lost many soldiers, he saw that now it had grown in content. Down below, big aquaculture machines from the city, and those of the prador commanders, had been brought in to be loaded with supplies and salvageable wounded. The lower carapace section of prador, which the Engineers had turned into rafts the day before, were mostly back in place on the vehicles. Other smaller harvesters rolled along too, still sporting harpoons and nets. Cyberat swarmed into the spaces between these, dotted through with the large war bodies of Old Guard travelling on treads or on huge balloon or cage wheels. Out ahead, the prador ground war machines stood in patient rows, being rearmed by Engineers, while to the right and left, spherical war drones lay on the ground recharging from reactors torn out of the installation's guts. All would be ready by the time they reached the next target.

Piper studied the battle sphere. The choices were many, since installations like this were scattered all about the planet, but now he'd chosen something harder. The nearest space port had been hit from orbit – the main targets there being the ships on the ground. The prador had been busy since then, clearing wreckage and working hard on one prador destroyer. He didn't want that thing back up in the sky, since it could become a threat but, also, it looked like an opportunity.

'Are we all ready for our next chores?' he enquired, then muted the answering roar to say, 'Then it is time to move out.' He sent coordinates and the ground war machines set in motion, while drones started launching from the sides. The Cyberat headed out at the fore, with many still coming in behind from the installation city, while the aquaculture machines began rolling. Numerous queries arrived about the order of the march and he ran his conversational program to connect and reply, but mostly drew their attention to the battle sphere scenario covering this very subject.

'Is it you actually speaking?' Mallon asked.

He located her in the crowd, rolling on cage wheels, surrounded by an entourage of Engineers and tens of thousands of Enforcers ranked behind her. Her question explained why he wasn't engaging with as many as before. And, peering into a selection of minds, he saw they'd also realized he couldn't be speaking personally with them all in their millions. He noted a degree of resentment about that too. He'd felt he had been cheating, and many felt they'd been cheated, but the whole thing was much more nuanced than that.

'It is and it isn't,' he replied to her, and in different ways to those others. 'When I respond to many of you, it's via a program within my mind that models the upper strata of my mind. I can also divide my focus over thousands of these conversations. But, it has to be said, I haven't tried to do it with all of them. I do have other things to think about.'

'It doesn't seem right,' she said ponderingly.

'No, it doesn't seem right to me either,' he said. 'And the reason for that is that it's machine-based and not human. Perhaps something to think on in regard to the Founder's ideas . . .'

At once that statement generated thousands more conversations for his program to handle, along with more engagement between Cyberat rather than with him. He noted wryly how this communication reflected all the problems that arose in the far past with the first social medias. But his interest strayed elsewhere, as he noted many talking who hadn't spoken before.

Enforcers were now engaging – like the strong silent soldiers finally forced to speak out. They were mostly monosyllabic, but the quantity was overwhelming. Notably, the general opinion coming across from them was directed towards the Old Guard and refugees: suck it up, at least you can talk. He smiled at that but also felt some caution, because all were now thinking outside of, and breaking away from, their programming. He could be seeing the beginning of the end of this force, with schisms forming . . . unless he reprogrammed them again through installed animuses.

He left the conversation to run, observing patterns and deciding he really didn't want to change anything. Over the ensuing hours, the army drew clear of the installation city and spread out to utilize dry ground where possible, a vast horde stretching from horizon to horizon.

'In two days we'll arrive at our next target,' he told them, bluntly interrupting this exchange and sending a battle sphere projection. 'As you can see, it may be that our target will come to us before then.'

The response to his army setting out had been desultory at first, but now a prador army was coalescing out from the space port, while other large movements of prador were converging there from around the world. He ran estimates and saw that at the likely time of contact, the prador would outnumber his force five to one. Even now, their masses were substantial and stretching hundreds of kilometres across.

'We will need to be engaged because of that,' said an Old Guard called Transter, well before anyone else noted the likely time of arrival of the new prador fleet. 'As an army out here away from any prador, we'll be too easy a target.'

Piper reviewed his forces again, now with a gap ten kilometres wide between it and the installation, and moving in good order. He made some calculations and saw that they were travelling at the pace of the slowest, which were the aquaculture machines and the prador war machines.

'Pick up the pace,' he said, detailing this. They decided to leave the aquaculture machines behind, guarded by the ground war machines. Much of their supplies and their wounded would be vulnerable. But it didn't matter. This was a battle that would go swiftly one way or the other. If he could reach out and seize control, as intended, they would win. If he couldn't, his army would soon enough be boiling the shallow seas.

Steam began to rise around the advancing Cyberat. As he flew above them, Piper watched them slowly overtaking the aquaculture machines and then flowing between the ground war machines. However, he did notice one of the former keeping up with the army and, querying that, discovered it to be the machine of the prador general, repaired during the night. The thing had some seriously powerful engines and had probably been that prador's personal transport when all they did here was harvest mudskippers and reaverfish, as well as hunt down stray humans.

The landscape here consisted mostly of water, no more than one or two metres deep, and spits of shingle or rock. In places, he saw the soldiers parting around the occasional deeper pools, but that changed at the behest of one Old Guard commander. He told his soldiers, 'You've fought hostile armoured aliens with weaponry as good as ours, and you're still frightened of deep water?' It was Transter again, and he shamed them into those pools, where they scared up shoals of flat reaverfish and sent them splashing between the ranks. Once the army was beyond the slower machines, there was a bit of back flow as soldiers discovered problems with their bodies, either human or machine, and had to return to the Engineers and Medics at the rear.

'Will you actually hear this?' wondered Tinsher, speaking to him. 'They can see you in their minds, but they need to see you with their eyes . . . if they have them.'

He focused on this Old Guard woman. Her human plug form sat in a recess to the fore of one of three conjoined cylinders. One of the other cylinders sported the ion cannon he'd seen her use to good effect, while the one she was in contained grav-engines, feeds and carousels for that weapon, as well as other armament attached all over it. The third held a linear fusion reactor of old Cyberat design. She reminded him of the one on Founder's World who'd taken a shot at him, and whom he'd destroyed. But he was more interested in what lay inside that form, and so eased into her mind, as he had done with Mallon.

His reprogramming had taken as well with her as with the Enforcers, because it wasn't at large variance from her original thinking. He found those elements of shame in her, as in Mallon, but in her case they were because of what she'd *not* done, rather than any heinous acts she'd committed. She had been there at the beginning with Castron, in the rebellion fifty years ago, but thereafter ducked out of what ensued. She'd rolled along with the regime, keeping her head down, as had so many. Now seeing her history gave Piper abrupt pause. He had always looked upon the Old Guard as authority, the establishment, something above him to be feared and resented, and latterly to be regarded with contempt. But now, as he began to understand them better, he realized that had been an over-simplification, not least because of memories surfacing from his reptile in his dreams – from the inadvertent copy of some portion of his father. It seemed evident now that his father had been an actor in that old rebellion, had known Castron, and had fought, but then gone his own way. His father, even though he'd chosen not to be part of the ruling hierarchy, had been Old Guard too.

Piper grimaced at that, feeling a wave of something running through him he could only describe as emotional cognitive dissonance. The hatred – certainly not his own – was intimately tangled with the same shame Tinsher felt. His influenced emotions had shaky foundations. The reality, he felt, would only be found by living free of that shadowy presence and, even then, he wasn't sure. Angry, he pushed the melange of emotions down and returned to concentrating on the moment, and what Tinsher had said. He examined conversations she'd had, and others throughout the army, then generalized thought streams and emotional content. She didn't have the kind of access he had and he was, at least for the moment, baffled how she'd seen it when he had not. But she was right.

Many were the questions of 'Where is he? Can you see him?' and an air of dislocation and uncertainty permeated the army. Enforcers knew where their own commanders were, but merely saw them as a conduit to him. And as their mental function continued to rise, they were developing not so much distrust for those commanders, as a lack of respect. He hadn't banished from their minds how they'd become Enforcers, nor the fact that those commanders had been part of that system. There wasn't so much of that amidst the refugees who made up most of the Engineers and Medics, but still they were searching the sky. He guessed that a moving dot picked out by their sensors wasn't quite what they wanted. And the Old Guard themselves in those large war bodies? They were mentally moving into the territory of ruling small kingdoms, while the high king was just a distant voice.

'You are correct,' he said to Tinsher.

'That you? Really?'

'It's always me, really.' As he said this, he formed a plan. He drew in data on Enforcers and Old Guard, but also allowed personal prejudice to inform his choice. Yes, this would do it. He found the necessity contemptible, but knew he couldn't simply do what he wanted without incorporating the regard of others. He began to prepare his entourage.

He sent out orders to the Engineers running the prador general's machine, and they at once began to clear a space on the thing by redistributing supplies aboard. Orders to specific Enforcers had them rising out of their ranks and heading in towards the machine. He viewed some of these. The Enforcers he'd chosen were of an old, blocky design. They were larger and more impressive than the more modern versions and, until their visit to Room 101, had been a lot more inefficient. But their size had enabled them to load up with large fusion reactors, laminar power and extra weapons. Latterly they'd added brassy prador armour, heavy Gatling cannons and in many cases, prador claws.

'Tinsher, Transter, Mallon and Drillain, you are with me – you can relay orders to your soldiers when battle is joined,' he said, detailing positioning as the aquaculture machine began to accelerate through the advancing army. Space also opened out around this, into which the big Enforcers began to descend, all of them lowering triangular caterpillar tread units. Piper, seeing space had now been cleared for him, descended too, with Enforcers buzzing and moving quickly out of his path. He halted twenty metres above the machine as his entourage fell in around him.

'While I agree with Tinsher on this,' said Mallon. 'You're putting a big red target dot on yourself now.'

He checked her thinking. She was proud to have been chosen, but also annoyed at that pride. He found similar pride in the others too but without the annoyance. Then he withdrew, because though he needed to know some of their thinking, it could also be a distraction.

'You too,' he sent personally to Anode, Triode and Aremer. 'Attend me.'

The entourage took shape as a spearhead oozing out at the front of the main force. He delivered new orders to watchers in the sky all along the kilometres-long front. Their job, to survey the terrain ahead and gather data on the prador, was redundant while Polity satellites constantly updated the battle sphere. He now wanted them delivering status updates on the army to its soldiers. And all would be able to see him, with some of his commanders and a guard of Enforcers, leading the way.

'Better?' he asked Tinsher.

'As best as can be managed at this scale,' Tinsher replied.

Piper dipped into the mood of his soldiers and felt it firming up. He had properly incorporated himself at the head and, knowing where he was now, they felt more sure of him. He settled down to the machine, folding out his war body's feet and initiating their remora function to stick to the armour. His force

403

was once more precisely organized. That would last at least another day or, he hoped, two.

The day drew slowly on and the sun, becoming visible at last in the cloudy sky, set on the horizon spectacularly because of all the dust and smoke in the atmosphere. Ahead the prador still gathered, but weren't advancing. Piper called a halt for rest and consolidation, since many were still as toxin-laden as he. It didn't matter if the prador army grew – numbers were now no longer the issue.

He left his war body and tended to human needs after stripping out of his suit, pondering on the organic inconvenience of having to void his bowels in the shade of the aquaculture machine, with prador-clawed Enforcers backed up around him. He compared that to plug-form Cyberat flicking out solid pellets of excrement when necessary. He preferred his human form, even if the form of the mind within in it might not be of that species.

'I've brought you food and drink,' Anode told him much later, as Triode stepped away. He wiped himself down with the fabric Triode had provided after scouring him head to foot with her sprayer – the water ran soapy into surrounding crevices on this outcrop in shallow seas.

'Put it there.' He pointed up to the edge of his war body.

She stared at him standing naked on this particular mushroom of rock. He saw the sheen to her eyes as she then quickly turned away and did as bid. The two were constant members of his 'staff' now, but the fact they'd become body servants too seemed cruel, for he was a constant reminder of what they had lost. He quickly put his suit back on, climbed up on the aquaculture machine to eat, and then returned to his war body to sleep and dream the emotional memories of someone else.

With the sunrise, the army advanced again and after fifty

kilometres, the waterscape began to change. They departed shallow seas and moved to marginally higher ground. Across this lay patchworks of pools laden with thick grey mud forming shiny drifts, the land around packed shingle. About these pools stood large silos, pumps and squat blocky machines, while the pools themselves stirred with the car-sized flopping bodies of giant mudskippers. Transter's admonition about deep water had to be abandoned when Cyberat became mired in the mud, and then damaged by the panicking creatures. Those with grav hopped over the pools when encountering them, and others just circumvented them. Engineers ran sprayers over those caked with mud and repaired the eight hundred and three Cyberat who'd been injured. Four drowned in their machine bodies, but their deaths were a negotiable thing, as their nanosuites vitrified them. Piper ordered them lifted out and transported back, since leaving them in place would do nothing for morale. His own method of transport didn't need to divert around the pools and simply ran over their occupants. Glancing back, he saw them rising up out of the mud unharmed by the experience. He did, however, have to divert around some of the tanks, pumps and other machines, and focused on the nodes they formed in his inner space.

Many silos contained great masses of food worms, growing in mud created by those machines as they slowly ground up the gravel. Other containers were full of dry eggs to be added and hydrated. Trailing those grinding machines, the pools were in slow, constant motion across this landscape, leaving a trail of mud, and he recognized how here the prador were reforming the world to their purpose. Years hence, barring the end of prador occupation, all this area would become mud and skippers. He traced a power grid buried in the ground running to the machinery, and relayed the information to the Engineers. As the army passed, they began uprooting cables and splicing in recharging stations that the troops could feed upon. They'd gone ten kilometres before the power went out. Obviously the prador were watching.

Fewer pools were in evidence further on – the ground rising higher and becoming drier. Piper slowed the natural acceleration of the march to the fore, until all his army was beyond the main concentration of pools, and focused ahead. In the hours of late afternoon, it seemed a bank of cloud had risen, but as it drew closer, it began to separate out into a rash of black dots. The prador forces were on the move now. The landscape here, consisting of slabs and drifts of gravel, interspersed with growths that resembled seaweed more than land plants, acquired a brassy metallic horizon line. Flare trails next appeared and, without any necessity for him to order them, war bodies began rising, trailing Enforcers like exhaust smoke. All those who had missile supplies on his side opened up too, drive flares across the whole army throwing Cyberat shadows. The battle had begun.

A roaring grew in volume, as engines ramped up power, and missiles hurtled in or out. The war bodies in the sky flung out hardfields and the roar peaked with hundreds of explosions building a wall of fire, blast by blast. Hardfields flickered and some blacked out. A war body blew armour out of its side and began to fall, its generator burned out, but Enforcers came in underneath it and supported it on the way down. All the Cyberat in the sky opened up on any approaching missiles with their other weapons. Two tactical nukes got through. One landed below his rising drones, wiping out floating reactors and Engineers on the ground, its cloud rising up into the drones but with little effect. Another landed nearby and rocked Piper's machine, while the blast swept up Cyberat in its infernal grasp. The reptile in him, or prador, or whatever it had become, filled his mind with the usual anger and demanded a reply. But Piper was now well accustomed to separating his emotions from his actions, and the beast from his consciousness.

Taking a battle sphere view beyond the explosions, he saw war machines in advance of the prador. Many of these were longer and heavier than he'd seen before and he registered their purpose only a second before it became apparent. The missile barrage was a distraction, unlikely to stop his army, but almost a necessary crossing of swords. The real first strike came from these machines and couldn't be stopped. They hit far over to his left: a smoking line running through Cyberat as far back as a kilometre, followed by a blast that tracked that line, showering out wrecked bodies and molten metal. Those machines had railguns. More strikes ensued and, detaching his war body's feet from the harvester, Piper rose up. He gave the order to the army to do the same, meanwhile sending his prador war drones to attack.

Ahead, the great mass of prador looked like a wave on an immense brassy sea, as they too began taking to the sky. The war drones he'd sequestered swept in and down, hurtling low over the landscape. And, with no sense in conserving fuel or armaments, they went to maximum and fired all their weapons continuously. Above, the prador war drones of the opposing force hurtled forwards and now, battle being joined, Piper could see no advantage in holding back on his aces. He flew higher, his entourage rising with him in a protective formation. The vast army ahead became clear to human vision, and adrenalin surged through him, excitement too and reptile – or prador – aggression. Still focused inwardly, he left his sequestered war drones to their program. They didn't slow at all and slammed hard into the railguns, flinging up huge machines or tearing off chunks of them, then bouncing on into the prador beyond, weapons still firing. He swept their nodes aside, and inspected the disposition of his forces, which was essentially now to disperse in the sky. Then he targeted thousands of alien nodes for his animuses and sent them.

The opposing prador drones all abruptly decelerated and looped down, at first still heading towards his forces, but then finishing a complete loop and hurtling back low towards the prador. He input instructions similar to those of the previous drones, and they kept on accelerating and firing, but towards their own side. Many of them then dropped acceleration, and some stopped firing as prador commanders tried to seize back control. But Piper's grip was wide and his animuses fought to retain their hold. And, almost like when he was conducting his multiple conversations with the Cyberat, he consigned this to a program and focused elsewhere. Now for the ground war machines.

They slowed to a stop and began moving back towards the prador, humanized upper bodies turning right around as they opened fire. As Piper observed this, a huge explosion blotted out his actual view, centred over three hexagonal hardfields. His war body rocked and two big Enforcers dropped from the sky, trailing smoke.

'My thanks,' he said to Tinsher, and saw that Old Guard raise a complete human hand under her dome of chain-glass. Mallon had been right about that painted target.

The prador rose up over their sequestered war machines, but the machines kept firing at them, creating a rain of armour and shattered bodies. The toll on the enemy was high, but nowhere near enough to decide the battle. When the prador then started firing on them, Piper ramped up the machines' attack to the maximum, with no need to seek out targets as so many prador filled the sky above. Again, he consigned his control of them to a program, wiping his slate clean for the next operation. Even as he did this, he noted he was losing more and more of the machines back to the prador, as doubtless more of their commanders focused on the code. He was right to bring this to a confrontation quickly, rather than stand back and set machine against prador, because his control of them had a limited effective time.

Into his clear inner space he now brought millions of nodes, for millions of other machines. This hadn't been something he'd tried before, but he knew it was possible. Prador suits were motorized. At one time, they could be remotely controlled by adults, but that had been stopped when Polity AIs had found a way to take control through the same route. But the suits still did have some primitive programs that could be run by the occupants, to keep the suits fighting when said occupant was injured or even dead. Piper opened up a series of nodes and now, speaking their language and knowing their code, he found himself looking at a similar scenario to one he'd had when facing the Enforcers for the first time. He smiled and mentally wrote the programs as the sky filled with debris and fire all around him. He charged up his bones, and ensured uninterrupted power to the substrate, then watched.

Prador and Cyberat met in the sky and the close-quarter fighting began. The great mass of creatures seemed a solid cloud, but not all were off the ground, where he wanted them. Beside him he saw Transter fall on a group of three prador, grappling one and hammering the two others with particle beams. The big Enforcers around him seemed heavily inclined for grappling too, and employed their new prador claws. Other Enforcers were running the usual routines and killing more efficiently now, but still the ground below was mounding with broken machine bodies and Cyberat, either dead or crying in pain. Piper himself, just waiting for the right moment, started to open up with his own weapons, firing particle cannon bursts selectively, then following through with fusillades of armour-piercers, launching programmed missiles to seek out prey. And then, finally, the moment arrived when all the prador were off the ground.

'Fly high and await instructions,' he ordered his army.

The Cyberat obeyed at once, en masse firing up thrusters and shooting upwards, and the prador followed. Piper went high too, and fast, his entourage swirling around him as he rose. Then he attended to the prador.

First he simply turned off their weapons, the light of them dying, and a moment later their formations fell into shadowed confusion. Then he shut off their grav.

It was as if a floating mountain had simply dropped out of the sky. Prador fell, some of them tugging opponents down with them. In two gravities, the hard impact exploded gravel and shards of rock into the air, and the whole landscape seemed to bounce. He watched prador falling on top of each other, tumbling from impact points and slamming against growing piles of their fellows. The creatures were of course heavily armoured but, still, Piper knew they'd come down hard enough to be stunned. He then ran in another instruction to load up queued fight programs inside them, to grapple and tear at anything nearby, and so they did. The ground over square kilometre after kilometre became a hellscape of armoured bodies ripping into each other. He sent another instruction for them to start firing their weapons. The sound wave from this shuddered through his war body and the scene acquired the addition of fire. Some shots speared up into the sky and hit Cyberat, but most firing spread at ground level. The prador disappeared under a haze of armour debris and shattered stone. Occasional detonations of reactors, or heavy munitions blowing, spread concentric ripples of destruction.

The chaos just seemed to go on and on, but Piper counted twenty-eight minutes of solid firing before the particle beams and Gatling cannons began to die. Movement down there died too: having drained power using their weapons, they were losing power to their suits. Just to be sure, like someone shaking a rug to free it of pests, he flicked back to the grav program. Many prador rose again, still fighting each other. He let them keep going until they came near to where his soldiers hovered, then shut off grav once more. They dropped again in bouncing chaos, and now with energy depleted, it seemed the fight had gone out of even their programs. Those still alive were just moving, turning, obviously confused, looking for enemies and often simply collapsing.

'Now kill them,' he coldly instructed his army.

This time there was a perceptible delay between his order and it being obeyed. Old Guard reacted first, reinforcing the instruction and running tactical scenarios. It was best, it seemed, to start at the near edge and roll them up. The army divided into waves and then formed into an extended cylindrical form of the milling wheel, each wave being one tooth. Coming down at one edge of the massed prador, the cylinder began to turn. Armour-softening particle beam shots went in first, armour-piercers and other explosive rounds next. Where the roller passed, it left smoking and immobile remains behind. The thing crunched on through the prador, but it wasn't nearly as wide as their mass. Observing this, Piper found memories in both his history lessons and the experiences of those in the four-year virtuality. Yes, this looked like a cylinder mower going across a lawn.

The roller finally reached the back edge, swinging round over ground out in front of the space port where prador lay widely scattered, and then started churning back again. Piper hovered in the sky there, looking towards the port, and saw prador fleeing – mostly adults with retinues of first-children.

'Fall in with me again,' he called.

His entourage swept in quickly, big Enforcers all around and the four Old Guard war bodies to the fore. With a near-simultaneous clang, Triode and Anode landed on his war body on either side and clung on, then shortly after that Aremer landed behind. All three had added weapons to their usual comple-ment and were scanning around protectively. He ignored them and concentrated on his inner space. Millions of prador nodes had gone out, along with over a quarter of the machines he'd seized.

'This cannot be sustained,' Tinsher told him privately, and sent detail.

She meant the roller steadily annihilating the prador. It was working efficiently but the Cyberat simply didn't have enough ammunition and power to kill them all. They were running out of bullets.

'Leave them,' he instructed, sending detail to everyone on what he wanted next. Those Cyberat without grav, and the aquaculture machines, began flowing through the path the roller had cut. The roller broke and rose with the soldiers, heading in streams behind him towards the space port, while one column sat protectively above the ground troops in case of attack from the prador on either side. Rather than go to the mass of interlinked nodes he'd been raising for the destroyer ahead, he banished it to one side and pulled in the prador nodes again. In mid-air, he halted and turned, his entourage sweeping round with him. Inspecting what he could control, he saw that his first attack on their armour had been informed by how he'd first attacked Enforcers on Founder's World. There was a better way, now and for the future. He sent a new instruction to the installed animuses.

The great mass of remaining prador shifted, raising a sound as of a thunderstorm. Since the process operated mainly on compressed air and not stored power, the armour opened hori-zontally on every one of them, then ejected them. Some jammed against others, some flipped over, and others ejected straight at the ground. A colour change swept across the mass, as purple and yellow prador bodies struggled clear of their brassy armour. He designated forces, and two streams of Cyberat coiled back and came down. Now ammo was no longer such a problem. With only their natural armour, the prador had no defence against single rotogun shots and particle beam bursts. It was a slaughter and he felt suddenly uncomfortable with this. Was it because he'd been so close to a prador mind and empathized with them? No, prador had little empathy with each other. The brutal nature of this warfare had been forced by an enemy fighting a war of extermination. And tactically, he could have conducted it no other way, whether prador or human. Perhaps he'd been unaffected by it precisely because he had incorporated prador thinking and his present discomfort actually arose from humanity, or perhaps a perception of what humanity should be? Next, noting weapons fire away from his troops, he saw humans with their perspective similarly altered by the prador, but via a different route.

In four different areas the ground had collapsed, while figures were flowing out of the tunnels below. The heavyworlder humans wore armoured diving suits and carried an array of prador weapons that a *normal* human couldn't have hauled. He saw one with a huge ammo pack on his back, running belt feeds to a Gatling cannon, marching through the chaos, killing prador with short bursts of fire. Others had shoulder-mounted missile launchers, and were firing one at a time, then calmly reloading from the missiles they carried on their backs. Focusing in, he saw one individual discard an empty weapon and pull an axe from his back. He hacked the legs off one side of a prador, leaped on top of it and struck again, shattering its head turret, and then reached inside it. The prador dropped an instant later, as if its power supply had been cut. This reminded him of Meersham's encounter, long ago in a mine. With a thought, Piper ordered in more Enforcers to assist, then he swung away and faced towards the space port again.

The enmeshed nodes formed the totality of the prador destroyer on the landing pad. He opened the nodes and absorbed data, tracing the state of its systems. The thing's grav was out, many of its weapons down, and a newly installed flash-frozen ganglion had yet to be connected. However, its thrusters still worked, and many of its weapons were still available. He connected at once – shaping animuses and installing them. Just seconds later, he fired up the thrusters and the thing was edging up off the pad, tearing away scaffolds and ripping out feed pipes. He turned it just so and allowed it to settle, meanwhile accessing its railguns. With an inner push, he brought up targeting for three railguns and put V-shaped prador targeting icons over those still fleeing, at the same time backing that up with his own frames to feed into targeting after each shot. The crackle, as of close lightning, reached his ears, with the destroyer silhouetted against the flash from each shot. In the far distance, the shapes fragmented, vapour trails belatedly appearing, spearing towards them. He consigned that to a program yet again, and turned his attention elsewhere.

'Priority to be given to Engineers and Medics, bar in the extermination behind,' he instructed, while his programs, or rather his extended cybernetic mind, filled in the detail. 'Resupply and repair on the move.' He also consigned a few thousand Engineers to the destroyer and, from his nodes on that thing, gave them its schematic and a repair list. Those Cyberat converged on the vessel, even as it ran out of targets at the horizon.

'And next?' Mallon enquired with an edge to her voice.

'An installation city like the first one,' he replied flatly. 'And then another and another, until no more prador remain.'

17

A prador dreadnought, turned inside out by U-space distortions, was an impressive demonstration of its armour's incredible strength and integrity. The armour – in a shape still vaguely resembling the original ship – had become a glowing nugget, sitting at the centre of an expanding cloud of the ship's innards. Piper could see tunnels, like worms, weaving amidst the structural girders and boulders of impact foam, armouries and factory cylinders, as well as prador. Peering closer at this armour, he noticed it was scattered with huge nodules, and realized they were the ball sockets of weapons that now all pointed inwards. The whole mess sat in silhouette against the gas giant and, while he watched, two squid-form attack ships slid into view. Heavy lasers cut out from them through the fog of vapour, and the prador who'd escaped their wrecked ship soon found that vacuum had become an even more hostile environment. He watched suits of armour bursting open, then a father-captain tracked across space, burning as he tried to flee.

When the attack ships moved off, leaving vacuum to kill any prador who'd been unsuited, Piper wondered about the necessity of killing that crew. He'd exterminated prador here on the surface because they were all potential soldiers in further battles. Out there, those prador represented little further threat to the Polity ships. Perhaps it wasn't all about cold calculations, and finding the least costly way of ending the war, and AIs could be as vengeful as anything organic.

He switched out to the larger view and watched the battle continue. The fleet of prador ships they'd feared would be coming here had been knocked out of U-space very close to the gas giant and had been trapped close to it. In essence, the Polity had the high ground here and were making good use of it. They even had another runcible weapon on site and it had delivered a total of eight punishing shots – some of them taking out more than one prador ship at a time. The threatened prador fleet was now rapidly turning into a meteor storm bombarding the gas giant.

'They are later than expected and somewhat pitiful,' said Albermech. 'Supposing one had pity to spare for them . . .'

Piper recognized the purpose of this leading comment and ignored it, still focusing on the imagery. Due to the U-space mines sown by the Polity, many of which had detonated and interfered with U-com, the battle sphere was updating gradually and intermittently. However, the *Albermech* had stayed in-system by Yannetholm's moon and was getting good tight-beam information directly from the ships involved.

'Why so few of them? Why was the battle sphere prediction so far off?' Piper asked.

'Our watchers saw the fleet gathering and had information that it was coming here, but just after that, the fleet broke up and half the ships dispersed. This has something to do with the odd occurrences going on within the Kingdom.'

'So there will be no interruption to my plans?'

'None at all.'

'Thank you for the update,' said Piper, and was about to disconnect.

'You have done well down there,' said Albermech.

'Better than expected,' Corisian added.

Almost inevitably, another link request arrived and Piper opened it.

'It might have been better than *you* expected,' said Inster.

'Oh but then I don't have your *experience*,' Corisian shot back.

Having listened, Piper now felt impatient. They were all so damned obvious in their attempt to engage and assess him. And, of course, the reason why was clear.

'If you have some questions to ask, then ask them,' he stated. 'You all might be twiddling your thumbs up there, but I have things to do.'

'Corisian?' Inster enquired.

'You go,' Corisian replied.

'So, General Piper Lagan,' said Inster. 'You've taken a fast intense road from being a brainwashed Cyberat youth to where you are now. How do you feel?'

'That's not the precise question you want to ask,' said Piper.

'So what is the question?'

'You want to know how ordering hundreds of thousands of Cyberat to their deaths and exterminating millions of prador has affected me.'

'You would agree it's a pertinent question,' interjected Corisian.

'Of course it is. You want this particular weapon to keep on functioning.'

'It's not quite so cold as that,' said Inster.

In passing, Piper noted that Albermech was easing open bandwidth on his link. He didn't like it. The touchy-feely approach, the careful sliding in to check on the mental condition of the patient. He hated their almost patronizing inspection of him. Internally, he opened out the bandwidth of all three links. To Albermech and Corisian, he began feeding through just as much as they could take of the whole mental telemetry of his war: all he had seen and experienced, the decisions made and

417

orders given, the shifting status of him and his reptile, the effect of all but absorbing a prador mind, everything. Albermech and Corisian slammed together under the tsunami, melding in AI–human synergy as they absorbed it. To Inster, he sent a limited version of the same, because the man was no AI and what he'd sent to the others would have broken his mind.

'I felt my soldiers dying as soon as we arrived in this system. Their pain, their fear and their slide into oblivion. And I feel it still, though necessarily muted so I can remain functional. I reamed out the mind of a prador and experienced its consciousness, and much of that is part of me now too. So I know that I'm not just killing cartoon monsters in some virtual game. I understand perfectly the hideous reality of killing millions of them. And I understand its necessity in our response to their war of extermination.'

'Fuck and fuck,' said Inster, obviously hammered down under the load – the silence of the other two indicated they were in the same position.

'There it is,' said Piper. 'Make of it what you will, but understand something further: I'm beyond your assessment now. I'm beyond you predicting my behaviour from your inputs into a naive young man and modelling from that.'

'Could that be arrogance?' Inster enquired, and Piper could feel the wince in his com.

'No it's not. Albermech feared my substrate was based on Jain tech. It's not, but its fractal, almost limitless nature remains and I have opened out into that. My mental processing now exceeds that of my war body substrate. And, in a mathematical sense, it would take more than a Polity ship AI, or agent, to predict the format of my mind across any more than just a few minutes. But you must also understand that I will continue doing what I must, because the reality of the prador remains.'

'We understand,' said the blend of Albermech and Corisian.

'I'm glad you do,' said Inster.

'And in future,' Piper added, 'I would prefer direct questions and communication without subterfuge. This particular Polity weapon has no patience with it.'

With that Piper slammed their links closed. He'd not lied about the complexity of his mind, though had perhaps exaggerated their inability to predict him. In all, his response to them had arisen from a simple basis: they needed to learn to respect him. He blinked away after-images of the war out there in space and returned to his own realm, with his own immediate concerns.

Engineers swarmed through the prador destroyer they'd captured, busily at work. Central control of the thing lay in a captain's sanctum deep inside, but Piper wanted access to his war body, and to be able to get it outside quickly. The sensory turret of the vessel turned out to be ideal. It had rear doors large enough to allow his war body through, and enough space for a prador crew, so room to accommodate it. Engineers had made a few changes, stripping some things out and applying screen paint around the interior, but otherwise the space remained the same.

From the cockpit of his war body, Piper gazed through an activated area of screen paint at the activity across the space port, re-establishing a sense of his immediate surroundings. Then, as he had been doing before the call from Albermech, he returned to checking the status of his army. Relatively speaking, the losses in this last battle had been very low, at just over fifty thousand Cyberat. Meanwhile, the Medics and Engineers were busily at work, their temporary factories set up, with repairs and restocking ongoing. Checking through the logistics, he found no problems with resupply, in fact the precise opposite. Such a wealth of weapons, munitions, power supplies, materials and food supply organics lay all around that the Engineers were struggling with the choices. He made some changes, putting in a time limit. Then, peering down from his war body and seeing he had visitors, he physically disengaged from its substrate. This time the disconnection felt merely physical and elicited no response from his reptile. Even as he unstrapped, removed connections from his suit and climbed down, he still felt completely linked in.

The Yannets were big bulky humans, larger than Meersham, and larger still in the armoured diving suits they wore. He could have spoken to them without this meeting, but had called them here just to make a face-to-face connection: it was more of benefit to him than them – a humanizing connection. Ten of them had wanted to come to him, but he'd instructed that there should only be two representatives. He had just one matter to discuss, but knew there was more they desired, and didn't want the protracted argument that would inevitably arise if he had to deal with more people. He also didn't want the physical threat. These people had been at war for decades and might have few moral barriers. They were also big, strong and armed. Coming to stand before the two, Piper did feel physically small. But, even outside of his war body, his mind still encompassed a world and, it seemed, a weary understanding of reality.

'He's just a young man,' said the girl who, despite her impressive bulk, looked no older than Piper. She took a step back as Triode and Anode clattered round the war body and moved in to either side of Piper. They were armed, as they had been before, and gazed at the two heavyworlders suspiciously. He glanced at them with curiosity. Their instructions had been to join Aremer and the other Engineers currently working on the ship's engines. He felt annoyed that they'd disobeyed him, but also pleased they were now showing a greater independence of mind.

'This young man has killed more prador in the last two days than we've managed since they took our world thirty years ago, Cinia. He can be whatever he wants to be.' The big old man, Groll, studied Piper. 'You wanted to speak to us?'

'Your people,' said Piper, recalling recorded imagery to his mind. 'The captives.'

'They are not salvageable,' said Groll, his expression twisting bitterly.

'That's not entirely the case,' Piper replied. 'And either way, I want to know what to do with them.'

Enforcers entering the space port buildings had found the pens, as well as the coring and thralling rooms, and the Yannets within them. He reviewed the memory of humans hung on frames, their bodies blue with the Spatterjay virus, the surgical benches, the racked thralls and a bin full of brains and spinal cords, writhing with alien life. He thought of those actually in the pens, also blue, still retaining the rags of clothing, ferocious and animalistic when they attacked the Cyberat who were trying to free them. They'd had to lock them down again.

He continued, 'There are about two thousand under the thrall and another thousand yet to be operated on, but who are infected with the Spatterjay virus. The latter are being held in a pen and are not . . . rational. One of my Enforcers went in to release them and only escaped by leaving most of his machine body behind him.'

'It's best to burn them all,' said Groll.

Piper stared at him. This meeting had been a mistake. It didn't humanize him to meet people he could assess, understand and become aggravated by, all within a couple of sentences. He wondered if this was how Inster, Corisian and Albermech had first thought of him, and had the humbling thought that they had more patience.

421

'You won't be hunted by prador any more,' he said, limiting it to just that, to assess their intelligence.

Groll's expression went through a number of changes but it was Cinia who replied, 'They are merely animals, even uncored. There's nothing we can do with them.'

Piper nodded to her and returned his attention to Groll.

'Will the Polity help?' the man asked.

'My Medics are synthesizing a viral suppressor even now, and will administer it,' Piper replied. 'Thereafter we'll hand your people over to you with enough of the suppressor to . . . deal with them.'

Groll looked abruptly tired and ashamed, while Cinia, whom Piper presumed had grown up knowing nothing but surviving the prador, gaped at him in confusion.

'We haven't been able to think this way in a long time. I hope you understand.'

'Oh I do.' People infected with the Spatterjay virus, without any form of suppression, were dangerous to be around, and dangerous to keep around while you were trying to stay alive under prador rule. Enough years of that and it became accepted practice to be rid of any who were recovered from the prador. Further years and it became just the way things were – as it was in Cinia's mind. There were lessons here for Piper.

'We'll deal with the ones who've been thralled,' he said, turning to the view but blind to it. There was no point asking if they had some ceremonial way of disposing of these walking corpses. That too would have been something lost over the years. 'I'll leave a few of my Medics here to deal with the rest. Some of your people should stay too.'

'But we've got to—' Cinia began.

Groll stilled her with a hand on her shoulder. Piper saw this through Triode's eyes, even while he watched, through other eyes and sensors out in the space port, the Enforcers respond to his immediate orders. They threw thermal grenades into the building where they'd confined the thralled Yannets. The mindless humans reacted at first, trying to get away from the fire, until Piper stilled them via the animuses he'd installed. Their movement had been a facsimile of an intelligent response, driven by the virus that had turned them blue, fibrous and grotesque. He continued watching, feeling it to be a duty, and sure the fire was burning in his eyes. He could perhaps have used them as he used the prador war machines, but felt that somehow, despite all he'd done, that would have been a step too far.

'So what happens now?' Groll asked.

Piper shrugged, knowing this wasn't about the human blanks in the space port. 'More of the same,' he said flatly, now actually integrating his physical view, even while the burning continued in his mind.

Ahead, he opened a wide swathe of the screen paint, and it seemed as if a hole had opened to the outer air. Piper looked out at the ruination lying all around: a landscape of shattered metal and broken organics, pillars of smoke rising into the sky, Cyberat buzzing above or moving through it all like insects over a great corpse. He turned back.

'There was something you wanted?' he asked next.

'We want to kill prador,' said the man, succinctly.

Piper gazed at the two here, while searching out all the other Yannets in the battle sphere. There were fifty or so around the destroyer and thousands more scattered across the battlefield, mostly still hunting down and killing prador. He noted their nodes forming up too. Their armoured diving suits were powered and he could seize control of them easily. But all this wasn't the information he sought. He checked their linkage to the battle sphere and, though many wore augs, they probably weren't as keyed into the data as he, his Cyberat and the forces above were. They didn't know what they didn't know.

'This is our world,' said the girl impatiently.

Piper nodded and checked some other things. Medics were moving aboard the ship any wounded who could be sufficiently cell welded and otherwise repaired to return to fighting in the near future. A supply train was also on the way in, with useful loot from the battlefield and the space port. And amidst the wounded were Yannet fighters – over three hundred of them.

'You took big losses,' he said. 'In total, there were fifteen thousand of you and you lost nearly four thousand.'

The man grimaced, and the girl turned her head aside, tears welling. She wiped them hurriedly then turned back with her expression hard.

'You have lost hundreds of thousands,' she said.

Before she could continue, the man said, 'There are millions of us remaining and we have communication. Forces like mine are moving into position at most major prador installations.'

'And many of them will die,' said Piper.

'So will your people!' said the girl.

Piper nodded thoughtfully. 'My people are fighting for a future the Polity can give them. And, though we've had initial losses, there won't be so many henceforth. But my people also come from a home world of eight hundred million.'

'I fail to see your point,' said the girl.

'It's simply a question: do you want to squander the future on avenging the past?'

The two had no immediate reply, so he continued, 'There's no need for you to throw your people into this. It won't be decided by the number of fighters.'

'But by what you do . . . by some power you have,' said the

man. 'We saw what happened. We've tried getting into their systems too but never could.'

'So maybe it's time for you to sit back and think about protecting your population and rebuilding?' He gestured outside. 'There'll be more of your people to be rescued too.'

'Are you playing games with us?' asked the girl. 'There's no future while the prador are here, and there's no future until they're defeated everywhere. Do you think that if you remove the prador from this world, we'll start rebuilding? We've all lost too many people. We'll go where the war is now.'

Piper gazed at them, saying nothing for a little while, then abruptly changed course. 'Transport is your main problem. We'll be setting out at nightfall in four hours. As you know, I'm moving wounded aboard this ship. There'll be room for about a thousand of you and the rest will have to use the aquaculture machines the wounded were on before.'

'And what will our role be?' asked the man.

Piper shrugged. 'The same role as everyone in my army: you will kill prador until there are no more here for you to kill.' He turned his gaze outside through the window, and via his bones. The two stood there for a long, uncomfortable silence, and then departed.

'I don't understand,' said Anode.

'There seemed no purpose,' Triode added.

He turned and winced a smile at them. 'I envy the both of you.'

From their perspective, it'd been a pointless conversation. There'd been no need to consult the Yannets about the captives, and of course these people would continue fighting, but he saw something else here. The war swept people up and changed them, became their lives. With his reprogramming of the Cyberat, he'd accelerated that process in them and he was very definitely not escaping it either. Seeing that father and daughter made him

425

think on his mother and what she must be doing now, but distantly, because from his perspective Founder's World was years behind him. He decided that he *should* think more about home, and about a future. The thought passed.

A stratum of cloud seemed to drop on the landscape – over skipper pools and silos – and changed it all at one stroke. A greenish-yellow fog concealed it as the first air shock rumbled, even reaching the destroyer which was now high in the sky. The second stratum came down next, raising yet another fog lit with the flashes of power supplies and munitions exploding. Then the stuff began to clear and, through the eyes and sensors of others, Piper observed kilometre after kilometre of twisted and broken prador armour, slick with the organic component of that fog, tangled over the shattered remains of the prador. Unarmoured prador were apparently not rugged enough to survive falling a kilometre in two gravities. Though, if any did, they didn't then survive Piper dumping the suits from which he'd ejected them on top of them.

The Cyberat roller passed over the mounded dead – a strange storm cloud issuing brief spurts of lightning for localized exterminations. These flashed through the darkness to Piper's human eyes, while the whole of the battle lay as clear as day in his mind. A spiral settled over the prador installation ahead, drilling in and killing survivors. Yannets, many of whom he'd earlier deposited on the ground, fought brief battles in the tunnels with prador who were trying to flee. They then came out on the surface ready to continue fighting, and trudged through the calf-deep exudates of the shattered creatures. As the army passed, it swept up more aquaculture machines and supplies.

'What's happening with their machines – the ones you control?' Mallon and ten thousand others asked.

'If we take one installation at a time like this, it'll take us twenty years to be finished here. I have redirected them to expand the front.' He sent detail on that.

'The prador might take them back,' Tinsher observed.

'No, they won't,' Piper replied, utterly sure.

The ground war machines were up to power and now heading out alone towards a row of smaller installation cities. Meanwhile the drones moved in the other direction, towards heavy lifter ports and a hundred square kilometres of warehouses. Piper still required line-of-sight to maintain links to his animuses in both the machines and Cyberat. However, once he was using the com system of the destroyer, he'd have another handle on them, even when those machines got out of sight. By sequestering conventional prador methods, along with those animuses functioning independently, he'd be able to keep a grip on them. Unfortunately, at that range, he wouldn't be able seize control of the prador they were attacking, though. He remembered now an earlier conversation with Tinsher.

'You can control their war machines, shut down their weapons, have them fighting each other and eject them from their armour. Why not do this all across the planet?' the old Cyberat had asked.

'My range is huge,' he'd replied. 'When I was in the *Albermech* I could reach out across the volume encompassing the fleet, which was larger than this world. And I can perceive much of this world via the battle sphere and my own links. However, warfare creates massive EMR and now there's U-space interference. The data corrupts and, even when it doesn't, I can't reach around the horizon line.'

'What about bouncing via satellites?'

'No. Polity satellites cannot retransmit what I do. Albermech tried that back on Founder's World and failed.' He smiled deprecatingly. 'I do have limitations.'

As with Albermech, he had yet to find a way to rebroadcast animuses. Eventually the machines he'd sent would run out of ammo, power or simply be destroyed. But then, that would be prador destroying prador . . .

'Are you done yet?' he enquired of the twins, who were scuttling around the base of his war body.

'Nearly there,' Anode replied.

'And why do you ask verbally?' Triode asked.

'Because I could sit up here godlike directing all and never actually talk to anyone,' he replied. 'Even the AIs seem to think it worthwhile for humans to hang onto humanity.'

'Strange dichotomies,' said Triode.

'In what sense?'

'It's something all Cyberat have discussed since you mentioned it . . . humans linking to technology behaving more like they think machines should behave.'

'Yes,' Piper added, 'while the machines themselves become more human.'

'I hope our home world hasn't resorted to its old ways,' she said.

'Indeed,' said Piper, but didn't elaborate.

The destroyer drifted along behind the army with brief spurts of thrusters as it changed course. Sunrise lay hours away and the next installation just an hour. Piper gazed ahead, completely in the battle sphere, and saw intermittently updated views of that next enemy city. Already prador and war drones from there were up in the sky, then he saw something odd happening: explosions down on the ground. He focused in and saw rows of ground war machines issuing smoke, top halves tilted over like arthritic old men. The prador knew he could take control of their machines, but destroying them indicated they felt they had no way of stopping him.

The two finished making the links he'd requested: a heavy optic connection to an interface now extruded from his war body, making hard connections to this ship and all its com gear. He was already connected via his ability in various areas of the emitted spectrum, but the hard link, through shielded optics, was much firmer. It was as if he had turned up the contrast on the data, and brought the ship's system to the fore. Linking into its communications gear upped his range.

He began to sample and test. Reaching out to the right, he touched on the war drones, as square kilometre upon kilometre of warehouses came into view for them, all clustered around the wreckage of launch pads and cargo haulers the Polity had hit upon arrival. The sky there was filling with prador hurtling up from the ground caches. He noted disruption in the drones, as the prador tried to shut them down and, via the destroyer com gear, he hardened them against that; for they were over the horizon and his animus links to them were shredding. The drones started firing at long range and prador fired back, particle beams lancing between them. Clouds of small missiles broke from the drones too, and Gatling cannons sparked. He also noted, beyond the prador force, other prador shooting into the sky and heading away.

Next he turned to the ground war machines. They were still far from their target, while Yannets came out of tunnels and moved in behind them. Far ahead prador watchers were up in the skies, while there seemed a good deal of activity around the row of installations. Closer view through the battle sphere showed him aquaculture machines heading out and away from his approaching machines.

'They're running!' said Transter, and thousands of others.

Focusing on the big installation ahead, Piper saw that the prador force he'd thought was coming up into the sky ready to meet him was now flowing away too.

'So it would seem,' he said. 'Let's see how my range is.'

He reached out and began incorporating the nodes of those lying ahead and in sight. Close to a million firmed in his internal space, while a million more faded in and out. He started to transmit animuses. In the sky all the prador jerked as one, as if strewn on a sheet that had been snapped. Armour through a wide swathe of them then opened and ejected them. Thousands upon thousands fell, while some still clung desperately to their still-floating armour. Via the animuses, he could hear their whistling squeals and clattering mandibles as, legs windmilling, they eventually dropped hard. Many hit the installation, shattering and splashing on the oyster-shell roofs, then breaking and collapsing those roofs. Others hit on the ground, blowing out gravelled craters lined with minced flesh and shell. Still others foamed up a shallow sea with green blood and dark flesh. There he noted some survivors, stunned and broken but still moving. The water began to foam as reaverfish fed.

The next part of the program kicked in, dropping the armour. Almost as an afterthought, he added a refinement to close up the armour and then run its fight programs. So, besides being potentially crushed by their own falling armour, the prador might find it trying to kill them. Falling armour churned up sea and ground and all but flattened the installation.

For the prador still in the sky beyond, he noted intermittent swirls of the armour opening, as well as some suits dropping that hadn't been opened. His animuses had reached other prador, but this marked the limit of his range at about fifty kilometres. Matching against the nodes available to him, he saw the pattern: these were the nodes that were partially formed, blinking in and out of existence. Those escaping had no nodes at all.

Piper frowned at his limitations and again began to speculate how he might overcome them. This situation was simply not good enough. He should be able to deliver his animuses all around the planet. They were, after all, only information and so should go as far as transmitters could reach. Albermech's failure to decode or copy what Piper had done on Founder's World didn't necessarily mean it was impossible for him. He then realized that when Albermech had tried to do this, the AI had feared Piper was occupied by Jain technology. So it had perhaps been reluctant to reach down too deeply into the programming.

He made space for himself inside, almost as though he was clearing a work bench, and raised a selection of animuses from his bones, peeling them up out of the reptile for examination. He already knew them well, but in the sense that a biologist knows the organs of a creature and their function intricately, but not completely. He wasn't really down into the DNA of his creations, and he couldn't visualize their full holistic function. He ran through all he did know: how he needed to maintain a thread of contact with them, to stop them rapidly disrupting under computer defences, and constantly to push their evolution in their victims. This process was almost unconscious. In fact, it was very much unconscious, since it mostly ran in the reptile in his bones – in his security and sequestration software, in that facsimile of his father.

He explored this further, feeling the reptile shift in discomfort as he drew out more clumps of code – *animalcules* – and examined them. Something Albermech had said impinged on his thoughts, about his point of penetration being the interface between the organic and the technologic. That became a puzzle when he considered how he was able to control machines without a cyborg basis. This led him off course for a while, as he worked out that his sequestration was purely mechanistic and little different to how Polity AIs seized control of machines. It was simple, in fact, and he knew he could at least rebroadcast *that* via satellites, or other relatively simple transceivers. Although, with their protection against AI attack, the prador suits still needed installed animuses for him to seize them.

Returning to the complex animuses, he delved deep and went deeper still, expanding vast models in his mind, and at last he began to get some hint of why he couldn't rebroadcast them through satellites. The animuses, arriving like parasites at the organic–technological interface, reinterpreted his mind's instructions for the computing to their own ends. The creatures were open-ended living things and blurred into those fractal spaces he knew so well. Yet, when copied or retransmitted through conventional computing, they lost that and became distinct – effectively running on prior programs and vulnerable to attack. The organic component was required for complete retransmission.

Piper had already tried retransmission through the prador and it had failed. He saw now this was because they weren't organically interfaced with their suits. He recognized he'd been looking in the wrong place, and there might be another solution. He had been designed to sequester Cyberat and bend them to his will, so could he not therefore make Cyberat his transceivers? Using their interfaces, the animuses wouldn't lose their fractal nature. And so thinking, he remembered the rebel Old Guard Geerand in his spherical com body. That individual was still back on Founder's World, but perhaps there would be others like him here?

Upon the thought, he ranged out and found hundreds of Cyberat in spherical machine bodies loaded with communications equipment. They'd been retrofitted for battle with many weapons attached, but still they retained their initial purpose. Some of them were Old Guard, but most were high-status Engineers, lying in the command chain rather than in overall command of any units in his army. And in that role they retransmitted battle plan detail for smaller conflicts in the overall larger ones. When he linked to them he found that, yes, their technology was so much more accessible than what lay in prador suits and war machines. They could act as solid relays.

Piper started designing a new battle plan, similar to one scenario and model he'd contemplated while in virtuality, applying swarm mathematics. And, in doing so, he accepted something that had been sitting on the periphery of his consciousness for some while: the war down here was now all but over; only extermination remained.

With this understanding that the prador defeat here had become all but inevitable, Piper ordered his army to encamp for the remainder of the night. He grounded the destroyer on a conglomeration of the mushroom stones, crushing them down, just a few kilometres from an abandoned installation city. Via the battle sphere, he observed the prador – all those within a hundred miles of his position were heading away, like ripples from a stone cast into a pool. Beyond this, he could see them consolidating in some installation cities, ports and a large industrial complex. They'd run, but even they knew there was a limit to how far they could go. He then drew his attention back and once again inspected his forces.

The ever-busy Medics and Engineers were catching up with their work. All around, the Engineers were repairing and rearming from the loads of materials and other supplies collected up from the battlefields and prador facilities they'd attacked. They had also swarmed into the nearby city to set up factories, utilizing the fusion power supplies there. Medics were in that city too, establishing hospital workshops where both they and the Engineers were working on Cyberat who'd been physically injured and mechanically damaged in battle.

They were in cleaner surroundings than the mud, grit and chaos of the first encampment.

Within the destroyer, other Medics worked on Cyberat in hibernation, actually bringing some out of their sleep. Closer inspection revealed they were carrying out more complex surgeries that they'd had no time for before. And those coming out of hibernation were often those whose problems had been solved by their Polity nanosuites. He considered investigating further, via installed animuses, but again decided on human contact. In a lower hold of the destroyer, he observed Medics operating on plug-form Cyberat supported in frames. They were piped and wired into equipment, crawling here and there with battlefield autodocs, much like the one Cheen had sent into those tanks on Founder's World to inspect the dead prador there.

'What's the situation here, Annel?' he asked the Medic in charge.

Annel was a plug form in the peak of a pyramidal body, bristling with the equipment found on an autosurgeon.

'General!' said Annel, his shock feeding back through his animus – a mixture of disbelief and a little in the way of fear.

Piper examined data on the patients here and continued speaking, allowing the Medic to recover his composure. 'As far as I can see, none of these Cyberat have battle injuries, while most are not Enforcers . . .'

'The Polity nanosuites,' Annel managed.

'Do explain.'

The Cyberat settled down on his treads, his upper plug form revolving as he looked around the room. Through his animus, Piper got the impression the Medic was surveying his patients to see if he'd done something wrong.

'Installed in Room 101, they were set for maintenance of the basic plug form, as well as defence against new pathogens, and to increase the chances of survival in the case of injury and even what we would have viewed as death.'

'Using the vitrification process,' Piper interjected.

'Yes, but these are less than fifty per cent of their function.'

'Really? So what's happened here?'

'We can access our suites. Our cyber enhancements enable us to alter their programming either by accident, as has been the case with Enforcers here, or through tinkering in the case of others. They've activated functions that are causing problems.'

'Give me some examples.'

Annel waved to the nearest plug form, from whom the Medics had removed a great deal of interface hardware. 'In every case here, they've fully activated their suites' injury response, and in some cases what I would call their "basic body form" schematic. But the injury response, fully activated, initiates healing processes that interfere with our interface tech. It assumes their amputations are injuries. The basic form schematic is something unexpected, however. The suite extrapolates the basic human form from DNA and then starts trying to rebuild it.'

'What?'

In his sudden enthusiasm for his subject, Annel seemed to forget his fear. 'The suites are running regenerative processes. Observe . . .' He reached out with a shiny eight-fingered hand to the nearby plug form and prodded at a translucent bubble over the shoulder section. Piper wasn't sure what was being pointed out. He routed through the Medic's senses to see inside the bubble. Extending from the shoulder joint was a skinless baby's arm. On seeing this, Piper immediately dived into Annel's mind, as well as the links to other Medics here and elsewhere, *and* their shared database. Thousands of Cyberat had activated their nanosuites this way. In many cases, the Medics had managed to shut them down again. Others had gone too far and been put

435

into hibernation. The ones in this room were intermediate – their suites were being shut down but they'd require surgery to return them to their previous state. Piper hated that what he was seeing here was *progression*, because to return them to that previous state meant cutting away the regrowing limbs.

'Some might not consider this a problem,' he said, pondering how it had been unnecessary to leave this nanosuite option open on his soldiers to keep them at their best function – the chaotic mind of the Room 101 AI was at play here, he realized.

'Some think that way, yes,' said Annel cautiously.

'In fact, many Cyberat would like to return to human form,' said Piper, testing.

'Most of those here.' Annel waved a hand at his surroundings. 'Our problem is that regeneration shuts down most of their interfaces and requires support. If we allow this to continue with these, they'll cease to be useful in your army. They'd need to go into regrowth tanks with high-input nutrient feeds, cooling and nanosuite oversight computing.'

Piper pulled back from his close inspection here and focused on the battle sphere and all his plans there. Deep down in the code, at its basis, was the logic of what Annel was doing. All the strategy and all the logistics of his war was predicated on functional soldiers; therefore the Medics were working to that end. Cyberat growing new limbs in tanks were not functional soldiers. But how much requirement did he have for them now? And how much right did he have to hold them to said requirements when, as seemed evident, some had chosen otherwise, despite his programming them to his ends?

'I'm going to make some changes,' he said.

'I wondered if you might,' said Annel.

Resources were oversupplied. Medics and Engineers were still busy but, if things continued as they were, they'd soon not have so much to do. He selected areas in the installation city currently unused, then raised schematics for the required equipment from medical databases and transmitted that to the Engineers and Builders. Within minutes he'd created a new plan, slotting it into the battle sphere. Data, logistics and strategy were reformed. Beyond building the tanks and the support infrastructure, more work was required to develop the defences for the city installation. At last he was going to make a more permanent base. Reassignments went out, diverting Cyberat to their tasks, and in turn he answered all the thousands of questions. The role for Annel arrived through that Cyberat's hardware a moment later and he jerked as if slapped.

'Me?' he queried.

'Yes, you,' Piper replied, eyeing where parties of Enforcers and Engineers were forming up with grav-rafts and other transport in tow. 'Move those you have here, and those in hibernation for the same reason, to the site I've indicated. Build regrowth tanks and keep on building them. Any Cyberat who chooses this course must be given the opportunity.'

'There could be millions,' Annel observed.

'Indeed. You will also shortly be receiving any injured Cyberat who we cached, including those who were vitrified.'

'I note that I cannot be one of those to choose this course while I'm running this.'

'Somebody has to.' Piper grimaced, understanding that Annel wanted his human body back, while wondering about the difficulties he'd given himself. He pulled his attention away from Annel and his patients, noting Medics there already getting to work demounting hardware. New flow patterns of Engineers and other Medics formed outside, with some bringing over aquaculture machines for transport of the injured. He withdrew his attention further – orders had been made and actions were being performed with great efficiency. He wouldn't broadcast this because he didn't want too many taking that route all at once, but knew the news would spread anyway.

Piper detached, his reptile objecting more strongly than usual because some of what he'd just done had penetrated it. With a bitter feeling, he pushed it down, knowing its objection was to a visceral sense of relinquishing power. There was confusion there too, about old objectives and surely his father's regret at losing his own body. With his threads drawing back into his body, Piper raised his hands and pulled away from the war body substrate. The reptile consolidated in him, again seeming more substantial, annoying, unresolved. It was time, he felt, for him to delve into this unwelcome guest in his mind and ream more data from it about its past, about his father, about Castron. But first he had something personal to deal with.

After detaching the feeds to his suit, Piper climbed out of the cockpit, walked down the war body and jumped onto the floor. His overall perception of his surroundings was never completely back to human senses, and he knew the precise locations of all aboard the destroyer.

'Anode, Triode!' he called, both in the sphere and with a voice turned slightly croaky.

He sensed them below and then quickly going into motion. A diagonally divided door opened in the place they'd made their home, and they came scrambling up a shaft on spider limbs. A short while later they were up on his level and clattering around the war body. They grinned at him, happy to be called and perhaps needed.

'What do you require, General?' Anode asked.

He studied the two sisters, feeling the obscenity of what had been done to them more intensely, just as he felt it for all Cyberat. He didn't know how many Cyberat would choose to have their human bodies back but, after his interaction with Annel, he'd extrapolated that it'd be many. It was detestable that people had been forced by social pressure, expectation and ideology to accept these mutilations in the first place. His thoughts strayed back to his own thinking before his accident, and from his present perspective he saw how, without his mother's education, he would've swallowed the indoctrination whole as well. Now he wondered about loss. It seemed the loss his father had felt translated across all Cyberat. Indoctrinated similarly to the way he would have been, they'd accepted the amputations and only later understood what they'd given up. But of course by then, without any Polity technology to rescue them, it was too late to object.

'You were deliberately injured by the Old Guard, as were many, and pushed into progression,' he stated.

'Yes, we were,' Triode replied, her smile diminishing.

'Your father grabbed you from the hospital and that is why you don't have the usual cerebral support and skull expansions, and run your hardware via aug.'

'Yes, that's so,' they both said simultaneously.

'You asked me before about having your bodies back. That's your wish?'

They shifted about on their spider limbs and looked uncomfortable. It annoyed him to know, via their animuses, that they were searching for replies they thought he'd want to hear. He gathered the data on what he'd just done, on what the nanosuites were capable of doing, and the work Annel would be carrying out in the installation city, briefly noting that the Medic was already moving his patients out of the destroyer. He then sent the information directly to them. They grew abruptly still, and both of them closed their eyes. While they absorbed this he went into them and inspected their minds, their reactions.

Drillain had raised them to be sceptical of the Cyberat thesis, while also working against it. He'd wanted them to have choices and remembered what he'd fought for alongside Castron. After the rebellion fifty years ago, he had been one of those working to change things from the inside, rather than opting out and stewing in resentment like Doge. The two girls hadn't wanted to sacrifice their limbs, and had never believed the machine to be superior. Rather, they'd liked the organic beauty of their bodies and he saw their attitude reflected in memories of a girl by a stream. Now they wanted their human bodies back.

'We serve and we obey,' said Anode, opening tearful eyes.

'We cannot choose that course while there's work to be done,' said Triode, her eyes dry and her tone pragmatic.

Piper got a hint of it then and, pushing deeper, saw that they had both, by dint of superior connection through their augs, explored the possibilities inherent in their nanosuites. They'd not activated them to that end, however. Their loyalty to him was so intense it made him flinch.

'Then you'll obey me now,' he said. 'You will activate the regenerative function of your nanosuites from this moment.'

They shifted about even more, feet clattering. In them he could feel their need warring with duty.

'You will do it right now,' he affirmed.

This was too much to ignore further, and they obeyed on the instant. Feeling that activation, and knowing it was a cascade they couldn't now stop, he withdrew from their minds and the discomfort of their regard.

'Now you will go and join Annel, and head over with him. The regrowth tanks are already being built and I expect you to be among the first in them.'

They hesitated, spider feet beating a tattoo against the floor.

440

Triode was now crying and, though he'd mostly withdrawn, he could still feel the warring emotions inside them.

'Go now,' he said, and via their animuses reinforced the order.

They finally turned and clattered away. Piper moved back to his war body and sat on the edge, breathing out a sigh as he tracked the two of them heading down through the destroyer. On reaching Annel they relayed their orders to him and he set them about loading patients onto grav-sleds. Next, flicking over to the installation city, he saw areas being cleared at speed and manufactories already producing the polymer to be shaped into regrowth tanks, while others assembled the support tech. The sense of power was remarkable. He could make a decision and deliver orders and, in just seconds of him doing so, see it taking on material form. Alone with their tools, the Engineers had the manufacturing capacity of small factories of ancient Earth; together, they were an industry. But a deep disquiet also came over him.

There was very little in a material sense he couldn't do. If he ordered the Cyberat to build a city, the foundations would be going in a minute later. If he ordered them to destroy the installation city there, it would be rubble in a very short time. Obviously, they were also obeying his orders to depopulate a world of alien invaders. His animuses bent them to his will and to his aims, but he now saw it went further than that. He sensed it all around him, and it was impinging on him more and more that the fanatical desire to serve him that he'd seen in the twins was reflected throughout. It occurred to him that he'd displaced one kind of ideology in them with another. He knew, with utter certainty, that there was very little he couldn't make them do for him, and he saw the danger in that.

Suddenly weary, he turned and climbed up onto the war body and went back to the cockpit. Resting in the seat again, he smiled wryly. Albermech and others were right to be concerned about the way all this was affecting him, but their fears of him becoming drunk on the power were unfounded. Throughout his most recent education, he'd understood how he had been manipulated; manipulating others had given him even deeper insight. And he didn't want either. He didn't want to be controlled and he didn't want to control others. He would, he decided, free his soldiers from his influence and allow them to make their own decisions. Polity be damned. In him, the AIs had the main weapon they wanted, and whoever slaughtered the disabled prador thereafter didn't matter. And now, he also decided, it was time to get to the root of the manipulator Doge had inadvertently installed in him. It was time to solve the reptile.

Piper leaned back, relaxed and closed his eyes, then queued the nanosuite to put him to sleep, also altering the process to his requirement. He would raise the unconscious state, the REM dream state, in his mind. But, being able to compartmentalize so much and run thousands of functions in parallel, he would also view his dreams consciously. Data on various animals that were able to sleep parts of their minds, like Terran cetaceans, rose for his inspection, but he waved this away as irrelevant. He needed to focus through his unconscious state on the thing that seemed to determine the course of his dreams. He put his hands down and connected to the war body substrate, while keeping the reptile in clear focus. As he sank into sleep yet remained conscious, he noted its function sliding into another state. Evidently his sleep initiated some version of the same in that being too. So they dreamed together.

18

'I'm a pragmatist and you're a romantic – an idealist,' said the man with stringy blond hair. Piper studied him – the slightly withered look of his torso and arms, his face, and the spider carrier body holding his plug form. Castron had aged, but there was no telling how much since the time of the younger pre-revolutionary version he'd seen in other dreams. Perhaps inspection of the dream form Piper himself now wore would elucidate that.

He *was* his father and, within himself, he sensed the complex arrays of factory control connections, extended mental storage and complex diagnostics. He inspected the partitioned research sections too – cut away and separated from the usual Cyberat com. Secret. Hidden. He traced down and, without even seeing it, built a picture, extrapolating from its control circuitry the cylindrical body into which he was plugged, and the composite treads it ran upon.

'And you have been very pragmatic in my absence, it would seem,' he replied. Of course it wasn't Piper replying, but Doge. He gestured with one hairy muscular arm to the massive factory that surrounded them, specifically to the weaponized policing-format bodies rolling off the productions line – all much the same as the four that had accompanied Castron here.

'Somebody had to be,' Castron replied. 'It seems that the

character traits which make good rebels do not make good organizers and leaders. Destroyers don't make builders.'

'Except of course in your case,' said Doge acidly.

'I had to get things done,' Castron said simply, giving a shrug. 'You were not available to consult.'

It was a dream, of course, but it wasn't. With conscious overview, Piper was both a spectator and participant. His awareness now was a thing akin to that of the four-year virtuality whereby he'd experienced episodes in a person's life along with the context. As Doge here, he knew about the executions of erstwhile rebels, the schisms and conflicts between factions, the abandonment of ideals for Castron's pragmatism that seemed to be recreating the very same regime they'd fought to bring down. But also as Doge, he felt anger and guilt. Losing such a large portion of his body had hit him hard and, by the time he'd accepted it, his influence on the course of the rebellion had waned. There was his source of anger: guilt rising from recognition of his own cowardice. How he had backed away from the infighting at the top to establish his own safety in bringing factories online and making himself useful.

'We need enforcement.' Castron gestured to the policing bodies. 'If you find it morally unacceptable to make these, it should be easy enough to find someone more inclined to the task.'

'Oh, I'll make your damned bodies, since you seem the least bad of the options. At least you're forming a council and some workable type of government.'

Deep within Doge, Piper felt shame that was an amalgamation of his own and his father's. His father had been brusque and assertive, but Piper had felt the stab of fear that'd engendered it. He knew, and his father knew, this was cowardice. Kowtowing to the new regime to avoid becoming a target. In his father, Piper saw reflected many of the Old Guard who were now part of his force on Yannetholm. Perhaps he wasn't as bad as Mallon had been, but he wasn't admirable. Now attempting to probe the further extent of this memory, he found it fizzling to nothing. This brought home to him that what was recorded here – the reptile – wasn't actually his father, with the breadth of a human being's mentality. It was a skeletal thing, mostly emotion, mostly subconscious. And from this new perspective, he now saw that he could explore it, that he didn't need to garner what he could from dreams.

He pushed further into the reptile and, since it was essentially asleep, he could see more of it. He did what he'd done before, building a model of it in his inner space. He mapped its points of connection and its distribution. And he tracked down those webs of neural mirror connections inside the thing that were experiences, copied across and dotted through it like metastases. He touched on one and brought it up.

'We should make that child,' said Reema, lying on a bed in a progression hospital. She was tubed and wired into support technology, the raw burns in, and excisions from, her body visible under polymer films.

'So you agree with me at last,' he replied as Doge.

'And many more thereafter, once the technology proves out.'

Threads of thought showed him the irritation Doge had with her. How only now she agreed with him after her 'accident', her decision made through emotion and not logic. Other threads hinted at Castron being the reason she'd ended up here. She'd been vocal in her objection to progression, and out of petty vengeance he'd put her there. And he'd put Doge in his place.

Piper didn't like the emotions here: the hatred, the guilt and the contempt. He copied memories across to his internal space and ran searches to align them in chronological order. Working with a fluidity beyond what was normal for him in a fully conscious state, he skimmed out relevant and pertinent detail, excised the emotional weight, then ran through them as an interwoven story, blandly told. Yes, Doge had been a rebel. After extreme injury, he'd retreated from a place in the new regime and grown resentful and angry because of the guilt he felt in doing so little about it turning into the old. He lost himself in his work and twisted that into an answer to his guilt, seeing it as a weapon he could deploy against Castron and his ilk. Reema had been another he'd twisted to his cause – naive, idealistic and easily manipulated. And she had become even more so when Castron punished him by severely injuring her. And that was it. There were no big revelations. Piper learned nothing new or life-changing. Rather, he realized how, similar to what might be styled as the evil of Mallon, or Castron, his father's motivations had simply been contemptible and prosaic.

Piper turned away, not wishing to pursue this any further, for he had nothing further to gain from the memories. However, while the reptile was in its somnolent state, he examined its connections to him again – back into his bones – and how it lay embedded within him. He saw with utter clarity how it was formed of the animuses and control programming of his weaponized mind. Before, he'd attempted to squeeze it out of his bones into the war body substrate, but in doing so found it ripped out his programming, his animuses and his power. This wasn't a method he could use if he wanted to be rid of it completely and retain power. However, did he want to retain power? Would losing that in order to be rid of this thing be so bad? All he needed to do was find a place outside of himself to put it . . .

Piper considered the Cyberat all around him, where the reptile had extended narrow threads through his links to their animuses. They didn't deserve to become hosts to his father's guilt and anger, not even the likes of Mallon. Also, their enhancements weren't in any way equivalent to the substrates where it presently resided. Perhaps he could push it out into the prador? No, that wouldn't work either, for the same reason. Anyway, he couldn't do this now, in the middle of a war.

Nevertheless, his father's guilt and anger were a burden he no longer wanted to carry, and he would find a way to be free of them.

In the heliotrope dawn of a red sun rising in swathes of dark green cloud, the Cyberat swarmed up into the sky. Still the army consisted of the best part of thirty million. Now it began dividing into streams led by Old Guard commanders and their subordinates. These were supported by Engineers and Medics, complemented with grav-rafts taken from the prador, and sometimes actually part of the prador, loaded down with supplies. Each stream was an army in itself, the numbers ranging from three hundred to six hundred thousand, since he'd retained his original command structure. Mallon was out there leading a force of four hundred thousand, Tinsher a force of six hundred thousand . . . Drillain and Transter too, along with fifty others. Each commander now had in his or her retinue an even division of the Cyberat carrying com gear. They would fly high to receive his animuses, and the tight beams of his programming feeds, to run these into the enemy. Piper had selected targets for each army – the most distant from each other lying three thousand kilometres apart.

'Can you maintain this spread?' asked Mallon.

'Absolutely,' Piper replied, utterly sure he could.

'I will be at my target in forty minutes,' Tinsher told him, while all the rest of the commanders gave their itineraries too.

Piper replied to them individually and conducted brief

conversations with them all. This time he didn't feel as if he was cheating in using his programming. It was part of him – it was what he was, unlike the reptile which he now entirely regarded as an interloper. He expanded out from the commanders, delivering lectures and homilies, and conducting brief chats with hundreds, then thousands, then tens of thousands of Cyberat, before winding that steadily down. As the armies spread out, starring across the sky towards their destinations, Piper raised the destroyer on grav, orienting it towards the best position to maintain his links to the animuses within his com Cyberat.

'You're covering a wider area,' said Aremer. 'We will scour the planet.'

Piper glanced at him squatting to one side on the war body, occupying Triode's position, and nodded agreement. Out of brief curiosity, he touched on the Engineer's mind to skim some of his thoughts on Triode and Anode. What he found there surprised him in its intensity. Aremer had had much internal conflict recently, his Cyberat indoctrination warring with his knowledge that it *was* indoctrination. He'd acquired great skill over the years in using the tools available to his Cyberat machine body and didn't want to lose any of that. Triode had informed him that he could control a machine body via an aug, but he had his doubts about the matter. What had finally swayed him was deep and integral – a feeling of loss and incompleteness that was wholly organic. And so Aremer had turned on the regenerative aspect of his nanosuite. Now, almost as expected, he felt guilty about that, because his purpose was to serve Piper.

Piper pulled out of him, perceiving that with this attitude reflected across the Cyberat, he'd initiated something major that would result in massive changes to his army, if not the end of it. And yet he felt it was right. When they were done on this world and probably moved on to another, it would be in a much-altered form. He wanted to play his part in the prador/human war, and he'd manipulated his soldiers to that end. But he was as uncomfortable manipulating them as he was with being manipulated. He didn't want an army of slaves. Thinking about slaves, he mentally touched on the prador flash-frozen ganglion in the destroyer to run instructions through it. This was a test, rendering much data from the animus he had on the thing.

'I obey,' it told him, firing up thrusters and taking the vessel higher.

Uncomfortable too was how closely his soldiers resembled prador entities like this mind.

Ten kilometres up was high enough for him to maintain direct line communications with his diverse armies spreading out into a ring. He flicked to the battle sphere and saw the perfection of his design establishing in it. His armies would, as Aremer had said, scour the planet. After these next battles, he'd expand the whole ring around the globe, while maintaining communication, obliterating any prador that lay in his path. If they continued running, as it seemed many were still doing – he could see prador abandoning the installation city Tinsher was heading to right now – then no matter. He would seize the machines and destroy the infrastructure they left behind, until only fleeing prador remained. Then he would raise higher, maintain com and spread his armies further, carrying on until the planet was clear. But then, even as his armies began to arrive at their targets, he saw something odd occurring.

'What the fuck?' he said.

Prador and war machines, which he'd thought were fleeing one installation city, were actually attacking another. He saw prador slamming into each other in mid-air, with very little in the way of weapons fire, but a lot in the way of straight claw-on-claw savagery. Some psychological reaction to imminent defeat? He couldn't find it in what he knew about them.

Two flashes ensued over to the other side of the three-thousand-kilometre area he covered, leaving after-images in the battle sphere. EMR disruption distorted things for a while, but when com cleared up he saw one space port and one installation were now glowing craters. Mushroom clouds rose and ring-shaped blast waves spread across the surrounding landscape. It made no sense. He'd seen no missiles fired and the Polity had delivered no orbital strikes. Had they committed suicide there?

Tinsher arrived at his target and, putting this strange behaviour out of his mind, Piper concentrated on his plan. What matter if the prador had decided to make this easier for him? A small army came out against the Cyberat. Piper sent animuses to seize control of a rising cloud of war drones, sending half into the installation and the other half to go after fleeing prador. He then eyed the force heading out to meet Tinsher, sending animuses there too. As they took hold, the arthropods rained down on slabs jutting out of the shallow sea like prehistoric beasts. Their armour hailed onto them next, pounding what survived of them to slurry. Piper sent a shutdown to the fight programs in that armour when he saw tunnels opening and Yannets coming out – those programs would be a danger to them.

'Continue,' he told Tinsher.

'Very little to continue with,' the Cyberat replied flatly.

Warehouses collapsed under the barrage elsewhere, with other installation cities and tactics changing, but not as a whole. Many prador armies now remained on the ground. Others flew up, as though they hadn't heard the bad news. Masses of prador fled through shallow seas to fall into pit traps opened by the Yannets, or to be fried in tactical nuclear blasts. Another city exploded. This major CTD burned Cyberat in the approaching army from the sky, and hurled out a boiling tsunami that left clear steaming ground behind. The losses there hardened Piper's resolve. Because, no matter the hatred and need for human survival Albermech and Corisian had raised in him, he could feel this annihilation sucking out his will. It was all perfectly logical in a fight against creatures whose aim was extermination, but Piper felt bloody.

'Tactical change,' he said succinctly, more to hear his human voice speaking than to deliver the message to his soldiers, who received the detail on it at once.

'What are you doing now?' asked Aremer, his eyes glassy as he doubtless watched the battle sphere.

'They are falling apart,' he replied. 'There is some loss by retransmission through my comlink Cyberat, but I don't think that matters any more.'

All the armies had now impacted, and though he'd lost Cyberat, especially at the edge of that CTD blast, there had been little in the way of fighting and the losses were meagre. Laying in real imagery in the battle sphere, he saw the colour change in the sky due to the fires, great columns of smoke, blast waves and tsunamis dying across the watery landscape. His orders took effect at once, the circle of armies breaking at one point and then folding out over the ensuing days into a line over ten thousand kilometres long. Even as it folded out, it rolled over more prador, at one point even over two prador armies tearing into each other. Encompassed in the battle sphere, the line scored nearly halfway across one visible face of the planet. And as he watched it set into motion, he received comlink requests.

'Not unexpected,' he said, opening the three of them at once.

The Albermech and Corisian links immediately expanded bandwidth. He allowed that, knowing he could shut it down immediately and, if he so wished, easily slap the AI–ship captain amalgamation away. He was so beyond them now. Though they'd opened that bandwidth, it was Inster who spoke.

'Remember when I stuck my gun against your forehead and told you to put that fucking thing on the ground?' the agent asked.

'I do indeed. It's a precious memory for me,' Piper replied dryly.

'Imagine I'm doing the same right now.'

Instead of asking questions, Piper thought hard about what this might mean, before replying, 'So we can afford to be merciful now?'

'Well, apart for some disagreeable elements, the Prador Kingdom did just surrender.'

'You fucking what?'

'Surrender, truce . . . it's all semantics and a lot gets lost in translation from a species who find the concepts of both words alien,' Inster said.

Corisian now interjected. 'Negotiations have begun at least and, as you may have noted down there, there is some disagreement on their side.'

'Albermech?' he asked, surprised that he needed confirmation from the AI.

'Yes, unbelievably, it may all be over,' the AI replied. 'Here, perhaps this will help you to understand. Corisian will run you through it. I'm rather busy.'

Through the wide bandwidth from Albermech came a virtuality attachment. Piper hesitated, some of his earlier paranoia about the Polity reawakened, then he plunged in. It wasn't so much that he trusted the Polity now, but he felt sure he could handle or dismiss their machinations. The virtuality expanded in his inner space and he at once found himself on another world.

He was standing on what looked vaguely like grassy mudflats, similar to those seen in some places on Founder's World. But here the sky was violet and, scattered around him, arched and domed organic buildings seemed to have grown from the mud and extended out into the sea. He of course recognized the design, since he'd been dropping prador on such buildings for weeks. He was also surrounded by prador. All of them seemed to be first-children and all wore armour with evident readjustments and extensions, and painted in black and white. More of the scene opened to his perception and now he saw the pillars of smoke, the fragments of prador armour, the blown-open suits and steaming remains. Amidst the black and white prador was an adult. He had prosthetic limbs, mandibles and claws of exotic metal that looked like polished purple-tinted gold. His limbs were moving but not touching the ground, for grav-motors buoyed him up. The other prador had run control skeins into its armour and were pulling on attached chains.

'The prador home world,' said Corisian, etched into being in the air beside him and obviously an addition to this scene. 'And that there' – the captain pointed to the chained prador – 'was their king.'

'Was?' Piper enquired.

'Just watch.'

His perspective bobbed and shifted, and he found himself moving, hints of a larger body around him and numerous legs rising and falling. Having delved so deeply into a prador mind, he understood he was getting the recorded perspective from one prador, as though he was inside its armour and looking out. This too caused distortions, because prador had more than simple human binocular vision.

He and the other prador moved along the mudflats to the edge of the sea where a jetty as wide as a highway stretched out, supported by legs much like those of the prador themselves. The apparent first-children towed the adult out to the end of this jetty, Piper's perspective following. Reaching the end, they knocked off the adult's grav. Sound kicked in now; it'd been absent before. He heard the clattering, hissing and bubbling of their speech. There wasn't much of it from the black-and-whites and just terse instructions from the one whose perspective he shared. He understood it perfectly.

'Don't wait for my order – just get it done,' was what this one said.

Meanwhile, the king issued a continuous stream of threats concerning the terrible punishments in store for those around him. It was, as Piper had understood with the adult whose mind he'd looted, the standard prador death song. One of the black-and-whites brought over a machine, while the others fought to hold onto the king's legs – fought to keep him in place. Piper couldn't identify the machine, until it extruded a spiral drill, glittering with braided shearfields. It sparked against the king's body armour and started to cut, spraying smoking swarf. The body armour, Piper noted, was not the same exotic metal as the limbs, else this wouldn't have been possible. After a lengthy struggle, the drill broke through, eliciting a shriek and a pained clattering of mandibles from the king.

'Percentage diatomic acid?' enquired another of the black-and-whites.

'Just ten per cent,' replied the leader, waving a claw that seemed unusually long, almost like that of a langoustine. Piper noted the size of the creature he was viewing from and realized it too was an adult, though its shape seemed odd.

Another machine was brought up to the hole through the king's armour, and a tube fixed in place. Piper watched, feeling almost a hint of amusement seeing the prador with that machine operating it – it turned out to be much like a stirrup pump, with vessels attached to hold the diatomic acid and its dilutant. The king started shrieking regularly, mandibles clattering so hard they threw up sparks. In his struggles, he managed to throw two of his captors off the side of the jetty. The one with the pump had to reattach the pipe twice and then, when done, began to inject resin to fill the hole.

'Float him,' said the leader.

'They are vicious creatures,' said Piper to Corisian.

'Yes, they are, and vicious methods are required to rule them. This spectacle wasn't just for us but for all the prador,' the ship captain replied.

Through a control skein, they turned on the grav of the king's suit. He rose into the air, kicking. With a heave of the chains, they sent him off the side of the jetty. He dropped a few metres, then stabilized a couple of metres above the surface of the ocean, his legs skittering against the water. The shrieking and clattering continued as he drifted out and, having already seen numerous examples of the same, Piper knew he was in agony. This carried on and on which, Piper understood, was the point of using such a low dilution of the acid. Top strength would have killed him in just a few minutes. Not wanting to wait for the resolution of this, Piper speeded up the virtuality package, pausing to see steam boiling out of the adult's anal vent, then pausing again when it broke out around its prosthetic limbs. The termination, after a death that took hours, was the prador leader whose perspective he shared walking out and bringing to bear a big heavy weapon. Piper recognized a Polity weapon – a rail launcher of specially designed armour-piercing missiles. One shot dipped the king into the ocean, to come back up with a massive smoking dent in his armour. The next shot penetrated and detonated inside – the internal explosion throwing limbs in every direction. The carapace continued to float until a third shot underneath blew the grav-motors. It finally dropped and sank out of sight rapidly. Then the virtuality ended and Piper came out of it.

'So I have just witnessed a usurpation?' he enquired.

'Yes, you have,' Corisian replied. 'The creature whose perspective you shared is now the new king of the prador. This individual is particularly intelligent and capable, not only in how he's managed so complete a usurpation, but in his immediate dealing with the Polity.'

'You mean surrender . . .'

'Yes and no. He understands that the prador cannot win the war. But he also understands the further cost to the Polity of winning it and therefore his bargaining position.'

'So the AIs will make bargains,' said Piper tightly.

'Cold calculations, boy. Cold calculations.'

Over the ensuing days, Piper brought the line to a halt and the destroyer down to the surface, landing just out from one installation city apparently occupied by *surrendered* prador. Having adopted some of their thinking, he found the concept difficult to encompass. He gazed at the battle sphere now incorporating the whole world, and turned the globe, with its artificial red and green markings. These indicated in the first case the small conglomerations of hostile prador and in the second those that were supposedly now no longer the enemy. Chaos was continuing to break out all around the globe as prador fought each other, and he saw many red areas fading out. It seemed war among themselves was a matter of extermination too.

Piper was quite ready to sit back and let this all play out, but knew he couldn't. He trusted none of this. Wars didn't simply finish with everyone laying down their weapons – which the prador had not done – slapping each other on the back and going their separate ways. He needed to remain on his guard, and now the war was supposedly coming to an end, he didn't want to lose any more of his soldiers pointlessly. He concentrated on the battle sphere and the disposition of his forces. Attack by any prador armies wasn't the danger now, since he could drop them out of the sky in an instant, but what he'd seen earlier was. If he brought all his armies together in one place, they were vulnerable to nuclear strikes.

'Distribute,' he said succinctly, filling in detail.

The line began to break up as his armies headed towards various green enclaves.

'The purpose of this?' Transter enquired.

Checking the Cyberat's position, Piper saw that Transter was leading his force to a place lying out from where two prador forces were fighting. Their orders – let them kill each other.

'Specifically surrender here.'

'I'm not sure what you mean.' Oddly this was a conversation he didn't need to repeat much at all through his programs. The Cyberat seemed subdued, in shock as they struggled to adapt to a new paradigm.

'As Inster told me: a lot is lost in translation. On Polity worlds like this one, the prador must surrender and wait for transport out. Elsewhere, it's basically a ceasefire, where prador ships and other forces are retreating. Overall they want a truce but aren't prepared to surrender the entire Prador Kingdom.'

'The red cities?' Mallon asked.

'We'll let the prador deal with their own, then we wait.'

'We could take out those cities,' she observed.

'But in doing so I would divide up our forces, putting too many supposedly surrendered prador at our backs.'

'You don't trust this?'

'Divisions amidst them are along familial lines. Those with greater investment in the old Kingdom, and related to the king's

457

family, are the hostiles. But they are all xenophobic and I don't trust that other families won't change their minds.' Piper paused, checking figures. 'We have lost over a million Cyberat on this world and I don't want to lose any more.'

'Polity forces will be down here shortly?' Transter asked.

'No,' Piper replied. 'They will be pulling out, only leaving a small contingent, since there are more critical areas that require them.'

'So what, precisely, are *we* waiting for?'

'An envoy from the Kingdom.'

Piper sat listening to the ticking of cooling metal and the sounds filtering up through the ship. The occasional clattering movement he put down to Aremer who, without his intervention, had eased into the position of personal attendant, with command over this part of the ship. With a small effort he focused on the Engineer. He had five recruits under him, rerouting conduits and installing Cyberat hardware to make things run more smoothly. They were keeping busy and had done some good work, but he realized he missed Triode and Anode. He thought about them, stuck in their bodies and in a life they hadn't chosen, then he considered himself, before sending a signal to open armoured hatches to the rear of the ship's sensory turret.

'Going outside again?' asked Aremer, looking directly towards him, even though he couldn't see him with his eyes from where he was inside the destroyer.

'Indeed I am,' he replied, pondering on the irony of that, being enclosed in his war body as he was.

It had become his habit to venture out as day merged into night, and then day again. During this time, he observed longer incremental changes. Meteor showers diminished steadily over the rhythmic world tides and the atmosphere lost its heat – the orange fading as the skies slowly returned to the original deep blue. But then cloud started to boil up and he noticed frost forming on surfaces, with ice sheathing pools deposited by rainstorms. A seasonal change? The Yannets said otherwise, for their world had never been cold enough for ice before. This was yet another fallout of the war and a result of the dust in the atmosphere.

Out in space, remaining Polity vessels had been spending their time directing larger debris on 'safe' courses – usually towards the sun – while grabbing up survivors, both human and prador. Just a few days previously, surviving Cyberat settled through atmosphere to slot back into his forces, annoyed to have missed the fighting. Meanwhile four heavy meteors had come down, blasting out craters that filled with water, to create four seas deeper than usual here.

There had been much to do to ensure his forces wouldn't be caught off guard should this surrender be false, but now it was all finalized. It seemed the surrender must be for real, because all across the massive battle front of interstellar war the prador had been putting themselves at a severe disadvantage with it. What did that leave for him? It was a question he'd posed many times and one for which he still had no real answer.

Moving outside was almost autonomous. He didn't have to focus on detaching the war body's feet from the floor, or disconnecting the telescopic bayonets plugging him into the surrounding system. The armoured hatches opened behind, exposing morning sky cut through with the smoke trails of industry and still showing the flashing glints of occasional meteors, but not the perpetual rain of earlier. He raised the body on grav and slid it towards that light, then out over the gentle curve of hull and down again to attach like a parasitic louse.

With the war body secured, he prepared to detach from the

thing itself. As usual, he raised his hands from the chair arms and waited until all the metallic dots on his palms had disappeared. But as they faded, the diminishment of his processing and connection simply didn't occur. Running a rough comparison soon revealed that the capacity in his bones had expanded so much that the war body substrate now seemed but a fraction of his overall self. The resultant processing and EMR expansion created the illusion of no disconnection at all. Despite the reptile remaining as intimate as ever, he could shut off his bones and be free of it. It didn't influence him any more. It was there and strong inside him, but the thing's power and influence in his mind had diminished now he understood it so well, too well. Also, his aims and its emotional drive were so in alignment that it didn't interfere too much. Grimacing, he detached feeds to his combat suit while the chain-glass bubble rose, then climbed out and walked down to stand on the hull. He had some thinking to do.

The question of *What the hell do I do now?* transitioned into *What do I actually want to do?* His purpose for existence – the purpose for which his father and mother had made him on Founder's World – had ceased to be relevant with the fall of the Old Guard. Then, as a weapon made for one war, he'd been repurposed for another by the Polity. And now that too was done.

Piper walked out along the hull, gazed across the mottled jigsaw of land and sea stretching in one direction, then over to the nearby installation city in the other. He raised nodes in his internal space and millions were easily accessible, with no reduction in his perception of them. He peered at the war body. He could leave it behind if he wished, but what did he wish? What did Piper Lagan, distinct from the reptile within, distinct from his father's influence, distinct from Polity indoctrination, want? He shook his head. He couldn't really know that person because he was a product of all those, combined with his experiences, and he really didn't now want to put any of it aside.

Also, through this introspection, he understood that his driving daemons had no force any more. Castron, in flying to the Prador Kingdom, was likely dead, as Inster had said. Piper's attitude to the Old Guard and others of the previous Founder's World regime had changed, now having been in the minds of many of them, and having fought with them. They were just people – just as much a product of their history as he was. And the prador too. He'd absorbed their language and code, seen into the mind of one of them and, in the process, understood them as a product of their particular evolution. They were dangerous creatures, of course, but no longer such a danger to humanity, and certainly not to him. That hatred was gone too. He understood, at last, that he'd outgrown his programming.

Piper sat down on the hull of the dreadnought and, after a time, Aremer and two other Engineers clattered out to join him.

'What's in the future for you three now?' he asked.

They made no immediate reply, though he was aware of the frenetic communication between them. Finally Aremer replied for all three of them.

'We want what was taken from us, then we want to go home,' he said.

He nodded, thinking about his mother, thinking about the new regime back on Founder's World and how it must not fall back into old patterns. He hoped it hadn't already. He thought about things taken from him, but found only additions and at last no reasons for resentment.

'I too want to go home,' he replied.

The sky grew dark in a few areas of the horizon, for it seemed storms were coming, but then the regular patterns of the clouds revealed something else. Piper had summoned four forces here, and they were the troops of Mallon, Tinsher, Transter and Drillain. Clouds then became distinct as columns and wedges of hundreds of thousands of Cyberat. The air filled with their power hum and concerted racket. Water vapour and stratified shimmering, as of heat haze, appeared below them, as the spill of their grav-engines stirred things up down there. Piper, mostly withdrawn to his human senses, felt sure he could smell them: machine oil and electronics, aromatic composites and a hint of fleshy putre-faction. Or perhaps he was imagining that, or it arose from the Engineers squatting around him on the hull of the destroyer. In short order they flooded the sky above, diminishing the light, and then began to come down to land all around. The racket grew to a roar and the ground vibrated. Vapour filled the air, making him lose sight of many of them in rising fog banks. Areas of ground and shallow sea disappeared underneath them.

It was a huge and impressive host, and still just a fraction of his entire army. Piper stood up and stretched, chewing on the nutrient bar Aremer had brought him. He switched easily to his full mind and senses to watch the four Old Guard falling together, along with those big old Enforcers – his retinue forming up. Soon they became visible to his human eyes, dropping out of the sky and settling at the base of the destroyer. The big Enforcers took up their designated spaces and then, with a shift of machine bodies, the horde opened a road leading to the installation city. Piper nodded – all was as it should be – and he increased the function of his bones to focus on the battle sphere.

He raised his attention high into orbit around the world and beyond. It still looked cluttered up there but that was mostly battle debris. The station the Polity had seized now had the *Albermech* docked to it, while half an orbit round sat a war runcible, brought in from further out in the system and apparently repurposed here. Around it were attack ships to protect it, not from prador assault, though, but from fast-flying debris. Even as he watched, the runcible activated, drawing a translucent meniscus across its ring. A few thousand kilometres out, two tugs were hauling in the badly damaged hulk of a prador destroyer. They drew it in closer and closer, then brought it to a halt a hundred kilometres out from the runcible. The ship then began spilling its contents: a great swarm of armoured prador flying on thrusters. They streamed towards the runcible and through it – their exit point being the Polity edge of a no man's land agreed between the two realms, where prador ships awaited to pick them up.

'What about the survivors further out in the system?' Piper asked, rather than explore the battle sphere to find out.

'Ah, you're back,' said Corisian.

'It hasn't been necessary to communicate,' Piper replied. 'The battle sphere, or perhaps com sphere now, provides enough data, and I've been busy down here.'

'Yeah, sure you have.'

'Perhaps I've also been finding the need for Polity commanders to still touch base with me a bit tiresome too.' Piper let that sink in, then reminded him, 'Prador survivors further out in the system?'

After a long pause Corisian replied, 'Those that there are, are being packed into two mostly intact dreadnoughts. The ships are incapable of flight but have enough air and supplies to enable the creatures to survive until we haul the runcible back out there.'

'It's nice that the prador are retrieving their soldiers,' said Piper flatly.

'The new king is smart enough to know his soldiers wouldn't surrender without guarantee of safe passage back to the Kingdom.

Even so, most of the evacuation of their kind is being organized by the Polity.'

'I wonder how many will actually get home?'

'Who cares – at least they will be off our worlds.' Corisian then added, 'That's the last of them here. And our visitor should be coming through in a moment.'

Piper watched the runcible as the last tail of prador went through the meniscus. He saw no visible change to the thing, but changes in the data landscape of the battle sphere indicated it had switched over to receiving. The nose of a ship then nudged through the meniscus, and the whole thing slid out into vacuum. Piper eyed the small destroyer, noting it was the largest prador ship that could get through, but put his suspicions on hold. If it attacked, it could do damage to his forces but wouldn't survive the Polity attack ships and the *Albermech*. It would be a pointless exercise for them. Its size was all about the status of the individual aboard.

'So, an envoy,' he said. 'Why the necessity?'

There had been so much to do since he heard the news this envoy was coming, he'd never asked the question. He'd also felt an odd depressive indifference about this event, which he alleviated by concentrating on his Cyberat; on their manufacturing and the steady expansion of the regrowth tank system, as well as ensuring they remained clear of the diminishing prador conflicts here. He understood the feeling as a truism of war, for he was in one of those 'long periods of boredom between moments of terror'. And it had been no lie about the Polity commanders here needing to touch base with him constantly. He had tired of their questions and obvious intent. But now he needed to re-engage and, instead of pondering and preparing for the future, start actually moving into it.

There was no reply for a short time, and then Corisian's link winked out and Inster's started blinking for attention. A second later, four other familiar links appeared. It seemed Meersham, Sloan, Cheen and Geelie were once again open to conversation. Cynical thoughts about the Polity wanting to draw him back into the fold compelled him to ignore them and open only Inster's comlink.

'Where did Corisian go?'

'Big AI shit occurring,' said the agent. 'Albermech, as you know, has been heavily engaged with organizing things here, but has now taken control of that runcible too – its AI just routed out elsewhere – and Corisian is engaged with all that too.'

The explanation seemed weak to Piper. This was again about pushing Piper into human engagement with Inster and the others. Corisian – older even than Inster – had doubtless read his irritation and pulled out, probably impatient with it. Now with Inster, it would be back to the assessing and manipulating. He understood it perfectly: they had activated a powerful weapon in him, and now, the war being over, they wanted to deactivate it. The process of decommission, which he'd expected, had started.

'Perhaps you can tell me why the necessity for an envoy, then,' he said, feeling old, a little jaded and very cynical.

'The prador on the surface lost their king and much of the chain of command leading down to them,' Inster explained. 'They're sufficiently indoctrinated to accept their new king, the order to cease fire and the promise of a return home. But for the next steps, they need a representative of authority in place. This creature will likely be one of the new king's family.'

'It will be interesting to meet him,' said Piper.

'It would be tactically unsound for that to happen,' Inster replied.

'What?'

'Yes, I see that you've prepared a path into the city and you have your personal bodyguard in place, but we would rather it wasn't you making the initial meeting.'

Piper felt a flash of annoyance and his reptile responded hard, actually increasing the function of his bones, or perhaps it was the other way around. He inspected himself internally and didn't like what he found there: righteous indignation, the expectation of him being dominant and angered arrogance. Was that him or his father? He pushed it down.

'And why not me?' he asked tightly, now eyeing the *Albermech* in the battle sphere.

A shuttle had detached and was moving out. Inster was aboard and no doubt the four of the Sparkind team.

'Firstly, because I have more experience with this sort of negotiation. It may also be that the prador, probably knowing where you came from, will not accept you as a valid representative of the Polity.'

'And yet I am the sum cause of their defeat down here . . .'

'Agreed, but my second point is relevant to that: one must never underestimate prador intelligence. Seeing Cyberat, they will know where you're from. They almost certainly know you are in prime control and, with what you did, they will have hurried to gather data on you. They'll know who you are and they'll fear your abilities.'

'How can they know?'

'You put yourself at the head of your army. They will have gathered data via your penetration of their systems. And, lest we forget, Castron went to the Prador Kingdom . . .'

'I see,' Piper replied, but the reasoning seemed specious to him. Castron would surely have been killed before any kind of collaboration . . . 'But why am I a danger if the war is over?'

'You are not that naive,' said Inster dryly. 'We don't want you to meet the envoy because where you are currently your forces protect you. You are a dangerous weapon to the prador. I wouldn't put it past them to sacrifice the envoy and all the prador on this world just to remove you from the game board.'

'Despite the war being over, and risking that entire peace?'

'A good commander, or king, prepares for future eventualities.'

'I see . . . So how are you all?' He abruptly changed the subject, opening the links to the Sparkind too. As the replies rolled in and he answered with a simple portion of his mind, aping easy jocular human interaction, he focused with the rest of his mind on the battle sphere and deliberately opened up his bones further.

The shuttle containing Inster and the rest was hovering out from the *Albermech* and delaying its approach. The prador destroyer, now escorted by two attack ships, fell into orbit around the world and descended. The attack ships stayed on station to either side of it as it passed down through cloud and shed vapour in atmosphere, and all seemed well. Then it suddenly changed course, simultaneous with Piper receiving numerous alerts. He dropped his conversation with the Sparkind, enhanced the battle sphere and saw through it the particle beam strikes and missile launches coming from remaining prador red areas. The beam strikes were first, searing along a mass of hardfields appearing below the destroyer – the thing ejecting the burning stars of failing hardfield generators. The attack ships broke off and separated, ramping a thousand gees to targets, spewing fire, sewing lines of missiles whose drives ignited. Apparently given permission, the destroyer opened fire too. Next, the *Albermech* sparkled with a thousand lights and shortly after the vapour trails of railgun shots sketched lines through atmosphere. From where he stood, Piper observed the evening sky igniting with flashes, while in the battle sphere missiles exploded under highly accurate railgun strikes. Then the strikes on the ground erupted.

Piper's caution to his army was instinctive, almost unconscious, but unnecessary. The vessels pounded the red areas. Nukes raised great balls of fire. Railgun strikes stitched across installations and selectively took out missile batteries. Particle beams seared the areas too, almost like cauterizing wounds. He detected launches from the prador green areas as well and observed swarms of missiles hurtling towards these last remaining aggressors. The rumbling air shock of this devastation reached Piper shortly after, as flashes lit all across the horizon. The firing from the ground stuttered and died in slews of magma and craters that boiled the sea spilling back into them.

Did this indicate the reality that his seizure of this world, while having its utility, had actually been a test of his potential? Had he not been entirely necessary? Because, surely after winning the battle in vacuum, the Polity ships could have annihilated the prador here from orbit, as they were now doing. No, it was more nuanced than that. Without him, the Polity would have planned some other way to take out those on the ground, but it would have required resources. The whole point of Albermech dragging Enforcers and others off Founder's World had been about that. And now, analysing further, he saw that an assault from the air or orbit would not have been as easy as this. The prador from the red areas had just made one last effort, a final stand. It didn't seem to be about changing outcomes. Judging by the desultory defence of their positions, they'd had little hope of it working. They had effectively committed suicide.

As the firing from below sputtered out, the attack ships swept up from close to the surface and hurtled for orbit and out. The destroyer, leaking smoke from a couple of strikes that had hit home, changed course and dropped lower. Tracking it in the sphere, Piper also turned to look towards a specific point on the horizon, and there picked out the expanding dot. Finally the vessel loomed into view and slid above him, feathering its thrusters to pause there for a short time, as if its passenger was inspecting him. Then, with a surge of grav, it slid on and descended over the other side of the installation city. Meanwhile, Inster's shuttle began its descent, illustrating that he had expected this brief conflict.

In the battle sphere Piper cleared up imagery even further – this being very easy since Polity satellites and many of his Cyberat were focused on this area. As the destroyer settled over there on a chequerboard of mudskipper ponds and began opening ports and dropping ramps, he saw a reception committee already on the way out. Three adults surrounded by first-children, trailed by columns of second-children, came to within a hundred metres of the ship and halted. The ship, meanwhile, began unrolling a mesh walkway from one major ramp, finally terminating on the drier ground on which the installation had been built, just at the feet of the reception committee. Perhaps this envoy didn't like getting his feet wet.

Prador came down the ramp. Two were adults walking on golden prosthetic limbs, their natural armour inset with metal patterns of the same gold, reminding Piper of the tattoos a girl by a river once showed him. First-children came next – their armour black and white and looking pristine compared to the battered state of those waiting. There were other prador here too, the size of second-children and clad in shiny chrome, carrying what Piper first mistook for armament, then upon analysis recognized. They were prador engineers. Then came the envoy.

The envoy had made himself easily identifiable by wearing bone-white armour. He was bigger than all the first-children Piper had seen so far and, knowing prador biology, he could tell that he had all his limbs. He'd also apparently not shed the rear set to expose his mating apparatus, to become an adult, though the limbs on a suit of their armour didn't necessarily reflect what lay inside. There was also something about his shape – flatter and wider, longer limbs and claws. Piper recognized this from the virtuality of the old king's execution: here was one of the new king's children.

The envoy proceeded along the walkway fast, as if impatient. The reception committee parted ahead and he went straight towards the city, the others flowing in behind him. However, on reaching an entrance he paused and turned, tilting back and looking up into the sky. In that moment, the animuses in a series of war machines Piper controlled received a programming link, much like those the prador had used when struggling to take back control of them. These links established without trying to seize back control and instead opened comlink portals. Piper smiled. Inster had been right about prador gathering information on him via his seizure of their machines, otherwise they wouldn't have been able to do this. The envoy, still tilted back and looking at the sky, gave confirmation. Piper gathered his links to those animuses and routed them into his virtual aug, as a comlink, then opened it.

'Piper Lagan,' said the envoy.

'And you are?'

'I'm called Orlik – a Polity terror drone gave me the name, out of spite I suspect, since it so little resembles my prador name and is impossible to say in prador speech.'

'How unkind, but it seems your translator handles human speech very well.'

'Yes, my translator, it does.'

Piper realized there was something unsaid there. Opening up a logic tree, he came to a variety of conclusions. One of them was that this prador didn't need a translator, but that of course was ridiculous. Even if it understood human language, it didn't have the vocal apparatus to speak it.

'So why are you contacting me?' he asked.

'A Polity negotiator is coming down from that ship up there . . . the *Albermech*. It will all be a staged event for the benefit of the prador here, with the main points of our surrender already hashed out. But I want to speak to you, face to face.'

'Why?'

'I had considered using the argument that the stratification of command in us prador makes it essential that the one who defeated us here should accept the surrender. That would have scanned well for humans, but is actually irrelevant to prador, for whom the concept of surrender is a difficult thing.'

'And you dismissed that argument, of course.' A surge of adrenalin had arrived and his bones were fizzing upon the comprehension that this prador was *smart*, and seemed nothing like the prador he had previously encountered. This keyed into what Corisian had said about the new kind – the intelligence. Now taking in the odd shape of this creature's armour, he wondered what else might be at play here. He was fascinated and curious.

'I did dismiss it. I am curious to meet you.'

'And perhaps, as is not unfeasible, anxious to see a future threat to your father's kingdom eliminated? For it could be that your father has an inclination to renew the war at some point.'

'No, I'm genuinely curious, but aware too that what you just said is an idea fed to you by the Polity. I should also note that your ability, since you are presently outside of that war body, is not confined to it.'

'Meaning?'

'Your power to destroy us will not be diminished by coming to see me. Come in your war body, with as much protection as you want. You can still seize control of our armour and otherwise eject us from it.'

'But you may be prepared to sacrifice yourself and all others there by detonating a nuke when I arrive.'

'I arrived in a destroyer and, since you have seized one, you know its capabilities. I know your location and just a short time ago was directly above you. If my aim is to kill you, why didn't I do it then?'

'Fair enough.' Piper reviewed this. Their destroyers were loaded with weaponry and, standing out on the hull outside his war body, he'd been vulnerable. Sure, his forces and his destroyer would have slung up defences, and there would have been a hell of a fight, but where he was standing would have been nevertheless turned into a nuclear furnace.

'And if that isn't enough for you, I can give you an additional lure.'

'That being?'

'Castron.'

19

The reaction to hearing Castron's name was immediate and, in retrospect, Piper should have expected it. The reptile solidified within him, distinct, angry, raising animuses and warfare programming. His overlay, always present, hardened over a clarification of thought. Ennui disappeared as he rose to a higher function; warfare function. But this time he became acutely aware of cause and effect. Previously, he'd always thought of the overlay as a product of the reptile, but now he recognized it for what it was: a product of his own mind and a defence *against* the reptile. It enabled him to subdue it. It enabled him at least to filter its effect on his thinking. And yet, he now understood that, should the correct circumstances prevail, it might not be enough.

'Attend me,' he snapped, turning and trotting back to his war body.

His order received, his retinue of big Enforcers shifted into the path he'd made from his destroyer towards the installation city. As he climbed up the side of his machine, Mallon, Tinsher, Drillain and Transter rose into view. He eyed the huge war bodies these Old Guard occupied, then considered the size of the Enforcers too, and looked towards the city. It simply wouldn't do. He wanted to meet this envoy but, despite his rationale that it probably didn't want to kill him, he wasn't going to walk into a potential trap. Nor did he want to go somewhere confined, where his guard couldn't follow.

'Here in one hour,' he said, sending a location outside the city a few kilometres beyond the vessel the envoy had arrived in. The forces of the four Old Guard were scattered there, but he flashed orders to them. These were relayed through the chain of command, and Cyberat soldiers began to clear a path, then opened out a large area around a mass of the mushroom stone a couple of kilometres long, and half as wide, nested amidst mudskipper pools.

'It seems suitable,' Orlik agreed. 'But that Polity shuttle will be down here before then.'

'Agreed – the matter will be resolved.' He stepped inside his war body, his hands hesitating over the chair arms. Then, with the physical hard link being almost superfluous now, he simply raised it into the sky with his mental connection. Leaving the comlink to the prador open, he focused his attention on the four Old Guard.

'What's happening?' asked Mallon, speaking for them.

'I'm going to meet this prador envoy.'

'Is that a good idea?'

Thinking on their past, Piper considered keeping information from them, but it didn't sit well with him. Such control and manipulation still keyed into his own dislike of how the same had been used with him. No lies any more. He also felt it was time, if the war was truly over, for him to sacrifice his godlike power over all the Cyberat.

'Keep this to yourselves for the present: the envoy has news about Castron who, as you know, fled into the prador realm.'

The words had a visible effect as their war bodies shifted in the air. Tinsher and Transter collided, then parted quickly as if embarrassed. He sensed their mixed emotions and the direction of their thoughts. Drillain's spurt of anger quickly resolved into prospects of vengeance, with the lurid fantasy of Castron being handed over to them and simply executed in the mud of this world. Tinsher and Transter entertained a similar vision but were not so vengeful and thought confusedly about Castron being taken back to Founder's World for trial. This then strayed into thoughts about their own position. Both were thinking about going back to face the consequences of their previous action or inaction. Meanwhile, Mallon had almost split in two. She felt loyalty to Castron, battling against Piper's programming of her mind. However, despite his programming of her being about fighting the prador, not eliminating Castron, that old loyalty was dying anyway. He realized it had been displaced by loyalty to him.

They weren't alone in their response; the reptile continued to thrash inside him. He felt anger at their prosaic and selfish thought processes, and saw them as they once were. He tracked their ideas about Castron and filled in some of his own – this line of thought fractured into visualizations of grotesque punishments. The impulse to adjust the latter three to the perspective of rebels like his father and mother, to ensure agreement and bend their thought to his own, came to him strongly. And then equally as powerful came his self-disgust. No, again no – the time for manipulation was over. He pushed back, feathering the slide switches to his bones down, and used the overlay to force the reptile into the shape of his mind. Confined, controlled, as if it had been physically trying to escape his body.

'Let's see what this is about,' he managed, sending his war body past them and down the side of the destroyer, sliding low above the massed Cyberat.

After a delay, they brought themselves behind him, while the Enforcers below rose into the air and moved in around him.

Soon they'd fallen into a formation, with him at the tip of a spearhead of Enforcers, and the four Old Guard spaced evenly all around him. Now viewing through other eyes and sensors towards the city, he saw the envoy coming out, surrounded by his entourage, along with the three prador adults and numerous local first- and second-children that had met him here. At the installation, other prador were coming out and settling on the roofs too. He could see how all of this might run out of control, if one were to suppose easily matched forces, but that wasn't the case. No matter the disposition of forces here, he could still seize control; he could still continue his extermination of the prador.

'I note that you've seen fit to ignore what I said earlier,' said Inster calmly.

'I am more than capable of dealing with this,' Piper replied. 'And to be frank, your fears for my safety are unfounded. I also submit that you wanting to take over here is more about putting me in my place as a small component of the Polity forces. Wouldn't want me getting all arrogant and totalitarian now, would we?'

'As I've observed before, you've acquired much cynicism for one so young,' said Inster dryly.

'It isn't my own.'

'And perhaps something of your parents' rebelliousness,' Inster added.

'Perhaps. Nevertheless, you will land your shuttle down by my destroyer and remain there until I summon you.'

'Perhaps the chain of command is unclear to you.'

'What is clear is that you put me and mine down here as an independent force, and let us do our own thing while you made your assessment of me. Now circumstances have changed, you're making unsubtle moves to try and put me back in my box.'

Piper and his entourage had soon rounded the city and now

the stone island lay in sight. They passed over to the left, in relation to the city, from where the envoy and his people were now making their way along the path. In total there were a hundred prador there, and they looked minuscule compared to the vast spread of surrounding Cyberat. He and his entourage came in over the slab and began spiralling down. Meanwhile, Inster's shuttle became visible in the sky, but whether it was heading where Piper had instructed, he didn't know. He landed, Enforcers positioned in an arc at his back, Old Guard on either side of him, facing towards the approaching envoy.

'Very well,' Inster finally replied. 'How do you plan to do this?'

'I'll play it by ear and you, Polity agent, will have to trust that I can get it right.' He shut off the links to Inster, Albermech, Corisian and the others and, knowing how they did it, ensured they wouldn't be able to open those links from their side. This was going to be his. He then opened the chain-glass bubble of his war body, accompanied by a babble of protest from the four Old Guard, and climbed out.

'Be silent,' he told them. He quashed the urge to shut down their ability to speak, adding, 'I know what I'm doing,' then climbed down to stand on the slick stone. Their protests died because his control of them extended beyond animuses and into the loyalty he'd instilled, and the fanaticism that had grown out of that.

The prador arrived, forming a similar arc to his retinue, with the envoy front and centre. Piper eyed the weapons they still carried and wondered at his impulse to put himself in such a vulnerable position here. He studied the big white-armoured Orlik and noted he seemed to be carrying no weapons, and then began to walk out. Orlik responded and walked forwards too, the other prador edging out behind him until he clattered at them to send them back. They came face to face at last. Piper studied the creature further, noting yellow eyes behind its visor and finding no memory of the same in all those fragments of lives he'd lived. There was definitely something off about this creature. He opened up bandwidth through the millions of nodes around him and scattered about the face of the planet, ensuring every Cyberat could see this scene and hear every word.

'It is a pleasure finally to meet you, Piper Lagan,' said Orlik politely.

'I very much doubt that. Unless you are the wrong species, your pleasure would be to see me glued to a rock while you pulled out my guts.'

Orlik shrugged in a very human manner. 'There are many pleasures in life and they are not necessarily mutually exclusive.' He waved a claw at their surroundings. 'So how do you want this to proceed?'

'I want to proceed to your comment about Castron, the previous dictator of Founder's World. But first there are some formalities we must get out of the way.'

He felt the mention of Castron hit home across the Cyberat, even the four who already knew. All around him the Enforcers shifted, their weapons tracking as they searched for targets beyond those directly ahead of them. Chatter between Cyberat ramped up to a mental cacophony which he had to mute. Beyond the slab, he could see them moving, pushing closer and then swirling away again. The ground started vibrating. It also hit home within himself, and yet again he found himself struggling with his reptile. The creature may not have understood much of what he did and said, being a thing of instinct and emotion, but it knew that name well.

'Like what?' Orlik asked.

Piper had absorbed enough of a prador mind to know the

requirements. Orlik had said that surrender was a difficult concept for them to grasp, but that wasn't the case. The previous king couldn't have united them had it really been so. He imagined there'd been many refusals and exterminations during the process, but the adult heads of prador families must have surrendered to his rule. The concept that was actually difficult for them was surrender to the alien.

'You will disarm yourselves. Here. Now. In front of me.' He didn't know whether it was him or the thing inside that relished these words.

Orlik clattered and bubbled at the prador behind. A long pause ensued, into which he added in prador speech that Piper might decide to do the job anyway by ejecting them from their suits. The black-and-whites went first, latches and fixings clicking open, and heavy Gatling cannons being deposited on the ground. Then the local prador did the same. Two of the chromed engineer kind began to move through them, collecting up these weapons and depositing them in a pile to one side of Orlik and Piper. Chatter amidst the Cyberat waned as they all watched this – the intensity of their regard was like a lead weight in the back of Piper's skull.

Next, simultaneously with the black-and-whites, claw tips opened. Piper resisted the urge to lash out at them and watched as they extruded the long, intricate glassy guts of particle cannons, and these too were collected up. He noted that all retained their ammunition and particulate feeds, and would doubtless acquire new weapons when back in the city. That didn't matter, since this was wholly symbolic. After ten minutes a large pile had accrued.

'Now you will show respect,' he told Orlik.

Another appreciable pause ensued, before the envoy told the rest what to do and lowered his claws, crashing the tips against the stone. The anger at this humiliation was evident to Piper and

479

it soon seemed his army sensed it too. Chatter rose again and Piper winced a smile at the raw joy arising from them. They had won and this was the absolute proof. Piper couldn't feel completely happy about their joy, though, because this was the way he'd programmed them – it wasn't entirely their own but that of Polity soldiers who might or might not still be alive now.

'I can arrange for all prador across the planet to do the same, if you so wish.' Exasperation and annoyance seemed evident in the envoy's tone.

'That will not be necessary,' Piper replied.

'Are you sure about that?' And now sarcasm.

'But what you can arrange is their departure from this world.' Piper pointed to the nearby installation city. 'Prador armour is vacuum capable, has grav and thrusters. You'll begin here and have them heading up to the runcible in orbit.'

'They cannot go through all at once,' said Orlik. Now Piper read tension and wariness. He wondered again about translation and why he was sensing so much. Did the creature's translator convey emotion in its voice, or was it deliberately adding these nuances?

'Which is why we will start with just here. Other installation cities will follow when feasible, but you'll depart this world just as fast as possible.'

Orlik turned to clatter and bubble at the three adults. They clattered back and shifted about. Piper observed stalked eyes swinging towards the weapons but then, a moment later, they all stabbed their claws down at the rock for a few seconds, before moving off towards the pathway back into the city. Their children stabbed their claws down too and followed them. It wasn't clear to Piper whether these shows of obeisance were for him or the envoy, but it didn't matter now. He smiled and felt some cruelty in it.

'Inster, a Polity agent, will be along in a while and you can finalize all the details of the removal of prador from this world with him.'

In the battle sphere, he watched Inster's shuttle descending next to his captured destroyer, with Cyberat clearing a space for it. A ramp came down fast and Inster strode down it with the four Sparkind at his back. Other human figures were coming through the Cyberat towards the ramp and Piper recognized the Yannets Groll and Cinia. He should have told them what he was doing, but in retrospect was glad he hadn't. Their presence would have complicated matters. Let Inster deal with all that.

'So now we get to what you really want here,' said Orlik.

'Indeed,' said Piper. The reptile pushed for prominence again, now seeming to harden out of a shadow through his being. His overlay felt like hardfields defending his consciousness from the thing, but he nevertheless knew his eyes had turned as yellow as Orlik's. He managed to keep it in check, but couldn't completely suppress it, for it seemed appropriate that it should be present now. In his internal space, he searched out the node for Orlik's suit and found it struggling to form up. The suit was all but impenetrable to most forms of scan, and had defences similar to those of Golem and other Polity AIs.

'Tell me about the scout ship your previous king sent to my home world.'

Orlik tilted slightly as if surprised. He'd expected a direct question about Castron rather than this slow lead-in. But Piper knew the facts about the old dictator would not take long to impart and wanted to learn something else now. The node finally consolidated and he opened it up, quickly finding its points of access. He then peeled up an animus, which the reptile eagerly offered, and transmitted it. Orlik's defences went to high alert and the envoy staggered back a little, but then straightened up. The animus engaged, defeating the repeated attempts to block its progress, and at last seized control of the suit system. No attack programs were available to run so, should he want the envoy to dance to his tune, he would have to do that by direct, focused control. But he could now eject Orlik from his suit. That wasn't what he was after, though.

'What are you doing?' the prador asked over their comlink.

'Satisfying my curiosity.'

'Very well. I cannot stop you. But for this war to end, the king my father must remain in control, so it would be best if you don't share what you find.' Orlik's security went off entirely, allowing complete access.

Out loud, Orlik launched into his explanation, as requested. 'With the war not going so well, the previous king sent out ships to look for other ways into the Polity and other resources to use. Your world was to form a base from which to drive a fast attack straight through to Earth. We would have seized your industrial capacity to build prador kamikazes for that purpose.'

Piper had only encountered prador kamikazes in the memories of others. They were small ships loaded with CTDs, controlled by flash-frozen ganglions. Such an attack might have worked.

'And the people of my world?'

As he asked the question, he began to see what the suit contained, using Orlik's suit internal sensors and turning the exterior scanning equipment inwards. From this he started building a virtual image of the creature. The internal program he was using had to correct continuously, for its expectation of what a prador *should* look like misaligned with the image gradually appearing.

'Most would have been exterminated. In alliance with Castron, we tested thrall technology on some subjects. However, despite using Cyberat methods and interface tech, it wouldn't work. The next objective was to infect subjects with the Spatterjay virus to make them durable enough to withstand the technology. It was at this stage that communications ceased.'

Piper nodded, still keeping an eye on the developing image. 'That would have been when Castron killed your scouts.'

'I see . . . interesting he killed them at this stage and not earlier.'

'What do you mean?'

'He waited until he had access to the virus . . .'

All other activity paused in Piper's mind as he worked his way through that. Castron had been using the prador as a source of technology, and acted once he had access to the Spatterjay virus. He thought about those test subjects in the old dictator's laboratories. Castron had obtained the prador thrall tech, then, with the virus that enabled it to work on humans, got the final piece he wanted. To what end? The answer was evident: complete and utter domination of the Cyberat.

'But his subjects rebelled,' said Piper, 'and he fled to the Prador Kingdom.'

As he restarted the process within, the image of Orlik rapidly built to completion and Piper gazed at the thing, saying no more. Orlik was heavily mutated and hardly looked like a prador at all. The hard divisions between sections of carapace had blurred and it had all taken on a fleshy look. His main body had become narrow, the legs and claws extended, while the head turret had shifted forwards. Internally, the organs had moved around, some expanding and some diminishing. The major ganglion ring had broken and was forming bulbous additions at the ends. Nerves had thickened, the lung-gill organ had separated and oddly resembled human lungs, while arteries had widened. And it all seemed bound up with fibrous growth, like some parasitic fungus. He studied the data on this and it soon drew comparisons with things he'd encountered over many lives: this prador was infected with the Spatterjay virus.

Piper flashed out more animuses, straight into the black-and-whites behind, punching through their defences now he knew the way. In the fast data render, he soon saw that similar beings occupied those suits too. They responded by opening claw tips and he wondered if, had they still possessed their particle cannons, he would be ash by now. Orlik spun and clattered at them angrily and they backed up, closing up those tips.

All the implications of this hit Piper at once. That these members of the king's family were infected indicated that the king was too. And normal prador would not accept this. They were vicious enough regarding aberrations. The selective extermination of their young in later life came on top of filial selection in earlier years. A mutated prador never lasted long amidst third-children. But it went beyond that. The mind he'd absorbed, now distributed through his own, responded with abhorrence. This was why Orlik didn't want this known. If normal prador found out, the new king would never be able to retain power.

'I will keep your secret,' he said over com.

'It is for the benefit of humanity, besides my own,' Orlik replied back through com, then out loud said, 'Your people rebelled against Castron – you tell me. I don't have much information about that, but suspect you were integral. However, Castron did not flee to the Prador Kingdom.'

'Explain.'

'The scout ship was detected the moment it entered prador space. It was boarded and its ganglion interrogated. The ship had been returned on the same course it took to your world. Castron was not aboard.'

★ ★ ★

As Piper returned to his prador destroyer, he damned his complacency regarding the reptile. Its power over him had begun to wane when its first main focus of hatred had gone out of reach: Castron. This process had then continued under the confusion of emotional input: the successful rebellion, the prador/human war, all that had happened to Piper since leaving Founder's World. His understanding of the reptile and his increased control via virtual aug and nanosuite had also brought it into check. But now it seemed to have become as substantial in him as his skeleton. It wanted to drive him after Castron and he necessarily fought it because his responsibilities couldn't allow him simply to run with the urge of this driving daemon. He also couldn't shut it down while he needed its function to carry out those responsibilities.

'Annel.' He made contact with the Medic currently setting up regrowth tanks in the installation city where Piper had left him. At the same time he raised alterations to his army's logistics. The effect of this began to kick in, with Engineers and Medics preparing to head into the sky from the four armies stationed around the destroyer, even as he landed on the hull. 'Your resources are now no longer constrained by preparedness for warfare. Expand your operation.' He sent detail on this directly to the Medic.

'What?' Annel paused while absorbing the data. 'I'm filling this city with regrowth tanks. You have indicated other cities too . . .'

'You're in charge and can choose subordinates for the other cities. All Medics currently not busy are heading to you. Engineers and Builders are going to your location too, as well as Cyberat with heavy com facility.'

'This is a great responsibility.'

Piper looked through Annel's eyes and sensors at his surroundings. He was in one of the warehouses where reaverfish had been hung. The fish were all gone but the rails and hooks still ran across the ceilings. They had been utilized to take skeins of pipes and wires that fed down into regrowth tanks already in position. A row of them disappeared into the distance and, touching on the Medic's mind, Piper saw that nearly one thousand eight hundred had been made and were ready. However, as yet only six hundred of them were occupied.

'I wouldn't have given it to you if I didn't think you capable,' said Piper and then, with his overlay tight over his emotions, 'How are the twins doing?'

Annel launched up into the air, a wall on one side and ceiling lights fleeing past above him. He came down to land between two rows of tanks and perambulated along a short distance, turning to gaze at two particular tanks, and aware of Piper's scrutiny through his senses. Inside were Triode and Anode. Originally honed down to plug form, they now had two protruding foetal legs, and were floating in amber fluid, with wires and tubes nested around them and plugged in.

'It will take another month. It's accelerated, obviously, but we can't do it faster until we install bigger cooling systems.'

'So you told me before. Now you can install those systems.'

'I will start at once.'

'Good.'

Piper pulled out into overview – a battle sphere perspective – and saw the massive shifts across all his army as Engineers, Builders and Medics headed to where he'd assigned them. He raised his war body from the hull and floated forwards, into the sensory turret of the vessel, then locked it down and climbed out, meanwhile noting other activity in the sphere. Walking outside, he looked towards the installation city to there see prador swirling up into the sky. He next focused on the four Old Guard and Enforcers still bobbing in the sky close to the destroyer. With a thought, he ordered them to land on the hull. He'd use them as the object of his address, translating that out to all the Cyberat.

Glancing down towards the shuttle, he switched sensor attention to the envoy and saw that Inster had arrived. The agent was there on a stool, sitting before Orlik, while the Sparkind were behind him, scattered through Yannets who had clustered round. Piper smiled to himself, seeing that the four soldiers weren't there because the prador might do something untoward, but to keep an eye on the heavyworlders. But that was all Polity business; he had his own concerns. He turned and faced the four war bodies and Enforcers.

'The war is over,' he announced, feeling a diminution of pressure from the reptile as, in some sense, it understood his overall intentions. 'It's now time to look to our future. But it's also my wish that you all look to your personal futures in full and proper understanding of events that have brought you here. Most of you are Enforcers, who were enslaved by the old regime and faced extermination under the new regime for crimes that were not your own. And many here are members of the old regime, even Old Guard, who equally wouldn't have done well under the new. Such a mix should not have worked as a disciplined military force. I made it work.'

He paused, mentally inspecting the reaction to his words. He could see the expansion and divergence from the dictates of the animuses he'd installed in them were having an effect. Many Enforcers expressed puzzlement at fighting either alongside or under Cyberat who had been their oppressors. Many others, like most of the old regime refugees, already understood that they'd been programmed to do this.

'My ability to seize control of Cyberat helped bring about victory for the rebellion on Founder's World. Then when the

Polity rescued you all and recruited you into this war, I used that ability to control you. I want all of you now to fully understand I put programming in your minds so you would comprehend the prador threat – so you could feel it concerned you. And I applied a command structure, with me at the head, that you couldn't diverge from. My actions were no more morally acceptable than the way in which the old regime programmed Enforcers.'

Millions of replies came in, also from most of those in front of him. He concentrated on those through his program – fracturing them out over all the Cyberat and ensuring everyone heard the exchanges.

'I think you're too hard on yourself, comparing what you've done to what my regime did to the Enforcers,' said Tinsher.

'Perhaps I am. I have justification in that the prador were waging a war of extermination, and all humans, in the Polity and on Founder's World, would have been its victims. But having been, in essence, programmed myself too, I find it immoral.' As his reply went out, Mallon jumped in with the data he had given her concerning his four-year virtuality, and this spread through the host.

'If you had not exerted such control, there would have been no Cyberat army and, freed of restraints, the Enforcers might have exterminated all of us old regime Cyberat,' said Transter.

'That is also true,' Piper replied to him and to the tens of thousands who made the same point. Most were old regime, but it surprised him to see just how many Enforcers also made it.

'I wonder at the extent of my reprogramming,' said Drillain. 'I have more information than before concerning the Polity and the prador. But I feel no different, and am sure the decisions I've made were no different from how they would have been without programming.'

That was another point made by almost three-quarters of the Cyberat host.

'The programming is deep, but more nuanced than was used on the Enforcers on Founder's World. For some it made few changes, other than providing the information you mention. For others, it has necessarily been more radical.' His gaze strayed to Mallon, who was one of those, and who it seemed inevitable would speak next.

'It seems to me,' she said, 'that you are preparing to relinquish this control. It also seems to me that once you do it, there will be a bloodbath here, with Enforcers turning on Old Guard like me.'

Massive objections to this arose from the horde. They didn't agree, for they had fought together. But with a leaden feeling in his stomach, Piper understood that those objecting now might well be thinking differently when he shut down all their animuses, as he indeed intended to do.

'Be that as it may,' Mallon continued, surprising him. 'In very many cases, including my own, such a response from the Enforcers would be justified. I am prepared to accept what is due. However, personally I would prefer that you didn't relinquish control of me. If I am to die, I would like to die as I am, and not as the person I was.'

Piper gaped at her and his legs felt abruptly weak, as thousands upon thousands agreed with her. Feedback from the Enforcers was unexpected too, for they didn't want to become killers of their own kind. They couldn't see themselves as that, after all they'd been through. His reptile responded to the opportunity: pushing up old hatreds of those who had been in the Founder's World regime, pressing for action, and somehow aware that his next move might lead to the eradication of the four in front of him. He recognized this drive as not his own, gritted his teeth and pushed back with the overlay. He had to stick to his own logic and the course he'd mapped out. But in choosing this course he also had to be aware that the reptile would try to push him along it destructively.

'I would add,' Mallon continued, 'that from the beginning I was aware of what you'd done to me. But now, having been part of the effort here, I've felt purpose in a morally justified cause I never felt in my old life. I would rather die with that in my mind than the resentments, anger and hatred I feel sure are ready to rise.'

It seemed like a version of Stockholm syndrome, or the programming of victims of a cult. He hated just how powerfully he'd altered their minds. But as an overwhelming consensus of replies and comments from all strayed into how they enjoyed who they now were, he questioned his idea of removing their animuses. Was he being hasty? His consciousness, influenced by the reptile, demanded action, while this required careful thought.

'You will have choices soon,' he said, abruptly changing course. 'Your actions will no longer be predicated on what is best for an army and for the defeat of the prador. Many of you are aware that Medics and Engineers are now building regrowth tanks in the installation cities here. Many may not be aware that the nanosuites installed in you at Room 101 can bring about regeneration of fully human bodies. So you can choose that, or to retain your present form. And you can choose to go into the Polity, or return to Founder's World, though some organization for that will be required—' Piper just stopped, realizing he was waffling and didn't really know what the Polity would do here. Finally, reluctantly, he opened up the comlinks to Corisian and Albermech, and then after a pause to Inster.

'Well that was rude,' said Inster, while the other two comlinks blended together and nothing came through. 'And don't you fucking dare drop control of those Cyberat.'

'You've been listening?'

'Of course I have, and Mallon has it right: you let those Enforcers off the leash and the old regime refugees won't last a day.'

'Are you so sure about that?'

'Don't be naive. It's a numbers game. Most won't be interested, but it'll only take a small percentage of the millions here to turn things nasty.' He paused, then continued, 'Anyway, you are not naive, you're just looking to cut your ties here – to disconnect yourself from your responsibilities.'

'Never could get much past you . . . Tell me, what about the Cyberat here? What do you see as the future for them?'

'Their deal was Polity citizenship if they want it, and that stands. They can go where they want from here, in whatever form they choose. It will, however, have to be after all the prador are gone. Albermech?'

The combined entity that was the AI and the ship's captain spoke up: 'Logistics are a problem and it will take time. However, your Engineers are capable of building hold tanks like those I originally transported here, and any who want to go back to Founder's World I will transport there. Once the prador are gone, the runcible here will be directed into the Polity to a military decommissioning world, where those others who want will be prepared for citizenship.'

'But still, they must have free will to make their choices.'

'Don't be obtuse,' said Inster. 'You know what you have to do.'

The conversation had taken seconds – speeding up after Inster's initial comment. In the meantime, debate among the Cyberat had risen to a peak he'd never seen before. He ran through

491

samples, hearing the fears of many about how they might change, the protestations of those who felt sure they wouldn't, concerns about the future, fears about a lack of structure in their lives. Yes, he knew what he had to do.

Piper focused on his links to millions of animuses. Through these things, he had changed the Cyberat's thinking and inserted them into their positions in his command structure. But the animuses also maintained their thinking, so they couldn't disobey in that structure. Viewing the components, he considered what he might remove and what replace, but in the end saw that there was a simpler way. If he removed the animuses instantly, chaos would ensue, while the command structure served a purpose even now. Hauling up programming, he began designing something new. The reptile resisted for a second but that died away as, in an emotional context, it saw his action as shrugging off a commitment that stood in the way of its ultimate goal.

'You've spoken and I have heard,' he said. 'There will be no conflict and the choices you have will remain.'

When he finally had the program ready, he sent it at once to every single animus. It hit home in those ahead of him, for each of them shifted, in fact shivered as it struck. Around the destroyer, he saw the ripple effect of it spreading, and felt it impacting beyond every horizon. Millions of questions came back to him and a general air of puzzlement.

'What have you done?' Mallon asked. 'I feel no different.'

'You will retain your animuses but, over a period of a month, the links I have to them will die and their programming will be yours to control. There will be no reversals to your thinking, but it will become yours to edit or alter thereafter. You'll be able to choose who you are going to be: you have free will.'

'Things could become chaotic here,' Mallon warned.

'Would you prefer not to pay the price for free will and remain slaves?'

She looked suddenly pained, and dipped her head. Piper continued, 'The command structure remains in place, but anyone can remove themselves from it. Instructions can be given, and they can be either ignored or obeyed. I have given you choices, and I recuse myself from command over you. Now it is up to you to make those choices.'

Another million questions arrived, and Mallon reflected them.

'What will you do?' she asked.

'I am going to take this destroyer to Founder's World. And I will need some volunteers.'

Predictably there were millions of them.

Piper walked down through the destroyer as it rumbled with activity. Engineers scuttled past him in the wide prador tunnel, smiling and saluting with whatever limbs they had available for that purpose.

'General!' they said. Over the last week he'd grown tired of correcting that.

Further along the corridor, one of the big Enforcers of his retinue halted and pushed his newly acquired prador claws down against the floor, in prador obeisance. He grimaced at the woman there under chain-glass, with ribbed pipes running into her eyes, and gestured her away as if in irritation. But he wasn't really irritated. The four thousand aboard, out of millions of volunteers, were happy to be here. Keeping a light-touch connection on them via their dying animus links, Piper knew that none of this was about obeisance or obedience, but respect. They did what he asked because they were happy to do so.

Ahead, sunlight shone in through a major ramp door where Cyberat were bringing in supplies. And Mallon, standing at the entrance, directed them where to take everything. She was coming with him, as was Tinsher. Transter and Drillain were staying here. If he reached out, he knew he'd find them amidst the rapidly expanding mass of regrowth tanks, in the first installation city that had been turned to that purpose. Drillain was helping build the place, while staying close to his daughters. Transter was already in one of the new tanks – his war body handed over to Engineers to dismantle for parts. There were no others aboard the ship Piper knew personally, though many of his retinue of Enforcers were here. But others were coming.

'Loading will be complete in one hour,' Mallon informed him. She hadn't scrapped her war body but had it stored on the vessel, while she wore only her blocky limbed transport body. 'Getting all aboard and closed up will take another half-hour.'

Piper moved past the line of Engineers and out onto the ramp. He gazed across the chaotic landscape of churned mud, slabs and mudskippers flopping about in bewilderment, searching for their once neatly divided pools. Over to his right, the few thousand yet to board were waiting, but elsewhere the armies that had been here had departed. He moved over to the side of the ramp and sat down, with his legs dangling over the edge. Reaching out with his mind through dying links, it satisfied him that he couldn't reach all the Cyberat any more. Things had changed out there, taking new courses.

Piper observed the grav-raft gliding in over the devastation from the installation city, to settle next to the nearby Polity shuttle. Two climbed off and entered the shuttle, and then the raft slid over, coming to the foot of the ramp and landing. Inster, Meersham and Geelie climbed from the thing and walked up the ramp towards him. He stood up.

'How is the envoy?' Piper asked.

'Efficient, irascible and decidedly odd,' Inster replied. 'He's pushing hard to get all the prador off world and through the runcible, while ensuring his dominance among the prador here. In the latter case, he's had about two hundred adults executed and first-children that were under them raised to that position.'

'Raised?'

'Once the hormonal suppression comes off, old first-children rapidly transition. Interestingly they go through a period of what can only be described as cowardice, which of course makes the envoy's job easier.'

'And the Yannets?' Piper asked.

'Seizing installation cities and prador tech, but they're stunned and only gradually perceiving that the world is theirs again, hence the continued assassinations of prador.'

Inster stepped from foot to foot, looked around, while rubbing his hands together.

'Is there something you require here?' Piper asked.

The agent turned back to him, bringing his hands down. 'We're coming with you.'

'What makes you think I want you to come? And anyway, don't you still have a lot to do here? It's going to take weeks, if not months, for the prador to leave this world.' He gestured into the distance, where it seemed smoke was rising into the sky, but in fact it was millions of prador heading for the runcible gate.

'No, my business is done here,' said Inster. 'Albermech and Corisian can oversee all this now.' He pointed back to the shuttle. 'And you have room for that in this thing.'

'You still haven't answered my initial question.'

'I ask that you allow us to come with you. Founder's World is as much unfinished business for me as it is for you.'

Piper raised an eyebrow. He'd expected some kind of pressure but not that. He looked to Meersham and Geelie. 'And you two?'

Meersham stabbed a big thumb at Inster. 'Someone has to be

there to drag his ass out of the fire.' Geelie just shrugged and smiled.

'Very well. I've no fear of you interfering with anything I decide to do.' He waved a hand towards the nose of the ship and, with a whumph, two big hold doors began to open there, exposing a space large enough to take their shuttle. Sloan and Cheen, aboard the thing, raised it from the ground on grav, and then on thrusters steered it towards the doors.

'Never actually been inside one of these things,' said Inster, walking into the ship assertively. Piper watched him go, Meersham hurrying to catch up with him. Geelie paused by Piper, looking to where the shuttle was now entering the prador destroyer.

'Lucky you had one hold you didn't pack with Cyberat and equipment,' she observed.

'Indeed,' he replied, concealing the happiness he felt.

As the ship rose through the clouds, Piper found his internal space emptying of nodes, with any remaining links to Cyberat on the surface stretched to breaking point. Annoyingly, however, new ones were appearing and, checking on them, he saw they were from Cyberat within range whose links had died, being offered up for sequestration again. With a thought, he instituted a program to delete them as they reappeared. He'd sacrificed that degree of control and didn't want it back. The command structure still remained in place aboard this ship and the level of communication was high. All he was losing was the ability to delve deeply into their minds and seize control of the same. For a second the reptile fought this, for it could feel its power, or perhaps its purpose, diminishing. He pushed it down, again pressing against something that had grown in substance, wiry and strong.

'I'll no doubt see you in the future,' he said, as a new transmission arrived through one comlink.

'One would hope so,' Albermech replied.

Piper inspected what the AI had sent. The package contained U-space coordinates for Founder's World, along with a translation to convert those to prador coordinates. He ran the translation and sent it through the animus link he maintained to the ship's flash-frozen ganglion – its mind.

'And the other package?'

'Waiting for you.' More information arrived, detailing the course of a cargo container the *Albermech* had dispatched into orbit. He at once relayed course changes to the ganglion, then instructions to Mallon.

'We're ready,' the Old Guard replied.

He peered through cams, seeing her in one of the holds, with Engineers and Enforcers gathered around her, supplies stacked and strapped behind, but still room enough for the new delivery. Even as he glimpsed this, he became aware of Mallon setting the system to evacuate the hold in preparation for opening its door.

'You'll need no more than the injectors,' said Albermech. 'Your Engineers have already demonstrated they have the knowledge and ability to build regrowth tanks.'

'How many doses in that container?'

'A million, but also nanofactors for making more.'

It had been a last-minute decision. The Cyberat here had had their nanosuites installed on Room 101, but there was no equivalent technology on Founder's World. It would be his gift for them, once his business there was done. And it'd be a gift that would ensure less likelihood of them lapsing into their old ways.

'Thank you,' he said.

'My pleasure,' said Albermech.

'Try not to get yourself killed,' Corisian added.

'I'll bear that in mind.'

'Look after him, Inster,' said the thing, which in that instant had become both the mind of a ship and a man.

Peering into one of the storage lockers he'd opened in the wall of the prador captain's sanctum, Inster replied out loud, 'I think he's a little beyond my care now.' He stood upright and looked around. 'I don't need to tell him that if Castron really didn't leave Founder's World, he likely made preparations.'

'You just did,' said Piper.

'I guess.' Inster closed up the hatch, turned and headed over.

They moved on through the ship as Inster inspected things Piper had already seen through the eyes of others. Cyberat were everywhere, scuttling or otherwise motoring through tunnels that matched their size. Some were ensconced in the quarters of first-children, or in larger volumes the second-children had occupied communally. Still others sat in rows down the sides of larger tunnels used previously for the transit of adult prador. All these were somnolent, or occupying themselves in the thousands of ways people with computing attached to their minds could. Perhaps they were also toying with their animuses, now in their power, deciding who they wanted to be. Most of those on the move were Engineers – fixing and converting things for Cyberat, installing food processors and body maintenance machines.

'Weapons?' Inster asked.

'All functional and controlled by my soldiers,' Piper replied.

'So essentially at your command?'

Piper acknowledged the observation with a nod. He didn't want to get into the detail of that. With the command structure now being a matter of choice, his soldiers could technically decide not to fire their weapons. However, he was also certain they wouldn't choose to do otherwise when required. He remained aware that, though his links to their animuses were dying or had died, his ability was the same as before – in an instant he could transmit more to seize control of the Cyberat around him again. He vowed not to, but even then understood the nuance. Could he, or would he stop himself if the decision was a life-and-death one?

Finally, they found themselves in the sensor turret where his war body was locked down. Piper activated the screen paint, opening the view back along the destroyer and all around. They were clear of atmosphere now, Yannetholm dropping away. Piper eyed the floating debris and distantly the moon still glowing like an ember. This system was strewn with wreckage and he knew it wasn't alone in that. It would be a scene mirrored across multiple worlds, and clearing up after interstellar war was a task of perhaps centuries.

'The others?' Piper asked.

'Not much inclined for exploring, since they've seen and fought in ships like this many times. They're back in the shuttle.'

Thrusters fired and a course change ensued. Piper keyed to the screen paint and pulled up another view there, showing down the side of the destroyer. The doors to one hold had already opened and Cyberat were gathered around it like insects coming out of a hole in a rotten log. Shortly, the cargo container fell into view, drifting towards the ship, and the ship drifting towards it. The thing was oblate and five metres long, with rounded corners and simply sealed. Piper found its node, opened it out and took control. Throwaway thrusters ignited on its surface, guiding it in. Two Cyberat out on the hull fired off gecko claw grabs that thwacked solidly in place on the thing, then reeled it in. The grabs were a new addition and it gladdened Piper to see such speed of adaptation to vacuum in the Cyberat, without him having had to drive it.

As the doors closed, clear starlit space opened ahead and

Inster staggered a little as the fusion drive kicked in. Piper, who'd expected it, did not. The ship ramped up acceleration and, still touching the ganglion mind of the ship, he observed the complex formulae interacting and fully occupying it, before next translating as instructions to the U-space nacelles. He recorded every detail, already seeing that, though this operation was conducted by specialized minds, it wasn't beyond him. Space twisted and, as before, all seemed to transition into infinities and singularities. Piper pulled back his range quickly, confining it to the ship. And they were on their way.

'Shall we join them in the shuttle?' Inster enquired.

Piper looked at his war body and then at the view. He could do all he needed to do from any location in the ship and didn't need to be here.

'Why not?' He shrugged.

20

The transition back to realspace was again like surfacing from a pool, though without the clean feeling he'd experienced the first time – as if the pool might be polluted. He compared it to a thousand such experiences, most in virtuality, but found none the same. From the prador captain's sanctum, Piper delivered his instructions and the ganglion lit fusion engines to bring them in around Founder's World. The arrays of hexagonal screens, some running prador code and some running Cyberat, flicked to hundreds of sensor inputs. Working the ship nodes, Piper cleared them and brought up a view of his home world across many screens, then he looked around.

Mallon and Tinsher were in similar transport bodies. The Sparkind were rigged out for fighting and casually carried their weapons. Inster had dumped his combat suit and now wore the clothing in which Piper had first seen him. He was more comfortable being an agent than a soldier. Other Cyberat were in the sanctum, while still more clustered in the corridor without. Piper nodded, then checked signal traffic.

The instruments showed that the ship was starting to be hit by EMR scanning from satellites in orbit, so he had no doubt that those below knew what was up here. There was no com as yet, but surely, having learned about them during the Polity recruitment of a large chunk of their population, they weren't

501

anxious to speak to what looked like prador arriving. Sorting frequencies, Piper found Cyberat com bands and began broadcasting. He walked forwards to stand nearer the screens and spoke so all could hear.

'This is Piper Lagan, the son of Doge and Reema. I would like to speak to whoever is in charge down there.'

After a short delay, thousands of replies came, and thousands of questions. A second later, the replies ramped up into the millions. Piper ran a search program looking for any specific Cyberat signatures he recognized. He found one and opened it to a cluster of screens.

'Geerand,' he said, meanwhile running data packages to all, detailing events on Yannetholm, while instituting his program to multiple replies. But he kept most of his focus on the old com Cyberat.

'So their war is over,' Geerand said, a human face and upper torso, sunk in technology, coming to occupy the screen cluster.

'Yes, *our* war is over,' Piper replied. As he did this, he ordered and sorted the data input from the world below, gradually sketching out the situation down there. The replies also included data packages and he began to get the shape of it all. 'And it seems order has been restored down there, too,' he added tightly.

He saw blasted landscapes and crews out collecting up the shattered remains of Enforcers, Old Guard war bodies and other Cyberat. Huge areas of lichen had become black scars, burned down to the rock. Cyberat in dozer bodies and other larger machines were clearing rubble. He noted odd clouds and, searching further, recognized swarms of flies – another one of those Earth imports that had seemed to serve no purpose, until now . . . A brief image of piled Enforcers struck him – crows feeding on the fleshy remains. Comparing imagery to what little he'd seen before departing Founder's World, he could tell that conflicts had continued. Flies and fleshy remains shouldn't be in evidence after this long.

Focusing next on all the data from Ironville, he observed even more activity. Here debris had been cleaned out and sat piled wherever possible, while rebuilding was in progress. He noticed recyclers pouring out steam and trolleys heaped with the re-processed. Next, focusing on areas he knew, he saw that the Polity Embassy had acquired antimissile rotogun towers and a wall. The original seat of government, a few kilometres away from there, was a wreck gutted by fire. He guessed he'd found the new home for the rulers here. Many of these images he sent to the screens, and to the minds of those all around him, including the Sparkind and Inster.

'I wish that were so,' Geerand replied. 'There has been much loss of life since the rebellion and we are attempting to establish a new and fairer regime. We of the Revolutionary Council are still arguing about the details here. Unfortunately groups in the mountains and at other locations far from Ironville are not much inclined to listen.'

Piper was getting that too. This revolutionary council had tried to impose planetary rule. Factions had risen in disagreement with that. Some factions slanted towards even less of the Founder's principles, and some were more inclined to enforcing the same. They had turned on each other, with many annihilated and the winners dividing off into smaller polities. Meanwhile the revolutionary council didn't have the power and support to put them down, though it had tried. The factions had now dug in and built defences, and he picked up warnings broadcast to keep others away. Though not in accord on many matters, they all agreed that they no longer wanted centralized rule. Precisely why, he didn't know – data from those outer factions were meagre since they weren't talking all that much.

The conflict, death and waste appalled him and he wondered if that was because he was as naive as he had been before, when Inster and the soldiers had expressed their doubts about 'revolution'. However, he analysed this and knew he wasn't naive but being influenced by those four virtual years he'd experienced; by the minds of those who had spent so much of their lives fighting an alien enemy. The idea of humans factionalizing and fighting like this was abhorrent. It was a mess, but at least he could comfort himself with the fact that the fighting had at least paused.

'And my mother?' he asked, studying his own emotions as he said the word.

'She is part of the council. She doesn't have Cyberat enhancements now but I've sent a message for her to get to a com unit.'

'Good . . . I want to bring this ship down. If you can give me a landing site near Ironville?' He felt an acknowledgement of her position but little more, and understood this to be the case because you felt most strongly about those in your proximity. She had never really been close and, of course, he had been away for years . . .

'Here,' said Geerand, sending a location. 'We'll speak further when you arrive.' He then shut off contact.

'Surprisingly terse,' said Inster, moving up beside him, his fingers up against his aug and his expression intense. 'But I'm presuming you have more data out of all this than I do?'

'It's pretty much as expected down there,' Piper replied, not quite able to put his finger on what was bothering him about everything he'd heard. Perhaps he had been concentrating too much on his own responses.

'Why did you say nothing about Castron?'

'Just not the right time, yet.' He turned to Inster and the four

Sparkind. 'I'm going to Ironville, but perhaps it would be a good idea to gather some data elsewhere too.'

The shuttle carrying Inster and the others slid out of its bay and dropped down into atmosphere, moving out on its own reconnaissance mission. As Piper entered the sensory turret of the destroyer, he ranged out, checking preparations. Cyberat were at the weapons and shield generators that needed to be manned, while he controlled the rest. He thought then about Inster's last words before heading for the shuttle.

'Best to maintain a healthy paranoia,' he'd said.

He felt that now, intensely. Gazing down at the world through ship's sensors, he fought an internal battle. The reptile was on one side, but he wasn't even sure if he was on the other. Where would be the harm in doing something he'd promised himself he would never do? Nobody would notice it and, despite him recusing himself from absolute power over the Cyberat aboard, he still bore responsibility for them. It would be a safety measure only, providing him with the option of control – easily dismissed at a later time. Feeling self-disgust, Piper abruptly strengthened animus links and re-established those that had broken, and then swore quietly.

Was this too much? What was he worrying about? He had a prador destroyer and four thousand heavily armed Cyberat aboard. He would land, properly assess the situation on the ground, see his mother and get her take on it. That Castron was somehow involved in all of this seemed certain – perhaps leading one of the factions, or secretly installed somewhere in Ironville. He'd find the man and reach the resolution he, and his reptile, required. It shouldn't otherwise concern him that things seemed so messy here, since that was human, and perhaps later he could help resolve things. Still, he maintained those links.

505

The destroyer dipped and rumbled into atmosphere. It swept down through cloud strata and the familiar shape of the land masses came into view. The roaring increased as he kept a light touch on the ship's ganglion – letting it do its job.

'I've got contact,' said Inster from the shuttle. 'An enclave of your people at the foot of the mountains. They're updating me on stuff from their side and have agreed to let me land. They're completely anti the Founder and pro-Polity. Lots of questions about nanosuites . . .'

Piper had ordered that a portion of the nanosuites be loaded aboard the shuttle, along with some of the nanofactors. These gave Inster something to bargain with and, as a precaution, ensured the suites weren't all in one place. Healthy paranoia.

'Anything on why they broke into factions and started fighting?'

'Ah, Piper, it's almost a historical precedent. Anyway, it seems that after the fights – more rabid elements and power seekers being put down – they were coming together under the revolutionary council. It then overstepped and started issuing diktats that the outer factions simply didn't agree with. One, it seems, was to not kill Enforcers and return them to Ironville.'

'I don't see that as wrong.'

'Think about that some more.'

Piper did, and felt a sinking sensation in his stomach. 'They're not gathering up Enforcers out of altruistic motives; out of any regard for their lives.'

'Seems policing is required and why not use what they already have?' The agent's sarcasm was heavy. 'Things change and yet remain the same.'

'Okay, keep me informed.'

Piper stepped up onto his war body and grimaced. He'd wanted simply to walk out of this ship, but now it didn't seem like such a good idea. Climbing inside, he felt the reptile eagerly pushing him again. He maintained *his* overlay like a hardfield over his consciousness, dampening its push to be hasty, but sometimes he questioned his aim here – would he have the same aims without the thing inside him? But then this was precisely the same issue that had occupied his thoughts for a long time: how much was free will? It was an endless debate. Trying at least to grasp something pragmatic, he examined the creature, this time using internal, precise measure rather than his visualization of the thing. He was right: the reptile had become more substantial ever since the mention of Castron back on Yannetholm. It occupied more processing, perhaps because his processing had expanded, and had now passed further Turing thresholds.

'You have grown strong,' he said, directing the words straight into the thing. The reptile surprised him with a reply, though without words. He felt it shift and express emotion: the anxious need to reach out and control the world beyond itself, frustration with limitations, guilt and anger of course, and huge restraint. Examining these, he felt a surge of his own anxiety, for he realized it was holding itself back. Yes, he could push the thing down and armour himself against it, but it had grown strong enough to resist him. Only its antecedents prevented it, for the guilt in part was his father's guilt about what he'd done to Piper, while it had some portion of other emotions a father would have for a son.

Piper huffed out a tense breath as he plugged in his suit. He didn't know how long those paternal emotions would continue to hold the thing back. It might at some point try to seize full control of him and he considered again how he intended to be rid of it. Even as that thought occurred, the reptile shifted again, peeling parts of itself out of his system and becoming a more distinct entity. Was this a demonstration of its strength and a warning, or was it a display of willingness? He couldn't know –

507

the emotions were too mixed up. He put his hands down on the chair arms, initiating the hard connection. It made no difference at all, though, so he physically disconnected and just ran the war body bare-brained.

Pulling his attention away from the reptile, because there was little he could do beyond resist it when it surged and otherwise hope it would remain obedient, he engaged his mind through sensors, to model the situation on the planet. There would be Enforcers down there, commanded by the revolutionary council. They seemed to be slipping back into old ways, so would almost certainly be averse to outside interference. Inevitably, and with distaste, his modelling shifted into the possibility of attack. A second later, he saw what he was doing and expanded the modelling into a battle sphere. Incorporating force strengths, tactics and logistics, and the extrapolations from those, he spread out fractal around him. Immediately included in this, the Cyberat aboard responded by sliding from prosaic concerns about a vague and chaotic future, into battle readiness. He saw how much they liked the familiarity, especially the Enforcers, for it gave them a simple structure. He had the passing thought about how many would choose to turn away from the responsibility of free will.

'I think you're right to be concerned,' said Mallon. 'They will have foreseen the degree of disruption you could cause, even without the nanosuites. Weak power structures abhor interlopers.'

Her comments surprised him, but illustrated how intimately entangled he and the minds of all around him were.

'Shields and active scanning instituted. Antipersonnel lasers and particle beams ready,' said Tinsher. 'I see that the landing site is far enough from the city for them to deploy tactical nukes.'

'Seems you are both as cynical as me,' Piper replied.

'I call it realistic,' Tinsher replied.

Piper looked towards the landing ground. It was an area where factories and greenhouses had been obliterated, and then dozered clear. He could see grids sketched out on the open ground with lines of red powder. It was obviously being prepared for new foundations to go in. From there, a path had been carved through debris to a nearby road which ran back into the city. He could now see Cyberat flowing in from city streets and moving along that road, while above them only Enforcers and a scattering of large war bodies flew. He didn't like that – it seemed too much like the no-fly order of the old regime at the start of the rebellion. He concentrated on the Cyberat there.

Geerand was one of those in the sky. The other war bodies Piper didn't recognize, and he found himself groping for data as the reptile pushed him. Identification arose from assorted minds, though in many cases signatures were different. A lot of these war bodies were recognizable to his Old Guard, but a good number weren't occupied by the plug forms that had owned them. The reptile seemed to concede this and waned again, though it remained intensely watchful. Piper meanwhile hated himself. Without consciously intending to do so, he'd garnered the information through animus links.

Those down on the road were mostly Engineers and other less militarized castes, crammed in around a scattering of ground vehicles. Out front ran an open car, driven at its head by a plug form, while in the seats sat a human figure, with two human-form Cyberat behind. He recognized his mother and scanning closer saw she remained whole. This last was a good sign, but a bad sign was that she'd yet to communicate with him. Again the reptile responded, and this time he felt a wash of regret.

The ship began to feather down grav, thrusters adjusting altitude as it lined up with the landing ground. Inside, his Cyberat gathered in readiness at the hold doors, while others remained at the weapons and shields. With a thought, Piper opened the sensory turret doors behind him and detached his war body's feet. As he slid it out and attached to the hull, he ordered his Cyberat to the next stage of readiness. It would be a tactical mistake to keep all the doors closed and all the Cyberat inside until they landed. Hold and personnel doors – made for prador – opened all around the ship. He saw Mallon and Tinsher, now occupying their war bodies, floating out first and matching their descent. Big Enforcers poured out too, spreading across the hull. Engineers and others, also armed, edged out directly around the doors.

The ship came down, shuddering and partially sinking into the ground. As its grav-engines and internal grav shut down, he felt abruptly light, and realized the ship had been set for Yannetholm, and they'd lived in the same gravity as that world while aboard. Now ramp doors and egress ways lowered. His Cyberat flooded out of them to spread out around the ship, while many of those that didn't launch into the sky moved higher up the hull. A perfect deployment to face threats from any direction. They were oriented towards those approaching from the city, but he also had them out behind the ship. Those on the hull could launch at any moment and would begin rotation with those in the sky, should they have to hold this position for long. Piper launched his war body and descended, bringing it down to the head of the primary formation, heavy Enforcers moving in on either side, while Mallon and Tinsher held station in the sky slightly ahead of him.

'Geerand,' he sent. 'I want to talk to my mother.'

After an odd fizzing delay, Geerand replied, 'She informs me that she will speak to you face to face. She wants to know what came back from that Polity war.'

Piper didn't like this, nor did the reptile. He and his mother should have been talking ever since his arrival. He would have expected her to be anxious for it, and questioning him interminably. It was quite possible she was a prisoner and they wanted to keep her quiet until they had something in position. He ordered a further rise in alertness and scanning. Data coming in seemed no more threatening than before, though. The approaching Enforcers and war bodies were armed, certainly, but his force completely outmatched them. He could detect no suspicious activations in the city, nor within a hundred-kilometre circle, that might indicate a missile battery. Perhaps his paranoia had strayed into being unhealthy? He watched the approaching Cyberat turn into the rough road and progress along it. Entering the cleared area, they spread out over on their side of it, like an army deploying. The car his mother was riding in drove ahead a little way then stopped. She climbed out – somewhat clumsily he felt – then walked a little way out from the car. The two human-form Cyberat climbed out too and held their position just behind her.

'Reema wants a face-to-face with you,' Geerand repeated.

'Why would I put myself in such danger?' Piper asked.

'It is what it is,' Geerand replied. 'At some point you must trust us and we must trust you. Once she has spoken to you, your mother, as leader of the revolutionary council, will give her assessment.'

'I see,' said Piper. He sat thinking. In essence, their leader was offering herself as a hostage and wanted him to do the same – all apparently part of the process of learning to trust. If his mother was truly a prisoner, then she was a hostage of another kind, and their aim was to take him out. And yet, if they did, his Cyberat would fall on them like a hammer, so that didn't seem to make sense. He gazed at her out there, now walking towards him, poised between the fronts of mechanized warfare, of tough metals and hard composites, human and vulnerable, and knew his decision was made. He grounded his war body, while ordering those around him to hold station. He disconnected his suit and opened the chain-glass bubble. However, before he climbed out, his gaze strayed down to his sidearm and disruptor, which had been gathering dust down by the side of his seat since he'd put them there what seemed like an age ago. He picked them up, and then climbed out, it only then occurring to him that Geerand hadn't mentioned that his mother was their leader before.

'This isn't a good idea,' said Mallon.

'Both of you stay in position just back from me and be ready with hardfields. Stay alert.' He paused, then added, 'Tinsher, if this turns to shit, I want you to grab her and get her back to the ship.'

'As you command,' said Tinsher tightly, 'but I am in agreement with Mallon.'

Still Piper felt unusually light as he walked down the war body and jumped off. The smell of the earth reminded him of his time building houses, when Mallon had caused his 'accident'. The background odour of lichen filled him with nostalgia, but perhaps for a childhood and youth he'd never really experienced – linked to dreams of the girl by the river, and in turn to the childhoods of others who hadn't been raised for amputation and installation in machines. He stuck the sidearm holster to his belt, casually shouldered the disruptor and began walking ahead, Tinsher and Mallon floating along on either side above.

'Are you busy?' Inster enquired through the link he'd kept open permanently.

'I have some time,' said Piper.

'I now know why the division between the revolutionary council and the factions has deepened,' he said. 'The last fight here was an alliance of the council and three factions close to Ironville, against a group that wanted to kill a lot more of the old regime which remained. That alliance is still in place – the revolutionary council absorbed its neighbours. The others, seeing the power shift, became more inclined to negotiate. That went on for a while over com, until the council asked for physical negotiators to be sent. This stopped when the negotiators went out of contact with their fellows.'

'They were being killed?'

'No, every single one of them changed sides.' After a pause Inster continued. 'They returned to their fellows and in three cases managed to assassinate faction leaders.'

Piper abruptly slowed. Data points were gathering in his mind and starting to connect up, much like they had when he'd taken on prador code and language, and begun working out how to control them. It would surely render results, but hadn't yet. He shrugged, picked up his pace and focused on his mother. As they drew closer together, he began to notice things. Her clothing was soiled, torn in a couple of places, while her skin had an unnatural hue. A second later, he realized she'd put on make-up – something never used on Founder's World in the past, what with the indoctrinated Cyberat contempt for the human body. This made no sense to him. She had always been clean and well-dressed when much of her body had been machine. Why she would now feel she needed make-up, after her body had been restored, was baffling.

'Mother,' he called. 'It's good to see you.'

Just then he sensed a mass of links to the animuses in his soldiers dropping out. The program he quickly instituted to re-establish them seemed to struggle. He halted, paranoia ramping up.

'It is good to see you too,' said Reema, her words flat.

Closer now, he could see where some of the face-paint had been smeared away on her chin. The skin looked blue there and horror loomed. He didn't want to face this and reached out to his soldiers as more links went down. He went into those whose links were still intact and found massive disruption, viral programs assembling something: animuses, swamping those he'd installed.

'Aaah! Fuck you!' Mallon screamed. Her miniguns fired two bursts, smashing the two human-form Cyberat behind Reema off their feet. Both Old Guard bobbed in the air. Tinsher surged forwards but dropped and ploughed into the ground. Mallon held for a moment, then came down like tons of scrap from a shredder claw. Tinsher fired her main weapon, the ionic blast carving through the ground and into the city Cyberat. Others of his Cyberat opened fire too, shots singing past him, particle beams spearing out, but then their weapons went out and those Enforcers in the air began crashing down.

Piper froze to the spot. Evidently someone now possessed the same ability as he did, and it didn't take much thought to know who it was. He then detected other activations that indicated missile batteries opening fire. But the reality of his mother standing there, and another node raised for inspection, drained him of will.

'Piper!' she said, holding out arms as if for a hug, despite all the surrounding chaos – something he'd never experienced from her.

He opened the node, almost reflexively, and recognized a prador thrall. The thing standing before him was no longer his mother, just as those negotiators sent back from Ironville had no longer been who they were. She had been cored and thralled. Horror and anger swirled up, but it paled in comparison to the rise of what came from the reptile. He shouldered and fired his disruptor in one. The practically invisible beam struck and sent her staggering back, with electric discharges webbing her body. The thrall node flickered and she dropped, and he didn't know

514

if it was he who'd fired, for the reptile was up and strong, indistinguishable from him.

Cold angry clarity banished horror, and data aligned. He suddenly remembered a dream of his father's laboratory having been raided and his work stolen. He recalled that when Inster had tried to retrieve his father's later work, it had gone missing. Someone was using his own technology against him, and it could only be one: Castron.

Piper peeled up animuses and sent them battling for ascendancy in his Cyberat and those ahead. Tinsher managed to tilt up and release another shot from her ion cannon. Mallon opened fire with miniguns but then this died. Others opened fire from behind, where they were still stuck to the ship's hull. And animuses fought for dominance. A particle beam shot scored across the ground beside him, carving a glowing trench. It had come from the destroyer. Castron had moved beyond subterfuge and was now directly trying to kill him, as Piper's animuses fought that instruction in the old dictator's animuses. It wouldn't be long before a shot caught him or, alternatively, one of those missiles cutting trails through the sky arrived. He looked ahead to where Tinsher's ion blast had annihilated Cyberat and saw Geerand on the ground, burning. A battle sphere prediction, based on limited data, indicated slaughter here. These were his people and innocent. Castron's objective was him, and if he stayed the slaughter would continue as they both fought for control of the Cyberat.

Piper turned and ran, and bounded up his war body. He paused for a second, seeing all the Cyberat on the hull peeling off and crashing to the ground on some new instruction, and it reminded him of what he'd done to the prador. He flicked a glance to converging missile trails and extrapolated their target. Dropping inside the war body, he instinctively slammed his hands down for full connection, while closing up the chain-glass and the armoured shutters over that. Connection brought dismay, as an animus concealed in the war body substrate fought him, already having seized control of his weapons. Piper fought back, pushing it down. He then reached out to the ship. Castron wasn't familiar with controlling the technology there and had only made inroads into the Cyberat aboard. Piper sent an instruction to the ganglion, and in response the ship began to rise on grav, tilting upwards, nose to the sky.

Where now? Flee to the ship? Behind, a beam blast carved through his Cyberat towards him – from the ship again. He threw his war body into the sky as the interloper animus fought to retain control of his war body's weapons. The old Cyberat had miscalculated, expecting him to start fighting. This at least gave him a breathing space. He reached out to those missiles, accruing nodes, but faced the same battle inside them as in the Cyberat. Two tumbled out of the sky but others remained on course.

No, not the ship.

Fully upright, the destroyer fired its fusion engines, incinerating the ground below it and accelerating. While it remained within Castron's range, its weapons could still be deployed against Piper. But the main reason he couldn't run for it was those missiles. Unless he halted them, the ship was done for, as were the Cyberat aboard it, and it seemed unlikely he could stop them. With cold anger, he accepted this but knew he needed to get out of that range to stop any further killing and then . . . he didn't know. He abruptly grabbed the straps and pulled them across.

'Going somewhere, boy?' enquired a dry, irritated voice issuing through the animus.

Piper reached back along the connecting thread and sent his own animus straight into Castron. The dictator swore and began his own internal battle, but Piper still got a data render: Castron was in the Embassy. Meanwhile, the animus Piper fought now released the weapons and went on full attack against his drive systems. The war body began to drop as grav stuttered out. It tilted nose down and at last he saw the way. Once again in control of the weapons, he charged the railgun for multiple firings. The seat slammed closed around him and he felt leaden and soggy as internal grav intensified its damping field. Castron's animus didn't respond to this, as it was still concentrating on shutting down his drive. He, or it, hadn't understood what this meant.

The railgun fired once, its shot slamming down into the ground ahead of the city Cyberat. Appalling recoil hurled his war body into the sky. Shadow loomed and then a shuddering impact as his war body glanced off the hull of his rising destroyer. Then the railgun fired again and again. Even with the dampening, he felt as if the acceleration was trying to drag his soft body from his unbreakable bones. The war body hurtled up and up, while he glimpsed the ground erupting below in huge explosions, cutting a line from the city Cyberat across the edge of Ironville.

The missiles closed on the destroyer as he stubbornly fought for control of them. He knocked out two more, seeing them tumble and crash into the ground, flying apart and doubtless spreading their radioactive load. But three arrived perfectly on target, slamming through open doorways and deep inside. The simultaneous triple blast ignited a sun inside the vessel, its hull visibly expanding before fire blasted out of cargo doors, airlocks and weapons ports. He felt hundreds of Cyberat go out in an instant. The ship ceased rising at once then dropped as if someone had cut its strings.

Piper sped away. He hadn't halted the killing down there but had at least ameliorated it. He had that comfort at least, as he edged into blackout but pushed his nanosuite to keep him conscious. Finally, the acceleration came off, while he was still travelling so fast the body was delivering heat warnings. The warnings then went out, not because his speed had waned, but because the war body had left atmosphere.

Piper focused on the animus. Its connection to Castron snapped and it became easy prey to the part of him that was reptile. He tore into and shredded it, squeezing down functions and erasing it, meanwhile firing up thrusters and grav to slow the war body down and alter course. Finally, when the animus was gone, he found himself in tight orbit.

What now?

What indeed. Piper, and the dark thing inside, had responded to the threat in the only way possible, without sacrificing thousands to conflict. Now it was time for both of them to make a reply. He sent his war body back down towards the planet, knowing what it would be.

The Cyberat town was a large one Piper felt sure he'd passed over on his route to Ironville, when controlling the first iteration of this war body. He saw it now had an armoured wall running round it, with twin cannon rotoguns mounted on that and scattered through the place. On the ground, just outside a recently installed city gate, rested the shuttle.

'Put down in the city square,' said the Cyberat called Everand.

'You have a city square?' Piper asked.

'We inclined to more human municipal structures after the rebellion gutted this place,' Everand replied. 'Now we would very much like human bodies to utilize them.'

Not feeling at all conversational, at least with this person, Piper made no reply to him, instead speaking to Inster via aug.

'You trust these people?' he asked.

'Their motivations are pretty clear – even more so with what happened at Ironville.' Inster paused for an uncomfortable moment. 'How are you doing?'

'Castron cored and thralled my mother. He took away my Cyberat, Tinsher, Mallon . . .' He grimaced at the sky. 'How do you think I feel?'

He had the war body above the indicated square now and brought it down. Cyberat were gathered there and he noted a high number of them were in apparently human form. Closer inspection revealed plug forms inserted into mechanical human bodies. That at least indicated a large change in the zeitgeist here.

'Castron is a somewhat larger problem than we supposed,' Inster observed.

'Indeed.' Piper landed. In the crowd, he could now see the agent and the four Sparkind. He opened the bubble and climbed out, making sure to bring his weapons with him.

'But the factions out here are in communication now,' Inster continued by aug. 'They know why their negotiators came back like they did and are gearing up for an alliance.'

'That could be useful,' Piper replied. 'As a distraction.'

He dropped to the ground and walked over. Though many here were in human-form mechanical bodies, the one called Everand occupied a quad form, with a pyramidal upper body and the Cyberat at the top, shoulders and head protruding. Three rotoguns ran down each side of the body and were directed towards Piper.

'So you are the child of Reema and Doge,' said Everand. 'I am sorry for your loss.'

'It will be repaid.'

Everand dipped his head, then gestured to a nearby building and led the way. Two human-form Cyberat moved quickly ahead, opening doors. Inster fell in beside Piper and the other four moved in behind. Piper found himself avoiding looking at them. Even though she was Golem, he found the compassion in Geelie's face unbearable.

The doors closed and they found themselves in a room with the two human forms and two other Cyberat in carrier bodies – one an Engineer loaded with tool arms. Human furniture had been scattered haphazardly here, as if they knew what they wanted but hadn't quite figured out how it all worked. Nobody sat down.

Everand halted beside a table and turned.

'The outer Cyberat are gathering,' he said. 'Nurkin's people will be here soon. It's time to go to war yet again.' He grimaced, hissing, 'Castron.'

'That's good.' Piper dipped his head in acknowledgement. 'But I need to talk with Inster and the Sparkind privately, because other preparations have to be made.'

'I understand you were integral in the rebellion,' said Everand tightly, 'but we are not the old regime. We speak openly here.'

Piper glanced towards the closed doors, then to Inster before focusing back on Everand.

'Understood,' he said, 'but what I know is that you have no real idea of what you're facing.'

'What do you mean by that?'

'The extent and speed of Castron's power.'

'What do you mean?' he repeated.

Piper's inclination would have been towards diplomacy, had he not seen his mother turned into an organic robot, and hadn't his Cyberat been snatched from his grasp, as well as his ship destroyed. He and his reptile were out of patience. So the animuses he sent now had more of a predatory nature, and little in the way of subtlety. One went into Everand's system hard, seizing control without any attempt at concealment. He made it spin up the magazines on his rotoguns and eject their ammunition – thousands of rounds bouncing and clattering across the floor – then froze him to the spot. The two human forms, he marched across to chairs and sat them down, holding them there. With the other two, he raised their mechanical arms to their heads, as if ready to rip open their faces, then froze them too. With all, he knocked out their ability to broadcast beyond this building.

'This is what Castron can do to you,' Piper said, as he went deeper into their animuses, running other programming to wipe out any recording facility and drop them into unconsciousness. He then turned to Inster and the others.

'Was that entirely necessary?' Inster asked.

'The demonstration?'

'No – knocking them out.'

Piper eyed them all. 'Castron's ability is not as advanced as my own, but he may be capable of penetrating minds. If there are plans that we don't want him to know, then any Cyberat he will almost certainly seize control of mustn't know them.'

Inster contemplated this for a moment, then asked, 'If his ability isn't as advanced as your own, why did you run?'

'Is that really a fair question, considering his mother?' Geelie asked.

Piper glanced at her expression again, then away. 'Tactically I could have taken him, eventually, but if I'd stayed to do that the result would have been a lot of dead Cyberat. And there is another way.'

Inster stared at him for a long moment, then gave a small nod. Piper guessed the two-hundred-year-old agent had already worked out his intentions. Inster gestured to the Cyberat in the room. 'Still, it was unnecessary for you to shut down these Cyberat. We could have had this discussion via aug.'

'Okay,' said Piper, pulling back from the turmoil he felt

and striving for clarity. Inster was quite right: the lesson of control had been delivered, but the fact he'd shut down these Cyberat had been a demonstration of power, in reaction to his recently having felt such a lack of it.

'So what do you have in mind?' Meersham threw into the pause.

'My guess would be murder,' said Sloan.

'The reality is this: if the people out here launch an attack against Ironville and I go along with it, the same situation will arise. Castron and I will be battling for control of the Cyberat, and during it many of them will kill each other. I intend to circumvent that.'

'Now I'm interested,' said Inster. 'Presumably when you're in range of each other again, you'll be able to locate him . . .'

'Quite.'

Piper now pulled up his inchoate plan and, with cold angry clarity, refined it. He transmitted it by aug to Inster and the Sparkind. They just stood there for a second, absorbing it; it was Cheen who spoke first.

'I see faults in this – there's a better version involving less risk – perhaps you need to elucidate why you choose this course,' he said.

'I think that's plainly obvious,' said Geelie.

'I agree, but it needs to be said,' Cheen replied.

'Because this is personal,' Piper replied.

The physiological reaction eventually hit in the night. Piper felt grief rising up through all his experiences and his years in virtuality to engulf him, and its strength surprised him. He cried and allowed it to run because he felt that he should – that this should be experienced and endured. But it reflected down and raised his father's loss, and anger, and began to spiral into something he knew might shut him down. The moment this thought occurred, his ever-active, extended mind focused through his aug on his nanosuite, and he studied the large changes these emotions had wrought in his body and brain. Then he started making the adjustments to bring himself back to optimum – the mere action of this raised suite programming to eliminate the changes. Exploring memories, both his own and others', he found that such programming had been extensively refined during the war, it being necessary to keep soldiers functional.

Next he slept dreamlessly for three hours, showered, ate food left in the cabin by Geelie, drank coffee and then headed out of the shuttle. On the land beyond the town, the lichens were muted in electric lights, having been trampled by metal and composite feet, wheels and treads, and spore spikes were broken or tipped over by the activity, all raising that familiar fungal and resinous odour. Piper sneezed and closed his visor. Visual enhancement kicked in, returning swathes of purple, blue and green, and revealing the clouds of spore dust amidst the swarms out there. Hundreds and then thousands of Cyberat had arrived during the night.

He went back in through the city gate, still standing open, and climbed a composite ramp up to the top of the city wall to watch them gather. He felt dry, wrung out, but reformed and refined into something tougher too. He knew his course now and there would be no diversion from it.

Everand, along with the Cyberat who'd been with him before, waited there. The Cyberat man had been infuriated by Piper's demonstration before. Piper didn't mind the anger but did feel uncomfortable with Everand's questions about how long he'd been unconscious. It'd been easy to slip the required programming into him and the others, and to pressure him through his animus. He had the power, so why not use it? Because it was wrong, morally wrong. He winced at the memory of a discussion he'd had on the matter with Albermech.

'You're wearing clothing like theirs,' Everand observed as he approached.

Piper waved a hand dismissively at the combat suit he now had on. 'I'd been in the other thing for longer than I care to remember, and they had this spare. One thing you'll learn if you choose to use those nanosuites they gave you for regeneration: Polity clothing is very comfortable.'

Everand frowned. 'Strange concept to grasp.' He looked over to where the shuttle rested outside the wall, crouching against the ground like a blunt-limbed lizard. 'Where did they go?' he asked.

'Polity soldiers are not Cyberat,' Piper replied. 'They would doubtless be effective during the coming fight, but more use to us doing things their own way.' He pointed out into the dawn. 'They're on their way to Ironville. Their sabotage of missile batteries and defensive guns will be make a huge difference.'

'I see.'

Piper glanced at him but also touched on the animus still installed in his mind. Everand didn't trust him but, in the end, that didn't matter, so long as the gathering Cyberat forces did what Piper required of them. He watched war bodies, Engineers and other castes of Cyberat still arriving beyond the wall. It was notable how few Enforcers there were. Though these people wanted more of that thing called 'freedom', it was well to remember that old hatreds endured. But that was something for the future . . .

Meanwhile, in conjunction with the reptile, he redesigned an animus for broadcast. He'd learned the lesson of how relinquishing control could lead to disaster and swore he wouldn't do so prematurely again. He would take control, keep and hold it as much as possible until his task here was done. It seemed apposite that the completion of his mission would end his ability to control those around him.

'Argan has arrived and they're ready for conference,' said Everand.

Piper dipped into Cyberat com, expanding his bandwidth through the link Everand offered. The virtuality that opened to his perception seemed primitive compared to the Polity variety, but it sufficed. In a limitless white space, he found himself floating in a circle of twenty-five Cyberat. They all hung there as simple plug forms, with identification labels hovering over their heads – the images shimmering occasionally and losing coherence.

'You say you have a way to prevent Castron seizing control of us, boy?' asked the Cyberat identified as Nurkin – an old woman with the appearance of Mallon.

Piper bridled under the use of 'boy'. It had a history from those he called friends, but more recently had been used by Castron. He gritted his teeth on his bitter response, though. It would be very easy to slide into contempt of these people and, as a consequence, value their lives less. That was one of the many lessons he'd learned.

'Yes,' said another. 'Everand has apprised us of what you can do and, by inference, of what Castron is capable.'

'I do have a way,' he replied. 'But if I'm to use it, we must first establish a chain of command.'

'With you at the top, presumably,' said another.

Piper gazed at this rather young-looking man – one who seemed too young to have been whittled down to plug form. He explored data gleaned from Everand's mind and learned that this man led a faction which wanted to dismiss as much of the organic human from their lives as possible. The choice was theirs, but Piper didn't like it, and did wonder if everyone in the faction actually had the power to choose. Freedom, he'd already seen with Everand's people, was at a factional level rather than an individual one.

'He may be powerful, but he's still a boy,' said Argan. 'A steadier and more experienced head should be in charge.'

'That would be you, of course,' said Everand. 'I for one am not interested in being led by someone who used to rule over me with such disregard of my rights.'

Piper kept his silence, cynical about the word 'rights'.

'Well, fuck the pure and wonderful Everand,' said another.

'This is not useful,' said one more.

And from then on, they were talking over each other, sometimes shouting one another down. So, they were all in agreement they didn't want the revolutionary council or Castron ruling over them, but couldn't settle on leadership of their alliance against him. Piper sighed, wishing he didn't have to be so dictatorial, then found the thousands of nodes within his range, and sent animuses to them all. As subtle as those he'd used on his own Cyberat on the journey to Yannetholm, they began establishing. The virtuality juddered and then steadied, gaining more detail as it started to run through superior programming. He sampled the minds, focusing on Argan, and translated his response to all the rest as required. The man rode in a large war body much like Mallon's – definitely Old Guard. He knew something had happened and was now becoming suspicious. Piper soothed him, going straight into his organics to pinch off neurochem and nudge other thought processes into predominance, quelling anger and fear. He then topped this off to them all by sending his battle plan. As they received this package, the distraction was enough for the animuses to establish completely.

'What did you do?' asked Nurkin.

The full degree of what he'd done wasn't evident to them, but he did still want them to know he had done something.

'I sent defensive programming to you all,' he stated. 'You will hardly notice it. It will fight to keep Castron from seizing control of you. But now, let's focus on the battle plan.'

'It's . . . interesting,' said Argan.

'Why the multiple feints?' asked another.

'Castron's range is about the same as mine, which is essentially to the horizon. I want you to keep him busy, attack and withdraw, while I try to disrupt his hold on those Cyberat he does control.'

'Surely a direct, fast attack right into the city while *you* distract him would be better?' suggested Argan.

Piper gave a tight smile, seeing how any talk about who sat at the top of the command chain had faded. The animuses were making other changes too: whittling down the anger and inclination for warfare, increasing the sense of personal risk, and other more subtle changes. He could see how many were now in agreement with making feints against Castron's forces, because that didn't actually involve a full-out attack and so much risk to themselves.

'Direct attack isn't a good idea until Castron and I are fully engaged. Only once we've got to that point will he not have full control of his soldiers, and I'll be able to give the order for the main assault. If you try a direct attack before then, he'll seize control of you. The defensive programs will protect you for a while, but he'll get round them. Better to make those feints, as detailed, then pull back out of his range to allow the programs to adjust your defences.'

'That doesn't make sense,' said Nurkin, looking painfully puzzled.

Others were in agreement, so Piper pushed. Dissent eventually fell away as he continued speaking: 'The programs will learn from Castron's attempts to seize control of you. If you put

527

yourselves in his range for too long, they'll not have a chance to apply what they've learned.'

'I think I understand,' said Nurkin, now losing all expression.

'We go in two hours,' said Piper, and pressed once again.

A moment later the virtuality faded and he found himself back on the wall standing next to Everand.

'That went well,' said the Cyberat, glassy-eyed.

Piper inspected him, not feeling very good about what he'd done.

'I need to go to my war body now and prepare,' he said.

21

Piper's war body rose out of the town, with other Cyberat spiralling up below it. Everand was there, plugged into a larger Old Guard body whose owner, apparently, lay rotting in a mass grave just out from the town. The gates opened and more Cyberat who couldn't fly streamed out. These included human forms who, in their mechanical bodies, might even be able to move as fast as Geelie and Cheen. They joined the force that had gathered during the night, while from there further large war bodies and others who'd weaponized for aerial combat rose up too. He moved his war body out, heading directly towards Ironville, and the forces formed up behind it. As he meandered out, those in the air queried this slow pace, but he informed them it was to allow the slower-moving Cyberat on the ground to keep up.

It was working. The force would arrive in sight of Ironville within a couple of hours and there begin making its feints, buzzing in towards the city, sometimes engaging, but then pulling out. He himself had to get there first, though. He grimaced, turned away from the distant view and walked over to the grav-sled Cheen had rigged with a couple of gas thrusters on the back, and climbed aboard. The seat and controls were much like those of an antediluvian motorbike. He raised the thing off the ground and sent it skimming out of the cluster of spore spikes in which the others had hidden it, then down to the road leading to

Ironville, kicked in the thrusters and accelerated. As far as the Cyberat heading there knew, he was inside his war body. Though they might question why he'd closed the armour shutters over the chain-glass bubble so soon.

As he sped along the road, he firmed the mental link with the combat suit he wore, closed over the armoured hood and sealed up the visor. A HUD lit up but he wiped it away again, since he controlled the thing with his mind. He accelerated the sled up to full speed, while still travelling mentally in his war body. The machine hovered a hundred metres up and he knew, should he so wish, he could really ramp up its acceleration, just as he'd once flown its previous iteration here on Founder's World, leaving the Cyberat force behind and being over Ironville in minutes. The temptation was there, but to achieve what he wanted here, his ostensible presence in an attacking force needed to be convincing.

Now he made some last checks. The animuses in the attacking force would continue to work, unless interfered with from outside. And his war body would follow the plan, with leeway for some variation, while he maintained a simpler link via satellite for telemetry. A few kilometres further on, all his animus connections from behind snapped. He would reacquire them later, as necessary.

The metalled road took him in through wildlands bright with lichens, to croplands. Most of the stuff growing in fields or orchards on either side had little to do with food. The willows to his right produced a fibre useful in the construction of Cyberat bodies, while in the fields to his left grew a form of peanut that provided lubricating oil. Both were genetic mods which somehow made these organic products more acceptable to those who wanted to forgo the organic. Next he was going past greenhouses, and these did contain plants that produced the bulk fats and proteins to be processed into food, for those damnable human remains within Cyberat bodies. Piper had a brief thought about the agricultural revolutions waiting to happen on his world.

Ironville finally came into sight in the dawn light, with Cyberat rising up out of it. Thousands of new nodes appeared in his internal space, but he prevented connection to any of his animuses that remained inside them. His reptile baulked at this, offering up new animuses and urging connection. He gritted his teeth and suppressed it, for it was all about want and need and control, while he knew that if he made links or sent animuses, Castron would at once be alerted to his presence close by.

He drove on down, further between the greenhouses and then into a warehouse district scattered with Cyberat homes. The city Cyberat now swarmed above him, while on the roads were one or two of those incapable of flight – mostly of the Agronomist Cyberat caste. Ahead, even more of mixed castes were crowding through. His destination sat highlighted in his mind and, turning into a side road, he dropped the sled by a warehouse wall, beside two others of the same design, then dismounted and moved away from them. Inster had chosen a good place. Too deep into the city he would be noticed, while out here he'd be taken as one of the many unprogressed Cyberat who worked in this area. Coming to a path leading into a stand of bamboo, its stems blue with lichen, he activated his suit's chameleoncloth, transitioning it from the beige of a Cyberat's overalls to match his surroundings. Walking in, he deactivated it again, since he wanted to be seen by those who were waiting here.

The path led to a clearing five metres across, with other paths starring off it. He could see movement there: distortions in the air and two disembodied hands, then they turned off their cloth and opened their visors. Inster gestured him over.

'I'm still not sure this is the best idea,' said the agent. 'There's

531

no guarantee Castron will stay in the Embassy – quite possibly he'll head up to direct his forces.'

Piper walked over and studied the group. Inster was back in combat gear. Cheen and Geelie had their swords again, which had been absent during his brief glimpses of them at Yannetholm. Meersham looked as big and brutal as ever, while Sloan was squatting down over neatly lined-up explosives, slotting them into bandoliers. It almost felt to Piper as if he was completing some circle of experience.

'I doubt Castron will join them. He didn't seem inclined to put himself at the forefront of fighting during the rebellion,' said Piper. 'Anyway, it doesn't matter. Judging by the building there and his presence there earlier, the Embassy is now his base and he'll return to it.'

'In the case of a return, that will mean he's defeated the factions . . .' said Meersham.

Piper focused on the big man. 'Even better. It'll mean he feels safe, victorious, and will therefore be negligent.' He kept to himself a stab of anxiety and regret about Mallon, Tinsher and the others. If they were not already dead, they might die in the coming battle, on the wrong side yet again.

'Y'know, on Yannetholm I saw you turning into a good soldier,' said Meersham. 'Now I'm not so sure.'

'Really?' Piper asked, knowing what he was going to say.

Meersham gestured at Inster. 'Now you're more like him.'

Piper nodded and looked across to Cheen and Geelie. 'Reconnaissance?'

'We've taken a look and mapped out a route,' said Geelie. 'There should be no problems unless we are directly seen by Cyberat controlled by Castron.' She gestured at her suit. 'This is advanced chameleoncloth, but not chameleonware, and Cyberat have more than human senses.'

'Hence the gun tower,' said Inster. 'I liked that touch.'

Piper acknowledged this with a dip of his head. 'If we're seen, Castron will assume our purpose is sabotage. He'll direct forces in the city to keep watch around defensive weapons.'

'Tricky,' said Sloan, standing up and handing Piper a bandolier.

Piper slipped it on and stuck it in place, plugging a lead from it into his suit. It was chameleoncloth too and would match the suit's function. His weapon didn't have that facility but with it hanging on his back, he could conceal it by turning towards anyone who might see – otherwise he'd be using it.

'The sabotage is just a distraction,' he said. 'But, as I learned when we went into Castron's villa, Cyberat detection systems have a large fault in that they're tuned only to look out for Cyberat machine bodies because they are the only threat Castron would visualize.' He looked around at the surrounding paths. 'Shall we go?'

They were all ready, with bandoliers in place. Each of them carried disruptors and were as armed and effective a team as he would have wanted. Inster gestured to one path and led the way. In a minute, they were out of the bamboo and heading along a narrow track between warehouses, with the map they were following loading to Piper's virtual aug. He studied it, glad he hadn't needed to say they should stay off main routes.

'We still don't want to be seen,' said Inster privately over comlink. 'The systems are set to look for Cyberat, but if we're detected . . .'

'Resetting to a different threat will take time, though Cyberat will be searching,' Piper replied. 'But after the gun tower, they'll be looking in the wrong places.'

'Plenty of guns on that Embassy,' Inster observed.

'You have a better plan?'

'Yes: you locate Castron and we drop a nuke on him.'

'No,' said Piper simply.

Sliding into virtual invisibility, Cheen and Geelie moved on ahead. Piper closed his visor, which brought them into visibility again, moving fast to check side routes and then coming back. He activated his suit once more as, with the sounds of visors closing, the others did too. Geelie halted them at one point, and they stood silent and still as two partially progressed Cyberat crossed ahead of them. Piper watched them – a boy and a girl – and saw with distaste that the boy had lost his hands, ready to be replaced with gleaming multifinger grabs, while the girl was already undergoing skull expansion. Perhaps that was something Castron had speeded up. His method of control, as Piper's own, required hardware interfaced with the organic.

Ahead, rising up out of the city, the gun tower came into sight. As they made their way towards it, they circumvented a square pond sheened with oil and stinking of chemicals – outflow from a nearby factory – then weaved through a junkyard of Enforcer bodies stacked one upon another, to which dry remains still clung. Memories of a similar junkyard in a shallow sea rose in Piper's mind, only there the remains had been fresher and sometimes screaming. As if instigated by the memory, a mass of nodes reacquired and he connected to their animuses.

The approaching forces, and the war body apparently containing him, had come back into his range, while the Cyberat rising from the city were starting to fire missiles. With the reptile snarling, Piper next reconnected with those animuses still available to him in the city force, and sent more to those within range of his war body, but not all within his *actual* range. Just a few seconds later, as expected, Castron's animuses began their attempt to seize control of the attackers. In the physical battle, the force replied with antimissile rotogun and particle beam fire. Sounds like a thunderstorm rolled across the city and the sky lit up with flashes. Piper halted and squatted by a mound of wreckage. The others paused and turned to watch him.

'You are persistent,' said Castron, while groping for control in Piper's war body. Piper instantly responded by widening the link back to that machine, one channel filling up with an extension of the reptile as it too reached back. The thing lashed at the man, all anger, hatred and guilt. It was essential he gain no more foothold there than disruption of the weapons and drive, because if he went deeper he'd find the thing empty. In that respect, Piper drew much of the function of Castron's animus back to his bones. The impression to Piper was of them fighting in some virtual nowhere space, giving Castron little time or processing to spare to know any different.

'Vicious,' Castron added, 'but to be expected.'

'So you stole my father's technology,' Piper replied, not because he felt any urge to engage but because the exchange was a further distraction.

Castron gave no reply, soon too lost in their battle for control and bludgeoned back by the reptile's rabid attack. Piper smiled grimly, reining it back as the thing seemed inclined to tear itself from his bones.

'Not yet,' he told it.

Animus attacked animus within all the Cyberat in the sky. Firing started to lose accuracy on both sides and Cyberat dropped, grav waxing and waning and thrusters firing intermittently. Seeing danger, Piper sought out other nodes in his internal space with a precision he doubted Castron possessed. The missiles being simple machines, he didn't need to install animuses. He flooded them with standard Polity interdiction programs, shutting down their detonation and switching off their engines. Many of them swept through the approaching force on their way towards the ground, crashing and fragmenting there. He sighed out a breath. He shouldn't forget the basics of warfare from the mental plain he occupied: just a few nukes detonating could have ended this attack on the first feint.

Piper stood up as the factions began retreating, pulling out of Castron's range. As they went, he observed his own animuses adjusting as he'd programmed, not destroying the ones Castron had sent but absorbing them. He then tracked threads back, triangulated signals, traced those to his own Cyberat now under Castron's control and at last located him. The old dictator was in his war body on a platform up on the top of the Embassy. Briefly he glimpsed the man through Mallon's eyes, for she was there too – still alive, he was happy to see. He was looking to the sky with arms folded and doubtless confident of his safety, for Cyberat had mounted hardfield projectors from the Embassy around that platform. It seemed Inster's favoured method of attack would not have succeeded and this gave his own approach greater veracity. He sent his companions the imagery, then snapped all his connections as his war body went out of range too.

'No trace on you?' Geelie asked, looking over at him.

'No – as far as Castron is concerned, I'm in my war body.'

She nodded, and they all moved on again.

Further wreckage lay ahead: burned-out and collapsed homes, two factory units with their walls shattered and composite roof sheets rucked up by the machines they'd collapsed on. Scattered through this were Cyberat bodies – some Enforcers and some not. That part of him born in the four-year virtuality felt angry about the disregard for the dead and for the environment Cyberat lived in. Nothing was cleaned up unless it served the purpose of machine bodies. The rest of him saw it as simply a messy way to leave useful materials. Soon they'd moved along to the end of a wall where Inster peered out, sending his view to each of them.

A wide area had been dozered clear for the erection of the tower. Its base lay twenty metres wide and it rose up like a tree trunk to ten metres thickness. Having seen these before, Piper knew it to be made of an alloy frame with composite sheets bolted on. It had no entrance at ground level, but a ring-shaped platform high up around the weapons, for flying Cyberat to service it. The turret at the top projected four heavy rotoguns – two each side of a missile battery. It would have been an easy target were it not for the Enforcers on the ground about its base. Inster pulled back.

'Little paranoid?' Sloan suggested.

'No,' Inster replied. He looked to Piper and raised an eyebrow.

Piper explained, 'Castron has no shortage of Enforcers – probably more than he needs for the factions – so why not put them here where they serve some purpose?' He paused, then added, 'They're not considered people and have no homes. They're garaged and parked like cars when not in for service and rearming.'

'Still,' said Sloan. 'Not going to be easy to get through them undetected.'

Piper reviewed the image of the Cyberat ringed around the base. There were ten human forms scattered between five heavier bodies – all sporting rotoguns. He guessed more of the first kind were here because they'd be of less use in the expected fight to come.

'Status out there?' Inster asked.

'Next feint in ten minutes,' Piper replied.

'Cheen,' said Inster.

The Golem moved off at a run, dodging through wreckage and leaping broken walls. Piper tracked him round the circumference of the cleared area, where he could see him, and saw minimal disturbance in his path. Visual feed showed him arriving over at two o'clock to their six on the circumference. There he deposited a series of charges under one edge of a composite roof piled with other wreckage, and then ran on round.

'Sloan, prepare to ring it,' said Inster. 'Geelie, you'll go with him.'

The reptile shoved at Piper, for it wanted him to go with them, but it was stupid to do so. The more of them that headed for the tower, the higher the likelihood of detection. This time he didn't force the thing down, but allowed it to rise to the limit just to the point beyond which he no longer controlled it. Again it became much more distinct, its angry yellow glare shining from his eyes, while his overlay clamped down solid. He reached inside now, to begin levering it up and squeezing out connections, and it writhed with irritation. It was worrying to him how it maintained integrity without the connections, becoming more firmly and substantially itself, because in this form it *did* have more power to seize control of him. But all of this was necessary for his purposes.

Piper turned his attention to the feint. The factions fired missiles ahead of their attack; below, the ground forces had come into view. Animus connections hammered home again from both him and Castron, and the mental battle recommenced. Piper included the Enforcers around the base of the tower in his. He could do nothing precise there, because Castron would detect that some of the Cyberat had been singled out for special attention, but the disruption helped their plans. The Enforcers began moving erratically, weapons tracking round and legs, if they had them, occasionally giving out.

'Now,' he said.

The explosion lifted roof panels and other debris, and showered them over the Enforcers, who oriented to this potential threat. Two opened fire on the debris – beam shots burning it from the air and rotogun slugs tracking across fallen roof panels to leave smoking holes. Hidden by chameleoncloth, Geelie and Sloan ran through the largest gap available. Sloan at once started to slap planar explosive charges around the base of the tower, while Geelie tracked with him, facing out, watching the Enforcers. They worked round out of sight, and only as they came back into view did one of the human-form Enforcers abruptly whirl round. Its rotogun fired, stitching along the tower, then slamming into Geelie. She staggered back, reached out to grab Sloan, and hurled him forwards. Sloan rolled smoothly as the U-capper he had been and came up out of that running, while Geelie shut down her 'ware and moved in the opposite direction.

'Hell,' said Piper.

Geelie fired her disruptor four times, dropping three human forms in loose-limbed disarray in which they lost any resemblance to humanity. She hit one of the larger ones too – a flattened cone of a thing held up on numerous stubby legs – before rotogun fire again sent her staggering. She rolled and came up, shattered weapon discarded, and drew her sword. A leap took her four metres up, as a particle beam scored across where she'd just been. Landing between two human forms, her sword then blurred and made a machine-gun sound. They collapsed sans limbs, and she leaped towards another of the larger ones. Here her cuts went through an armoured cylindrical body, which blew its guts out of its side as she jumped again. By then Sloan was back with them.

'Blow it,' said Inster. 'We're out of here.' He gestured behind with his thumb.

Geelie, after demolishing yet another of the Enforcers, ran into a gap on the far side of the clearing, disappearing from sight.

The charges blew, and Piper ducked back, running after the others. A blast wave showered them with debris and one partially dismembered Enforcer, scrabbling at the ground with the stubs of its limbs. Glancing back, Piper saw the tower tottering, then falling – the Cyberat up there launched from the platform.

'Geelie, are you . . . hurt?' Piper asked via aug.

'Nothing that can't be fixed. However, I no longer have any concealment so will be a liability.'

'Then find somewhere to hide.

'That's not my inclination,' she replied. 'I'll keep at least some of these that are chasing me busy. Go and do your job, Piper.'

She shut off the comlink.

With Inster leading, they ran back along their approach path, Cheen dropping from the top of a wall to join them, then back on the route towards the Embassy. Piper glanced at the Golem, wondering what his thoughts were on Geelie, but didn't know to what end, and he had other things to occupy his mind.

The latest feint began its retreat and Castron concentrated his mental attack on those in which his animuses had the most advantage: sixty of them. Piper responded with the same strategy, which encompassed Cyberat who'd been under his control before. He opened bandwidth to his animuses in them, feeding in some of the reptile, and managed to seize back control of over a hundred of what had been his Cyberat in the Embassy grounds. Their actions thereafter differed. Castron turned his sixty against their erstwhile fellows, rotoguns hammering and particle beams stabbing out. The factions swirled away from them, while four big war bodies on Piper's side opened up with ion cannons – wiping out the computing of the sixty with non-destructive shots that nevertheless dropped them hard from the sky.

Piper gritted his teeth, fighting to control the reptile, or perhaps himself. He could have fought back there, but he had to stick with the overall strategy and, as ever, collateral damage was inevitable. The hundred original Cyberat he controlled he too could turn against the 'enemy', but morality was his disadvantage. Instead he went deep into eighty of them with something new and more aggressive in the computing realm. He created feedback loops, disrupting programs and burning out hardware, rendering them incapable of movement until their repair systems dealt with it, which wouldn't happen for some hours. They would remain noncombatants until this was all over.

The remaining twenty in the Embassy grounds he sent against the wall. Tinsher was among the big Enforcers who hammered that wall with rotogun slugs, tearing at it with prador claws, then crushing it flat as they went out over it and into the city. Tinsher paused to turn her ion cannon on two rotogun platforms – metal frameworks melting and buckling to send the guns crashing to the ground.

'General Piper!' she said.

'Yes, it's me,' he replied regretfully.

The factions retreated further and soon his war body went back out of range, and he snapped all connections again. He had no doubt that Tinsher's moment of freedom lasted only a few seconds after his disconnection. He felt bad about using her in what had just been another distraction and, grimacing, he speeded up to run beside Inster as they now moved into the city centre streets.

'Geelie?' Piper enquired over aug.

'Is a professional and will survive or not – that is the nature of war,' Inster replied.

They slowed in the streets where, seeing the number of Cyberat about, Piper had to alter the map. Inster nodded and they headed out into a wider street. With more space, they'd be able to avoid Cyberat, whereas in narrower streets they'd be running straight into them. In one avenue, they went along an arched path for those in human form, while larger Cyberat traversed the main avenue – a necessary safety precaution in Cyberat city planning. There they paused in some shadows, completely still, and watched a heavily armed war body roll past on cage wheels, trailed by a party of twenty Enforcers. Doubtless Castron had tired of the feints and was now moving more of his Cyberat into play. The game out there wouldn't last much longer.

Soon, at the end of another avenue, the main gate through the wall around the Embassy came into sight. They moved along to the end of this, crouched behind columns fronting a nearby building, and once again Inster looked out and sent them his view. Human-form Cyberat, scattered through with larger Enforcers, crowded the area. Piper swore. In having Tinsher and those others knock down the wall, he'd only concentrated more Cyberat around the Embassy. He moved out past Inster and peered along to the break. Tinsher was there, standing in it, while the big Enforcers that had broken it were gathered in the compound behind. He moved back out of sight.

'Sloan, Meersham and Cheen.' Inster pointed towards the main gate, meanwhile offering an update to Piper's protean plan.

Sloan unshouldered his pack and put it on the ground, pulling out more explosives and handing them to the other three. Piper felt slightly sick as he watched them. He'd known his choice in the method of attack would put them in severe danger. But why did that matter now, when he'd been doing the same with millions of Cyberat on Yannetholm? Did he consider these four more human? No, it wasn't that. On that world, there had been few choices beyond full-frontal warfare and he'd still felt the pain of his soldiers dying, still regretted the losses and still feared losing those he'd come to know. Here his objective was essentially selfish and he was putting other people at risk for it. In fact, many had already died during those feints.

'There has to be another way,' he said.

'You can see the situation as clearly as I can.' Inster pointed towards the Embassy gate. 'The place is swarming with Cyberat and we'll be seen if we simply try to sneak in. We need a distraction like the one back at that tower.'

'There will be a distraction during the next feint.'

'It may be enough, but we can't bet on that. Come on.'

He headed back the way they'd come. Piper hesitated, glancing to the other three who were peering towards the gate.

'Take care.'

Meersham turned to him. 'We've survived against the prador for decades,' he said. 'You must trust in us to do our job, while I trust that you will do yours.'

Piper nodded once and moved quickly after Inster.

Halfway down the avenue, the agent gestured for them to cross, sending an update to the map. Piper absorbed this, reminded of route changes when they'd attacked Castron's villa. Then he had taken charge, but did it now seem Inster was usurping him? No, Polity command structures in situations like this were more plastic, while he had become accustomed to virtual autocracy.

'Surely better to head towards the gap,' he said.

'Subterfuge within subterfuge,' the agent replied. 'Lots of smart Cyberat here and Castron is no pushover. Someone might be second-guessing us, so we have to stay ahead of that.' They crossed, freezing to a halt three-quarters of the way when three human forms came out of an arched entrance and crossed nearby. He and Inster faced them to conceal the disruptors on their backs. Once the Enforcers had crossed, they moved on, into a side street, then along another towards the wall. Here at the end Piper could just see the gate further down.

'They coming again?' Inster of course knew but was ensuring Piper remained focused.

'Yes.'

The army on the ground came first, disrupted by animuses but now partially immune as his own in them had adjusted, and they were struggling on. His war body appeared next over the horizon, at the head of the flying Cyberat. The factions brightened the sky with thrusters firing up – coming much faster now because this was it.

Piper reconnected to them and to animuses installed in Castron's forces where they hadn't yet been erased, as well as in his own erstwhile troops and others, while launching yet another into the old dictator himself. The forces hurtled together, firing intermittently, and many Cyberat dropped from the sky. It was inefficient warfare, chaotic and crazy, but still Piper knew many were dying, for he could feel them.

'Interesting what you did with the programming,' said Castron as their animuses battled, again seeming to be neither in him nor in Piper, but occupying some realm in between. 'But though you've made them more resistant, the numbers are on my side and you will follow your mother into reprocessing . . . or at least that part I removed.'

Psychology, of course. Piper suppressed the reptile, battled on with cold clarity and chose not to make an angry response.

'Interesting too how you can only keep control with some method of enslaving those you rule over. And even then, you have to steal that method.' Piper remembered his dreams, his father's memories, and took this opportunity to give the impression he knew more than expected. 'Lucky my father had developed his technology as far as he did when you sent Enforcers to steal it.'

'It wasn't *that* developed. Anyway, I found an up-to-date data cache when I split him open. I hope he understood the cache would bring about the downfall of his rebellion, as now, and your destruction . . . while he slowly died.'

This was pointless – ridiculously melodramatic. But Piper couldn't resist another barb: 'You will fail, old man – you don't have the bones for this. Time for you to die.'

If all of that wasn't enough to signal this was ostensibly the real attack, Piper pushed his war body forwards and opened up with its weapons, though his shots weren't particularly accurate. Pulling even further ahead, he then fired the railgun directly towards Castron's position, recoil hurling his war body up and back over the factions. The shot drew a vapour trail line and Piper felt the crump through his feet as it exploded against hardfields. The ejection trail of one generator rose from the Embassy, boiling and sparking, but Castron had more generators to spare.

'I like . . . this Polity technology,' said the old Cyberat.

'You can only fend off so many shots,' Piper replied.

Just then an explosion blew the gate, throwing its armoured doors into the compound. Disruptor fire ensued, dropping Cyberat, and a particle beam seared along the wall. Meersham and the others had begun their distraction.

'Gecko function,' said Inster, moving out.

Piper initiated this in his gloves, but held off on his boots until they'd reached the wall. A Cyberat – an Engineer on spider legs loaded with additional weaponry – ran straight for them from the left. It then skidded to a halt, swinging from side to side in puzzlement, the female under chain-glass frowning at something being fed in through the optic links sunk into her eyes. Inster fired once with his disruptor and she collapsed. Piper understood the risk of their detection had been small, since the shot could easily have come from the fight over by the gate.

They reached the wall and climbed with palms and boot soles sticking. In Piper's skull the animus battles continued, while his war body, pulling ahead from the factions and taking numerous hits from the opposing forces, fired its railgun again. Once more, a hardfield intercepted the shot but this time deflected it and didn't blow its generator. Instead the shot slammed down in the city beyond the Embassy and, as he reached the top of the wall, Piper saw a building drop in dusty ruin over there. From this vantage, he looked to the gate. It and part of the wall were gone now, and disrupted Cyberat lay scattered all around. Explosions and shots continued in the city beyond, steadily drawing away while further Cyberat converged on that point – many heading out of the compound. Further along from the gate, he could see where the wall was down, with Tinsher and the Enforcers remaining on station there. It seemed Inster had been right about that.

Piper dropped from the wall into the compound. They headed across without difficulty to a long wall, deeply inset with chain-glass windows. Inster hung his disruptor by its strap and drew one of his thin guns. He dialled it way down and then took precise shots around the rim of the window, burning out objects invisible to Piper. He next slapped a decoder on the window and turned it to collapsing white powder, and they were in.

'Bring back memories?' he asked.

Piper reached out and caught his shoulder. Signal strength had diminished the moment he stepped inside. The place was heavily shielded, which would be helpful as they moved through it, but not yet. If he started to lose connection with his animuses, while apparently plainly visible in the sky out there, it might give away the ruse. Back in the window space, he concentrated on his personal battle sphere.

The ground forces had met in chaotic battle. Still the animus war inside them caused problems with coordination and aim – which was mirrored up in the sky. Though lethal weapons burned the air and filled it with slugs, shrapnel and debris blown from mechanical bodies, the kill rate stayed low. But still, there was a death toll and that needed to end. And it would be Castron who ended it. Piper fired the war body's railgun once more – another shot that was deflected, this time spearing up into the sky.

'Fuck you, Castron!' he bellowed, allowing the reptile greater connection to the animus battle. The thing pulled from him, seeming to lose substance in his bones as it peeled up and spread much of itself through all the animuses. He again almost lost control of the thing but, in essence, so long as he could retrieve it, the impression of a lack of control was good. It took with it its anger, hatred and humiliation. Castron's response was laughter.

'Come out and face me!' Piper drove his war body hard out of the swirling battle towards the Embassy. He then struggled to pull the reptile back and regain some control. With as many of the airborne fighters as he could, he pushed them to descend to the ground. The factions started to go down first, Castron's force following them. The cries for him to pull back were an undercurrent he ignored while, in the battle sphere, he could see missile batteries and other weapons on the Embassy tracking his war body. He recalled a brief exchange with Inster:

'If Castron has made the Embassy his base, he'll control the Polity weapons there,' Inster had said.

'I know,' Piper had replied. 'I'm counting on that.'

Swarms of missiles rose up as his war body came over the city. He began evading and shooting some of them down, but huge chemical blasts blinded sensors and sent him tumbling.

Of course, Castron had not gone *fully* nuclear with them, since he wanted to survive this, so most simply exploded. Two, however, came apart; they must have been fissile warheads. Next, a particle beam lanced up, locked onto him and tracked him. This was no old Cyberat weapon but a Polity one with little diffusion. Armour began to ablate, and instruments to die as the temperature climbed. Then came the tactical nuke blast, just a hundred metres away. The flash lit the sky and the heat blast slammed into his already weakened war body. Piper noted severe damage but rolled the war body out, stunned to find it still functional. Prador armour and Polity technology were something. However, when the particle beam found him again, he focused on pulling back and suppressing the reptile as he shut off grav. He fed in erratic firing to the thrusters and, a second later, disconnected from *all* animuses.

Piper moved forwards, the reptile back inside him and thrashing, and looked up, knowing the precise part of the sky to find. There was his war body, picked out at the tip of the particle beam, falling through the air with missiles closing in. It went beyond the city as one hit, the bright flash darkening his visor. A minute later, the blast wave from the nuke sent him staggering back into the Embassy. Leaning against one wall, he continued suppressing the reptile – still raging at this loss – and pushed down the slide control on his bones. Then he glanced up at Inster.

'One has to hope Castron isn't vengeful,' said the agent.

Piper shook his head. 'I bet most of the Cyberat he controls are against him, and I doubt he wants to waste resources. Those of the factions that can retreat will do so. In the rest, his animuses will eventually seize control and they'll be his.' He had to believe that. He didn't want to imagine Castron going on to slaughter Cyberat who'd been his enemy, even if the need to eliminate them had passed. After all, the old dictator's most dangerous enemy was now apparently dead. They moved on into the Embassy.

Inster knew the way and took them on a convoluted route, avoiding main corridors more likely to be occupied by the larger Cyberat. Human-sized corridors here were strewn with debris, and in places walls had been torn down in the process of adapting it all for the Cyberat. Piper felt utterly cut off, disconnected, and wished there had been some way to remain in connection with his animuses. But then, as Inster opened a hidden door and led them into a small storage room, he felt stupid to neglect a non-Cyberat channel that was available. He raised the switch on his bones just enough to access the virtual aug.

'What's your situation?' he asked Geelie, scared she might not reply – the question acting as a comlink request.

'Crouching in a city drain after the pretty fireworks,' she replied.

'So not a source of information for me?'

'No, not really.'

'Sloan, Meersham, Cheen?'

'Looking for a drain cover,' Meersham replied.

'We want sight on the factions,' Inster interrupted. 'And you're not looking for a drain cover.'

'You know us too well,' Meersham replied. 'We're up in one of the towers. Cheen and Sloan are presently taking control of the weapons here, just in case.'

'The factions?' Inster reminded.

'Pretty much as expected,' Meersham continued. 'A chaotic fight now dying off as, I've no doubt, Castron seizes control of more of them. Separate contingents retreating just as fast as they can. No pursuit, but then Castron won't want to put his own forces out of his range. And anyway, he probably thinks he can take control of those who escaped at his leisure. The boy got it right.'

'Hold position till you get my signal, then head in.'

'And if we don't get your signal?'

'I think you know the answer to that.'

'Understood.'

With nothing further said, Piper turned his attention to what Inster was doing. The agent faced a wall at the end of the room, fingers up against his aug. He then stepped back and, with a soft hissing, a door slid open. Beyond lay a narrow corridor, but when Piper tried to find it on the Embassy map it wasn't there.

'Something you neglected to mention?' Piper asked.

'Just as you didn't want the factions to know your plan, because Castron might ream it out of their minds, I didn't want you to know about this. Though I doubted it, the possibility remained that you might lose in a mind-on-mind battle with him.'

'I see.'

They stepped in, with the door hissing closed behind them, and traversed corridors only just big enough for a man to stand upright. Meersham would have been uncomfortable in here and, Piper suspected, *would be* uncomfortable here if Inster didn't send that signal. He had no doubt that Inster's orders to the Sparkind were to take Castron out, if he and Piper failed to do so. The corridors took them on through and his tension rose as they closed in on the location of the platform. Soon Inster brought them to another door, which opened at the foot of a shaft leading to the roofs.

'So here we are,' said the agent, stepping onto a ladder leading up. 'You ready?'

Piper focused inwardly. His connection to the whole function of his bones was muted, but still the reptile felt solid in him, like a thorn jammed into a hand. Yet it wasn't wholly distinct, because it consisted of much of the programming and memory beyond his organic mind. He searched for analogies and one came up, an ancient one, and he now saw the thing as a cancer, for it was both part of him and not.

'Yeah, I'm ready.'

He climbed up after Inster, reviewing what he'd ascertained up there through Mallon's and Castron's senses and sensors, and comparing it to the Embassy map. The platform jutted from the side of a peaked roof, steel frameworks supporting it and running energy feeds up to the hardfield generators which ringed it. This shaft led up on the other side of the roof. They could cross lower down to the frameworks and climb up. Five Cyberat were up there: Castron, Mallon and three old-style Enforcers, though not any of those who had gone with him to Yannetholm. Perhaps Castron was unsure of his ability and didn't trust that he had full control of them. Piper might have been right in his jibe about bones. Castron's substrate didn't occupy a full human skeleton, after all. No, that was wrong – otherwise why would he have Mallon up there? It occurred to Piper that Castron might be giving her close attention. She'd been Castron's ally and what Piper had done to her mind would be of special interest to the old Cyberat, considering his aims.

'Same method of attack?' Inster asked.

'Yes, unless you have suggestions and feel the urge to take over again.'

'Any plan would work because of these.' Inster slapped a hand against his disruptor. 'But I would have preferred the others here too.'

The top of the shaft stood open to the sky. Piper couldn't divine the purpose of the thing, until he searched the schematic underlying the map and got an explanatory label. It was an entry point for small surveillance drones.

They reached the top, where Inster hit a control to open an iris lid, then crawled out onto a flat roof and moved up against a wall below the peaked one. The edge of the platform was just visible and they shifted along towards it. Piper closed his visor and deactivated the HUD again. He could target via his virtual aug. His reptile, even muted, offered up animuses, but using them melded it more into his system and he didn't want that. He dismissed them.

Reaching the framework, Piper climbed, moving back to where the platform rested against the sloping roof. Inster went in the opposite direction, ready to come in from the other side. Piper's stomach churned with tension, but his intellect negated it. He and Inster carried disruptors, so five clear shots should be enough to end the danger. He moved right up to the lip, a shield generator looming above to his left.

'Ready?' Inster enquired over aug.

'Yes.'

'Three, two, one and go!'

Piper hauled himself up, coming straight up to face one of the Enforcers. He fired as it swivelled a gun towards him, the air distorting between them and discharges running from where he hit it. Its gun fired in return, slamming shots into the sloped roof as he dived and rolled behind the generator. Coming out the other side, he fired again, hitting Mallon as she began to turn. Inster was firing too. The two other Enforcers collapsed down on blocky legs over there and, simultaneously, he and Inster fired on Castron. The war body rose, then guns slumped and it crashed down again, juddering the platform.

'Well that wasn't so—' began Inster, but a rotogun swivelled towards him and fired. The agent spun, shattered armour lifting in a spray of blood, and he disappeared over the side of the platform.

Piper froze. In just a second, they'd gone from finishing this to disaster. The shot had come from Castron's war body, now swinging weapons back towards him. In that moment, the reptile rose up and demonstrated how little control he now had over it as it nudged up the slide switches on his bones. He felt it occupying him as it threw him into a dive back behind the Enforcer, while shots stitched across the platform. Out the other side, he fired two more shots at Castron, both on target, but both seemingly having no effect, as rotogun shots slammed into the Enforcer, skidding it backwards. He caught a breath, the reptile ceding control to him again, then kicked his suit into assist and ran, shots following him across the platform. He leaped. A particle beam seared past as his foot came down on the top of Mallon's war body, and he tumbled over the other side of it. He glimpsed her under chain-glass, head bowed, muttering to herself.

'Do you think I didn't prepare for those weapons?' Castron asked. 'I neglect nothing.'

Piper risked a glance round Mallon. Final discharges were leaving Castron's war body, but it seemed his preparation had not countered all the effects. Rotogun shots scored past Piper, way out, so targeting was off, while it seemed the chain-glass shield and armoured shutters had jammed only part of the way out. This last Piper had hoped for, but with all the rest deactivated too. What now? Castron was there and, though he had weapons, he was still accessible. Nothing had changed. Inster was almost certainly dead, yet this seemed to make it even more critical that Piper complete what he'd come here to do.

He peered out, seeing Castron's war body up on grav and drifting forwards. No doubt he intended to push Mallon off the side. Piper fired twice more. Grav went out again and Castron crashed down. Piper then ran out, finger down on the trigger, firing continuously. He jumped, foot coming down on a rotogun as it fired. Castron's body jerked, but moved up again. Piper next went down, gun clattering away, and grabbed the rotogun. He was now clinging just a few metres away from Castron, as the war body dropped away from the platform, then rose and accelerated.

With gecko function engaged, Piper climbed up the war body towards the old dictator. Its guns swivelled and shifted, and a series of shots passed over him. But their movement limited them to targets beyond the war body; they couldn't hit something actually on it. This was a safety protocol and another hole in Cyberat defences. Black-eyed, Castron stared at him, his old face registering recognition, then twisted with a fear Piper had never seen there before. Piper crawled closer, and grabbed onto a partially protruding armoured screen, as Castron flipped the war body over and ramped up acceleration. Down below, the city slid from view. Piper clung on, opening up the sliders all the way to send the animus immediately presented to him. Castron replied, and again the two creations battled in that virtual space between them.

'You didn't prepare for this, did you?' Piper enquired.

The dictator's only reply was to fight harder in the virtual space. In subtext, Piper noted him snapping animus links elsewhere to apply more resources here. Even under such acceleration, Piper started moving again, around the edge of the armoured shield, heading round behind Castron. The man tracked him, as far as he could, eyes watering in the wind blast, but reached the point where the cerebral support attached to the back of his skull allowed no further movement.

'I have an old friend of yours with me,' said Piper, now coming over the shield and onto the area where the blocky legs of Castron's transport body were hooked in. Within himself, he tore up the reptile, levered it out and squeezed off connections. Just for a second, it fought him, then its anger and need for control drove it towards predominance. At that moment it could have seized control of him, but now with its perception through him increased, he felt its acknowledgement and understanding. Bringing one gecko-stick boot down on a limb of the transport body, and shedding his gauntlets, Piper propelled himself forwards. But now the war body flipped upright again and Castron's plug form abruptly spun round to face him, the transport body rising from its recess. Even as Piper reached for Castron's skull, two multifingered hands closed on his forearms and stopped him dead.

'Naive,' said the old man.

Piper's legs kicked out, but then he managed to get them under him. He glanced at where the mechanical arms had folded up out of the transport body. He heaved with full suit assist and all his boosted muscle, managing to push closer, the hydraulics of the arms whining, but he still couldn't get his hands any closer.

'You did well,' Castron conceded. 'You did the unexpected and have come this close, which is why I won't kill you.'

Piper interrupted him before he could move on to a lengthy description of what he would do. 'And I am not going to kill you,' he replied.

His bones ached in the seconds of preparation, and his hands hurt. It seemed likely this was all psychological. Mentally, he sent the detach order to the sleeves of his suit, and pulled back. His arms slid free and he lunged forwards again, slamming both palms against Castron's support unit. As his threads went in, automatically seeking connection, he gazed into the man's watering eyes. The grabs came up again, clamping on both his biceps, digging into his flesh. Too late.

The reptile tore free of the final connections and poured through into Castron's processing. The huge pressure of the data even heated some threads so much they blew like fuses, gusting the smoke of burned flesh past Piper's face. Castron's grabs tried to break his bones, tearing muscle and running with blood. They next attempted to pull him away, but with the threads so deeply linked this only dragged Castron's head and upper body forwards. The threads wound further in through his support unit and into his mind, pouring in Piper's dark passenger, until finally it arrived at the source of all its anger, hatred and guilt. Castron's mouth gaped and he screamed.

It was so quiet. Piper had never known such quiet, at least inside him. He lay flat on rock with the sounds of waves crashing nearby. The intensity and detail of their sound amazed him. The flight and the crash here were evident to him, but seemed just a sketchy overlay on internal events. He had just ripped out a large part of himself, and it had ripped itself out of him. Behind it, the detritus of programming and memory swirled, sometimes crystallizing in fractal patterns, then breaking apart to flow to new positions. Was it healing? He didn't know. All he did know was that his internal space was gone, along with all the tools he'd used to manipulate what lay within it. His virtual aug was down too. He abruptly sat upright, without using his arms, and looked down at them. At least the nanosuite was still working and had stopped the pain and the bleeding. The flesh was ripped but bloodless, skinned over with a pink sheen of scar tissue and his biceps in twisted lumps. He tried raising one arm and it responded weakly. The other didn't move at all, and both his hands felt like jelly. He turned and looked further along the rocky coast.

Perhaps some final instinct had driven Castron here, some need of the injured animal to run for home, for just half a kilometre away stood the old dictator's villa. Taking care, Piper stood up, noting that the suit's systems were down and it hung leaden on him. Dimly, in recent memory, he saw that the war body had been heading down as he finally retracted the threads, leaving the reptile behind. He'd slid from the limp grabs, along the face of the war body, and ended up tumbling through the air. The visor had closed automatically and the suit had softened his landing, though he did remember his forearm snapping at that point. He got his bearings. Castron had been heading home, but memory of the sounds of a war body crashing indicated he hadn't made it. Piper headed over towards the sea.

He came to a two-metre drop. Below, more whorled stone slanted down into the waves, spotted with limpets and growths of mussels within the narrow tide band. A hundred metres away, towards the villa, lay the first armoured chunk of the war body, with a rotogun jutting up into the sky from it. Further debris sketched a trail from that to the bulk of the thing, smoke still issuing from numerous holes. Piper walked along to find an easier place to climb down and headed over.

The remains of the war body lay tilted over, having issued a wheel from the other side, perhaps in a belated attempt at landing. Castron hung in view, hands up in front of his chest twitching, his head jerking occasionally too, with eyes closed and an expression of someone wincing, as though in deep embarrassment. Piper walked over, groping down at his waist, but at some point he'd lost his sidearm. He doubted he had the strength to use it anyway. Hand up to his bandolier, he did find a grenade, so detached and readied it. He didn't think he'd need it, though.

'Castron,' he said. 'Hey, Castron!'

The old man's nightmares continued for a few seconds more, then his head came up, black eyes glaring.

'Piper,' he said.

Piper stepped back, sudden guilt surging through him. With a series of clonks, Castron's transport body detached from the war body. It came out like a trapdoor spider, heaved clear, then turned as it dropped to the stone, swaying slightly as it stabilized.

'Piper,' said the old man again, staring at him.

Piper raised his hand and looked at the grenade he could only just grip. He lowered his hand. He didn't have it in him to use the thing, especially with what he had heard in that voice.

'No, not that,' said Castron, and the voice was entirely different.

The transport body began walking sideways like a crab, jerkily, hardly under control. It reached the water's edge and turned so Castron was facing him. Piper read terror writ large in the old man's expression, as the body started walking backwards into the sea.

'No,' said Castron. 'No, you can't . . .'

But he could. Castron's arms flailed at the water as the transport body took him down. He tilted his head back at the last to try for one last breath, and then he was gone. Piper went over to the war body and sat down with his back against it. That his father had said his name one last time was evident by his own reaction to it.

Epilogue

Piper stared down into the large chamber recently cleared out and reappointed. The Cyberat down there were in a variety of carrier bodies and one of them was Geerand. The man had survived the destruction of much of his main com body, and had gone into a progression hospital. He now stood in human form, though it appeared mostly mechanical. Geerand was using one of the nanosuites but at a low setting, growing those missing parts of his body into the temporary mechanical shell he wore. He would like to have done it more quickly, but that meant tank regrowth and right now he had too much to do. Many had made similar decisions, but all Piper thought about then was how the word 'progression' had begun to take on a more positive meaning. Meanings, he well understood, were one of the first casualties of ideology.

'Are you ready to join them?' asked a voice behind.

'I thought you were still recovering from vitrification,' Piper replied without looking round.

'I am, but the view isn't so entertaining from a regrowth tank.'

Piper turned and eyed Inster. The man was back in his standard agent clothing but his skin did look a bit grey and scaly, while he seemed a lot thinner than before. The rotogun shots had punched out a good third of his torso, including one lung and a portion of his heart. This would have killed him, were it not for his nanosuite. Piper should also have been aware of that possibility, having seen it multiple times on Yannetholm, but it would have made no difference to his actions after seeing the agent shot. Geelie, herself stripped down to a skeletal Golem, had carried him back to the shuttle.

'Come to watch the boy enter the world of Cyberat politics?' Piper asked.

'You'll do well enough.'

Piper frowned. 'I thought so. It all seemed clear enough for me: everyone free to choose their own destiny, whether that's in human form or honed down to a fleshy nub inside a mechanical body. Minimal government and policing and so forth.'

'Seems a good idea to me.'

'Yes, but then Geerand asked me about the children. How and when should they be given their choices and, of course, what about them being indoctrinated by their parents?'

'A quite pertinent concern for you, I imagine.'

'That was just the first,' said Piper, ignoring the implication as he turned and walked past Inster off the balcony. 'What is the purpose of government? The greatest good for the greatest number seems right in a society where zero sum largely doesn't apply, and the aforementioned do not impinge on the rights of the individual to the territory of his mind, body and property.' Piper glanced at Inster as they progressed down the wide Cyberat corridor.

Inster smiled tiredly. 'But of course there will be disagreement on what is the greatest good and what those rights mean.'

'Yes. Those here who still agree with the founding principles still see human amalgamation with machine as the greater good, for example.'

'It's complicated,' Inster observed. He paused, then continued, 'Luckily not as complicated as it could have been. If yours and

Castron's animuses had still been fighting each other inside them, they would still be killing each other now.'

'People make it more complicated than it needs to be.' Piper stuck with just saying that. He didn't want to lie to Inster, mainly because the man would know.

'Why did you accept the offer?' the agent asked.

'Because I'm going to make damned certain this new regime won't become the old.'

'I'm sure you have that capability, but it's well to be aware that regimes consist of people, and it is they who revert . . .'

Piper glanced at him again, wondering if he knew, but could read nothing in his expression. He probably did because he'd asked no direct questions about the matter – just made oblique comments, like the one about the animuses.

They reached a ramp spiralling down. Cyberat passed them going up to the balconies. These mostly carried recording and sensing gear, so what occurred within the chamber below could be broadcast to all Cyberat. Single Cyberat within the chamber could do this too, but no one trusted that the information wouldn't be distorted and a narrative imposed.

'There's our boy!' shouted Meersham from the foot of the ramp.

Piper eyed the big man, and the other three walking into the atrium beyond him. They still wore combat gear and were armed, but then there was no one here who wasn't, except, apparently, Piper himself. Geelie was new-minted, having clad herself in another covering of syntheflesh and skin. As he reached the atrium, they all gathered round.

'Ready for your big day?' Geelie gazed at him speculatively.

'As ready as I can be.'

'So what is on your agenda for today?' asked Cheen tersely.

He peered at the Golem. 'Preparations for the others. The

Albermech will be here in fifteen days with twenty-three million soldiers coming home.'

'A party, then,' said Sloan with a wink.

'And perhaps with a toast to the lost,' said Piper, looking to Meersham.

Meersham shrugged, reached out and clapped him on the shoulder. 'You'll do fine.' He pointed to the ramp. 'We're going up to watch. Come on, guys.' With that, they headed up.

'I can think of a thousand pieces of advice to give you,' said Inster. 'But in the end I'll stick with one: resist the easy option.'

'I'll bear that in mind.'

Piper turned and headed for the arch leading from the atrium into the council chamber, while Inster followed the others up the ramp. It was as if a thread had now been broken. He became more aware of the Cyberat crowding the area, and how they separated to give him a clear path. Here he saw some of his Enforcers, their stolen prador claw tips down against the floor. Mallon was near the arch in a small carrier body too. She raised a metal hand in salute – she'd already assured him that, as she'd once been part of the old regime, she would keep public distance from him, so no associations could be made.

He moved into the chamber. Geerand stood back from the long table loaded with holographic projectors and other hardware they could access during discussions. Some chairs had been provided for those who could use them, with one further chair at the end. Piper acknowledged greetings and looked dispassionately into many angry expressions. He headed for the end chair, pulled it out and sat down. Others sat too, while carrier bodies moved in close. Still other Cyberat shifted back, clearing a space around those at the table. He now recognized faction Cyberat included here, and some of them clearly didn't look happy with his presence – obviously still angry about how he'd used them.

He closed his eyes for a second, then brought up the slide control in his bones. His inner space opened and expanded massively to encompass millions of nodes. His programs ordered them, categorized them, connected them in chains and expanded logic trees from them. Animuses queued up like bullets ready to go into thousands of breeches. Massive power lay here, ready for him to order the world to his will. And without a reptile imposing itself between him and his hardware, it was all so much clearer. He gazed internally upon all this, feeling larger than Founder's World and larger than the Cyberat scattered across its face. It was power more extreme than any other single human possessed, and what Castron had wanted to seize. Piper viewed it with dispassion, and then shut it down.

'We have much to discuss,' he said quietly.

Power was the temptation, he now understood, while strength was not using it.

About the Author

Neal Asher divides his time between Essex and Crete, mostly at a keyboard and mentally light years away. His full-length novels are as follows. First is the Agent Cormac series: *Gridlinked*, *The Line of Polity*, *Brass Man*, *Polity Agent* and *Line War*. Next comes the Spatterjay series: *The Skinner*, *The Voyage of the Sable Keech* and *Orbus*. Also set in the same world of the Polity are these standalone novels: *Prador Moon*, *Hilldiggers*, *Shadow of the Scorpion*, *The Technician*, *Jack Four*, *Weaponized* and *War Bodies*. The Transformation trilogy is also based in the Polity: *Dark Intelligence*, *War Factory* and *Infinity Engine*. Set in a dystopian future are *The Departure*, *Zero Point* and *Jupiter War*, while *Cowl* takes us across time. The Rise of the Jain trilogy is comprised of *The Soldier*, *The Warship* and *The Human*, and is also set in the Polity universe.